Travelling to Utopia

The Michael Moorcock Collection

The Michael Moorcock Collection is the definitive library of acclaimed author Michael Moorcock's SF & fantasy, including the entirety of his Eternal Champion work. It is prepared and edited by John Davey, the author's long-time bibliographer and editor, and will be published, over the course of two years, in the following print omnibus editions by Gollancz, and as individual eBooks by the SF Gateway (see http://www.sfgateway.com/authors/m/moorcock-michael/ for a complete list of available eBooks).

ELRIC

Elric of Melniboné and Other Stories

Elric: The Fortress of the Pearl

Elric: The Sailor on the Seas of Fate

Elric: The Sleeping Sorceress

Elric: The Revenge of the Rose

Elric: Stormbringer!

Elric: The Moonbeam Roads
comprising –
Daughter of Dreams
Destiny's Brother
Son of the Wolf

CORUM

Corum: The Prince in the Scarlet Robe
comprising –
The Knight of the Swords
The Queen of the Swords
The King of the Swords

Corum: The Prince with the Silver Hand
comprising –
The Bull and the Spear
The Oak and the Ram
The Sword and the Stallion

HAWKMOON

Hawkmoon: The History of the Runestaff
comprising –
The Jewel in the Skull
The Mad God's Amulet
The Sword of the Dawn
The Runestaff

Hawkmoon: Count Brass
comprising –
Count Brass
The Champion of Garathorm
The Quest for Tanelorn

JERRY CORNELIUS

The Cornelius Quartet
comprising –
The Final Programme
A Cure for Cancer
The English Assassin
The Condition of Muzak

Jerry Cornelius: His Lives and His Times (short-fiction collection)

A Cornelius Calendar
comprising –
The Adventures of Una Persson and Catherine Cornelius in the Twentieth Century
The Entropy Tango
The Great Rock 'n' Roll Swindle
The Alchemist's Question
Firing the Cathedral/Modem Times 2.0

Von Bek
comprising –
The War Hound and the World's Pain
The City in the Autumn Stars

The Eternal Champion
comprising –
The Eternal Champion
Phoenix in Obsidian
The Dragon in the Sword

The Dancers at the End of Time
comprising –
An Alien Heat
The Hollow Lands
The End of all Songs

Kane of Old Mars
comprising –
Warriors of Mars
Blades of Mars
Barbarians of Mars

Moorcock's Multiverse
comprising –
The Sundered Worlds
The Winds of Limbo
The Shores of Death

The Nomad of Time
comprising –
The Warlord of the Air
The Land Leviathan
The Steel Tsar

Travelling to Utopia
comprising –
The Wrecks of Time
The Ice Schooner
The Black Corridor

The War Amongst the Angels
comprising –
Blood: A Southern Fantasy
Fabulous Harbours
The War Amongst the Angels

Tales From the End of Time
comprising –
Legends from the End of Time
Constant Fire
Elric at the End of Time

Behold the Man

Gloriana; or, The Unfulfill'd Queen

SHORT FICTION

My Experiences in the Third World War and Other Stories: The Best Short Fiction of Michael Moorcock Volume 1

The Brothel in Rosenstrasse and Other Stories: The Best Short Fiction of Michael Moorcock Volume 2

Breakfast in the Ruins and Other Stories: The Best Short Fiction of Michael Moorcock Volume 3

Travelling to Utopia

The Wrecks of Time
The Ice Schooner
The Black Corridor

MICHAEL MOORCOCK

Edited by John Davey

This edition published in Great Britain in 2014 by
Gollancz
An imprint of the Orion Publishing Group
Orion House, 5 Upper St Martin's Lane,
London WC2H 9EA

An Hachette UK Company

The authorised representative in the EEA is Hachette Ireland,
8 Castlecourt Centre, Dublin 15, D15 XTP3, Ireland (email: info@hbgi.ie)

5 7 9 10 8 6

A CIP catalogue record for this book is available from the British Library

ISBN 978 0 575 09277 8

Typeset by Jouve (UK), Milton Keynes

Printed and bound in Great Britain by Clays Ltd, Elcograf S.p.A.

The Orion Publishing Group's policy is to use papers that are natural, renewable and recyclable products and made from wood grown in sustainable forests. The logging and manufacturing processes are expected to conform to the environmental regulations of the country of origin.

www.multiverse.org
www.sfgateway.com
www.gollancz.co.uk
www.orionbooks.co.uk

Introduction to *The Michael Moorcock Collection*

John Clute

HE IS NOW over 70, enough time for most careers to start and end in, enough time to fit in an occasional half-decade or so of silence to mark off the big years. Silence happens. I don't think I know an author who doesn't fear silence like the plague; most of us, if we live long enough, can remember a bad blank year or so, or more. Not Michael Moorcock. Except for some worrying surgery on his toes in recent years, he seems not to have taken time off to breathe the air of peace and panic. There has been no time to spare. The nearly 60 years of his active career seems to have been too short to fit everything in: the teenage comics; the editing jobs; the pulp fiction; the reinvented heroic fantasies; the Eternal Champion; the deep Jerry Cornelius riffs; NEW WORLDS; the 1970s/1980s flow of stories and novels, dozens upon dozens of them in every category of modern fantastika; the tales of the dying Earth and the possessing of Jesus; the exercises in postmodernism that turned the world inside out before most of us had begun to guess we were living on the wrong side of things; the invention (more or less) of steampunk; the alternate histories; the *Mitteleuropean* tales of sexual terror; the deep-city London riffs: the turns and changes and returns and reconfigurations to which he has subjected his oeuvre over the years (he expects this new Collected Edition will fix these transformations in place for good); the late tales where he has been remodelling the intersecting worlds he created in the 1960s in terms of twenty-first-century physics: for starters. If you can't take the heat, I guess, stay out of the multiverse.

His life has been full and complicated, a life he has exposed and hidden (like many other prolific authors) throughout his work. In *Mother London* (1988), though, a non-fantastic novel published at what is now something like the midpoint of his career, it may be possible to find the key to all the other selves who made the 100 books. There are three protagonists in the tale, which is set from about 1940 to about 1988 in the suburbs and inner runnels of the vast metropolis of Charles Dickens and Robert Louis Stevenson. The oldest of these protagonists is Joseph Kiss, a flamboyant self-advertising fin-de-siècle figure of substantial girth and a fantasticating relationship to the world: he is Michael Moorcock, seen with genial bite as a kind of G.K. Chesterton without the wearying punch-line paradoxes. The youngest of the three is David Mummery, a haunted introspective half-insane denizen of a secret London of trials and runes and codes and magic: he too is Michael Moorcock, seen through a glass, darkly. And there is Mary Gasalee, a kind of holy-innocent and survivor, blessed with a luminous clarity of insight, so that in all her apparent ignorance of the onrushing secular world she is more deeply wise than other folk: she is also Michael Moorcock, Moorcock when young as viewed from the wry middle years of 1988. When we read the book, we are reading a book of instructions for the assembly of a London writer. The Moorcock we put together from this choice of portraits is amused and bemused at the vision of himself; he is a phenomenon of flamboyance and introspection, a poseur and a solitary, a dreamer and a doer, a multitude and a singleton. But only the three Moorcocks in this book, working together, could have written all the other books.

It all began – as it does for David Mummery in *Mother London* – in South London, in a subtopian stretch of villas called Mitcham, in 1939. In early childhood, he experienced the Blitz, and never forgot the extraordinariness of being a participant – however minute – in the great drama; all around him, as though the world were being dismantled nightly, darkness and blackout would descend, bombs fall, buildings and streets disappear; and in the morning, as though a new universe had taken over from the old one and the world had become portals, the sun would rise on glinting rubble, abandoned tricycles, men and women going about their daily tasks as though nothing had happened, strange shards of ruin poking into altered air. From a very early age, Michael Moorcock's security reposed in a sense that everything might change, in the blinking of an eye, and be *rejourneyed* the next day (or the next book). Though as a writer he has certainly elucidated the fears and alarums of life in Aftermath Britain, it does seem that his very early years were marked by the epiphanies of war, rather than the inflictions of despair and beclouding amnesia most adults necessarily experienced. After the war ended, his parents separated, and the young Moorcock began to attend a pretty wide variety of schools, several of which he seems to have been expelled from, and as soon as he could legally do so he began to work full time, up north in London's heart, which he only left when he moved to Texas (with intervals in Paris) in the early 1990s, from where (to jump briefly up the decades) he continues to cast a Martian eye: as with most exiles, Moorcock's intensest anatomies of his homeland date from after his cunning departure.

But back again to the beginning (just as though we were rimming a multiverse). Starting in the 1950s there was the comics and pulp work for Fleetway Publications; there was the first book (*Caribbean Crisis*, 1962) as by Desmond Reid, co-written with his early friend the artist James Cawthorn (1929–2008); there was marriage, with the writer Hilary Bailey (they divorced in 1978), three children, a heated existence in the Ladbroke Grove/Notting Hill Gate region of London he was later to populate with Jerry Cornelius and his vast family; there was the editing of NEW WORLDS, which began in 1964 and became the heartbeat of the British New Wave two years later as writers like Brian W. Aldiss and J.G. Ballard, reaching their early prime, made it into a tympanum, as young American writers like Thomas M. Disch, John T. Sladek, Norman Spinrad and Pamela Zoline found a home in London for material they could not publish in America, and new British writers like M. John Harrison and Charles Platt began their careers in its pages; but before that there was Elric. With *The Stealer of Souls* (1963) and

Stormbringer (1965), the multiverse began to flicker into view, and the Eternal Champion (whom Elric parodied and embodied) began properly to ransack the worlds in his fight against a greater Chaos than the great dance could sustain. There was also the first SF novel, *The Sundered Worlds* (1965), but in the 1960s SF was a difficult nut to demolish for Moorcock: he would bide his time.

We come to the heart of the matter. Jerry Cornelius, who first appears in *The Final Programme* (1968) – which assembles and co-ordinates material first published a few years earlier in NEW WORLDS – is a deliberate solarisation of the albino Elric, who was himself a mocking solarisation of Robert E. Howard's Conan, or rather of the mighty-thew-headed Conan created for profit by Howard epigones: Moorcock rarely mocks the true quill. Cornelius, who reaches his first and most telling apotheosis in the four novels comprising *The Cornelius Quartet*, remains his most distinctive and perhaps most original single creation: a wide boy, an agent, a *flaneur*, a bad musician, a shopper, a shapechanger, a trans, a spy in the house of London: a toxic palimpsest on whom and through whom the *zeitgeist* inscribes surreal conjugations of 'message'. Jerry Cornelius gives head to Elric.

The life continued apace. By 1970, with NEW WORLDS on its last legs, multiverse fantasies and experimental novels poured forth; Moorcock and Hilary Bailey began to live separately, though he moved, in fact, only around the corner, where he set up house with Jill Riches, who would become his second wife; there was a second home in Yorkshire, but London remained his central base. *The Condition of Muzak* (1977), which is the fourth Cornelius novel, and *Gloriana; or, The Unfulfill'd Queen* (1978), which transfigures the first Elizabeth into a kinked Astraea, marked perhaps the high point of his career as a writer of fiction whose font lay in genre or its mutations – marked perhaps the furthest bournes he could transgress while remaining within the perimeters of fantasy (though *within* those bournes vast stretches of territory remained and would, continually, be explored). During these years he sometimes wore a leather jacket constructed out of numerous patches of varicoloured material, and it sometimes seemed perfectly fitting that he bore the semblance, as his jacket flickered and fuzzed from across a room or road, of an illustrated man, a map, a thing of shreds and patches, a student fleshed from dreams. Like the stories he told, he seemed to be more than one thing. To use a term frequently applied (by me at least) to twenty-first-century fiction, he seemed equipoisal: which is to say that, through all his genre-hopping and genre-mixing and genre-transcending and genre-loyal returnings to old pitches, *he was never still*, because 'equipoise' is all about *making stories move*. As with his stories, he cannot be pinned down, because he is not in one place. In person and in his work, it has always been sink or swim: like a shark, or a dancer, or an equilibrist…

The marriage with Jill Riches came to an end. He married Linda Steele in 1983; they remain married. The Colonel Pyat books, *Byzantium Endures* (1981), *The Laughter of Carthage* (1984), *Jerusalem Commands* (1992) and *The Vengeance of Rome* (2006), dominated these years, along with *Mother London*. As these books, which are non-fantastic, are not included in the current *Michael Moorcock Collection*, it might be worth noting here that, in their insistence on the irreducible difficulty of gaining anything like true sight, they represent Moorcock's mature modernist take on what one might call the rag-and-bone shop of the world itself; and that the huge ornate postmodern edifice of his multiverse *loosens* us from that world, gives us room to breathe, to juggle our strategies for living – allows us ultimately to escape from prison (to use a phrase from a writer he does not respect, J.R.R. Tolkien, for whom the twentieth century was a prison train bound for hell). What Moorcock may best be remembered for in the end is the (perhaps unique) interplay between modernism and postmodernism in his work. (But a plethora of discordant understandings makes these terms hard to use; so enough of them.) In the end, one might just say that Moorcock's work as a whole represents an extraordinarily multifarious execution of the fantasist's main task: which is to *get us out of here*.

Recent decades saw a continuation of the multifarious, but with a more intensely applied methodology. The late volumes of the long Elric saga, and the Second Ether sequence of meta-fantasies – *Blood: A Southern Fantasy* (1995), *Fabulous Harbours* (1995) and *The War Amongst the Angels: An Autobiographical Story* (1996) – brood on the real world and the multiverse through the lens of Chaos Theory: the closer you get to the world, the less you describe it. *The Metatemporal Detective* (2007) – a narrative in the Steampunk mode Moorcock had previewed as long ago as *The Warlord of the Air* (1971) and *The Land Leviathan* (1974) – continues the process, sometimes dizzyingly: as though the reader inhabited the eye of a camera increasing its focus on a closely observed reality while its bogey simultaneously wheels it backwards from the desired rapport: an old Kurasawa trick here amplified into a tool of conspectus, fantasy eyed and (once again) rejourneyed, this time through the lens of SF.

We reach the second decade of the twenty-first century, time still to make things new, but also time to sort. There are dozens of titles in *The Michael Moorcock Collection* that have not been listed in this short space, much less trawled for tidbits. The various avatars of the Eternal Champion – Elric, Kane of Old Mars, Hawkmoon, Count Brass, Corum, Von Bek – differ vastly from one another. Hawkmoon is a bit of a berk; Corum is a steely solitary at the End of Time: the joys and doleurs of the interplays amongst them can only be experienced through immersion. And the Dancers at the End of Time books, and the Nomad of the Time Stream books, and the Karl Glogauer books, and all the others. They are here now, a 100 books that make up one book. They have been fixed for reading. It is time to enter the multiverse and see the world.

September 2012

Introduction to *The Michael Moorcock Collection*

Michael Moorcock

By 1964, after I had been editing NEW WORLDS for some months and had published several science fiction and fantasy novels, including *Stormbringer*, I realised that my run as a writer was over. About the only new ideas I'd come up with were miniature computers, the multiverse and black holes, all very crudely realised, in *The Sundered Worlds*. No doubt I would have to return to journalism, writing features and editing. 'My career,' I told my friend J.G. Ballard, 'is finished.' He sympathised and told me he only had a few SF stories left in him, then he, too, wasn't sure what he'd do.

In January 1965, living in Colville Terrace, Notting Hill, then an infamous slum, best known for its race riots, I sat down at the typewriter in our kitchen-cum-bathroom and began a locally based book, designed to be accompanied by music and graphics. *The Final Programme* featured a character based on a young man I'd seen around the area and whom I named after a local greengrocer, Jerry Cornelius, 'Messiah to the Age of Science'. Jerry was as much a technique as a character. Not the 'spy' some critics described him as but an urban adventurer as interested in his psychic environment as the contemporary physical world. My influences were English and French absurdists, American noir novels. My inspiration was William Burroughs with whom I'd recently begun a correspondence. I also borrowed a few SF ideas, though I was adamant that I was not writing in any established genre. I felt I had at last found my own authentic voice.

I had already written a short novel, *The Golden Barge*, set in a nowhere, no-time world very much influenced by Peake and the surrealists, which I had not attempted to publish. An earlier autobiographical novel, *The Hungry Dreamers*, set in Soho, was eaten by rats in a Ladbroke Grove basement. I remained unsatisfied with my style and my technique. *The Final Programme* took nine days to complete (by 20 January, 1965) with my baby daughters sometimes cradled with their bottles while I typed on. This, I should say, is my memory of events; my then wife scoffed at this story when I recounted it. Whatever the truth, the fact is I only believed I might be a serious writer after I had finished that novel, with all its flaws. But Jerry Cornelius, probably my most successful sustained attempt at unconventional fiction, was born then and ever since has remained a useful means of telling complex stories. Associated with the 60s and 70s, he has been equally at home in all the following decades. Through novels and novellas I developed a means of carrying several narratives and viewpoints on what appeared to be a very light (but tight) structure which dispensed with some of the earlier methods of fiction. In the sense that it took for granted the understanding that the novel is among other things an internal dialogue and I did not feel the need to repeat by now commonly understood modernist conventions, this fiction was post-modern.

Not all my fiction looked for new forms for the new century. Like many 'revolutionaries' I looked back as well as forward. As George Meredith looked to the eighteenth century for inspiration for his experiments with narrative, I looked to Meredith, popular Edwardian realists like Pett Ridge and Zangwill and the writers of the *fin de siècle* for methods and inspiration. An almost obsessive interest in the Fabians, several of whom believed in the possibility of benign imperialism, ultimately led to my Bastable books which examined our enduring British notion that an empire could be essentially a force for good. The first was *The Warlord of the Air*.

I also wrote my *Dancers at the End of Time* stories and novels under the influence of Edwardian humourists and absurdists like Jerome or Firbank. Together with more conventional generic books like *The Ice Schooner* or *The Black Corridor*, most of that work was done in the 1960s and 70s when I wrote the Eternal Champion supernatural adventure novels which helped support my own and others' experiments via NEW WORLDS, allowing me also to keep a family while writing books in which action and fantastic invention were paramount. Though I did them quickly, I didn't write them cynically. I have always believed, somewhat puritanically, in giving the audience good value for money. I enjoyed writing them, tried to avoid repetition, and through each new one was able to develop a few more ideas. They also continued to teach me how to express myself through image and metaphor. My Everyman became the Eternal Champion, his dreams and ambitions represented by the multiverse. He could be an ordinary person struggling with familiar problems in a contemporary setting or he could be a swordsman fighting monsters on a far-away world.

Long before I wrote *Gloriana* (in four parts reflecting the seasons) I had learned to think in images and symbols through reading John Bunyan's *Pilgrim's Progress*, Milton and others, understanding early on that the visual could be the most important part of a book and was often in itself a story as, for instance, a famous personality could also, through everything associated with their name, function as narrative. I wanted to find ways of carrying as many stories as possible in one. From the cinema I also learned how to use images as connecting themes. Images, colours, music, and even popular magazine headlines can all add coherence to an apparently random story, underpinning it and giving the reader a sense of internal logic and a satisfactory resolution, dispensing with certain familiar literary conventions.

When the story required it, I also began writing neo-realist fiction exploring the interface of character and environment, especially the city, especially London. In some books I condensed, manipulated and randomised time to achieve what I wanted, but in others the sense of 'real time' as we all generally perceive it was more suitable and could best be achieved by traditional nineteenth-century means. For the Pyat books I first looked back to the great German classic, Grimmelshausen's *Simplicissimus* and other early picaresques. I then examined the roots of a certain kind of moral fiction from Defoe through Thackeray and Meredith then to modern times where the picaresque (or rogue tale) can take the form of a road movie, for instance. While it's probably fair to say that Pyat and *Byzantium Endures* precipitated the end of my second marriage (echoed to a degree in *The Brothel in Rosenstrasse*), the late 70s and the 80s were exhilarating times for me, with *Mother London* being perhaps my own favourite novel of that period. I wanted to write something celebratory.

By the 90s I was again attempting to unite several kinds of fiction in one novel with my Second Ether trilogy. With Mandelbrot, Chaos Theory and String Theory I felt, as I said at the time, as if I were being offered a chart of my own brain. That chart made it easier for me to develop the notion of the multiverse as representing both the internal and the external, as a metaphor and as a means of structuring and rationalising an outrageously inventive and quasi-realistic narrative. The worlds of the multiverse move up and down scales or 'planes' explained in terms of mass, allowing entire universes to exist in the 'same' space. The result of developing this idea was the *War Amongst the Angels* sequence which added absurdist elements also functioning as a kind of mythology and folklore for a world beginning to understand itself in terms of new metaphysics and theoretical physics. As the cosmos becomes denser and almost infinite before our eyes, with black holes and dark matter affecting our own reality, we can explore them and observe them as our ancestors explored our planet and observed the heavens.

At the end of the 90s I'd returned to realism, sometimes with a dash of fantasy, with *King of the City* and the stories collected in *London Bone*. I also wrote a new Elric/Eternal Champion sequence, beginning with *Daughter of Dreams*, which brought the fantasy worlds of Hawkmoon, Bastable and Co. in line with my realistic and autobiographical stories, another attempt to unify all my fiction, and also offer a way in which disparate genres could be reunited, through notions developed from the multiverse and the Eternal Champion, as one giant novel. At the time I was finishing the Pyat sequence which attempted to look at the roots of the Nazi Holocaust in our European, Middle Eastern and American cultures and to ground my strange survival guilt while at the same time examining my own cultural roots in the light of an enduring anti-Semitism.

By the 2000s I was exploring various conventional ways of story-telling in the last parts of *The Metatemporal Detective* and through other homages, comics, parodies and games. I also looked back at my earliest influences. I had reached retirement age and felt like a rest. I wrote a 'prequel' to the Elric series as a graphic novel with Walter Simonson, *The Making of a Sorcerer*, and did a little online editing with FANTASTIC METROPOLIS.

By 2010 I had written a novel featuring Doctor Who, *The Coming of the Terraphiles*, with a nod to P.G. Wodehouse (a boyhood favourite), continued to write short stories and novellas and to work on the beginning of a new sequence combining pure fantasy and straight autobiography called *The Whispering Swarm* while still writing more Cornelius stories trying to unite all the various genres and sub-genres into which contemporary fiction has fallen.

Throughout my career critics have announced that I'm 'abandoning' fantasy and concentrating on literary fiction. The truth is, however, that all my life, since I became a professional writer and editor at the age of 16, I've written in whatever mode suits a story best and where necessary created a new form if an old one didn't work for me. Certain ideas are best carried on a Jerry Cornelius story, others work better as realism and others as fantasy or science fiction. Some work best as a combination. I'm sure I'll write whatever I like and will continue to experiment with all the ways there are of telling stories and carrying as many themes as possible. Whether I write about a widow coping with loneliness in her cottage or a massive, universe-size sentient spaceship searching for her children, I'll no doubt die trying to tell them all. I hope you'll find at least some of them to your taste.

One thing a reader can be sure of about these new editions is that they would not have been possible without the tremendous and indispensable help of my old friend and bibliographer John Davey. John has ensured that these Gollancz editions are definitive. I am indebted to John for many things, including his work at

Moorcock's Miscellany, my website, but his work on this edition has been outstanding. As well as being an accomplished novelist in his own right John is an astonishingly good editor who has worked with Gollancz and myself to point out every error and flaw in all previous editions, some of them not corrected since their first publication, and has enabled me to correct or revise them. I couldn't have completed this project without him. Together, I think, Gollancz, John Davey and myself have produced what will be the best editions possible and I am very grateful to him, to Malcolm Edwards, Darren Nash and Marcus Gipps for all the considerable hard work they have done to make this edition what it is.

Michael Moorcock

Contents

The Wrecks of Time

For Jimmy Ballard

When all the world dissolves,
And every creature shall be purified,
All place shall be hell that is not heaven.

– Christopher Marlowe,
Doctor Faustus

Prologue

THERE THEY LAY, outside of space and time, each hanging in its separate limbo, each a planet called Earth. Fifteen globes, fifteen lumps of matter sharing a name. Once they might have looked the same, too, but now they were very different. One was comprised almost solely of desert and ocean with a few forests of gigantic, distorted trees growing in the northern hemisphere; another seemed to be in perpetual twilight, a planet of dark obsidian; yet another was a honeycomb of multicoloured crystal and another had a single continent that was a ring of land around a vast lagoon. The wrecks of Time, abandoned and dying, each with a decreasing number of human inhabitants for the most part unaware of the doom overhanging their worlds. These worlds existed in a kind of subspacial *well* created in furtherance of a series of drastic experiments...

Chapter One
The Great American Desert

In Professor Faustaff's code-book this world was designated as Earth 3. The professor steered his flame-red Cadillac convertible along the silted highway that crossed the diamond-dry desert, holding the wheel carefully, like the captain of a schooner negotiating a treacherous series of sandbanks.

The desert stretched on all sides, vast and lonely, harsh and desolate beneath the intense glare of the sun swelling at its zenith in the metallic blue sky. On this alternate Earth there was little but desert and ocean, the one a flat continuation of the other.

The professor hummed a song to himself as he drove, his bulk sprawling across both front seats. Sunlight glinted off the beads of sweat on his shiny red face, caught the lenses of his polaroid glasses and brightened those parts of the Cadillac not yet dulled by the desert dust. The engine roared like a beast and Professor Faustaff chanted mindlessly to its rhythm.

He was dressed in an Hawaiian shirt and gold beach shorts, a pair of battered sneakers on his feet and a baseball cap tilted on his head. He weighed at least twenty stone and was a good six and a half feet tall. A big man. Though he drove with care his body was completely relaxed and his mind was at rest. He was as at home in this environment as he was in more than a dozen others. The ecology of this Earth could not, of course, support human life. It did not. Professor Faustaff and his teams supported human life here and on all but two of the other alternates. It was a big responsibility. The professor carried it with a certain equanimity.

The capital of Greater America, Los Angeles, was two hours behind him and he was heading for San Francisco where he had his headquarters on this alternate Earth. He would be there the next day and planned to stop at a motel he knew en route, spend the night there, and continue in the morning.

Peering ahead of him Faustaff suddenly saw what appeared to be a human figure standing by the side of the highway. As he drove closer he saw that it was a girl dressed only in a swimsuit, waving at him as he approached. He slowed down. The girl was a pretty redhead, her hair long and straight, her nose fairly sharp and freckled. Her mouth was large and pleasant.

Faustaff stopped the car beside the girl.

'What's the trouble?'

'Truck driver was giving me a lift to Frisco. He dumped me when I wouldn't go and play amongst the cactus with him.' Her voice was soft and a trifle ironic.

'Didn't he realise you could have died before someone else came along?'

'He might have liked that. He was very upset.'

'You'd better get in.' Most young women attracted Faustaff and the redhead particularly appealed to him. As she squeezed into the passenger seat beside him he began to breathe a little more heavily than usual. Her face seemed to assume a more serious expression as he glanced at her but she said nothing.

'My name's Nancy Hunt,' she said. 'I'm from LA. You?'

'Professor Faustaff, I live in Frisco.'

'A professor – you don't look like a professor – a businessman more, I guess, but even then – a painter, maybe.'

'Well, I'm sorry to say I'm a physicist – a physicist of all work you could say.' He grinned at her and she grinned back, her eyes warming. Like most women she was already attracted by Faustaff's powerful appeal. Faustaff accepted this as normal and had never bothered to work out why he should be so successful in love. It might be his unquestioning enjoyment of love-making and general liking for women. A kindly nature and an uncomplicated appreciation for all the bodily pleasures, a character that demanded no sustenance from others, these were probably the bases for Faustaff's success with women. Whether eating, boozing, smoking, love-making, talking, inventing, helping people or giving pleasure in general, Faustaff did it with such spontaneity, such relaxation, that he could not fail to be attractive to most people.

'What are you going to Frisco for, Nancy?' he asked.

'Oh, I just felt like travelling. I was with this swimming party, I got sick of it, I walked out onto the street and saw this truck coming. I thumbed it and asked the driver where he was going. He said Frisco – so I decided to go to Frisco.'

Faustaff chuckled. 'Impulsive. I like that.'

'My boyfriend calls me moody, not impulsive,' she smiled.

'Your boyfriend?'

'Well, my ex-boyfriend as from this morning I suppose. He woke up, sat up in bed and said "Unless you marry me, Nancy, I'm going now". I didn't want to marry him and told him so. He went.' She laughed. 'He was a nice guy.'

The highway wound on through the barren world and Faustaff and Nancy talked until naturally they moved closer together and Faustaff put his arm around the girl and hugged her and a little later kissed her.

By late afternoon they were both relaxed and content to enjoy one another's company silently.

The convertible sped on, thudding tyres and pumping pistons, vibrating chassis, stink and all, sand slashing against the windscreen and the big yellow sun in the hot blue above. The vast, gleaming desert stretched for hundreds of miles in all directions, its only landmarks the few filling stations and motels along the rare highways, the occasional mesa and clumps of cactus. Only the City of Angels, in the exact centre of the desert, lay inland. All other cities, like San Francisco, New Orleans, Saint Louis, Santa Fe, Jacksonville, Houston and Phoenix, lay on the coast. A visitor from another Earth would not have recognised the continental outline.

Professor Faustaff chanted wordlessly to himself as he drove, avoiding the occasional crater in the highway, or the places where sand had banked up heavily.

His chant and his peace were interrupted by a buzzing from the dashboard. He glanced at the girl and made a decision with a slight shrug of his shoulders. He reached inside the glove compartment and flicked a hidden switch there. A voice, urgent and yet controlled, began to come from the radio.

'Frisco calling Professor F. Frisco calling Professor F.'

'Professor F. receiving,' said Faustaff watching the road ahead and easing off a little on the accelerator. Nancy frowned.

'What's that?' she asked.

'Just a private radio – keep in touch with my headquarters this way.'

'Crazy,' she said.

'Professor F. receiving you,' he said deliberately. 'Suggest you consider Condition C.' Faustaff warned his base that he had someone with him.

'Understood. Two things. A U.M. Situation is anticipated imminent on E-15, Grid areas 33, 34, 41, 42, 49 and 50. Representatives on E-15 have asked for help. Would suggest you use I-effect to contact.'

'It's that bad?'

'From what they said, it's that bad.'

'Okay. Will do so as soon as possible. You said *two* things.'

'We found a tunnel – or traces of one. Not one of ours. A D-squader we think. He's somewhere in your area, anyway. Thought we'd warn you.'

Faustaff wondered suddenly if he'd been conned and he looked at Nancy again.

'Thanks,' he said to the radio. 'I'm arriving in Frisco tomorrow. Keep me informed of any emergency.'

'Okay, professor. Cutting out.'

Faustaff put his hand into the glove compartment again and flicked the switch off.

'Phew!' grinned Nancy. 'If that was a sample of the kind of talk you physicists go in for I'm glad I only had to learn Esperanto at school.'

Faustaff knew that he should feel suspicious of her but couldn't believe that she was a threat.

His Frisco office did not use the radio unless it was important.

They had told him that an Unstable Matter Situation was imminent on the fifteenth and last alternate Earth. An Unstable Matter Situation could mean the Total Break-up of a planet. Normally, representatives of his team there could cope with a U.M.S. If they had asked for help it meant things were very bad. Later Faustaff would have to leave the girl somewhere and use the machine that lay in the trunk of his car – a machine called an invoker, which could summon one of Faustaff's representatives through the subspacial levels so that Faustaff could talk with him directly and find out exactly what was happening on Earth Fifteen. The other piece of information concerned his enemies, the mysterious D-squad who were, Faustaff believed, actually responsible for creating the U.M. Situations wherever they arose. At least one of the D-squad was already on this Earth and could be after him. That was why he knew he should suspect Nancy Hunt and be cautious. Her appearance on the highway *was* mysterious, after all, although he was still inclined to believe her story.

She grinned at him again and reached into his shirt pocket to get cigarettes and his lighter, putting a cigarette between his lips and cupping the flame of the lighter so that he was forced to bend his large head towards it.

As evening came and the sun began to set the sky awash with colours, a motel-hoarding showed up. The sign read:

LA PLEJ BON AN MOTELON
Nagejo – Muziko – Amuzoj

A little later they could just make out the buildings of the motel and another sign.

'PLUV ATA MORGAU'
Bonvolu esti kun ni

Faustaff read Esperanto fluently enough. It was the official language, though few people spoke it in everyday life. The signs offered him the best motel, swimming, music and amusements. It had humorously been called The Rain Tomorrow and invited him to join the host.

Several more hoardings later they turned off the road into the car park. There were only two other cars there under the shade of the awning. One was a black Ford Thunderbird, the other was a white English MG. A pretty girl in a frilly ballerina skirt that was obviously part of her uniform, a peaked cap on her head, strode towards them as they got stiffly out of the car.

Faustaff winked at her, his body dwarfing her. He put his sunglasses in his pocket and wiped his forehead with a yellow handkerchief.

'Any cabins?' he asked.

'Sure,' smiled the girl, glancing quickly from Faustaff to Nancy. 'How many?'

'One double or two singles,' he said. 'It doesn't matter.'

'Not sure we've got a bed to take you, mister,' she said.

'I curl up small,' Faustaff grinned. 'Don't worry about it. I've got some valuables in my car – if I close the roof and lock it will they be safe enough?'

'The only thieves in these parts are the coyotes,' she said, 'though they'll be learning to drive soon when they find that cars are all that's left to steal.'

'Business bad?'

'Was it ever good?'

'There are quite a few motels between here and Frisco,' Nancy said, linking her arm in Faustaff's. 'How do they survive?'

'Government grants mainly,' she replied. 'There've got to be filling stations and motels through the Great American Outback, haven't there? Otherwise how would anyone get to Los Angeles?'

'Plane?' the redhead suggested.

'I guess so,' said the girl. 'But the highways and motels were here before the airlines, so I guess they just developed. Anyway some people actually *like* crossing the desert by car.'

Faustaff got back into the car and operated the hood control. It hummed and extended itself, covering the automobile. Faustaff locked it and got out again. He locked the doors. He unlocked the trunk, flipped a switch on a piece of equipment, relocked it. He put his arm around the redhead and said: 'Right, let's get some food.'

The girl in the cap and the skirt led the way to the main building. Behind it were about twelve cabins.

There was one other customer in the restaurant. He sat near the window, looking out at the desert. A big full moon was rising.

Faustaff and the redhead sat down at the counter and looked at the menu. It offered steak or hamburger and a variety of standard trimmings. The girl who'd first greeted them came through a door at the back and said: 'What'll it be?'

'You do all the work around here?' asked Nancy.

'Mostly. My husband runs the gas pumps and does the heavy chores. There isn't much to do except maintain the place.'

'I guess so,' said Nancy. 'I'll have a jumbo steak, rare with fries and salad.'

'I'll have the same, but four portions,' said Faustaff. 'Then three of your Rainbow Sodas and six cups of coffee with cream.'

'We should have more customers like you,' the girl said without raising an eyebrow. She looked at Nancy. 'Want anything to follow, honey?'

The redhead grinned. 'I'll have vanilla ice-cream and coffee with cream.'

'Go and sit down. It'll be ten minutes.'

They crossed to a window table. For the first time Faustaff saw the face of the other customer. He was pale, with his close-cropped black hair growing in a widow's peak, a neat, thin black beard and moustache, his features ascetic, his lips pursed as he stared at the moon. He turned suddenly and glanced at Faustaff, gave a slight inclination of the head and looked back at the moon. His eyes had been bright, black and sardonic.

A little while later the girl came with the order on a big tray. 'Your other steaks are in that dish,' she said as she set it on the table. 'And your trimmings are in those two smaller dishes. Okay?'

'Fine,' Faustaff nodded.

The girl put all the contents of the tray onto the table and then stood back. She hesitated and then looked at the other customer.

'Anything else you want – er – Herr Kloset… sir…?'

'Klosterheim,' he said smiling at her. Although his expression was perfectly amiable, there was still a touch of the sardonic gleam Faustaff had seen earlier. It seemed to faze the girl. She just grunted and hurried back to the counter.

Klosterheim nodded again at Faustaff and Nancy.

'I am a visitor to your country I am afraid,' he said. 'I should have invented some sort of pseudonym that could be more easily pronounced.'

Faustaff had his mouth full of steak and couldn't respond at once, but Nancy said politely: 'Oh, and where are you from, Mr…?'

'Klosterheim,' he laughed. 'Well, my present home is in Sweden.'

'Over here on business or holiday?' Faustaff asked carefully. Klosterheim was lying.

'A little of both. This desert is magnificent isn't it?'

'Hot, though,' giggled the redhead. 'I bet you're not used to this where you come from.'

'Sweden does have quite warm summers,' Klosterheim replied.

Faustaff looked at Klosterheim warily. There was very little caution in the professor's make-up, but the little there was now told him not to be forthcoming with Klosterheim.

'Which way are you heading?' asked the girl. 'LA or Frisco?'

'Los Angeles. I have some business in the capital.'

Los Angeles – or more particularly Hollywood, where the presidential Bright House and the Temple of Government were situated – was the capital of the Greater American Confederacy.

Faustaff helped himself to his second and third steaks. 'You must be one of those people we were talking about earlier,' he said, 'who prefer to drive than go by plane.'

'I am not fond of flying,' Klosterheim agreed. 'And that is no way to see a country, is it?'

'Certainly isn't,' agreed the redhead, 'if you like this sort of scenery.'

'I am very fond of it,' Klosterheim smiled. He got up and bowed slightly to them both. 'Now, please excuse me. I will have an early night tonight, I think.'

'Goodnight,' said Faustaff with his mouth half-full. Once again Klosterheim had that secret look in his black eyes. Once again he turned quickly. He left the restaurant with a nod to the girl who was still behind the counter, fixing Faustaff's sodas.

When he had gone the girl came over and stood by their table.

'What you make of him?' she asked Faustaff.

Faustaff laughed. The crockery shook. 'He's certainly got a talent for drawing attention to himself,' he said. 'I guess he's one of those people who go in for making themselves seem mysterious to others.'

'No kidding,' the girl agreed enthusiastically. 'If you mean what I think you mean, I'm with you. He certainly gives me the creeps.'

'Which way did he drive in from?' Faustaff asked.

'Didn't notice. He gave an LA hotel as his address. So maybe he came from LA.'

Nancy shook her head. 'No – that's where he's going. He told us.'

Faustaff shrugged and laughed again. 'If I read him right this is what he wants – people talking about him, wondering about him. I've met guys like him before. Forget it.'

Later the girl showed them to their cabin. In it was a large double bed.

'It's bigger than our standard beds,' she said. 'Just made for you, you might say.'

'That's kind of you,' Faustaff smiled.

'Sleep well,' she said. 'Goodnight.'

'Goodnight.'

The redhead was eager to get to bed as soon as the girl had left. Faustaff hugged her, kissed her and then stood back for a moment, taking a small, green velvet skull-cap from his shorts' pocket and fitting it on his head before undressing.

'You're crazy, Fusty,' giggled the redhead, sitting on the bed and shaking with amusement. 'I'll never make you out.'

'Honey, you never will,' he said, as he stripped off his clothes and flipped out the light.

Three hours later he was awakened by a tight sensation round his head and a tiny, soundless vibration.

He sat upright, pushing back the covers, and getting as gently as possible out of bed so as not to disturb the girl.

The invoker was ready. He had better lug it out into the desert as soon as possible.

Chapter Two

Three Men in T-shirts

Professor Faustaff hurried from the cabin, carrying his huge naked bulk with extraordinary grace and speed towards the car park and his Cadillac.

The invoker was ready. It was a fairly compact piece of machinery with handles for moving it. He heaved it from the Cadillac's trunk and began hauling it out of the car park, away from the motel and into the desert.

Ten minutes later he squatted beneath the moon, fiddling with the invoker's controls. He set dials and pressed buttons. A white light blinked and went out, a red light blinked, a green light blinked, then the machine seemed still again. Professor Faustaff stood back.

Half-seen traceries of light now seemed to spring from the invoker and weave geometric patterns against the darkness. At length a figure began to materialise amongst them, ghostly at first but steadily becoming more solid. Soon a man stood there.

He was dressed in a coverall and his head was bandaged. He was unshaven and gaunt. He fingered the disc, strapped wristwatch fashion to his arm, and said nothing.

'George?'

'Hello, professor. Where are we? – I got the call. Can you make it fast? – we need everybody at the base.' George Forbes spoke tonelessly, unlike his normal self.

'You really are in trouble there. Give me the picture.'

'Our main base was attacked by a D-squad. They used their disruptors as well as more conventional weapons, helicopters flying in low. We missed them until they were close. We fought back, but the bastards did their usual hit-and-run attack and were in and out again in five minutes – leaving us with five men alive out of twenty-three, wrecked equipment and a damaged adjustor. While we were licking our wounds they must have gone on to create a U.M.S. We're trying to fight it with a malfunctioning adjustor – but it's a losing battle. Four others just won't be enough. We'll get caught in the U.M.S. ourselves if we're not careful – then you can write off E-15. We need a new adjustor and a full replacement team.'

'I'll do my best,' Faustaff promised. 'But we've no spare adjustors – you know how long one takes to build. We'll have to risk shipping one from somewhere else – E-1 is the safest, I guess.'

'Thanks, professor. We've given up hope – we don't think you can do anything for us. But if you can do anything…' Forbes rubbed his face. He seemed so exhausted that he didn't really know where he was or what he was saying. 'I'd better get back. Okay?'

'Okay,' said Faustaff.

Forbes tapped the disc on his wrist and began to dematerialise as the E-15 invoker tugged him back through the subspacial levels.

Faustaff knew he had to get to Frisco quickly. He would have to travel tonight. He began to haul the invoker back towards the motel.

When he was quite close to the car park he saw a figure in silhouette near his Cadillac.

The figure seemed to be trying to open the car door. Faustaff bellowed: 'What d'you think you're trying to do, buster?' He let go of the invoker and strode towards the figure.

As Faustaff approached the figure straightened and whirled round and it wasn't Klosterheim as Faustaff had suspected but a woman, blonde, tanned, with the shapely synthetic curves of a dressmaker's dummy – the kind of curves an older woman bought for herself. This woman seemed young.

She gasped when she saw the fat giant bearing down on her, dressed only in a green velvet skull cap, and she moved away from the car.

'You haven't any clothes on,' she said. 'You could be arrested if I screamed.'

Faustaff laughed and paused. 'Who'd arrest me? Why were you trying to get into my car?'

'I guess I thought it was mine.'

Faustaff looked at the English MG and the Thunderbird. 'It's not dark enough to make that kind of mistake,' he said. The big yellow moon was high and full. 'Which is yours?'

'The Thunderbird,' she said.

'So the MG's Klosterheim. I still don't believe you could make a mistake like that – a red Cadillac for a black Thunderbird.'

'I haven't broken into your car. I guess I was just peeking inside. I was interested in that equipment you've got in there.' She pointed to a small portable computer in the back seat. 'You're a scientist aren't you – a professor or something?'

'Who told you?'

'The owner here.'

'Here. I see. What's your name, honey?'

'Maggy White.'

'Well, Miss White, keep your nose out of my car in future.' Faustaff was not normally so rude, but he was sure she was lying, as Klosterheim had been lying, and his encounter with George Forbes had depressed him. Also he was puzzled by Maggy White's total sexlessness. It was unusual for him to find any woman unattractive – they were always attractive in some way – but he was unmoved by her. Subconsciously he also realised that she was unmoved by him. It made him uncomfortable without realising quite why.

He watched her flounce on high heels back towards the cabins. He saw her enter one, saw the door close. He went to get his invoker and hauled it into the trunk, locking it carefully.

Then he followed Maggy White towards the cabins. He would have to wake Nancy and get going. The sooner he contacted his team in Frisco the better.

Nancy yawned and scratched her scalp as she climbed into the car. Faustaff started the Cadillac up and drove out onto the highway, changed gear and stepped on the accelerator.

'What's the rush, Fusty?' She was still sleepy. He had had to waken her suddenly and also wake the motel owner to pay him.

'An emergency in my Frisco office,' he said. 'Nothing for you to worry about. Sorry I disturbed you. Try and get some sleep as we drive, huh?'

'What happened tonight? You bumped into a girl or something in the car park. What were you doing out there?'

'Got a buzz from the office. Who told you?'

'The owner. He told me while he was filling the tank for you.' She smiled. 'Apparently you hadn't any clothes on. He thought you were a nut.'

'He's probably right.'

'I get the idea that the girl and that Klosterheim character are connected – have they anything to do with this emergency of yours?'

'They just might have.' Faustaff shivered. He had no clothes but the shirt and shorts he wore and the desert night was cold. 'Might just be salvagers, but...' He was musing aloud.

'Salvagers?'

'Oh, just bums – some kind of con team. I don't know who they are. Wish I did.'

Nancy had fallen asleep by the time dawn came. The rising sun turned the desert into an expanse of red sand and heavy black shadows. Tall cactus, their branches extended like the arms of declamatory figures, paraded into the distance; petrified prophets belatedly announcing the doom that had overtaken them.

Faustaff breathed in the cool, dawn smells, feeling sad and isolated suddenly, retiring into himself in the hope that his unconscious might produce some clue to the identities of Herr Klosterheim and Maggy White. He drove very fast, egged on by the knowledge that unless he reached Frisco quickly E-15 was finished.

Later, Nancy woke up and stretched, blinking in the strong light. The desert shimmered in the heat haze, rolling on for ever in all directions. She accepted the bizarre nature of the continent without question. To her it had always been like this. Faustaff had known it as very different five years before – when a big U.M.S. had only just been checked. That was something he would probably never fully understand – tremendous physical changes took place on a planet, but the inhabitants never seemed to notice. Somehow the U.M. Situations were accompanied by a deep psychological change in the people – similar in some ways, perhaps, to the mass delusions involving flying saucer spottings years before on his own world. But this was total hallucination. The human psyche seemed even more adaptable than the human physique. Possibly it was the only way the people could survive and protect their sanity on the insane planets of subspace. Yet the mass delusion was not always complete, but those who remembered an earlier state of existence were judged insane, of course. Even on a mass level things took time to adapt. What the inhabitants of Greater America didn't realise now, for instance, was that theirs was the only inhabited land mass, apart from one island in the Philippines. They still talked about foreign countries, though they would forget little by little, but the countries were only in their imagination, mysterious and romantic places where nobody actually went. Klosterheim had given himself away immediately he said he was from Sweden, for Faustaff knew that on E-3 a gigantic forest grew in the areas once called Scandinavia, Northern Europe and Southern Russia. Nobody lived there – they had been wiped out in the big U.M.S. which had warped the American continent too. The trees of that area were all grotesquely huge, far bigger than North American redwoods, out of proportion to the land they grew on. And yet these were one of the best results of the partial correction of a U.M.S.

On all the fifteen alternate Earths with which Faustaff was familiar Unstable Matter Situations had manifested themselves and been countered. The result of this was that the worlds were now bizarre travesties of their originals and the further back down the subspacial corridor you went the more unearthly were the alternate Earths. Yet many of the inhabitants survived and that was the important thing. The whole reason for Faustaff's and his team's efforts was to save lives. It was a good reason as far as they were concerned, even though it seemed they were fighting a slow, losing battle against the D-squads.

He was convinced that Klosterheim and Maggy White were representatives of a D-squad and that their presence heralded trouble for himself, if not the whole of his organisation. Frisco might have some new information for him when he got there. He hoped so. His usual equanimity was threatening to desert him.

Frisco's towers were at last visible in the distance. The road widened here and cactus plants grew thicker in the desert. Behind Frisco was the blue and misty sea, but the only ships in her harbour were coast-going freighters.

The sedate pace of Frisco compared to the frenetic mood he had left behind in LA made Faustaff feel a little better as he drove through the peaceful old streets that had retained a character that was somehow redolent of an older America, an America that had only really existed in the nostalgic thoughts of the generation which had grown up before the First World War. The streets were crammed with signs lettered in Edwardian style, there was the delicious smell of a thousand delicatessens, the tolling of the trolley cars echoed amongst the grey and yellow buildings, the air was still and warm, people sauntered along the sidewalks or could be seen leaning against bars and counters within the cool interiors of little stores and saloons. Faustaff liked Frisco and preferred it to all other cities in Greater America, which was why he had chosen to set up his headquarters here rather than in the capital of LA. Not that he minded an atmosphere of noise, bustle and neurosis – in fact he rather enjoyed it – but Frisco had a greater air of permanence than elsewhere on E-3 so that psychologically at any rate it seemed the best place for his HQ.

He drove towards North Beach and soon drew up beside a Chinese restaurant with dark-painted windows with gold dragons on them. He turned to the redhead.

'Nancy, how would you like a big Chinese meal and a chance to wash up?'

'Okay. But is this a brush off?' She could see he didn't intend to join her.

'Nope – but there's that urgent business I must attend to. If I don't come in later, go to this address.' He took a small notebook from his shirt pocket and scribbled the address of his private apartment. 'That's my private place. Make yourself at home.' He handed her a key. 'And tell them you're a friend of mine in the restaurant.'

She seemed too tired to question him any further and nodded, getting out of the car, still in her swimsuit, and walking into the restaurant.

Faustaff went up to the door next to the restaurant and rang the bell.

A man of about thirty, dark-haired, saturnine, wearing a T-shirt, white jeans and black sneakers, opened the door and nodded when he saw Faustaff. There was a large old-fashioned clock face stencilled onto the front of his T-shirt. It looked like any other gimmick design.

Faustaff said: 'I need some help with the equipment in the trunk. Anyone else here?'

'Mahon and Harvey.'

'I guess we can get the stuff upstairs between us. Will you tell them?'

The man – whose name was Ken Peppiatt – disappeared and came back shortly with two other men of about the same age and build, though one of them was blond. They were dressed the same, with the clock design on their T-shirts.

Helped by Faustaff they manhandled the electro-invoker and the portable computer through the door and up a narrow stairway. Faustaff closed the door behind them and kept an eye on the young men until they had set the equipment down in a small room on the first floor. The boards were bare and the room had a musty smell. They went up more uncarpeted stairs to the next floor which was laid out like a living room, with old, comfortable furniture untidily crammed into it. There were magazines and empty glasses littered about. The three men in T-shirts flopped into chairs and looked up at Faustaff as he went to an art deco cocktail cabinet and poured himself a large glass of bourbon. He spooned ice cubes into the drink and sipped it as he turned to face them.

'You know the problem they have on E-15.'

The three men nodded. Mahon had been the man who had contacted Faustaff the day before.

'I gather you're already arranging for a team to relieve the survivors?'

Harvey said: 'They're on their way. But what they really need is an adjustor. We haven't a spare – it'll be dangerous to let one go from another alternate. If a D-squad attacks a world without an adjustor – you can say goodbye to that world.'

'E-1 hasn't had an attack yet,' Faustaff mused. 'We'd better send their adjustor.'

'Your decision,' said Mahon getting up. 'I'll go and contact E-1.' He left the room.

'I'll want reports on the situation whenever possible,' Faustaff told him as he closed the door. He turned to the two others. 'I think I've been in touch with the people who made that tunnel you found.'

'What are they – salvagers or D-squaders?' Harvey asked.

'Not sure. They don't seem like salvagers and D-squaders usually only turn up to attack. They don't hang about in motels.' Faustaff told about his encounter with the pair.

Peppiatt frowned. 'That's not a real name – Klosterheim – I'd swear.' Peppiatt was one of their best linguists. He knew the root tongues of all the alternates, and many secondary languages as well. 'It doesn't click. Just possibly German, I suppose, but even then...'

'Let's forget about the name for the time being,' Faustaff said. 'We'd better put a couple of people on to watching them. Two Class H agents ought to be okay. We'd better have recordings, photographs of them, everything we can get for a file. All the usual information – normal whereabouts and so on. Can you fix that, Ken?'

'We've got a lot of Class H agents on retainer. They'll think it's a security job – Class H still believe we're some kind of government outfit. You might as well use half a dozen – they're available.'

'As many as you think. Just keep tabs on the pair of them.'

Faustaff mentioned that they were probably in LA or Frisco judging by what they had said. Their cars shouldn't be hard to trace – he'd taken the numbers as he left the car park that morning.

Faustaff finished his drink and picked up a clipboard of schedules lying on a table. He flipped through them.

'Cargoes seem to be moving smoothly enough,' he nodded. 'How's the fresh-water situation here?'

'We'll need some more. They're recycling already, of course, but until we get those big sea-water condensers set up we'll have to keep shipping it in from E-6.' E-6 was a world that now consisted of virtually nothing but freshwater oceans.

'Good,' Faustaff began to relax. The E-15 problem was still nagging him, though there was little he could do at this stage. Only once before had he experienced a Total Break-up – on the now extinct E-16 – the planet that had taken his father when a U.M.S. got completely out of hand. He didn't like to think of what had happened there happening anywhere else.

'There's a new recruit you might like to talk to yourself,' Harvey said. 'A geologist from this world. He's at main HQ now.'

Faustaff frowned. 'This will mean a trip to E-1. I guess I'd better see him. I need to go to E-1, anyway. They'll want an explanation about the adjustor for one thing. They'll be nervous, quite rightly.'

'They sure will, professor. I'll keep you in touch if anything breaks with this Klosterheim and the girl.'

'Have you got a bed free? I'll get a couple of hours sleep first, I think. No point in working tired.'

'Sure. The second on the left upstairs.'

Faustaff grunted and went upstairs. Though he could last for days without sleep, it was mainly thanks to his instinct to conserve his energy whenever he had the chance.

He lay down on the battered bed and, after a pang or two of conscience about Nancy, went to sleep.

Chapter Three
Changing Times

Faustaff slept for almost two hours exactly, got up, washed and shaved and left the house, which was primarily living quarters for a section of his E-3 team.

He walked down towards Chinatown and soon reached a big building that had once been a pleasure house, with a saloon and a dance floor downstairs and private rooms for one-night rental upstairs. Outside, the building looked ramshackle and the old paint was dull and peeling. A sign in ornate playbill lettering could still be made out. It read, somewhat unoriginally, The Golden Gate. He opened a side door with his key and went in.

The place was still primarily as it had been when closed down by the cops for the final time. Everything that wasn't faded plush seemed tarnished gilt. The big dance hall, with bars at both ends, smelled a little musty, a little damp. Big mirrors still lined the walls behind the bars, but they were fly-specked.

In the middle of the floor a lot of electronic equipment had been set up. Housed in dull metal casings, its function was hard to guess. To an outsider many of the dials and indicators would have been meaningless.

A wide staircase led from the floor to a gallery above. A man, dressed in standard T-shirt, jeans and sneakers, was standing there now, his hands on the rail, leaning and looking at the professor below.

Faustaff nodded to the man and began to climb the stairs.

'Hi, Jas.'

'Hi, professor.' Jas Hollom grinned. 'What's new?'

'Too much. They said you had a new recruit.'

'That's right.' Jas jerked his thumb at a door behind him. 'He's in there. It was the usual thing – a guy getting curious about the paradoxes in the environment. His investigations led him to us. We roped him in.'

Faustaff's team made a point of drawing its recruits from people like the man Hollom had described. It was the best way and ensured a high standard of recruits as well as a fair amount of secrecy. The professor didn't court secrecy for its own sake but didn't approach governments and declare himself simply because his experience warned him that the more officials who knew about him and his organisation the more spanners there would be in his organisation's works.

Faustaff reached the gallery and moved towards the door Hollom had indicated, but before he entered he nodded towards the equipment below.

'How's the adjustor working? Tested it recently?'

'Adjustor and tunneller both in good shape. Will you be needing the tunneller today?'

'Probably.'

'I'll go down and check it. Mahon's in the communications room if you want him.'

'I saw him earlier. I'll talk to the recruit.'

Faustaff knocked on the door and entered.

The new recruit was a tall, well-built, sandy-haired young man of about twenty-five. He was sitting in a chair reading one of the magazines from the table in the centre. He got up.

'I'm Professor Faustaff.' He held out his hand and the sandy-haired man shook it a little warily.

'I'm Gerry Bowen. I'm a geologist – at the university here.'

'You're a geologist. You found a flaw in the plot of the Story of the Rocks, is that it?'

'There's that – but it was the ecology of Greater America – not the geology – that bothered me. I started enquiring, but everybody seems to be in a half-dream when it comes to talking about some subjects. A sort of...'

'Mass hallucination?'

'Yes – what's the explanation?'

'I don't know. You started checking, eh?'

'I did. I found this place – found it was turning out a near-endless stream of goods and supplies of all kinds. That explained what was supporting the country. Then I tried to talk to one of your men, find out more. He told me more. It's still hard to believe.'

'About the alternates, you mean?'

'About everything to do with them.'

'Well, I'll tell you about it – but I've got to warn you that if we don't get loyalty from you after you've heard the story we do what we always do…'

'That's…?'

'We've got a machine for brainwashing you painlessly – not only wiping your memory clean of what you've learned from us, but getting rid of that bug of curiosity that led you to us. Okay?'

'Okay. What happens now?'

'Well, I thought I'd give you a good illustration that we're not kidding about the subspacial alternate worlds. I'm going to take you to another alternate – my home planet. We call it E-1. It's the youngest of the alternates.'

'The youngest? That seems a bit hard to figure.'

'Figure it out after you've heard more. There isn't much time. Are you willing to come along?'

'You bet I am!' Bowen was eager. He had an alert mind and Faustaff could tell that in spite of his enthusiasm his intellect was working all the information out, weighing it. That was healthy. It also meant, Faustaff thought, that it wouldn't take long for positive information to convince him.

When Faustaff and Gerry Bowen got down to the ground floor Jas Hollom was working at the largest machine there. A faint vibration could be felt on the floor and some indicators had been activated.

Faustaff stepped forward, checking the indicators. 'She's doing fine.' He looked at Bowen. 'Another couple of minutes and we'll be ready.'

Two minutes passed and a thin hum began to come from the machine. Then the air in front of the tunneller seemed full of agitated dust which swirled round and round in a spiral until delicate, shifting colours became visible and the part of the room immediately ahead of the tunneller became shadowy until it disappeared.

'Tunnel's ready,' Faustaff said to Bowen. 'Let's go.'

Bowen followed Faustaff towards the tunnel that the machine had created through subspace.

'How does it *work*?' Bowen asked incredulously.

'Tell you later.'

'Just a minute,' Hollom said, making an adjustment to the machine. 'There – I was sending you to E-12.' He laughed. 'Okay – *now*!'

Faustaff stepped into the tunnel and grabbed Bowen, pulling him in too. Faustaff propelled himself forward.

The 'walls' of the tunnel were grey and hazy, they seemed thin and beyond them was a vacuum more absolute than that of space. Sensing this Bowen shuddered; Faustaff could feel him do it.

It took ninety seconds before, with an itching skin but no other ill effects, Faustaff stepped out into a room of bare concrete – a storeroom in a factory, or a warehouse. Bowen said: 'Phew! That was worse than a ghost train.'

But for one large piece of equipment that was missing, the equipment in this room was identical to that in the room they'd just left. It was all that occupied the dully lit room. A steel door opened and a short, fat man in an ordinary lounge suit came in. He took off his glasses, a gesture that conveyed surprise and pleasure, and walked with a light, bouncing step towards Faustaff.

'Professor! I heard you were coming.'

'Hello, Doctor May. Nice to see you. This is Gerry Bowen from E-3. He may be coming to work with us.'

'Good, good. You'll want the lecture room. Um...' May paused and pursed his lips. 'We were a bit worried by E-15 requisitioning our adjustor, you know. We have some more being built, but...'

'It was on my orders. Sorry, doctor. E-1 has never had a raid, after all. It was the safest bet.'

'Still, a risk. This could be the time they pick. Sorry to gripe, professor. We realised the emergency was acute. It's odd knowing at the back of your mind that if a U.M.S. occurs we've nothing to fight it with.'

'Of course. Now – the lecture room.'

'I take it you won't want to be disturbed.'

'Only if something bad crops up. I'm expecting news from E-3 and E-15. D-squad trouble on both.'

'I heard.'

The corridor seemed to Bowen to be situated in a large office block. When they reached the elevator he guessed that that must be what it was – outwardly, anyway.

The building was, in fact, the central headquarters for Faustaff's organisation, a multistorey building that stood on one of Haifa's main streets. It was registered as the offices of the Trans-Israel Export Company. If the authorities had ever wondered about it, they hadn't done anything to let Faustaff know. Faustaff's father was a respected figure in Haifa – and his mysterious disappearance something of a legend. Perhaps because of his father's good name, Faustaff wasn't bothered.

The lecture room was appropriately labelled LECTURE ROOM. Inside were several rows of seats facing a small cinema screen. A desk had been placed to one side of the screen and on it was mounted a control console of some kind.

'Take a seat, Mr Bowen,' said Doctor May as Faustaff walked up to the desk and squeezed his bulk into a chair. May sat down beside Bowen and folded his arms.

'I'm going to be as brief as I can,' Faustaff said. 'And use a few slides and some V-clips to illustrate what I'm going to say. I'll answer questions, too, of course, but Doctor May will have to fill you in on any particular details you want to know. Okay?'

'Okay,' said Bowen.

Faustaff touched a stud on the console and the lights dimmed.

'Although it seems that we have been travelling through the subspacial levels for many years,' he began, 'we have actually only been in contact with them since 1971 – that's twenty-eight years ago. The discovery of the alternate Earths was made by my father when he was working here, in Haifa, at the Haifa Institute of Technology.'

A picture came onto the screen – a picture of a tall, rather lugubrious man, almost totally unlike the other Faustaff, his son. He was skinny, with melancholy, overlarge eyes and big hands and feet. He looked like the gormless feed-man for a comedian.

'That's him. He was a nuclear physicist and a pretty good one. He was born in Europe, spent some time in a German concentration camp, went to America and helped on the Bomb. He left America soon after the Hiroshima explosion, travelled around a little, had a job directing an English Nuclear Research Establishment, then got this offer to come to Haifa where they were doing some very interesting work with high-energy neutrinos. This work particularly excited my father. His ambition – kept secret from everyone but my mother and me – was to discover a device which would counter a nuclear explosion – just stop the bomb going off. A fool's dream, really, and he had sense enough to realise it. But he never forgot that that was what he would like to work on if he had the chance. Haifa offered him that chance – or he thought it did. His own work with high-energy neutrinos had given him the idea that a safety device, at very least, could be built that would have the effect of exerting a correcting influence on unstable elements by emitting a stream of high-energy neutrinos that on contact with the agitated particles would form a uniting link, a kind of shell around the unstable atoms which would, as it were, "calm them down" and allow them to be dealt with easily and at leisure.

'Some scientists at Haifa Tech had got the same idea and he was offered the job of directing the research.

'He worked for a year and had soon developed a device which was similar to our adjustors in their crudest form. In the meantime my mother died. One day he and several others were testing the machine when they made a mistake in the regulation of the particles emitted by the device. In fiddling with the controls they accidentally created the first "tunnel". Naturally they didn't know what it was, but investigation soon brought them the information of the subspacial alternate Earths. Further frenzied research, which paralleled work on the adjustor, the tunneller and the invoker, produced the knowledge of twenty-four alternate Earths to our own! They existed in what my father and his team called "subspace" – a series of "layers" that are "below" our own space, going deeper and deeper. Within a year of their discovery there were only twenty alternates and they had actually witnessed the total extinction of one planet. Before the end of the second year there were only seventeen alternates and they knew, roughly, what was happening.

'Somehow the complete disruption of the planet's atomic structure was being effected. It would start with a small area and gradually spread until the whole planet would expand into gas and those gasses drift away through space leaving no trace of the planet. The small disrupted areas we now call Unstable Matter Locations and are able to deal with. What at first my father thought was some sort of natural phenomenon was later discovered to be the work of human beings – who have machines that create this disruption of matter.

'Although my father's scientific curiosity filled him, he soon became appalled by the fantastic loss of life that destruction of these alternate Earths involved. Whoever was destroying the planets was cold-bloodedly killing off billions of people a year.

'These planets, I'd better add, all had similarities to our own – and your own, Mr Bowen – with roughly similar standards of civilisation, roughly similar governmental institutions, roughly similar scientific accomplishments – though all, in some way or another, had come to a dead end – had stagnated. We still don't know why this is.'

A picture came onto the screen. It was not a photograph but an artist's impression of a world the same size as Earth, with a moon the same as Earth's. The picture showed a planet that seemed of a universally greyish colour.

'This is E-15 now,' Faustaff said. 'This is what it looked like ten years ago.'

Gerry Bowen saw a predominantly green-and-blue world. He didn't recognise it. 'E-1 still looks like this,' Faustaff said.

Faustaff flashed the next picture. A world of green obsidian, shown in close-ups to be misty, twilit, ghastly, with ghoul-like inhabitants.

'And this is what E-14 looked like less than ten years ago,' came Faustaff's voice.

The picture Bowen saw next was exactly the same as the second picture he'd seen – a predominantly green-and-blue world with well-marked continental outlines.

'E-13, coming up now,' said Faustaff.

A world of blindingly bright crystal in hexagonal structures like a vast honeycomb. Deposits of earth and water had been collected in some of the indentations. Vs showed the inhabitants living hand-to-mouth existences on the strange world.

'E-13 as it was.'

A picture identical to the two others Bowen had already seen.

The pattern was repeated – worlds of grotesque and fantastic jungles, deserts, seas, had all once been like E-1 was now. Only E-2 was similar to E-1.

'E-2 is a world that seemed to stop short, in our terms, just around 1960 and the expansion of the space programmes. You wouldn't know about those, even, since E-3 stopped short, as I remember, just after 1950. This sudden halting of all kinds of progress still mystifies us. As I said, a peculiar change comes over people as well, on the whole. They behave as if they were living in a perpetual dream and a perpetual present. Old books and Vs that show a different state to the one they now know are ignored or treated as jokes. Time, in effect, ceases to exist in any aspect. It all goes together – only a few, like you, Mr Bowen, break out. The people are normal in all other respects.'

'What's the explanation for the changes of these worlds?' Bowen asked.

'I'm coming to that. When my father and his team first discovered the alternate worlds of subspace they were being wiped out, as I mentioned, rapidly. They found a way of stopping this wholesale destruction by building the adjustors, refinements of the original machines they'd been working on which could control the U.M. Situations where they occurred.

'In order to be ready to control the U.M.S. where and when it manifested itself, my father and his team had to begin getting recruits and had soon built up a large organisation – almost as large as the one I now have. Well-equipped teams of men, both physically and mentally alert, had to be stationed on the other alternates – there were fifteen left by then, not fourteen as now.

'Slowly the organisation was built up, not without some help from officials in the Israeli government of the time, who also helped to keep the activities of my father and his team fairly secret. The adjustors were built and installed on all the worlds. By means of an adjustor's stabilising influence they could correct, to some extent, a U.M.S. – their degree of success depending on the stage the U.M.S. had reached before they could get their machine there and get it working. Things are much the same nowadays. Though we can "calm down" the disrupted matter and bring it back to something approximately its original form, we cannot make it duplicate its original at all perfectly. The deeper back you go through the subspacial levels, the less like the original the planet is and the more U.M. Situations there have been. Thus E-15 is a world of grey ash that settles on it from thousands of volcanoes that have broken through the surface, E-14 is nothing but glassy rock, and E-13 is primarily a crystalline structure these days. E-12 is all jungle and so on. Nearer to E-1 the worlds are more recognisable – particularly E-2, E-3 and E-4. E-4 had it lucky – it stopped progressing just before the First World War. But it mainly consists of the British Isles and Southern and Eastern Europe now – the rest is either wasteland or water.'

'So your father founded the organisation and you carried it on, is that it?' Bowen asked from the darkness.

'My father died in the Total Break-up of E-16,' Faustaff said. 'The U.M.S. got out of control – and he didn't get off in time.'

'You said the U.M.S. weren't natural – that somebody caused them. Who?'

'We don't know. We call them the D-squad – the Demolition Squad. They make it their business to attack our stations as well as creating U.M. Situations. They've killed many people directly, not just indirectly.'

'I must say it's hard to believe that such a complicated organisation as yours can exist and do the work it does.'

'It has built up over the years. Nothing strange about that. We manage.'

'You talk all the time about alternate Earths – but what about the rest of the universe? I remember reading the theory of alternate universes some years ago.'

'We're pretty sure that the only alternates are of Earth and the moon in some cases. It's a pity spaceflight is not yet sufficiently sophisticated, otherwise we could put the theory to the test. My father reached this conclusion in 1985 when the second manned spaceship reached Mars and "disappeared". It was assumed it had gone off course into a meteor storm on its return flight. Actually it turned up on Earth 5 – its crew dead due to the stresses of passing through subspace in a most unorthodox way. This seemed to prove that some distance beyond Earth there are no subspacial alternates. Whether this is a natural phenomenon or an artificial one, I don't know. There's a lot we don't understand.'

'You think there is a force at work, apart from you?'

'I do. The D-squad speaks of that. But though we've done some extensive checking up, we haven't found a trace of where they come from – though it must be from somewhere on E-1. Why they should murder planets – and more specifically the inhabitants of those planets – the way they do, I cannot understand. It is inhuman.'

'And what is your real reason for doing all this, professor, risking so much?'

'To preserve human life,' said Faustaff.

'That is all.'

Faustaff smiled. 'That's all.'

'So it's your organisation against the D-squad, basically.'

'Yes.' Faustaff paused. 'There are also the people we call salvagers. They came from several different alternates – but primarily from E-1, E-2, E-3 and E-4. At different stages they have discovered our organisation and found out what it does. Either they have found us out of curiosity, as you did, or stumbled upon us by accident. Over the years they have formed themselves into bands who pass through the subspacial alternates looting what they can and selling it to worlds that need it – using E-1 as their main base, as we do. They are pirates, freebooters using stolen equipment that was originally ours. They are no threat. Some people are irritated by them, that's all.'

'There's no chance that they are connected with these D-squads.'

'None. For one thing it wouldn't be in their interest to have a planet destroyed.'

'I guess not.'

'Well, that's the basic set-up. Are you convinced?'

'Convinced and overwhelmed. There are a few details I'd like filled in.'

'Perhaps Doctor May can help you?'

'Yes.'

'You want to join us?'

'Yes.'

'Good. Doctor May will tell you what you want to know, then put you in touch with someone here who'll show you the ropes. I'll leave you now, if you don't mind.'

Faustaff said goodbye to Bowen and May and left the little lecture room.

Chapter Four
The Salvagers

FAUSTAFF DROVE HIS Cadillac towards the centre of San Francisco where he had his private apartment. The sun was setting and the city looked romantic and peaceful. There wasn't much traffic on the roads and he made good speed.

He parked the car and walked into the old apartment house that stood on a hill giving a good view of the bay.

The decrepit elevator took him up to the top and he was about to let himself in when he realised he'd given his key to Nancy. He rang the bell. He was still wearing the beach shirt and shorts and sneakers he had been wearing the day before when he left Los Angeles. He wanted a shower and a change before anything.

Nancy opened the door. 'So you made it,' she smiled. 'Is the emergency over?'

'The emergency – oh, yes. It's in hand. Forget about it.' He laughed and put his arms around her, lifting her up and kissing her.

'I'm hungry,' he said. 'Is my icebox well-stocked?'

'Very well-stocked,' she grinned.

'Well, let's have something to eat and go to bed.' He had now forgotten about wanting a shower.

'That seems a good idea,' she said.

Later that night the VC started ringing. Faustaff woke up instantly and picked it up. Nancy stirred and muttered but didn't wake.

'Faustaff.'

'Mahon. Message from E-15. Things are bad. They've had another visit from the D-squad. They want help.'

'They want me, maybe?'

'Well, yes, I think that's about the size of it.'

'Are you at HQ?'

'Yes.'

'I'll be over.'

Faustaff put the VC down and got up. Once again he was careful not to disturb Nancy who seemed a good sleeper. He put on a black T-shirt and a pair of dark pants and socks, then laced up his old sneakers.

Soon he was driving the Cadillac towards Chinatown and not much later was in The Golden Gate, where Mahon and Hollom were waiting for him.

Hollom was working on the tunneller, his face screwed up in impatience.

Faustaff went behind the bar and reached under it, putting a bottle of bourbon and some glasses on the counter.

'Want a drink?'

Hollom shook his head angrily.

Mahon looked up from where he was intently watching Hollom. 'He's having trouble, professor. Can't seem to drive the tunnel deep enough. Can't reach E-15.'

Faustaff nodded. 'That's sure proof that a big D-squad is working there. It happened that time on E-6, remember?' He poured himself a large drink and swallowed it down. He didn't interfere with Hollom who knew as much about tunnellers as anyone and would ask for help if he needed it. He leaned on the bar, pouring himself another drink and singing one of his favourite old numbers, remembered from when he was a youngster. 'Then take me disappearing through the smoke rings of my mind, down the foggy ruins of time, far past the frozen leaves, the haunted, frightened trees, out to the windy beach, far from the twisted reach of crazy sorrow...' It was Dylan's 'Mr Tambourine Man', Faustaff preferred the old stuff, didn't care much for modern popular music which had become too pretentious for his taste.

Hollom said tight-faced: 'D'you mind, professor? I'm trying to concentrate.'

'Sorry,' said Faustaff shutting up at once. He sighed, trying to remember how long it had taken them to break through to E-6 the last time there had been a heavy block.

Hollom shouted wildly, suddenly: 'Quick – quick – quick – I won't hold it long.'

The air in front of the tunneller began to become agitated. Faustaff put down his drink and hurried forward.

Soon a tunnel had manifested itself. It shimmered more than usual and seemed very unstable. Faustaff knew that if it broke down he would be alone in the depths of subspace, instantly killed. Though possessing very little fear of death Faustaff did have a strong love of life and didn't enjoy the prospect of having to give up living. In spite of this he stepped swiftly into the subspacial tunnel and was soon moving along past the grey shimmering walls. His journey was the longest he had ever made, taking over two minutes, then he was through.

Peppiatt greeted him. Peppiatt was one of several volunteers who had gone with the replacement team to E-15. Peppiatt looked haggard.

'Glad to see you, professor. Sorry we couldn't use the invoker – it's busted.'

'You are having trouble.'

The invoker was a kind of subspacial 'grab', working on similar principles to the sister machines, that could be used primarily to pull agents out of U.M.S. trouble spots, or get them through the dimensions without needing a tunnel. A tunnel was safer since the invoker worked on the principle of forming a kind of shell around a man and propelling it through the layers in order to break them down. Sometimes they resisted and didn't break down. Then a man 'invoked' was lost for good.

Faustaff looked around. He was in a large, natural cave. It was dark and the floor was damp, neon lighting sputtering on the walls, filling the cave with lurid light that danced like firelight. Pieces of battered electronic equipment lay everywhere, much of it plainly useless. Two other men were by the far wall working at something that lay on a bench. Cables trailed across the floor. Several more men moved about. They carried laser-rifles, their power-packs on their backs. The rifles had been stolen from the US government on E-1 and technicians in Haifa were trying to mass-produce them, but hadn't had much success as yet. Faustaff's men were not normally armed and Faustaff had given no order to fight back at the D-squad. Evidently someone had decided it was necessary. Faustaff didn't like it, but he decided not to question the order now that it had been made. The one thing the professor ever seemed adamant about was the fact that like physicians their business was to save, not take, life. It was the entire *raison d'être* of the organisation, after all.

Faustaff knew that his presence on E-15 wasn't likely to serve any particular practical purpose since the men working here were trained to cope with even the most desperate situation, but gathered that he was needed for the moral support the men might get from thinking about it. Faustaff was not a very introspective man on the whole. In all matters outside of his scientific life he acted more according to his instinct than his reason. 'Thinking causes trouble' was a motto he had once expressed in a moment of feeling.

'Where's everyone else?' he asked Peppiatt.

'With the adjustor. Areas 33, 34, 41, 42, 49 and 50 were calmed down for a while, but the D-squad came back. Evidently those areas form the key-spot. We're still trying to get them under control. I'm just going back there, now.'

'I'll come along.'

Faustaff grinned encouragingly at the men he passed on his way to the exit.

Peppiatt shook his head wonderingly. 'Their spirit's better already. I don't know what you do, professor, but you certainly manage to make people feel good.'

Faustaff nodded absently. Peppiatt operated a control beside a big steel door. The door began to slide back into the wall, revealing a bleak expanse of grey ash, a livid sky from which ash fell like rain. There was a stink of sulphur in the air. Faustaff was familiar with the conditions on E-15, where because of the volcanic upheavals almost everywhere on the planet, the people were forced to live in caves such as the one they'd just left. Their lives were fairly comfortable, however, thanks to Faustaff's cargoes brought from more fortunate worlds.

A jeep, already covered by a coating of ash, stood by. Peppiatt got into it and Faustaff climbed into the back seat. Peppiatt started the engine and the jeep began to bounce away across the wasteland of ash. Apart from the sound of the jeep the world was silent. Ash fell and smoke rolled in the distance. Occasionally when the smoke cleared a little the outline of an erupting volcano could be seen.

Faustaff's throat was clogged by the ash carried on the sulphurous air. It was a grey vision of some abandoned hell and infinitely depressing.

Later a square building, half buried in the ash, came in sight.

'That's one of our relay stations, isn't it?' Faustaff pointed.

'Yes. It's the nearest our copters can get to the main base without having a lot of fuel difficulties. There should be a copter waiting.'

A few men stood about outside the relay station. They were dressed in protective suits, wearing oxygen masks and heavy, smoked goggles. Faustaff couldn't see a copter, just a small hovercraft, a useful vehicle for this type of terrain. But even as they drew up, an engine note could be heard in the air above and soon a helicopter began to come down nearby, its rotors thrumming as it settled in the dust.

Two men ran from the station as the copter landed. They were carrying flapping suits, similar to those that all the men here wore. They ran up to the jeep.

'We'll have to wear these, I'm afraid, professor,' Peppiatt said.

Faustaff shrugged. 'Well, if we must.' He took the suit offered him and began to pull it over his bulk. It was tight. He hated feeling constricted. He slipped mask and goggles over his face. At least breathing and seeing were easier.

Peppiatt led the way through the clogging, soft ash to the helicopter. They climbed into the passenger seats. The pilot turned his head. 'They're coming out with fuel pellets now. Won't be long.'

'How are things up at the U.M.S.?' Faustaff asked.

'Pretty bad, I think. There are some salvagers here – we've seen them once – drifting around like buzzards.'

'There can't be much for them to salvage here.'

'Only spare parts,' the pilot said.

'Of course,' said Faustaff.

Using stolen or salvaged equipment belonging to Faustaff's organisation, the salvagers needed to loot spare parts whenever possible. In the confusion following a major D-squad attack this could be done quite easily. Though they resented the salvagers, Faustaff's team had orders not to use violence against them. The salvagers were apparently prepared to use violence if necessary, thus the going was pretty easy for them.

'Do you know which gang is here?' Faustaff asked as the copter was fuelled.

'Two gangs working together, I think. Gordon Ogg's and Cardinal Orelli's.'

Faustaff nodded. He knew both. He had encountered them several times before. Cardinal Orelli was from E-4 and Gordon Ogg was from E-2. They were both men whose investigations had led them to discover Faustaff's organisation and had worked for it for a while before going 'rogue'. Most of their gangs were comprised of similar men. Faustaff had a surprisingly few number of deserters and most of those were now salvagers.

The helicopter began to lift into the ash-laden air.

Within half an hour Faustaff could see signs of the U.M.S. ahead.

The Unstable Matter Situation was confined in a rough radius of ten miles. Here there was no grey ash, but boiling colour and an ear-shattering, unearthly noise.

Faustaff found it hard to adjust his eyes and ears to the U.M.S. He was familiar with the sight and sound of disrupted, unstable matter, but he never got used to it.

Great spiralling gouts of stuff would twist hundreds of feet into the air and then fall back again. The sounds were almost indescribable, like the roar of a thousand tidal waves, the screech of vast sheets of metal being tortured and twisted, the rumble of gigantic landslides.

Around the perimeter of this terrifying example of nature's death throes there buzzed land craft and helicopters. A big adjustor could be seen, trained on the U.M.S., the men and machines completely dwarfed by the swirling fury of the unstable elements.

They were now forced to use the radios in their helmets to speak to one another, and even then words were difficult to make out through the crackles of interference.

The helicopter landed and Faustaff got out, hurrying towards the adjustor.

One of the men near the adjustor was standing watching the instruments, arms folded.

Faustaff tapped him on the shoulder.

'Yes,' came a distant voice through the crackle.

'Faustaff – what's the situation like?'

'More or less static, professor. I'm Haldane.'

'From E-2 isn't it?'

'That's right.'

'Where are the original E-15 team – or what's left of them?'

'Shipped back to E-1. Thought it best.'

'Good. I hear you had another D-squad attack.'

'That's right – yesterday. Unusual intensity for them. As you know, they usually attack and run, never risk the chance of getting themselves hurt – but not this time. I'm afraid we killed one of them – died instantly – sorry to have to do it.'

Faustaff controlled himself. He hated the idea of dying, particularly of violent death. 'Anything I can do here?' he asked.

'Your advice might be needed. Nothing to do at present. We're hoping to calm Area 50 down. We might do it. Ever seen something like this?'

'Only once – on E-16.'

Haldane didn't comment, although the implication must have been clear. Another voice came in. It was an urgent voice.

'Copter 36 to base – U.M.S. spreading from Area 41. Shift adjustor round there – and hurry.'

'We need another dozen adjustors,' Haldane shouted as he

waved a hovering copter down to pick up the adjustor with its magnetic grab.

'I know,' Faustaff shouted back. 'But we can't spare them.' He watched as the grab connected with the adjustor and began to lift it up and away towards Area 41. Adjustors were hard to build. It would be folly to take others from more subspacial Earths.

The dilemma was insoluble. Faustaff had to hope that the one adjustor would finally succeed in checking and reversing the U.M.S.

A distorted voice that he eventually recognised as Peppiatt's said: 'What do you think, professor?'

He shook his head. 'I don't know. Let's get back to that copter and go round the perimeter.'

They stumbled back towards the copter and climbed in. Peppiatt told the pilot what to do. The copter rose into the air and began to circle the U.M.S. Looking it over carefully Faustaff could see that it was still possible to get the U.M.S. under control. He could tell by the colours. While the whole spectrum was represented, as it was now, the elements were still in their natural state at least. When they began to transform the U.M.S. would take on a purple-blue colour. When that happened it would be impossible to do anything.

Faustaff said: 'You'd better start getting the native population assembled in one place as soon as possible. We'll have to anticipate evacuation.'

'We won't be able to evacuate everyone,' Peppiatt warned him.

'I know,' Faustaff said tiredly. 'We'll just have to do what we can. We'll have to work out the best place to ship them to, as well. Perhaps an uninhabited land area somewhere – where they won't come in contact with the natives of another world. This has never happened before – I'm not sure what a meeting between two different populations would produce and we don't want more trouble than we have.' A memory of Klosterheim popped into his mind. 'The Scandinavian Forests on E-3 might be okay.' Already, tacitly, he was accepting that E-15 was finished. He was half-aware of this but his mind was struggling against the defeatist attitude beginning to fill him.

Suddenly the pilot broke in. 'Look!'

About six copters in close formation were coming through the ash-rain in the distance. 'They're not ours,' the pilot said, banking steeply. 'I'm going back to the base.'

'What are they?' Faustaff asked.

Peppiatt answered. 'Probably D-squaders. Might be salvagers.'

'D-squaders! Again!' The D-squads rarely attacked more than once after they had started the initial U.M.S.

'I think they're out to destroy E-15,' Peppiatt said. 'We'll have to defend, you know, professor. Lots of lives at stake.'

Faustaff had never quite been able to make the logical step which excused the taking of life if it saved life. His mind was slightly confused as he nodded and said, with a tight feeling in his chest, 'Okay.'

The copter landed near the adjustor and the pilot got out and spoke to Haldane the chief operator. Haldane came hurrying to where Faustaff and Peppiatt were climbing down. He was fiddling with his helmet. Then his radio blasted on all the frequencies they were using.

'Alert! Alert! All guards to Area 41. D-squad about to attack adjustor.'

Within seconds helicopters began to move in towards Area 41 and land, disgorging armed men.

Faustaff felt infinitely depressed as he watched them take up their defensive positions around the adjustor.

Then the D-squad copters began to come in.

Faustaff saw black-clad figures, seemingly faceless with black masks completely covering their heads. They had weapons in their hands.

The barely seen lance of concentrated light from a laser-rifle suddenly struck down from one of the leading D-squad copters. A man on the ground fell silently.

The guards around the adjustor began to aim a criss-cross lattice of laser rays at the coming copters. The copters dodged, but one of them exploded.

Like tiny, lethal searchlights the beams struck back and forth. The fact that the D-squads used E-1 equipment for all their attacks indicated to Faustaff that that was their origin. The only device they had which Faustaff and his men didn't have was the Matter Disrupter. Faustaff could make out the copter which carried it, flying well behind the others and rather lower.

More of Faustaff's men fell and Faustaff could barely stop himself from weeping. He felt a helpless anger, but it never once occurred to him to strike back at the men who had done the killing.

Another copter exploded, another went out of control and flew into the U.M.S. Faustaff saw it become incredibly luminous and then its outline grew, becoming fainter as it grew, until it vanished. Faustaff shuddered. He wasn't enjoying his visit to E-15.

Then he saw several of his guards fall in one place and realised that the attacking D-squad were concentrating their fire. He saw laser beams touch the adjustor, saw metal smoulder and burst into white flame. The helicopters rose and fled away, their mission accomplished.

Faustaff ran towards the adjustor. 'Where's Haldane?' he asked one of the guards.

The guard pointed at one of the corpses.

Faustaff cursed and began checking the adjustor's indicator dials. They were completely haywire. The adjustor was still powered and its central core hadn't been struck, but Faustaff could see immediately that it would take too long to repair. Why had the D-squads intensified their attacks so much, risking their lives – indeed, losing their lives – to do so? It wasn't like them. Normally they were strictly hit-and-run men. Faustaff pushed this question from his mind. There were more immediate problems to be solved.

He switched his helmet mike to all frequencies and yelled. 'Begin total population assembly immediate. Operate primary evacuation plan. The U.M.S. is going to start spreading any time – and when that happens we won't have much notice before the whole planet breaks up.'

The copter with the grab began to move down towards the

adjustor but Faustaff waved it away. The adjustor was heavy and it would take time to get it back to base. The evacuation of all the men from the area was more important. He told as much to the pilot over his radio.

Against the background of the vast, undulating curtain of disrupted matter, the team worked desperately to get out of the area, Faustaff helping men into copters and giving instructions wherever they were needed. There weren't enough copters to get everyone out at once. The evacuation would have to be organised in two lifts.

As the last of the copters took off, a handful of men, including Faustaff and Peppiatt, were left behind.

Faustaff turned to look at the U.M.S. with despair, noting that the spectrum was slowly toning down. It was the danger signal.

He looked back and saw some land vehicles bumping across the grey wasteland towards them. They didn't look like his organisation's jeeps or trucks. As they drew closer he could make out figures sitting in them, dressed in a strange assortment of costumes.

Sitting high in the back of one jeep was a man dressed in red – a red cap on his head, a red smock covering most of his body. He had a small oxygen mask over his nose and mouth, but Faustaff recognised him by his clothes. It was Orelli, leader of one of the biggest teams of salvagers. He had a laser-rifle pack on his back, and the rifle across his knees.

Peppiatt's voice came through the crackle of static in his ear piece. 'Salvagers. Not wasting much time. They must be after the adjustor.'

The remaining guards raised their weapons, but Faustaff shouted: 'No firing. The adjustor's no use to us. If they want to risk their lives salvaging it, it's up to them.'

Now Faustaff could make out a figure in a jeep just behind Orelli's. An incredibly tall, incredibly thin figure, in a green, belted jacket covered in ash, black trousers and ash-smeared jackboots. He carried a machine gun. He had a mask but it hung against his chest. His face was like a caricature of a Victorian aristocrat's, with thin, beaklike nose, straggling black moustache and no chin. This was Gordon Ogg who had once ranked high in Faustaff's organisation.

The jeeps came to a halt close by and Orelli waved blandly to the little group standing near the ruined adjustor.

'Rights of salvage are ours, I think, professor. I gather that *is* Professor Faustaff in the bulky suit and helmet. I recognise the distinguished figure.' He had to shout this through the noise of the raging U.M.S.

Orelli leaped down from the jeep and approached the group. Ogg did likewise, approaching at a loping gait reminiscent of a giraffe. While Orelli was of average height and inclined to plumpness, Ogg was almost seven feet tall. He cradled his machine gun in his left arm and stepped forward, extending his right hand towards Faustaff. Faustaff shook it because it was easier to do that than make a display of refusing.

Ogg smiled vaguely and wearily, brushing back dirty, ash-covered hair. Except in extreme cases he normally scorned any kind of protective gear. He was an Englishman in love with the early-nineteenth-century mystique of what an Englishman should do and be, a romantic who had originally opposed Faustaff purely out of boredom inspired by the well-organised routine of Faustaff's organisation. Faustaff still liked him, though he felt no liking for Orelli, whose natural deceit had been brought to full flower by his church training on E-4. Even his high intelligence could not counter the rare loathing that Faustaff felt for this man whose character was so preternaturally cruel and treacherous. Faustaff found it bewildering and disturbing.

Orelli's eyes gleamed. He cocked his head to one side, indicating the adjustor.

'We noted the D-squad flying back to its base and gathered you might have an old adjustor you didn't want, professor. Mind if we look at it?'

Faustaff said nothing and Orelli minced towards the adjustor, inspecting it carefully.

'The core's still intact, I note. Seems mainly a question of ruined circuits. I think we could even repair it if we wanted to – though we haven't much use for an adjustor, of course.'

'You'd better take it,' Faustaff said grimly. 'If you hang around talking you'll be caught by the U.M.S.'

Ogg nodded slowly. 'The professor's right, Orelli. Let's get our men to work. Hurry up.'

The salvagers instructed their men to begin stripping the adjustor of the essential parts they wanted. While Faustaff, Peppiatt and the rest looked on wearily, the salvagers worked.

Ogg glanced at Faustaff and then glanced away again. He seemed embarrassed momentarily. Faustaff knew he didn't normally work with Orelli, that Ogg despised the ex-cardinal as much as Faustaff did. He assumed that the difficulty of getting a tunnel through to E-15 had caused the two men to join forces for this operation. Ogg would have to be very careful that he was not betrayed in some way by Orelli when the usefulness of the partnership was over.

Faustaff turned back to look at the U.M.S. Slowly but surely the spectrum was toning down towards the purple-blue that would indicate it was about to spread in full force.

Chapter Five

The Break-up of E-15

When the copters had returned and taken Faustaff and the rest back to base, leaving the salvagers still picking the bones of the adjustor, Faustaff immediately took charge of the evacuation plans. It was proving difficult, he was informed, to get many of E-15's natives to the central base. Being in ignorance of Faustaff and his team, they were suspicious and reluctant to move. Some were already at the base, gathered from the nearby underground communities. Looking dazed and unable to comprehend where they were and what was happening, they even seemed to be losing touch with their own individual identities. Faustaff was interested to see this, since it gave him additional data on their reactions which might help him understand the queer psychic changes that took place amongst the populations of the inhabitants of subspace. His detached interest in their state didn't stop him from approaching them individually and trying to convince them that they were better off at the centre. He realised he would have to put several sympathetic members of his team in with their group when they were re-located on E-3's gigantic forest areas.

With some difficulty the group had succeeded in putting a tunnel through to E-3. The evacuees were already beginning to be shuttled through.

In dribs and drabs they came in and were escorted through the tunnel. Faustaff felt sorry for them as they moved, for the most part, like automata. Many of them actually seemed to think they were experiencing a strange dream.

Eventually the last of the evacuees were through and the team began to gather up its equipment.

Peppiatt was in charge of the tunneller and he began to look worried as the subspacial 'opening' flickered.

'Can't hold it open much longer, professor,' he said. The last few guards stepped forward into the tunnel. 'We're the last,' he said with some relief, turning to Faustaff.

'After you,' said Faustaff.

Peppiatt left the tunneller's controls and stepped forward. Faustaff thought he heard him scream as the tunnel collapsed. He rushed back to the tunneller and desperately tried to bring the tunnel back to normal. But a combination of the subspacial blocks and the steadily increasing disruption on E-15 made it impossible. Eventually he abandoned the tunneller and checked the invocation-disc on his wrist. There wasn't much hope of that working, either, under these conditions.

It looked as if he was trapped on the doomed world.

Faustaff, as usual, acted instinctively. He rushed from the cavern-chamber and out to where a copter still stood. He had had some training in piloting the copters. He hoped he could remember enough of it. He forced his huge frame into the seat and started the engine. Soon he had managed to get the copter into the air. On the horizon the peculiar purple-blue aurora indicated that there was little time left before the whole planet broke up.

He headed east, to where he had gathered the salvagers had their camp. He could only hope that they hadn't yet left and that their tunnel was still operating. There was a good chance that even if that were the case they would refuse to help him get off the planet.

He could soon see the shimmering, light plastic domes of a temporary camp that must be that of the salvagers. He could see no signs of activity and at first thought that they had left.

He landed and went into the first tent he came to. There were no salvagers there, but there were black-clad corpses. This wasn't the salvagers' camp at all – it was the camp of the D-squad. Yet as far as he could tell the D-squaders were dead for no apparent reason. He wasted time checking one of the corpses. It was still warm. But how had it died?

He ran from the tent and climbed back into the copter.

Now he flew even more urgently, until he saw a small convoy of jeeps moving below him. With some relief he realised that they had not yet even reached their base. They seemed to be heading towards a smoking volcano about ten miles away. He guessed that the salvagers had no copters on this operation. They were risking a lot in using the comparatively slow-moving turbojeeps. Had they killed the D-squaders? he wondered. If so, it still didn't explain how.

Soon he saw their camp – a collection of small inflated domes which he recognised as being made of the new tougher-than-steel plastic that seemed as flimsy as paper. It was used by the more advanced nations on E-1, mainly for military purposes.

Faustaff landed the copter with a bump that half-threw him from his seat. An armed guard, dressed in a heavy greatcoat and a helmet that looked as if it had been looted from some nineteenth-century fire station, moved cautiously towards him.

'Hey – you're Professor Faustaff. What are you doing here? Where are Ogg and Orelli and the others?'

'On their way,' Faustaff told the man, who seemed amiable enough. He recognised him as Van Horn, who had once worked for the organisation as a cargo control clerk. 'How's it going, Van Horn?'

'Not so comfortable as when I worked for you, professor, but more variety – and more of the good things of life, you know. We do pretty well.'

'Good,' said Faustaff without irony.

'Situation bad here, is it, professor?'

'Very bad. Looks like there's going to be a break-up.'

'Break-up! Phew! That is bad. Hope we get off soon.'

'It'll have to be soon.'

'Yes… What are you doing here, professor? Come to warn us? That's pretty decent.' Van Horn knew Faustaff and knew he was capable of doing this.

But Faustaff shook his head. 'I've already done that. No – I came to ask for help. My tunneller went wrong. I'm finished unless I can get through your tunnel.'

'Sure,' Van Horn said with a grin. Like most people he liked

Faustaff, even though his gang and Faustaff's organisation were somewhat opposed. 'Why not? I guess everybody will be pleased to help. For old times' sake, eh?'

'All except Orelli.'

'Except him. He's a poison snake, professor. He's so mean. I'm glad my boss is Ogg. Ogg's a weird guy, but okay. Orelli's a poison snake, professor.'

'Yes,' Faustaff nodded absently, seeing the jeeps approaching through the smoke and falling ash. He could make out Orelli in the leading jeep.

Orelli was the first salvager to encounter Faustaff. He frowned for a second and then smiled blandly. 'Professor Faustaff again. How can we help you?'

The question was rhetorical, but Faustaff answered directly. 'By giving me a chance to use your tunnel.'

'Our tunnel?' Orelli laughed. 'But why? Your father invented tunnellers – and now you come to us, the despised salvagers.'

Faustaff bore Orelli's amused malice. He explained how his tunnel had broken down. Orelli's smile grew bigger and bigger as he listened. But he said nothing.

Orelli looked like a cat who'd been handed a mouse to play with. 'I'll have to talk this over with my partner, you understand, professor. Can't make a hasty decision. It could affect our whole lives in one way or another.'

'I'm asking you for help, man, that's all!'

'Quite.'

Gordon Ogg came loping up, looking vaguely astonished to see Faustaff there.

'What are you doing here, professor?' he asked.

'The professor is in trouble,' Orelli answered for him. 'Serious trouble. He wants to use our tunnel to get off E-15.'

Ogg shrugged. 'Why not?'

Orelli pursed his lips. 'You are too casual, Gordon. Too casual. "Why not?" you say. This could be a trap of some kind. We must be careful.'

'Professor Faustaff would not lay *traps*,' Ogg said. 'You are over-suspicious, Orelli.'

'Better safe than sorry, Gordon.'

'Nonsense. There is no question of the professor not coming through with us – assuming that we *can* get through.'

Faustaff saw Orelli's expression change momentarily to one of open anger and cunning, then the smile returned.

'Very well, Gordon. If you wish to be so reckless.' He shrugged and turned away.

Ogg asked Faustaff what had happened and Faustaff told him. Ogg nodded sympathetically. Originally some sort of British soldier-diplomat on E-2, Ogg's manner was gentle and remote and he was still an essentially kindly man, but the romantic mind of a Byron lay behind the mild eyes and courteous manner. Ogg saw himself, even if others did not quite see him in the same way, as a freebooter, a wild adventurer, risking his life against the warped and haunted landscapes of the subspacial alternates. Ogg lived this dangerous life and no doubt enjoyed it, but his outward appearance was still that of a somewhat vague and benign British diplomat.

Ogg led Faustaff to the main tent where his men were already going through the tunnel with their loot.

'The tunnel's to E-11,' Ogg said. 'It seemed no good in trying to get through to E-2 or E-1 under current conditions.'

'Perhaps we should have realised that,' Faustaff murmured, thinking of Peppiatt dead in subspace. E-11 wasn't a pleasant world, being comprised primarily of high mountains and barren valleys, but he could contact his base on E-11 and soon get back to E-1.

Orelli came into the tent smiling his brotherly love to everyone. 'Are we ready?' he asked.

'Just about,' said Ogg. 'The men have to collapse the other tents and get the heavy stuff through.'

'I think it might be wise to leave the rest of the jeeps behind,' Orelli said. 'The professor's prediction appears to have been accurate.'

Ogg frowned. 'Accurate?'

'Outside,' Orelli waved a hand. 'Outside. Look outside.'

Faustaff and Ogg went to the entrance of the tent and looked. A great, troubled expanse of purple-blue radiance filled the horizon, growing rapidly. Its edges touched a blackness more absolute than the blackness of outer space. The grey ash had ceased to fall and the ground close by had lost its original appearance. Instead it was beginning to seethe with colour.

Wordlessly Ogg and Faustaff flung themselves back towards the tunneller. Orelli was no longer in the tent. Evidently he hadn't waited for them. The tunnel was beginning to look unsteady, as if about to close. Faustaff followed Ogg into it, feeling sick as he remembered Peppiatt's death earlier. The grey walls flickered and threatened to break. He moved on, not walking or propelling himself by any normal means, but drifting near-weightlessly until, with relief, he found himself standing on a rocky mountain slope at night-time, a big, full moon above him.

Silhouetted in the darkness, other figures stood around on the mountainside. Faustaff recognised the outlines of Ogg and Orelli.

Faustaff felt infinitely depressed. E-15 would soon be nothing more than fast-dissipating gas.

Even the salvagers seemed moved by their experience. They stood around in silence with only their breathing to be heard. In the valley below Faustaff could now make out a few lights, probably those of the salvagers' camps. He was not sure where this camp was in relation to his own base on E-11.

Faustaff saw a couple of men begin to climb down the slope, feeling their way carefully. Others followed and soon the whole party was beginning to pick its way down towards the camp, Faustaff in the rear.

At length they got to the valley and paused. Faustaff could now see that there were two camps – one at either side of the short valley.

Ogg put his hand on the professor's arm. 'Come with me, professor. We'll go to my camp. In the morning I'll take you to your base here.'

Orelli gave a mock salute. '*Bon voyage*, professor.' He led his men towards his own camp. 'I will see you tomorrow on the matter of spoil-division, Gordon.'

'Very well,' Ogg said.

Ogg's camp on E-11 had the same impermanent air as the hastily abandoned one on E-15. Ogg took Faustaff to his personal quarters and had a extra bed brought in for him.

They were both exhausted and were soon asleep in spite of the thoughts that must have occupied both their minds.

Chapter Six

Klosterheim on a Mountain

JUST AFTER DAWN Faustaff was awakened by the sounds of activity in Gordon Ogg's camp. Ogg was no longer in the tent and Faustaff heard his voice calling orders to his men. It sounded like another panic. Faustaff wondered what this one could be.

He went outside as soon as he could and saw Ogg supervising the packing up of tents. A tunneller stood in the open air, and the salvager technicians were working at it.

'You're going through to another world,' Faustaff said as he reached Ogg. 'What's happening?'

'We've had word of good pickings on E-3,' Ogg said, stroking his moustache and not looking directly at Faustaff. 'A small U.M.S. was corrected near Saint Louis – but parts of the city were affected and abandoned. We can just get there before the situation's properly under control.'

'Who told you this?'

Ogg said: 'One of our agents. We have quite good communications equipment, too, you know, professor.'

Faustaff rubbed his jaw. 'Any chance of coming through your tunnel with you?'

Ogg shook his head. 'I think we've done you enough favours now, professor. We're leaving Orelli's share of the loot behind us. You'll have to make some sort of deal with him. Be careful, though.'

Faustaff would be careful. He felt somewhat vulnerable, being left to the doubtful mercies of Orelli, yet he had no intention of pressing Ogg to let him through the tunnel to E-3. He watched numbly as the salvagers got their equipment and themselves through the subspacial tunnel and then witnessed the peculiar effect as the tunneller itself was drawn through the tunnel it had created. Within seconds of the tunneller's disappearance, Faustaff was alone amongst the refuse of Gordon Ogg's camp.

Ogg had left him behind knowing that he ran a fifty-per-cent risk of being killed outright by the malicious Orelli. Perhaps in Ogg's mind this was a fair chance. Faustaff didn't stop to wonder about Ogg's psychology. Instead he began to walk away from the camp towards the mountains. He had decided to try to make his way to his own base rather than trust Orelli.

By midday Faustaff had sweated his way through two crooked canyons and halfway up a mountain. He slept for an hour before continuing. His intention was to reach the upper slopes of the mountain, which was not particularly hard to climb and there was no snow to impair his progress. Once there, he would be able to get a better idea of where he was and plan his route. He knew that his base lay somewhere to the north-east of where he was, but it could be halfway around the world. Barren, and all but completely covered by bleak mountain ranges though it might be, this planet was still Earth, with the same approximate size as Earth. Unless his base was fairly close, he couldn't give himself very good odds on his surviving for much more than a week. He still consoled himself that he was better off here than with Orelli and that there was a slim chance of search parties being sent out for him, though probably he was already thought to have been killed. That was the worst part of it. Without being self-important, he was aware that with him dead there was a good chance of his organisation losing heart. Though he did little but co-ordinate his various teams and advise where he could, he was an important figurehead. He was more than that – he was the dynamic for the organisation. Without him it might easily forget its purpose and turn its attention away from the real reason for its existence, the preservation of human life.

Sweating and exhausted Faustaff at last reached a point less than thirty feet from the mountain peak where he could look out over what seemed to be an infinity of crags. There was none he recognised. He must be several hundred miles from his base.

He sat down on the comparatively gradual slope and tried to reason out his predicament. Before long, he fell asleep.

He awoke in the evening to the sound of a muted cough behind him. Turning, unbelievingly, towards this human sound, he saw with some astonishment the dapper figure of Klosterheim sitting on a rock just above him.

'Good evening, Professor Faustaff,' Klosterheim smiled, his black eyes gleaming with ambiguous humour. 'I find this view a trifle boring, don't you?'

Faustaff's depression left him and he laughed at the ludicrousness of this encounter. Klosterheim seemed bewildered for a second.

'Why do you laugh?'

Faustaff continued to laugh, shaking his large head slowly. 'Here we are,' he said, 'with no human habitation to speak of in hundreds of miles…'

'That's so, professor. But…'

'And you are going to try to pass this meeting off as coincidence. Where are you on your way to now, Herr Klosterheim? Paris? Are you just waiting here while you change planes?'

Klosterheim smiled again. 'I suppose not. In fact I had a great deal of difficulty locating you after E-15 was eliminated. I believe E-15 is your term for that particular Earth simulation.'

'It is. Simulation, eh? What does that mean?'

'Alternate, if you like.'

'You're something to do with the D-squads, aren't you?'

'There is some sort of link between myself and the Demolition squads – an apt term that. Coined by your father wasn't it?'

'I think so. Well, what *is* the link? What are the D-squads? Who do they work for?'

'I didn't take the trouble of visiting this planet just to answer your questions, professor. You know, you and your father have caused my principals a great deal of trouble. You would never believe how much.' Klosterheim smiled. 'That is why I am so reluctant to carry out their orders concerning you.'

'Who are your "principals" – what orders?'

'They are very powerful people indeed, professor. Their orders were for me to kill you or otherwise make you powerless to continue interfering in their plans.'

'You seem to approve of the trouble I have caused them,' Faustaff said. 'You're opposed to them, then? Some sort of double agent? You're on my side?'

'On the contrary, professor – your aims and theirs have many similarities. I am opposed to both of you. To them, there is some purpose in all this creation and destruction. To me, there is none. I feel that everything should die slowly, sweetly rotting away...' Klosterheim smiled, more wistfully this time. 'But I am a dutiful employee. I must carry out their orders in spite of my own aesthetic fancies...'

Faustaff laughed, once again struck by the comedy of Klosterheim's affectation. 'You are in love with death, then?'

Klosterheim seemed to take the question as a statement carrying some sort of censure.

'And you, professor, are in love with life. Life, what is more, that is imperfect, crude, half-formed. Give me the overwhelming simplicity of death to *that*!'

'Yours seems a somewhat adolescent rejection of the tangle of being alive,' Faustaff said, half to himself. 'You could try to relax a bit – take it more as it comes.'

Klosterheim frowned, his assurance leaving him even more, while Faustaff, calm, for some reason, and in fairly good spirits, pondered on what Klosterheim had said.

'I think you are a fool, Professor Faustaff, a buffoon. I am not the adolescent, believe me. My life-span makes yours seem like the life-span of a mayfly. You are naïve, not I.'

'Do you get no enjoyment from being alive, then?'

'My only pleasure comes from experiencing the decay of the universe. It *is* dying, professor. I have lived long enough to *see* it dying.'

'If that is true, does it matter to you or me?' Faustaff asked bemusedly. 'Everything dies eventually – but that shouldn't stop us enjoying life while it is there to be enjoyed.'

'But it has no purpose!' shouted Klosterheim, standing up. 'No purpose! It is all meaningless. Look at you, how you spend your time, fighting a losing battle to preserve this little planet or that – for how long? Why do you do it?'

'It seems worthwhile. Have you no sympathy, then, for the people who are destroyed when a planet breaks up? It's a shame that they shouldn't have the chance to live as long as possible.'

'But to what use do they put their stupid lives? They are dull, fuddled, materialistic, narrow – life gives them no real pleasure. The majority do not even appreciate the art that the best of them have produced. They are dead already. Hasn't that occurred to you?'

Faustaff debated this. 'Their pleasures are perhaps a little limited, I'd agree. But they do enjoy themselves, most of them. And living is enough in itself. It is not just the pleasures of life that make it worthwhile, you know.'

'You talk like one of them. Their amusements are vulgar, their thinking obtuse. They are not worth wasting time for. You are a brilliant man. Your mind is tuned to appreciating things they could never appreciate. Even their misery is mean and limited. Let the simulations die, professor – let the inhabitants die with them!'

Again Faustaff shook his head in baffled amusement. 'I can't follow you, Herr Klosterheim.'

'Do you expect their gratitude for this stupid dedication of yours?'

'Of course not. They don't realise what's going on, most of them. I am a little arrogant, I suppose, now that you mention it, to interfere in this way. But I am not a thinking man in most spheres, Herr Klosterheim.' He laughed. 'You may be right – I am probably something of a buffoon.'

Klosterheim seemed to pull himself together, as if Faustaff's admission had restored his assurance.

'Well, then,' he said lightly. 'Will you agree to let the planets die, as they must?'

'Oh, I'll continue to do what I can, I think. Assuming I don't starve out here, or fall off a mountain. This conversation is a little bit hypothetical when you consider my circumstances, isn't it?' he grinned.

It seemed rather incongruous to Faustaff that at that point Klosterheim should reach into his jacket and take a gun out.

'You puzzle me, I admit,' said Klosterheim. 'And I should like to watch you caper a little more. But since the moment is convenient and I have tiresome orders to carry out, I think I will kill you now.'

Faustaff sighed. 'It would probably be better than starving,' he admitted, wondering if there was any chance of making a dash at Klosterheim.

Chapter Seven
Cardinal Orelli's Camp

In a manner that was at once studied and awkward, Klosterheim pointed the gun at Faustaff's head while the professor tried to think of the best action to take. He could rush Klosterheim or throw himself to one side, risking falling off the mountain ledge. It would be best to rush him.

He probably would not have succeeded if Klosterheim hadn't looked up at the moment he ran forward, crouching to keep as much of his great bulk out of the line of fire as possible. Klosterheim had been distracted by the sound of a helicopter engine above him.

Faustaff knocked Klosterheim's gun to one side and it went off with a bang that echoed around the peaks. He hit Klosterheim in the stomach and the bearded man went down, the gun falling out of his hand.

Faustaff picked up the gun and levelled it at Klosterheim.

Klosterheim frowned and gasped in pain. It was obvious that he expected Faustaff to kill him and a peculiar expression came into his eyes, a kind of introspective fear.

The helicopter was nearer. Faustaff heard it behind him and wondered who the pilot was. The noise of its engine became louder and louder until it deafened him. His clothes were ruffled by the breeze created by its rotors. He began to sidle round Klosterheim, keeping him covered, so he could see the occupant of the helicopter.

There were two. One of them, wearing a smile of infinite cruelty, was the red-robed Cardinal Orelli, his laser-rifle pointing casually at Faustaff's stomach. The other was a nondescript pilot in brown overalls and helmet.

Orelli shouted something through the roar of the motor, but Faustaff couldn't hear what he was saying. Klosterheim got up from the ground and looked curiously at Orelli. Momentarily

Faustaff felt more closely allied to Klosterheim than to Orelli. Then he realised that both were his enemies and that Klosterheim was much more likely to side with Orelli. Orelli must have come looking specifically for him, Faustaff decided, watching the pilot skilfully bring the helicopter down on the slope a little below him. Orelli's rifle was still pointing at him.

The engine noise died and Orelli climbed from the cockpit to the ground, walking up towards them, the fixed, cruel smile still on his lips.

'We missed you, professor,' he said. 'We were expecting you at our camp much earlier. You lost your way, eh?'

Faustaff could see that Orelli had guessed the truth; that he had deliberately chosen to enter the mountains rather than join the malicious ex-clergyman.

'I haven't had the pleasure,' said Orelli, turning a warier smile on Klosterheim.

'Klosterheim,' said Klosterheim looking quizzical. 'And you are...?'

'Cardinal Orelli. Professor Faustaff calls me a "salvager". Where are you from, Mr Klosterheim?'

Klosterheim pursed his lips. 'I am something of a wanderer,' he said. 'Here today, gone tomorrow, you know.'

'I see. Well, we can chat at my camp. It is more comfortable there.'

Faustaff realised that there was little point to arguing. Orelli kept him and Klosterheim covered a they walked down to the helicopter and climbed in, squeezing into the scarcely adequate back seats. With the gun cradled in his arm so that the snout pointed in their general direction over his shoulder, Orelli settled himself in the seat next to the pilot and closed the door.

The helicopter took to the air again, banked and began to fly back in the direction from which it had come. Faustaff, grateful for his reprieve, though expecting a worse fate, perhaps, from Orelli, who hated him, looked down at the grim mountains that stretched, range upon range, in all directions.

Quite soon he recognised the valley, and Orelli's camp came

into sight, the collection of grey dome-tents hard to make out against the scrub of the valley floor.

The helicopter descended a short distance from the camp and landed with a bump. Orelli climbed out and signalled for Klosterheim and Faustaff to go ahead of him. They got down onto the ground and began to walk towards the camp, Orelli humming faintly what sounded like a Gregorian chant. He seemed in good spirits.

At Orelli's signal they bent their heads and entered his tent. It was made of material that permitted them to see outside without being visible themselves. There was a machine in the centre of the tent and Faustaff recognised it. He had also seen, once before, the two bodies that lay beside it.

'You recognise them?' Orelli asked casually, going to a large metal chest in one corner of the tent and producing a bottle and glasses. 'A drink? Wine only, I'm afraid.'

'Thank you,' said Faustaff, but Klosterheim shook his head.

Orelli handed Faustaff a glass filled to the brim with red wine. 'St Émilion, 1953 – from Earth Two,' he said. 'I think you'll find it pleasant.'

Faustaff tasted it and nodded.

'Do you recognise them?' Orelli repeated.

'The bodies – they're D-squaders, aren't they?' Faustaff said. 'I saw some like them on E-15. And the machine looks like a disrupter. I suppose you have plans to use it in some way, Orelli.'

'None as yet, but doubtless I shall have. The D-squaders are not dead, you know. They have been at a constant temperature ever since we found them. We must have passed through that camp of theirs on E-15 shortly before you. The body temperature is low, but not that low. Yet they aren't breathing. Suspended animation?'

'That's nonsense,' said Faustaff, finishing his drink. 'All the experiments tried in that direction have proved disastrous. Remember the experiments at Malmö in '91 on E-1? Remember the scandal?'

'I would not remember, of course,' Orelli pointed out, 'since I am not a native of E-1. But I read about it. However, this seems to be suspended animation. They live, and yet they are dead. All our attempts to wake them have been useless. I was hoping that you, professor, might help.'

'How can I help?'

'Perhaps you will know when you have inspected the pair.'

As they talked, Klosterheim had bent down and was examining one of the prone D-squaders. The man was of medium height and seemed, through his black overalls, to be a good physical specimen. The thing that was remarkable was that the two prone figures strongly resembled one another, both in features and in size. They had close-cropped, light brown hair, square faces and pale skins that were unblemished but had an unhealthy texture, particularly about the upper face.

Klosterheim pushed back the man's eyelid and Faustaff had an unpleasant shock as a glazed blue eye appeared to stare straight at him. It seemed for a second that the man was actually awake, but unable to move. Klosterheim let the eyelid close again.

He stood up, folding his arms across his chest. 'Remarkable,' he said. 'What do you intend to do with them, Cardinal Orelli?'

'I am undecided. My interest is at present scientific – I wish to learn more about them. They are the first D-squaders we have ever managed to capture, eh, professor?'

Faustaff nodded. He felt strongly that the D-squaders should have fallen into any hands other than Orelli's. He did not dare consider the uses which Orelli's twisted mind could think of for the disrupter alone. With it he would be able to blackmail whole worlds. Faustaff resolved to destroy the disrupter as soon as he received a reasonable opportunity.

Orelli took his empty glass from his hand and returned to the metal chest, pouring fresh drinks. Faustaff accepted the second glass of wine automatically, although he had not eaten for a long time. Normally he could hold a lot of liquor, but already the wine had gone slightly to his head.

'I think we should return to my headquarters on E-4,' Orelli said. 'There are better facilities for the necessary research. I hope you will accept my invitation, professor, and help me in this matter.'

'I assume you will kill me if I refuse,' Faustaff replied tiredly.

'I should certainly not take it kindly,' smiled Orelli, sharklike.

Faustaff said nothing to this. He decided that it was in his interest to return to E-4 with Orelli since once there he would stand a much better chance of contacting his organisation once he had escaped.

'And what brought you to this barren world, Mr Klosterheim?' Orelli asked, with apparent heartiness.

'I had word that Professor Faustaff was here. I wanted to talk to him.'

'To talk? It appeared to me that you and the professor were engaged in some sort of scuffle as I came on the scene. You are friends? I should have thought not.'

'The argument was temporarily settled by your appearance, cardinal,' said Klosterheim, his eyes matching Orelli's for cynical guile. 'We were discussing certain philosophical matters.'

'Philosophy? Of what kind? I myself have an interest in metaphysics. Not surprising, I suppose, considering my old calling.'

'Oh, we talked of the relative merits of living or dying,' Klosterheim said lightly.

'Interesting. I did not know you were philosophically inclined, Professor Faustaff,' Orelli murmured to the professor. Faustaff shrugged and moved closer to the prone D-squaders until his back was to Klosterheim and Orelli.

He bent and touched the face of one of the D-squaders. It was faintly warm, like plastic at room temperature. It didn't feel like a human skin at all.

He had become bored with Orelli's and Klosterheim's silly duelling. They evidently enjoyed it sufficiently to carry on with it for some time until Orelli theatrically interrupted Klosterheim in the middle of a statement and apologised that time was running short and he must make preparations for a tunnel to be made through subspace to his headquarters on E-4. As he left the tent a guard entered, covering the two men with his gun. Klosterheim darted Faustaff a sardonic look but Faustaff didn't feel like taking Orelli's place in the game. Although the guard would not let him approach too closely to the disrupter he contented himself with studying it from where he was until Orelli returned to say that a tunnel was ready.

Chapter Eight
The D-squaders

Even more tired and very hungry, Faustaff stepped through the tunnel to find himself in what appeared to be the vault of a church, judging by the Gothic style of the stonework. The stone looked old but freshly cleaned. The air was cold and a trifle damp. Various stacks of the salvagers' field equipment lay around and the room was lighted by a malfunctioning neon tube. Orelli and Klosterheim had already arrived and were murmuring to one another. They stopped as Faustaff came up.

The D-squaders and the disrupter arrived soon after Faustaff, the prone D-squaders carried by Orelli's men. Orelli went ahead of them, opening a door at the far end of the vault and leading the way up worn, stone stairs into the magnificent interior of a large church, alive with sunshine pouring through stained glass. The only obvious change in the interior was the absence of pews. This gave the whole church an impression of being even larger than it was. It was a place that Faustaff could see easily compared to the finest Gothic cathedrals of Britain or France, an inspiring tribute to the creativeness of mankind. The church furniture remained, with a central altar and pulpit, an organ, and small chapels to left and right, indicating that the church had probably been Catholic. The wine was still affecting Faustaff slightly and he let his eyes travel up the columns, carved with fourteenth-century saints, animals and plants, until he was looking directly up at the high, vaulted roof, crossed by a series of intricate stone cobwebs, just visible in the cool gloom.

When he looked down again he saw Klosterheim staring at him, a light smile on his lips.

Drunk with the beauty of the church Faustaff waved his hand around at it. 'These are the works of those you would have destroyed, Klosterheim,' he said, somewhat grandiosely.

Klosterheim shrugged. 'I have seen finer work elsewhere. This is pitifully limited architecture by my standards, professor – clumsy. Wood, stone, steel or glass, it doesn't matter what materials you use, it is always clumsy.'

'This doesn't inspire you, then?' Faustaff asked rather incredulously.

Klosterheim laughed. 'No. You are naïve, professor.'

Unable to describe the emotions which the church raised in him, Faustaff felt at a loss, wondering to what heights of feeling the architecture with which Klosterheim was familiar would raise him if he ever had the chance to experience it.

'Where is this architecture of yours?' he asked.

'In no place that you are familiar with, professor.' Klosterheim continued to be evasive and Faustaff once again wondered if he could have any connection with the D-squads.

Orelli had been supervising his men. Now he approached them. 'What do you think of my headquarters?'

'Very impressive,' said Faustaff for want of something better to say. 'Is there more?'

'A monastery is attached to the cathedral. Those who live there follow somewhat different disciplines to those followed by the earlier occupants. Shall we go there now? I have a laboratory being prepared.'

'I should like to eat before I do anything,' Faustaff said. 'I hope your cuisine is as excellent as your surroundings.'

'If anything it is better,' said Orelli. 'Of course we shall eat first.'

Later the three of them sat in a large room that had once been the abbot's private study. The alcoves were still lined with books, primarily religious works of various kinds; there were reproductions framed on the walls. Most of them showed various versions of *The Temptation of St Anthony* – Bosch, Brueghel, Grünewald, Schöngauer, Huys, Ernst and Dalí were represented, as well as some others whom Faustaff did not recognise.

The food was almost as good as Orelli had boasted and the

wine was excellent, from the monastery's cellar. Faustaff pointed at the reproductions. 'Your taste, Orelli, or your predecessor's?'

'His and mine, professor. That is why I left them there. His interest was perhaps a little more obsessive than mine. He went mad in the end, I hear. Some thought it possession, others –' he smiled his cruel smile and raised his glass somewhat mockingly to the Bosch – 'delirium tremens.'

'And what caused the monastery to become deserted – why isn't the cathedral used now?' Faustaff asked.

'Perhaps it will be obvious if I tell you our geographical location on E-4, professor. We are in the area once occupied by North Western Europe. More precisely we are near where the town of Le Havre once stood, although there is no sign of the town and none of the sea, either, for that matter. Do you remember the U.M.S. that you managed to control in this area, professor?'

Faustaff was puzzled. He had not yet seen outside the monastery walls and where, logically, windows should look beyond the cathedral or the monastery, they were heavily curtained. He had assumed he was in some rural town. Now he got up and went to the window, pulling back the heavy velvet curtain. It was dark, but the gleam of ice was unmistakeable. Beneath the moon, and stretching to the horizon, was a vast plain of ice. Faustaff knew that it extended through Scandinavia, parts of Russia, Germany, Poland, Czechoslovakia and parts of Austria and Hungary, covering, in the other direction, half of Britain as far as Hull.

'But there is ice for hundreds of miles about,' he said, turning back to where Orelli sat, sipping his wine and smiling still. 'How on earth can this place have got here?'

'It was here already. It has been my headquarters since I discovered it three years ago. Somehow it escaped the U.M.S. and survived. The monks fled before the U.M.S. developed into anything really spectacular. I found it later.'

'But I've never heard of anything quite like this,' Faustaff said. 'A cathedral and a monastery in the middle of a waste of ice. How did it survive?'

Orelli raised his eyes to the ceiling and smirked. 'Divine influence, perhaps?'

'A freak, I suppose,' Faustaff said sitting down again. 'I've seen similar things – but nothing so spectacular.'

'It took my fancy,' Orelli said. 'It is remote, roomy and, since I installed some heating, quite comfortable. It suits me.'

Next morning, in Orelli's makeshift laboratory, Faustaff looked at the two now naked D-squaders lying on a bench in front of him. He had decided that either Orelli was playing with him, or else Orelli believed his knowledge to extend to biology. There was very little he could do except what he was doing now, having electroencephalographic tests made on the subjects. It was not expedient to disabuse Orelli altogether, for he was well aware that, if there was no likelihood of his coming up with something, Orelli would probably kill him.

The skins still had the quality of slightly warm plastic. There was no apparent breathing, the limbs were limp and the eyes glazed. When the assistants had placed the electrodes on the heads of the two subjects he went over to the electroencephalograph and studied the charts that began to rustle from the machine. They indicated only a single wave – a constant wave, as if the brain were alive but totally dormant. The test only proved what was already obvious.

Faustaff took a hypodermic and injected a stimulant into the first D-squader. Into the second he injected a depressant.

The electroencephalographic charts were exactly the same as the previous ones.

Faustaff was forced to agree with Orelli's suggestion that the men were in a total state of suspended animation.

The assistants Orelli had assigned to him were expressionless men with as little apparent character as the subjects they were studying. He turned to one of them and asked him to set up the X-ray machine.

The machine was wheeled forward and took a series of X-ray plates of both men. The assistant handed the plates to Faustaff.

A couple of quick glances at the plates were sufficient to show that, though the men on the table seemed to be ordinary human beings, they were not. Their organs were simplified, as was their bone structure.

Faustaff sat down. The implications of the discovery swam through his mind but he felt unable to concentrate on any one of them. These creatures could have come from outer space, they could be a race produced on one of the parallel Earths.

Faustaff clung to this last thought. The D-squaders did not function according to any of the normal laws applied to animals. Perhaps they *were* artificial; robots of some kind. Yet the science needed to create such robots would be far more advanced than Earth One's.

Who had created them? Where did they come from? The extra data had only succeeded in making everything more confusing than it had been.

Faustaff lit a cigarette and made himself relax, wondering whether to mention any of this to Orelli. He would discover the truth for himself soon enough anyway.

He got up and asked for surgical instruments. With the aid of the X-ray plates he would be able to carry out some simple surgery on the D-squaders without endangering them. He cut through to the wrist of one of them. No blood flowed from the cut. He took a bone sample and a sample of the flesh and the skin. He tried to reseal the incision with the normal agents, but they refused to take. Finally he had to cover the incisions with ordinary tape.

He took his samples to a microscope, hoping he had enough basic biology to be able to recognise any differences they might have to normal skin, bone and flesh.

The microscope revealed some very essential differences which didn't require any specialised knowledge for him to recognise. The normal cell structure was apparently totally absent. The bone seemed composed of a metal alloy and the flesh of a dead, cellular material that resembled foam plastic, although the cells were much more numerous than on any plastic he was used to.

The only conclusion he could draw from this evidence was that the D-squaders were not living creatures in the true sense and that they were, in fact, robots – artificially created men.

The appearance of the materials that had gone into their construction was not familiar to Faustaff. The alloy and the plastic again indicated a superior technology to his own.

He began to feel perturbed for it was certain that the creatures had not been manufactured on any Earth that he knew. Yet they were capable of travelling through subspace and had obviously been designed for the sole purpose of manipulating the disrupters. That indicated the only strong possibility – that the D-squaders were the creation of some race operating outside subspace and beyond the solar system, from a base in ordinary space-time. The attack, then, probably did not come from a human source, as Faustaff had always believed. This was the reason for his uneasiness. Would it be possible to think out the motives of an unhuman race? It was unlikely. And without an indication of why they were trying to destroy the worlds of subspace, it seemed impossible to invent ways of stopping them for any real length of time.

He came to a decision then. He must destroy the disrupter, at least. It lay in one corner of the laboratory, ready for investigation.

To destroy it would at least stop Orelli using it, or threatening to use it in some attempt at blackmail. That would get rid of one of the factors bothering him.

He walked towards it.

At that moment he felt a tingling sensation in his wrist and the room seemed to fade. He felt sick and his head began to ache. He found it impossible to draw air into his lungs. He recognised the sensations.

He was being invoked.

Chapter Nine

E-Zero

Doctor May looked relieved. He stood wiping his glasses in the bare concrete room which Faustaff recognised as being in Earth One's headquarters at Haifa.

Faustaff waited for his head to clear before advancing towards May.

'We never thought we'd get you back,' said May. 'We've been trying for the last day, ever since you disappeared in the break-up of E-15. I heard our adjustor was destroyed.'

'I'm sorry,' said Faustaff.

May shrugged and replaced his glasses. His pudgy face looked unusually haggard. 'That's nothing compared to what's going on. I've got some news for you.'

'And I for you.' Faustaff reflected that May's invocation had come at exactly the wrong time. But it was no use mentioning it. At least he was back at his own base and could perhaps conceive a plan that would permanently put Orelli out of action.

May walked towards the door. Technicians were disconnecting the big invoker which had been used to pull Faustaff through sub-space once they had picked up the signal from the invocation-disc on his wrist.

Faustaff followed May out into the corridor. May led the way to the lift. On the fourth floor, they found the man's office.

Several other men were waiting there. Faustaff recognised some of them as heads of Central Headquarters departments and others he knew as communications specialists.

'Have you something to tell us before we begin?' May said, picking up a VC after introductions and greetings. He ordered coffee and replaced the VC.

'It won't take me long to fill you in,' Faustaff said. He settled himself into a chair. He told them of Klosterheim's attempt to kill him and how it was plain that Klosterheim knew much more about the worlds of subspace than he had admitted, that he had referred to his 'powerful principals' and indicated that the Faustaff organisation couldn't stand a big attack – and neither could the worlds of subspace. He then went on to describe Orelli's 'specimens' and what he had discovered about them.

The reaction to this wasn't as startled as he had expected. May simply nodded, his lips set tightly.

'This fits in with our discovery, professor,' he said. 'We have just contacted a new alternate Earth. Or I should say part of one. It is at this moment being formed.'

'An alternate actually being created!' Faustaff was excited now. 'Can't we get there – see how it happens. It could tell us a lot...'

'We've tried to get through to E-Zero, as we've called it, but every attempt seems to have been blocked. This Earth isn't being created naturally – there is an intelligence behind it.'

Faustaff took this easily. The logical assumption now could only be that some non-human force was at work not only, as was now obvious, destroying worlds, but creating them as well. Somewhere the D-squaders, Klosterheim and Maggy White fitted in – and could probably tell them a lot. All the events of recent days showed that the situation was, from their point of view, worsening. And the odds that faced them were bigger than they had guessed.

Faustaff helped himself to a cup of coffee from the tray that had been brought in.

Doctor May seemed impatient. 'What can we do, professor? We are unprepared for the attack, we are certainly ill-equipped to deal with even another big D-squad offensive of the kind you have just experienced on E-15. It is obvious that up to now these forces have been playing with us.'

Faustaff nodded and sipped his coffee. 'Our first objective must be Orelli's headquarters,' he said. He felt sick as he made his next statement. 'It must be destroyed – and everything that is in it.'

'Destroyed?' May was well acquainted with Faustaff's obsessive views about the sanctity of life.

'There is nothing else we can do. I never thought – I hoped I would never find myself in a situation like this, but we shall just have to follow the line of killing a few for the sake of the many.' Even as Faustaff spoke he heard his own voice of a short time ago talking about the dangers of justifying the taking of life under any conditions.

Doctor May seemed almost satisfied. 'You say he's on E-4. The area would be covered by grid sections 38 and 62 roughly. Do you want to lead the expedition? We shall have to send copters and bombs, I suppose.'

Faustaff shook his head. 'No, I won't go with it. Give them a five-minute warning, though. Give them that, at least. That won't allow them time to set up a tunneller and escape with the disrupter. I told you about the place – it'll be easy to spot, a cathedral.'

After Doctor May had gone off to arrange the expedition Faustaff sat studying the information that had so far been gathered about Earth Zero. There was very little. Apparently the discovery had been almost accidental. When E-15 was breaking up and it was becoming increasingly difficult to get tunnels between the worlds the technicians on E-1 found data being recorded on their instruments that was unusual. A check had led to contact with E-0. They had sent out probes and had found a planet that was still unstable, at that stage only a sphere consisting of elements still in a state of mutation. Soon after this their probes had been blocked and they had been unable to get anything but faint indications of the existence of the new body. All they really knew was that it was there, but they did not know how it had come there or who was responsible for it. Faustaff wanted to know *why* above everything else.

It was perhaps an unscientific attitude, he reflected as he got up. He had never before had quite such a strong sense of being unable to control a situation he found himself in. There was so little he could do at this stage. Philosophically he decided to give up and go to his house in the outer suburbs of Haifa, get a full night's sleep – the first he would have had in some time – hoping to have some ideas in the morning.

He left the building and walked out into the midday sunshine of the busy modern city. He flagged down a taxi and gave his address. Wearily he listened to the taxi driver talking about the 'crisis' which seemed to have developed in his absence. He couldn't quite follow the details and made no serious attempt to, but it appeared that the East and West were having one of their periodic wrangles, this time over some South-East Asian country and Yugoslavia. Since Tito's death Yugoslavia had been considered fair game for both blocs and although the Yugoslavs had steadfastly resisted any attempts at colonialism on the part of both East and West their situation was getting weaker. A revolution – from what appeared to be an essentially small group of fundamentalist Communists – had given the USSR and the USA an excuse for sending in peacekeeping forces. From what the taxi driver was saying there had already been open fighting between the Russians and the Americans and the Russian and American ambassadors had just withdrawn from the respective countries. Faustaff, used to such periodic events, was not able to feel the same interest in the situation as the taxi driver. In his opinion the man was unnecessarily excited. The thing would die down eventually. It always had. Faustaff had more important things on his mind.

The taxi drew up outside his house, a small bungalow with a garden full of orange blossom. He paid the driver and walked up the concrete path to the front door. He felt in his pockets for the key, but as usual he had lost it. He reached up to the ledge over the door and found the spare key, unlocked the door, replaced the key and went in. The house was cool and tidy. He rarely used most of the rooms. He walked into his bedroom which was in the same state as he'd left it several weeks before. Clothes lay everywhere, on the floor and the unmade bed. He went to the window and opened it. He picked a towel off the V that faced the foot of his bed and went into the bathroom. He began to shower.

When he returned, naked, to his room, there was a girl sitting on the bed. Her perfect legs were crossed and her perfect hands lay folded in her lap. It was Maggy White, whom Faustaff had encountered at the same time as he had first met Klosterheim in the desert motel on E-3.

'Hello, professor,' she said coolly. 'Do you never wear clothes, then?'

Faustaff remembered that the first time he'd met her he had been naked. He grinned and in doing so felt immediately his old relaxed self.

'As rarely as possible,' he smiled. 'Have you come to try to do me in, too?'

Her humourless smile disturbed him. He wondered if making love to her would produce any real emotion. Her effect on him was far deeper than Klosterheim's. She didn't reply.

'Your friend Klosterheim had a bash at it,' he said. 'Or have you been in touch with him since then?'

'What makes you think Klosterheim is my friend?'

'You certainly travel together.'

'That doesn't make us friends.'

'I suppose not.'

Faustaff paused and then said: 'What's the latest news concerning the simulations?' The last word was one Klosterheim had used. He hoped that he might trick her into giving him more information if he sounded knowledgeable.

'Nothing fresh,' she said.

Once again Faustaff wondered how a woman so well-endowed on the surface could appear to be so totally sexless.

'Why are you here?' he asked, going to the wardrobe and getting fresh clothes out. He pulled on a pair of jeans, hauling the belt around his huge stomach. He was putting on weight, he thought, the belt could hardly be pulled to the first notch.

'A social visit,' she said.

'That's ridiculous. I see that a new Earth is taking shape. Why?'

'Who can explain the secrets of the universe better than yourself, professor, a scientist?'

'You.'

'I know nothing of science.'

Out of curiosity Faustaff sat on the bed beside her and stroked her knee. Once again she smiled coolly and her eyes became hooded. She lay back on the bed.

Faustaff lay beside her and stroked her stomach. He noticed that her breathing remained constant even when he stroked her breasts through the cloth of her buttoned-up grey suit. He rolled over and stood up.

'Could you be Mark Two?' he asked. 'I dissected a D-squader a while ago. They're robots, you know – or androids, I think the term is.'

Perhaps he spotted a flash of anger in her eyes. They certainly widened for a moment and then half-closed again.

'Is that what you are? An android?'

'You could find out if you made love to me.'

Faustaff smiled and shook his head. 'Sweetheart, you're just not my type.'

'I thought any young woman was your type, professor.'

'So did I till I met you.'

Her face remained expressionless.

'What are you here for?' he asked. 'You didn't come because you felt randy, that's certain.'

'I told you – a social visit.'

'Orders from your principals. To do what, I wonder?'

'To convince you of the silliness of continuing this game you're playing.' She shrugged. 'Klosterheim was unable to convince you. I might be able to.'

'What line are you going to take?'

'A reasonable one. A logical one. Can't you see that you are interfering with something that you will never understand, that you are just a minor irritant to the people who have almost total power over the parallels...'

'The simulations? What do they simulate?'

'You are dull, professor. They simulate Earth, naturally.'

'Then which Earth is it that they simulate. This one?'

'You think yours is any different from the others? They are all simulations. Yours was, until recently, simply the last of many. Do you know how many simulations there have been?'

'I've known of sixteen.'

'More than a thousand.'

'So you've destroyed nine hundred and eighty-six altogether. I suppose there were people on all of them. You've murdered millions!' Faustaff could not stop himself from feeling shocked by this revelation.

'They owed their lives to us. They were ours to take.'

'I can't accept that.'

'Turn on the V. Get the news,' she said suddenly.

'What for?'

'Turn it on and see.'

He went to the set and switched it on. He selected the English-speaking channel for convenience. Some people were being interviewed. They looked grim and their voices were dull with fatalism.

As Faustaff listened he realised that war must have been declared between the East and West. The men were not talking about the possible outcome. They were discussing which areas might survive. The general effect was that they didn't expect anywhere to survive.

Faustaff turned to Maggy White who was smiling again. 'Is this it? The nuclear war? I didn't expect it – I thought it was impossible.'

'Earth One is doomed, professor. It's a fact. While you were worrying about the other simulations your own was nearing destruction. You can't blame anyone else for this, professor. Who caused the death of Earth One...?'

'It must be artificially done. Your people must have...'

'Nonsense. It was built into your society.'

'Who built it in?'

'They did, I suppose, but unknowingly. It is not in their interest, I assure you, to have this happen to a planet. They are hoping for a utopia. They are desperately trying to create one.'

'Their methods seem crude.'

'Perhaps they are – by their standards, but certainly not by yours. You could never comprehend the complicated task they have set themselves.'

'Who are they?'

'People. In the long run your ideals and theirs are not so different. Their scheme is vaster, that is all. Human beings must die. It is thought to be unfortunate by many of them. They aren't unsympathetic...'

'Not unsympathetic? They destroy worlds casually, they let this happen – this war – when from all you say they could stop it. I can't have much respect for a race that regards life so cheaply.'

'They are a desperate race. They are driven to desperate means.'

'Haven't they ever – reflected?'

'Of course, many thousands of your years ago, before the situation worsened. There were debates, arguments, factions created. A great deal of time was lost.'

'I see. And if they are so powerful and they want me out of the way, why don't they destroy me as they destroy whole planets? Your statements appear to be inconsistent.'

'Not so. It is a very complicated matter to eliminate individuals. It must be done by agents, such as myself. Usually it has been found expedient to destroy the whole planet if too many irritating individuals interfered in their plans.'

'Are you going to fill me in – tell me everything about these people? If I'm going to die because of a nuclear war, it shouldn't matter.'

'I wouldn't run the risk. You have a large share of pure luck, professor. I would suffer if I told you more and you escaped.'

'How would they punish you?'

'I'm sorry. I've told you enough.' She spoke rapidly, for the first time.

'So I'm to die. Then why did you come here to dissuade me if you knew what was going to happen?'

'As I said, you may not die. You are lucky. Can't you simply accept that you are complicating a situation involving matters that are completely above your head? Can't you accept that there is a greater purpose to all this?'

'I can't accept death as a necessary evil, if that's what you mean – or premature death, anyway.'

'Your moralising is naïve – cheap.'

'That's what your friend Klosterheim says. But it isn't to me. I'm a simple man, Miss White.'

She shrugged. 'You will never understand, will you?'

'I don't know what you mean.'

'That's what I mean.'

'Why didn't you kill me, anyway?' He turned away and began to put on a shirt. The V continued to drone on, the voices becoming hollower and hollower. 'You had the opportunity. I didn't know you were in the house.'

'Both Klosterheim and myself have a fairly free hand in how we handle problems. I was curious about these worlds, particularly about you. I have never been made love to.' She got up and came towards him. 'I had heard that you were good at it.'

'Only when I enjoy it. It seems odd that these people of yours understand little of human psychology from what I've gathered.'

'Do you understand the psychology of a frog in any detail?'

'A frog's psychology is a considerably simpler thing than a person's.'

'Not to a creature with a much more complex psychology than a person's.'

'I'm tired of this, Miss White. I must get back to my headquarters. You can write me off as an irritant from now on. I don't expect my organisation to survive the coming war.'

'I expected you to escape to some other simulation. It would give you a respite anyway.'

He looked at her curiously. She had sounded almost animated, almost concerned for him.

In a softer tone he said: 'Are you suggesting that?'

'If you like.'

He frowned, looking into her eyes. For some reason he suddenly felt sympathy for her without knowing why.

'You'd better get going yourself,' he said tersely, turning and making for the door.

The streets outside were deserted. This was unusual for the time of day. A bus stopped nearby. He ran to catch it. It would take him close to his headquarters. He was the only person on the bus apart from the driver.

He felt lonely as they drove into Haifa.

Chapter Ten
Escape from E-1

FAUSTAFF AND DOCTOR May watched as men and equipment were hurried through the tunnel which had been made to E-3. The expression on May's face was one of hopelessness. The bombs had already started to drop and the last report they had seen had told them that Britain had been totally destroyed, as had half of Europe.

They had given themselves an hour to evacuate everything and everyone they could. Doctor May checked his watch and glanced at Faustaff.

'Time's up, professor.'

Faustaff nodded and followed May into the tunnel. It took a great deal to depress him, but to see the organisation he and his father had built up crumbling, forced to abandon its main centre, made him miserable and unable to think clearly.

The trip through the grey tunnel to the familiar gilt-and-plush dance hall of The Golden Gate, which was their main transceiving station on E-3, was easily made. When they arrived, the men just stood around, murmuring to one another and glancing at Faustaff; he knew that he was expected to cheer them up. He forced himself out of his mood and smiled.

'We all need a drink,' was the only thing he could think of to say as he walked towards the dusty bar. He leaned across it and reached under, finding bottles and glasses and setting them on the counter. The men moved forward and took the glasses he filled for them.

Faustaff hauled himself up so that he was sitting on the bar.

'We're in a pretty desperate situation,' he told them. 'The enemy – I've hardly any better idea of them than you have – have for some reason decided to launch an all-out attack on the subspacial worlds.

It's plain now that all their previous attacks, using the D-squaders, have hardly been serious. We underestimated the opposition, if you like. Frankly my own opinion is that it won't be long before they succeed in breaking up all the subspacial alternates – that's what they want.'

'Then there's nothing we can do,' Doctor May said wearily.

'Only one thing occurs to me,' Faustaff said. 'We know that the enemy considers these worlds as something to be destroyed. But what about E-Zero? This has just been created – either by them or by someone else like them – and I gather they aren't normally willing to destroy a recently created world. Our only chance is in getting a big tunnel through to E-Zero and setting up our headquarters there. From then on we can evacuate people from these worlds to E-Zero.'

'But what if E-Zero can't support so many?' a man said.

'It will have to.' Faustaff drained his glass. 'As far as I can see our only course of action is to concentrate everything on getting a tunnel through to E-Zero.'

Doctor May shook his head, staring at the floor.

'I don't see the point,' he said. 'We're beaten. We're going to die sooner or later with everyone else. Why don't we just give up now?'

Faustaff nodded sympathetically. 'I understand – but we've got our responsibilities. We all took those on when we joined the organisation.'

'That was before we knew the extent of what we'd let ourselves in for,' May said sharply.

'Possibly. But what's the point of being fatalistic at this stage? If we're due to be wiped out, we might at least try the only chance we have.'

'And what then?' May looked up. He seemed angry now. 'A few more days before the enemy decides to destroy E-Zero? Count me out, professor.'

'Very well.' Faustaff glanced at the others. 'Who feels the same as Doctor May?'

More than half of the men there indicated that they shared May's views. At least half of the remainder seemed undecided.

'Very well,' he said again. 'It's probably best that we sorted this out now. Everyone who is ready to start work can remain here. The rest can leave. Some of you will be familiar with E-3, perhaps you can look after those who aren't.'

When May and the others had left, Faustaff spoke to his chief of Communications on E-3, John Mahon, telling him to call in all operatives from the other subspacial alternates and get them working on an attempt to break through to E-Zero.

Class H agents – those who worked for the organisation without realising what it was – were to be paid off. When Faustaff brought up the subject of Class H, Mahon snapped his fingers. 'That reminds me,' he said. 'You remember I put some Class H men on to checking up on Klosterheim and Maggy White?'

It seemed a long time ago. Faustaff nodded. 'I suppose nothing came of it.'

'The only information we got indicates that they have a tunneller of their own – or at least some method of travelling through the subspacial levels. Two Class H agents followed them out to LA to a cottage they evidently use as their base on E-3. They never came out of that cottage, and a check showed that they weren't there. The agents reported finding a lot of electronic equipment they couldn't recognise.'

'It fits with what I found out,' Faustaff said. He told Mahon about his encounters with the two. 'If only we could get them to give us more information we might stand a better chance of getting a concrete solution to this mess.'

Mahon agreed. 'It might be worth going out to this cottage of theirs, if we could find the time. What do you think?'

Faustaff debated. 'I'm not sure. There's every likelihood that they'd have removed their equipment by now anyway.'

'Right,' said Mahon. 'I'll forget about it. We can't spare anyone now to go out and have a look for us.'

Faustaff picked up a tin box. It contained the information gathered about E-Zero. He told Mahon that he was going to his apartment to go through it again and could be contacted there.

He drove his Cadillac through the sunny streets of Frisco, his enjoyment of the city's atmosphere now somewhat tainted by his mood of unaccustomed grimness.

It was only as he entered his apartment and saw how tidy the place was that he remembered Nancy Hunt. She wasn't there now. He wondered if she had given him up and left, although the indications were that she was only out temporarily.

He went to his desk and settled down to work, the VC beside him. As he studied the data, he called ideas through to his team at The Golden Gate.

Nancy came in around midnight.

'Fusty! Where have you been? You look dreadful. What's been happening?'

'A lot. Can you make me some coffee, Nancy?'

'Sure.'

The redhead went straight into the kitchen and came out later with coffee and doughnuts. 'Want a sandwich, Fusty? There's Danish salami and liver sausage, rye bread and some potato salad.'

'Make me a few,' he said. 'I'd forgotten I was hungry.'

'There must be something important up, then,' she said, laying the tray down on a table near him and returning to the kitchen.

Faustaff thought there might be a way of creating a new kind of warp in subspace, something they'd thought of in the past but dismissed since their methods had then been adequate. He called through to The Golden Gate and spoke to Mahon about it, telling him to find all the notes that had been made at the time. He realised that it was going to be several days before anything could be worked out properly and more time would be wasted in adapting the tunnellers, but his team was good, if depleted, and if anything could be done, they'd do it.

His brain was beginning to get fuzzy and he realised he would have to relax for a while before continuing. When Nancy came back with the sandwiches he went and sat next to her on the couch, kissed her and ate his way through the food. He sat back feeling better.

'What have you been doing, Nancy?'

'Hanging around, waiting for you. I went to see a V-drama today.'

'What was it about?'

'Cowboys. What have *you* been doing, Fusty? I was worried.'

'Travelling,' he said. 'Urgent business, you know.'

'You could have called.'

'Not from where I was.'

'Well, let's go to bed now and make up for all that time wasted.'

He felt even more miserable. 'I can't,' he said. 'I've got to go on with what I'm doing. I'm sorry, Nancy.'

'What's all this about, Fusty?' She stroked his arm sympathetically. 'You're really upset, aren't you? It's not just a business problem.'

'Yes, I'm upset. D'you want to hear the whole story?' He realised that he needed Nancy's comforting. There would be no harm now in telling her the whole story. Briefly he outlined the situation.

When he'd finished she looked incredulous. 'I believe you,' she said. 'But I can't – can't take it all in. So we're all going to die, is that it?'

'Unless I can do something about it. Even then, most of us will be destroyed.' The VC began to ring. He picked it up. It was Mahon. 'Hello, Mahon. What is it?'

'We're checking the new warp theory. It seems to be getting somewhere, but that wasn't why I called. Just thought I'd better tell you that E-14 and E-13 are in Total Break-up. You were right. The enemy's getting busy. What can we do?'

Faustaff sighed. 'Assign emergency teams to evacuate as many as possible from the deeper worlds. Evidently the enemy are working systematically. We'll just have to hope we can consolidate on here and E-2 and make a fight of it. Better order all the adjustors brought to E-2 and E-3. We'll spread them out. There might be a chance. We'll have to fight.'

'There was one other thing,' Mahon said. 'I think May organised an expedition to E-4 before you left E-1.'

'That's right. They were going to bomb Orelli's headquarters. Were they successful?'

'They couldn't find it. They came back.'

'But they must have found it – they couldn't have missed it.'

'The only thing they found was a crater in the ice. It could just be that the whole cathedral had vanished – been shifted. You said Klosterheim was with them, they had two D-squaders and a disrupter. It could easily mean that Klosterheim is helping Orelli. He probably knows the potentialities of the disrupter. Or maybe something went wrong and the cathedral was destroyed in some way. The only thing that's certain is that they've vanished.'

'I don't think they've destroyed themselves,' Faustaff replied. 'I think we'll have to watch for them in the near future. The combination of Orelli and Klosterheim is a bad one for us.'

'I won't forget. And I'll get the evacuation scheme moving. Any more details for us?'

Faustaff felt guilty. He'd spent too much time talking to Nancy.

'I'll let you know,' he said.

'Okay.' Mahon put the receiver down.

'Got to get on with it now, Nancy,' he said. He told her what he'd heard from Mahon.

He settled himself at his desk and began work again, making notes and equations on the pad beside him. Tomorrow he would have to go back to the centre and use the computers himself.

As he worked, Nancy kept him supplied with coffee and snacks. By eight the next morning he began to feel he was getting somewhere. He assembled his notes, put them in a folder, and was about to say goodbye to Nancy when she said:

'Mind if I come along, Fusty? I wouldn't like to have to hang around here for you again.'

'Okay,' he said. 'Let's go.'

As they arrived at The Golden Gate they found that the place had a visitor. It was Gordon Ogg. He came forward with John Mahon, through a confusion of technicians and machinery that now filled the dance hall.

'Mr Ogg wants to see you, professor,' Mahon said. 'He's got some news about Orelli, I think.'

'We'd better go upstairs, Gordon,' Faustaff said. They climbed the staircase to the second floor and entered a small, cluttered room where old furniture had been piled. 'This'll have to do,' Faustaff said as they sat down where they could. Nancy was still with them. Faustaff didn't feel like asking her to wait anywhere else.

'I must apologise for leaving you behind on E-11.' Ogg stroked his long moustache, looking even more mournful than usual. 'But then I had no conception of what was going on. You know it all, I suppose – the destruction of E-14 and E-13, the war that is destroying E-1?'

'Yes.' Faustaff nodded.

'And you know that Orelli has leagued himself with this chap with a funny name…?'

'Klosterheim. I suspected it. Though I'm still unable to think what mutual interest they have. It is in yours and Orelli's for things to remain basically unchanged.'

'As salvagers, yes. But Orelli has other schemes. That's why I came to see you. He contacted me this morning, at my base on E-2.'

'So he is alive. I thought so.'

'This other chap – Klosterheim – was with him. They wanted my help. From what I can gather Klosterheim was working for another group, but he's turned traitor. That was a little obscure. I couldn't quite make out who the other group were. There's a new parallel been formed, I gather…'

'E-Zero, that's right. Did they tell you anything about it?'

'Nothing much. Klosterheim said something about its not having been "activated" yet, whatever that means. Anyway they have plans for going there and setting up their own government, something like that. Orelli was cautious, he didn't tell me much. He concentrated mainly on telling me that all the other worlds are due to break up soon and nothing will be able to stop this happening, that I might just as well throw in my lot with him and Klosterheim since I had everything to lose and something to gain. I told him that I wasn't interested.'

'Why did you do that?'

'Call it a psychological quirk. As you know, professor, I have never felt any malice towards you and have always been careful never to attack you or any of your men by using violence. I preferred to leave you and work on my own – that's part of the same psychological quirk. But now it looks as if the crunch is coming, I wondered if I could help.'

Faustaff was touched by Ogg's statement. 'I am sure you could. Just the act of offering has helped me, Gordon. I suppose you have no idea how Orelli and Klosterheim intend to get through to E-Zero?'

'Not really. They did refer to E-3 at one point, I think they might have had some equipment here. They certainly boasted of a refined tunneller – Klosterheim seemed to link it with a disrupter that Orelli had captured. They can shift much bigger masses through subspace, I gathered.'

'So that's what happened to the cathedral. But where is it now?'

'The cathedral?'

Faustaff explained. Ogg said he knew nothing of this.

'I have the feeling,' Faustaff said, 'that the shifting of the cathedral has no real significance. It would have been done simply to exhibit the power of the new tunneller. But it is difficult to see why Klosterheim has reneged on his own people. I'd better fill you in on this.' He repeated all he knew about Klosterheim and Maggy White.

Ogg took all the information expressionlessly. 'An alien race manipulating human beings from somewhere beyond Earth. It sounds too fantastic, professor. Yet I'm convinced.'

'I think I've been foolish,' Faustaff said. 'You say they mentioned a base on E-3. We know about it. There might be a chance of finding something after all. Do you want to come and see, Gordon?'

'If you'd like me along.'

'I would. Come on.'

The three of them left the room. Faustaff enquired about air transport, but there was none available. He did not dare wait on the off chance of a copter coming through and he was not sure enough of himself to requisition one being used for evacuation purposes. He got into his Cadillac and they drove out of San Francisco, heading for Los Angeles.

They looked a strange trio, Faustaff driving, his huge body squeezed into the inadequate seat of the car, Nancy and Ogg in the back seats. Ogg had insisted on bringing the antiquated machine gun he always carried. His tall, thin body was held erect, the gun cradled in his arm. He looked like a Victorian nobleman on safari, his eyes staring straight ahead down the long road that stretched into the Great American Desert.

Chapter Eleven
The Way Through

THEY FOUND THE house that had been marked for them on their map by Mahon before they left.

It lay in a quiet Beverly Hills cul-de-sac about fifty yards from the road. A well-kept lawn lay in front and a gravel drive led to the house. They drove up it. Faustaff was too tired to bother about secrecy. They got out of the car and a couple of heaves of Faustaff's body broke the door open. They moved into the hall. It was wide and an open staircase led up from it.

'Mahon said they'd found the equipment in the back room,' Faustaff said, leading the way there. He opened the door. Orelli stood there. He was alone, but his rifle was pointing straight at Faustaff's head. His thin lips smiled.

'Professor Faustaff. We'd missed you.'

'Forget the villainous dialogue, Orelli.' Faustaff skipped suddenly to one side and rushed at the ex-cardinal who pulled the trigger. A beam went high and pierced the outer wall. Faustaff began to grapple the gun from Orelli who was now snarling.

Orelli plainly hadn't expected such sudden action from Faustaff who was normally loath to indulge in any sort of violence.

Ogg stepped in behind him while Nancy hovered in the doorway. He pushed the muzzle of his machine gun into Orelli's back and said softly: 'I shall have to kill you unless you are sensible, Orelli. Drop your rifle.'

'Turncoat!' Orelli said as he dropped the gun. He seemed offended and surprised by Ogg's allying himself with Faustaff. 'Why have you sided with this fool?'

Ogg didn't bother to reply. He tugged the laser-rifle's cord from the power-pack on Orelli's back and threw the gun across the room.

'Where's Klosterheim and the rest of your men, Orelli?' Faustaff asked. 'We're impatient – we want to know a lot quickly. We're ready to kill you unless you tell us.'

'Klosterheim and my men are on the new planet.'

'E-Zero? How did you get through when we couldn't?'

'Klosterheim has far greater resources than yours, professor. You were stupid to offend him. A man with his knowledge is worth cultivating.'

'I wasn't interested in cultivating him, I was more interested in stopping him from killing me, if you remember.'

Orelli turned to Ogg. 'And you, Gordon, taking sides against me, a fellow salvager. I am disappointed.'

'We have nothing in common, Orelli. Answer the professor's questions.'

Just then Nancy shouted and pointed. Turning, Faustaff saw that the air behind him seemed to glow and the wall beyond became hazy. A tunnel was being formed. Klosterheim must be coming through. He picked up the useless laser-rifle and stood watching the tunnel as it shimmered and took shape. It was of a glowing reddish colour, unlike the dull grey of the tunnels he was used to. Out of it stepped Klosterheim, he was unarmed. He smiled, apparently unperturbed, when he saw what had happened.

'What are you trying to do, professor?' Behind him the tunnel began to fade.

'We're after information primarily, Herr Klosterheim,' Faustaff answered, feeling more confident now that it was plain Klosterheim had no more men with him. 'Are you going to give it to us here, or must we take you back to our headquarters?'

'What sort of information, Professor Faustaff?'

'Firstly we want to know how you can get through to E-Zero when we can't.'

'Better machines, professor.'

'Who made the machines?'

'My erstwhile principals. I could not tell you how to build one, only how to work one.'

'Well, you can show us.'

'If you wish.' Klosterheim shrugged and went to a machine that was evidently the main console for the rest of the devices in the room. 'It is a simple matter of tapping out a set of co-ordinates and setting a switch.'

Faustaff decided that Klosterheim was probably telling the truth and he didn't know how the advanced tunneller worked. He would have to get a team down here immediately and have them check it over.

'Can you keep them covered, Gordon?' he said. 'I'll call my headquarters and get some people here as soon as possible.'

Ogg nodded and Faustaff went into the hall where he'd seen the VC.

He got through to the operator and gave her the number he wanted. The VC rang for some time before someone answered. He asked for Mahon.

At length Mahon came on the line and Faustaff told him what had happened. Mahon promised to send a team up by copter right away.

Faustaff was just going back into the room when he heard footsteps on the path outside. He went to the door and there was Maggy White.

'Professor Faustaff,' she nodded, as seemingly unsurprised by his presence as Klosterheim had been. Faustaff began to think that all his recent actions had been anticipated.

'Were you expecting me to be here?' he asked.

'No. Is Klosterheim here?'

'He is.'

'Where?'

'In the back room. You'd better join him.'

She went ahead of Faustaff, looked at Nancy curiously and then stepped into the room.

'We've got them all now,' Faustaff said, feeling much better. 'We'll wait for the team to arrive and then we can get down to business. I suppose,' he turned to Klosterheim, 'you or Miss White wouldn't like to tell us the whole story before they come?'

'I might,' Klosterheim said, 'particularly since it would now be best if I convinced you to throw in your lot with Cardinal Orelli and myself.'

Faustaff glanced at Maggy White. 'Do you feel the same as Klosterheim? Are you prepared to tell me more?'

She shook her head. 'And I shouldn't believe too much of what he tells you, either, professor.'

Klosterheim glanced at his wristwatch.

'It doesn't matter now,' he said, almost cheerfully. 'We appear to be on our way.'

Suddenly it seemed that the whole house was lifted by a whirlwind and Faustaff thought briefly that Orelli had rightly called him a fool. He should have realised that what could be done with a gigantic cathedral could also be done with a small house.

The sensation of movement was brief, but the scene through the window was very different. Amorphous, it gave the impression of an unfinished painted stage set. Trees and hedges were there, the sky, sunlight, but none of them seemed real.

'Well, you wanted to get here, professor,' smiled Klosterheim, 'and here we are. I think you called it E-Zero.'

Chapter Twelve

The Petrified Place

MAGGY WHITE GLOWERED at Klosterheim who seemed very full of himself at that moment.

'What do you think you're doing?' she said harshly. 'This goes against...'

'I don't care,' Klosterheim shrugged. 'If Faustaff could get away with so much, then so can I – we, if you like.' He turned a light-hearted eye on Faustaff who had still not completely recovered from the shock of transition between E-3 and E-Zero.

'Well, professor,' Faustaff heard Klosterheim say. 'Are you impressed?'

'I'm curious,' said Faustaff slowly.

Orelli began to chuckle and moved towards Faustaff, but was stopped short by Ogg's now somewhat nervous gun nudging at him. Ogg's expression had become resolute, but he seemed baffled. Nancy looked rather the same.

Orelli said sharply: 'Gordon! Put the gun away. That was a silly gesture. We are in the position of power now, no matter how many guns you point at us. You realise that? You must!'

Faustaff pulled himself together. 'What if we order you to return us to E-3? We could kill you if you refused.'

'I am not so sure you would kill us, professor,' Klosterheim smiled. 'And in any case it takes hours to prepare for a transition. We would need technical help too. All our people are at the cathedral.' He pointed out of the window to where a spire could be seen over the tops of roofs and trees. The spire seemed unnaturally solid in the peculiarly unreal setting. Part of the impression was gained, Faustaff realised, by the fact that the whole landscape, aside from the spire, looked unused. 'Also,' Klosterheim continued, 'they are expecting us and will come here soon if we do not turn up there.'

'We still have you,' Ogg reminded him. 'We can barter your lives for a safe transport back to where we came from.'

'You could,' Klosterheim admitted. 'But what would that gain you? Isn't E-Zero where you wanted to come?' He glanced at Faustaff. 'That's true, isn't it, professor?'

Faustaff nodded.

'You will have to be careful here, professor,' Orelli put in. 'I am serious. You had better throw in with us. United we stand, eh?'

'I prefer to stay divided, particularly if you fall as well,' Faustaff replied dryly.

'This antagonism is unrealistic, professor. Cut your losses.' Klosterheim looked somewhat nervously out of the window. 'The potential danger here is great; this is an unactivated simulation – it's delicate. A few wrong moves on your part would, among other things, make it almost impossible to return to any one of the other simulations…'

'Simulations of what?' said Faustaff, still trying to get concrete information from Klosterheim.

'The original…'

'Klosterheim!' Maggy White broke in. 'What are you doing? The principals might easily decide to recall us!'

Klosterheim responded coolly. 'How will they reach us?' he asked her. 'We are the most sophisticated agents they have.'

'They can recall you – you know that.'

'Not easily – not without some co-operation from me. They will never succeed with the simulations. They have tried too many times and failed too many times. With our knowledge we can resist them – we can become independent – live our own lives. We can leave this world only semi-activated and rule it. There would be nothing to stop us.'

Maggy White lunged towards Ogg and tried to grab the machine gun from him. He backed away. Faustaff got hold of the woman, but she already had both hands on the gun. Suddenly the gun went off. It had been set to semi-automatic. A stream of bullets smashed through the window.

'Careful!' shrieked Klosterheim.

As if startled by the firing, Maggy White took her hands away. Orelli had moved towards Ogg, but the tall Englishman turned the gun on him again and he stopped.

Klosterheim was staring out of the window.

Faustaff looked in the same direction, and saw that where the bullets had struck the nearest house its walls were falling. One had cracked and was crumbling, but the others fell neatly down, to lie on the ground in one piece. The impression of a stage set was retained – yet the walls, and the revealed interior of the house, which was now falling slowly, were evidently quite solid and real.

Klosterheim turned on Maggy.

'You accuse me – and cause that to happen,' he said, pointing out at the wreckage. 'I suppose you were going to try to kill me.'

'I still intend to.'

Klosterheim swung the pointing finger at Faustaff. 'There is the one you should kill. One of us should have done it long since.'

'I am not so sure now,' she said. 'He might even be of use to the principals. Not you, though.'

'No indeed,' smiled Klosterheim, lowering his arm. 'You realise what your action might have started?'

She nodded. 'And that wouldn't be to your advantage, would it, Klosterheim?'

'It would be to no-one's advantage,' Klosterheim said, rubbing his eyes. 'And it would be very unpleasant for Faustaff and the others – including you, Orelli, as I've explained.'

Orelli smiled to himself. It was a wickedly introspective smile as if he looked into his own soul and was pleased with the evil he found there. He leaned against one of the pieces of machinery and folded his arms. 'What you told me sounds almost attractive, Klosterheim.'

Faustaff became impatient. He felt that he should be taking some sort of action but he could think of nothing to do.

'We'll pay a visit to the cathedral I think,' he said on impulse. 'Let's get going.'

Klosterheim was plainly aware of Faustaff's uncertainty. He did not move as Ogg waved the gun towards the door. 'Why would the cathedral be better, Professor Faustaff?' he asked lightly. 'After all, there are more of our men there.'

'True,' Faustaff answered. 'But we might just as well go. I've made up my mind, Klosterheim. Move, please.' His tone was unusually firm. Hearing it, he was not sure that he liked it. Was he compromising himself too much? he wondered.

Klosterheim shrugged and walked past Ogg towards the door. Orelli was already opening it. Maggy White and Nancy followed Ogg with Faustaff keeping an eye on Maggy.

They went out into the hall and Orelli pulled the front door wide.

The lawn and gravel path looked only slightly different from what they had left on E-3. Yet there was something hazy about them, something unformed. Faustaff thought that the feeling they aroused was familiar and as they began to walk down the path towards the street he realised that, for all their apparent reality, they had the effect of making him feel as if he were experiencing a particularly naturalistic dream.

The effect was made perfect by the stillness of the air, the complete silence everywhere. Though he could feel the gravel beneath his feet, he made no sound as he walked.

Even when he spoke, his voice seemed so distant that he had the impression its sound carried around the whole planet before it reached his ears.

'Does that street lead to the cathedral?' he asked Klosterheim, pointing to the street at the bottom of the lawn.

Klosterheim's lips were tight. His eyes seemed to express some kind of warning as he turned and nodded at Faustaff.

Orelli appeared more relaxed. He also turned his head while he walked jauntily towards the street. 'That's the one, professor,' he said. His voice sounded far away, too, although it was perfectly audible.

Klosterheim looked nervously at his partner. To Faustaff it seemed that Klosterheim was privately wondering if he had made a mistake in joining forces with Orelli. Faustaff had known Orelli much longer than Klosterheim and was well aware that the ex-cardinal was at best a treacherous and neurotic ally, given to moods that seemed to indicate a strong death-wish and which led him and anyone associated with him into unnecessary danger.

Wanting something to happen, something he could at least try to deal with, Faustaff almost welcomed Orelli's mood.

They reached the street. Cars were parked there. They were new and Faustaff recognised them as the latest on E-1. Evidently, whoever created these 'simulations' didn't start from scratch.

There was no-one about. E-Zero seemed unpopulated. Nothing lived. Even the trees and plants gave the impression of lifelessness.

Orelli stopped and waved his arms, shouting. 'They're here, professor! They must have heard the shots. What are you going to do now?'

Turning a corner came about a dozen of Orelli's brigandly gang, their laser-rifles ready in their hands.

Faustaff bellowed: 'Stop! We've got Klosterheim and Orelli covered!' He felt a bit self-conscious, then, and looked at Ogg, feeling he was better able to take the initiative.

Ogg said nothing but he straddled his legs slightly and moved his machine gun a little. His expression was abnormally stern. Orelli's men stopped.

'What are you going to do now, Faustaff?' Orelli repeated.

Faustaff glanced at Ogg again but Ogg apparently refused to meet his gaze. There was a big hovercar close by. Faustaff contemplated it.

Klosterheim said softly: 'It would be unwise to do anything with the automobile. Please, professor, don't use any of the things you find here.'

'Why not?' Faustaff asked in the same tone.

'To do so could trigger a sequence of events that would snowball until nobody could control them. I'm speaking the truth. There is a ritual involved – every simulation has its ritual before it becomes completely activated. The gun going off doesn't appear to have had any result – but starting a car could begin the initial awakening…'

'I'll kill him if you come any closer!'

Ogg was talking to Orelli's men who had begun to stir. He was pointing the gun directly at Orelli, Klosterheim apparently forgotten. The normally stoical Ogg now seemed to be under stress. He must have hated Orelli for a long time, Faustaff reflected. Or perhaps he hated what Orelli represented in himself. It was quite plain to them all that Ogg hoped to kill Orelli.

Only Orelli himself seemed relaxed, grinning at Ogg. Ogg frowned now, sweating. His hands shook.

'Gordon!' Faustaff said desperately. 'If you kill him, they'll start shooting.'

'I know,' Ogg replied, and his eyes narrowed.

Behind them Maggy White had started to run up the road, away from Orelli's men. Klosterheim was the only one to turn his head and watch her, his face thoughtful.

Faustaff decided to go to the car. He gripped the door handle. He pressed the button and the door opened. He noticed that the keys were in the ignition. 'Keep them covered, Gordon,' he said as he got into the driving seat. 'Come on, Nancy.'

Nancy followed him, sitting next to him.

'Gordon!' he called. He started the engine. He realised that he hadn't considered the possibility that the car wouldn't work. The motor began to turn over.

Faustaff called to Ogg again and was relieved to see that he was edging towards the car. Nancy opened the back door for him and he slid in. His gun was still pointing directly at Orelli.

Faustaff touched a button. The car rose on its air-cushion and they began to move down the road, slowly at first.

One shot came from a laser-rifle. The beam went high.

Faustaff put his foot down, hearing Klosterheim order the men to stop firing.

'Faustaff!' Klosterheim yelled, and although they were now some distance away he could hear him perfectly. 'Faustaff – you and your friends will suffer most from this!'

They passed Maggy White on the way, but they didn't stop for her.

Chapter Thirteen
The Time Dump

As Faustaff drove into downtown Los Angeles he realised that everything was not as normal as he had thought. Much of the area was unfinished, as if work on the 'simulation' had been abandoned or interrupted. Houses were intact, stores bore familiar signs – but every so often he would pass something that clashed with the effect.

A tree in a garden, for instance, was recognisable as a Baiera tree with sparse, primitive foliage. The tree had flourished during the Jurassic, up to 180 million years in the past. A block that Faustaff remembered as having once been taken up with a big movie theatre was now a vacant lot. On it were pitched Indian wigwams reminiscent of those that had been used by the Western plains Indians. The whole appearance of the settlement did not give the impression of its having been built as an exhibit. Elsewhere were wooden houses of a style typical of three centuries earlier, a brand new 1908 Model T Ford with gleaming black enamel, brass fittings, and wheel-spokes picked out in red. A store window displayed women's fashions of almost two hundred years before.

Although, in general appearance, the city was the modern Los Angeles of 1999 on E-1, the anachronisms were plentiful and easily noticed standing out in sharp contrast to everything else. They added to Faustaff's impression that he was dreaming. He began to experience vague feelings of fear and he drove the car away very fast, heading towards Hollywood for no other reason than because that was where the highway was leading him.

Nancy Hunt gripped his arm. Evidently close to hysteria herself, she tried to comfort him. 'Don't worry, Fusty,' she said. 'We'll get out of this. I can't even believe it's real.'

'It's real enough,' he said, relaxing a little. 'Or at least the threat is. You just can't – I don't know – get to grips with the place. There's something basically intangible about it – the houses, the street, the scenery – it isn't one thing or another.' He addressed Gordon Ogg who was still grim-faced, hugging his machine gun to him, eyes hooded.

'How do you feel, Gordon?'

Ogg moved in his seat and looked directly at Faustaff whose head was half-turned towards him. Faustaff saw that there were tears in Ogg's eyes.

'Uncomfortable,' Ogg replied with some effort. 'It's not just the scenery – it's me. I can't seem to control my emotions – or my mind. I feel that this world isn't so much unreal as...' He paused. 'It's a different quality of reality, perhaps. We are unreal to *it* – we shouldn't be here. Even if we had a right to be here, we shouldn't be behaving as we are. It's our state of mind, if you like. That's what's wrong – our state of mind, not the place.'

Faustaff nodded thoughtfully. 'But do you think you'd be willing to enter the state of mind you feel this world demands?'

Ogg hesitated. Then he said: 'No, I don't think so.'

'Then I know what you mean,' Faustaff went on. 'I'm going through the same thing. We've got to try to hang on, Gordon – this world wants us to alter our identities. Do you want to alter your identity?'

'No.'

'Do you mean personality?' Nancy asked. 'That's the feeling I've got – that at any moment if I relaxed enough I just wouldn't be me any more. It's like dying, almost. A sort of dying. I feel that something of me would be left but it would be – naked...'

Their attempts to express and analyse their fears had not helped. Now the atmosphere in the car was one of terror – they had brought their fears to the surface and they were unable to control them.

The car rushed down the highway, carrying a frightened cargo. Above them, the featureless sky added to their impression that time and space as they knew it no longer existed, that they no longer possessed a fragment of potential influence over their situation.

Faustaff tried to speak again, to suggest that perhaps after all they should turn round and throw themselves on Klosterheim's mercy, that he at least would have an explanation of what was happening to them, that they might accept his suggestion of their combining forces with him until they saw an opportunity of escaping from E-Zero.

The words that came out of his mouth held no meaning for him. The other two did not hear him, it seemed.

Faustaff's large hands shook violently on the steering wheel. He barely resisted the urge to let the car crash.

He drove on a while longer and then, with a feeling of hopelessness, stopped the car suddenly. He leaned over the steering wheel, his face contorted, his mouth gibbering while another part of his mind sought the core of sanity that must still be within him and which might help him resist the identity-sapping influence of E-Zero.

Did he want to resist? The question kept entering his mind. At length, in trying to answer, he recovered partial sanity. Yes, he did – at least, until he understood what he was resisting.

He looked up. There were no houses in the immediate vicinity. There were some seen in the distance behind and ahead of him, but here the highway went across sparse grassland. It looked like a site that had been levelled for development and then left. What caught his eye, however, was the dump.

At first glance it looked like a garbage dump, a huge hill of miscellaneous junk.

Then Faustaff realised that it wasn't junk. All the objects looked new and whole.

On impulse he got out of the car and began to walk towards the vast heap.

As he got closer he could see that it was even bigger than he had first thought. It rose at least a hundred feet above him. He saw a complete Greek Winged Victory in marble; a seventeenth-century arquebus, gleaming oak, brass and iron; a large Chinese kite painted with a dragon's head in brilliant primary colours. A Fokker Triplane of the type used in the 1914–18 war lay close to the top, its wood and canvas as new as the day it left its factory. There were wagon wheels and what looked like an Egyptian boat; a throne that might have belonged to a Byzantine emperor; a big Victorian urn bearing a heavy floral pattern; an Indian elephant howdah; a stuffed Timber Wolf; a sixteenth-century arbalest – a crossbow made of steel; a late-eighteenth-century electric generator; a set of Japanese horse armour on a beautifully carved wooden horse, and a North African drum; a life-size bronze statue of a Sinhalese woman; a Scandinavian runestone and a Babylonian obelisk.

All history seemed to have been piled together at random. It was a mountain of treasure, as if some mad museum curator had found a way of upending his museum and shaking its contents out onto the ground. Yet the artefacts did not have the look of museum pieces. Everything looked absolutely new.

Faustaff approached the heap until he stood immediately beneath it. At his feet lay a near-oval shield of wood and leather. It looked as if it belonged to the fourteenth century and the workmanship seemed Italian. It was richly decorated with gold and red paint and its main motif showed an ornate mythical lion; beside it, on its side, was a beautiful clock dating from around 1700. It was of steel and silver filigree and might have been the work of the greatest clockmaker of his time, Thomas Tompion. Few other craftsmen, Faustaff thought abstractedly, could have created such a clock. Quite close to the clock he saw a skull of blue crystal. It could only have been fifteenth-century Aztec. Faustaff had seen one like it in the British Museum. Half-covering the crystal skull was a grotesque ceremonial mask that looked as if it came from New Guinea, the features painted to represent a devil.

Faustaff felt overwhelmed by the richness and beauty – and the sheer variety – of the jumble of objects. Somehow it represented an aspect of what he had been fighting for since he had taken over the organisation from his father and agreed to try to preserve the worlds of subspace.

He reached down and picked up the heavy Tompion clock, running his fingers over the ornate silver. A key hung by a red cord from the back. He opened the glass door at the front and inserted the key. Smoothly the key turned and he started to wind the clock. Inside a balance wheel began to swing with a muted tick-tock.

Faustaff set the hands to twelve o'clock and, holding the clock carefully, put it down.

Although the sense of unreality about his surroundings was still strong, this action had helped him. He squatted in front of the clock and tried to think, his back to the great mound of antiques.

He concentrated his whole attention on the clock as, with an effort, he considered what he knew about E-Zero.

It was fairly obvious that E-Zero was simply the latest 'simulation' created by whoever had employed Klosterheim, Maggy White and the D-squaders. It was also almost certain that this simulation was no different from what the other thousand had been like at the same stage. His own world, E-1, must therefore have been created in the same way, its history beginning at the point where E-2's history had become static. That would mean that E-1 had been created in the early sixties, shortly before his own birth, but certainly not before his father's birth – and his father had discovered the alternate worlds in 1971. It was unpleasant to consider that his father, and many of the people he had known and some of whom he still knew, must have been 'activated' on a world that had originally been a world like E-Zero. Had the inhabitants of his own world been transported from one subspacial world to another? If so, how had they been conditioned into accepting their new environment? There was no explanation as he wondered again why the inhabitants of all the worlds other than E-1 accepted without question the changes in their society and their geography resulting from a series of Unstable Matter Situations. He had often wondered about it. He had once described them as seeming to live in a perpetual dream and a perpetual present.

The difference on E-Zero was that *he* felt real enough, but the whole planet seemed to be a dreamworld also in a state of static time. For all the bizarre changes that had taken place on the other subspacial worlds, he had never got this impression from them – only from the inhabitants.

Evidently the conditioning that occurred on the drastically altered worlds would be applied more or less in reverse on E-Zero.

He could not consider who had created the alternate Earths. He would have to hope that at some time he would be able to get the answers once and for all, from either Maggy White or Klosterheim. He could not even guess why the worlds had been created and then destroyed. The kind of science necessary for such a task would be far too sophisticated for him to comprehend immediately, even if he never learned its principles.

The creators of the subspacial worlds seemed unable to interfere with them directly. That was why they had created the android D-squaders, obviously – to destroy their work. Klosterheim and Maggy White had made a more recent appearance. Plainly, they were either human or robots of a much more advanced type than the D-squaders and their job was not directly concerned with demolishing the subspacial Earths but with eliminating random factors like himself.

Therefore the creators, whoever and wherever they were, were not able to control their creations completely. The inhabitants of the worlds must have a fair degree of free will, otherwise he and his father would never have been able to set up the organisation they had used to preserve and bring relief to the other alternates. The creators, in short, were by no means omnipotent – they were not even omniscient, otherwise they would have acted sooner than they had in sending Klosterheim and Maggy White in to get rid of him. That was encouraging, at least. It was obvious, too, that Klosterheim believed they could be disobeyed, for Klosterheim had plainly reneged on them and was out to oppose them. Whether or not this opposition would succeed Faustaff could not tell since only Klosterheim and Maggy White knew exactly what was opposed. Maggy White was still loyal. Perhaps she had some way of contacting her 'principals' and had already warned them of Klosterheim's treachery. Klosterheim hadn't appeared to be worried by this possibility. Could these principals be relying solely on Klosterheim and Maggy White? Why, if that were the case, were they so powerful and at the same time so powerless? Another question he could not yet begin to answer.

Faustaff remembered that he had recently considered temporarily taking Klosterheim up on his offer. Now he rejected the idea. Klosterheim and Orelli had both proved untrustworthy – Klosterheim to his employers, Orelli to him. But Maggy White seemed loyal to her principals and she had once said that Faustaff's ideals and theirs were not so different in the long term.

Maggy White then, must be found. If he were going to seek anyone's help – and it was evident that he must – then she was the one. There was a strong possibility, of course, that she had now left E-Zero or been captured by Klosterheim.

All that he could hope for now, he thought, would be a chance of contacting the creators. Then at least he would know exactly what he fought. Perhaps Maggy White could be convinced. Hadn't she said to Klosterheim that he, Faustaff, would be of more use to her principals than Klosterheim now? Faustaff had failed to thwart them, but he could still hope to find a way of convincing them of the immorality of their actions.

He had no idea where Maggy had gone. The only course open to him was to retrace his journey and see if he could find her.

All this time he had been staring at the clock, but now he noticed the position of the hands; exactly an hour had passed. He got to his feet and picked up the clock.

Looking about him he still felt disturbed by the continuing unreality of his surroundings; but he felt less confused by them, less at their mercy.

He began to walk back towards the car.

It was only when he had reached it and climbed in that he realised Nancy Hunt and Gordon Ogg were no longer there.

He looked in all directions, hoping that he would see them; but they were gone.

Had they been captured by Klosterheim and Orelli? Had Maggy White found them and forced them to go with her? Or had they simply fled, totally demoralised by their fear?

Now there was an additional reason for finding Maggy White as soon as possible.

Chapter Fourteen
The Crucifixion in the Cathedral

As he drove back down the highway, seeing the spires of the cathedral over the roofs of the houses ahead, Faustaff wished that he had brought one of the guns he had seen on the dump. He would have felt better for possessing a weapon of some kind.

He slowed the car suddenly as he saw some figures approaching him down the middle of the highway. They were behaving in a peculiar way and seemed oblivious to his car.

When he got closer he recognised them as Orelli's men, but differently dressed. They wore unfamiliar, festive costumes of the kind normally seen at carnivals. Some were dressed as Roman soldiers; some, he gathered, as priests, and others as women. They came down the highway performing an exaggerated high-stepping walk and they wore rapt, uncomprehending expressions.

Faustaff felt no fear of them and sounded the car's horn. They did not appear to hear it. Very slowly, he drove the car around them, looking at them as closely as he could. There was something familiar about the costumes; what they represented struck a chord in him, but he could not analyse what it was, and he did not feel he had the time to work it out.

He passed them and then passed the house in which he'd been transported to E-Zero. The house still looked much more real in contrast to the others near it. He turned a bend in the street and saw the cathedral ahead. It was in its own grounds, surrounded by a stone wall. Let into the wall were two solid gateposts and the big wrought-iron gates were open. He drove straight through them. He felt that caution would be useless.

He stopped the car at the west-front of the cathedral where the main entrance lay, flanked by tall towers. Like most cathedrals, this one seemed to have been built and rebuilt over several centuries though in general appearance it was Gothic, with the unmistakeable arches of its stained-glass windows and heavy, iron-studded doors.

Faustaff mounted the few steps until he stood at the doors. They were slightly ajar and he pushed them partially open, just enough for him to pass through. He walked into the nave, the vast ceiling rising above him, and it was as empty of seats as when he had last been in it. But the altar was there and candles burned on it. It was covered by an exquisite altar cloth. Faustaff barely noticed these, for it was the life-size crucifix behind the altar which drew his attention. Not only was it life-size but peculiarly lifelike, also. Faustaff walked rapidly towards it, refusing to believe what he already knew to be true.

The cross was of plain wood, though well-finished.

The figure nailed to it was alive.

It was Orelli, naked and bleeding from wounds in his hands and feet, his chest rising and falling rapidly, his head hanging on his chest.

Now Faustaff realised what Orelli's men had represented – the people of Calvary. They must certainly have been the ones who crucified him.

With a grunt of horror Faustaff ran forward and climbed on the altar reaching up to see how he could get Orelli down. The ex-cardinal smelled of sweat and his body was lacerated. On his head was a thorn garland.

What had caused Orelli's men to do this to him? It was surely no conscious perversion of Christianity; no deliberate blasphemy. Faustaff doubted that Orelli's brigands cared enough for religion to do what they had done.

He would need something to lever the nails out. Then Orelli raised his head and opened his eyes.

Faustaff was shocked by the tranquillity he saw in those eyes. Orelli's whole face seemed transformed not into a travesty of Christ but into a living representation of Christ.

Orelli smiled sweetly at Faustaff. 'Can I help you, my son?' he said calmly.

'Orelli?' Faustaff was unable to say anything else for a moment. He paused. 'How did this happen?' he asked eventually.

'It was my destiny,' Orelli replied. 'I knew it and they understood what they must do. I must die, you see.'

'This is insane!' Faustaff began trying to tug at one of the nails. 'You aren't Christ! What's happening?'

'What must happen,' Orelli said in the same even tone. 'Go away, my son. Do not question this. Leave me.'

'But you're Orelli – a traitor, murderer, renegade. You – you don't deserve this! You've no right...' Faustaff was an atheist and to him Christianity was one of many religions that had ceased to serve any purpose, but something in the spectacle before him disturbed him. 'The Christ in the Bible was an idea, not a man!' he shouted. 'You've turned it inside out!'

'We are all ideas,' Orelli replied, 'either our own or someone else's. I am an idea in their minds and I am the same idea in my own. What has happened is true – it is real – it is necessary! Do not try to help me. I don't need any help.'

Though he spoke distantly, Faustaff had the impression that Orelli also spoke with preternatural lucidity. It gave him some insight into what he feared on E-Zero. The world not only threatened to destroy the personality – it turned a man inside out. Orelli's outer persona was buried within him somewhere (if he had not lost it altogether) and here was revealed his innermost self; not the Devil he had tried to be but the Christ he had wanted to be.

Slowly, Faustaff got down from the altar while Orelli's calm face smiled at him. It was no idiot's smile, it was not insane – it was a smile of fulfilment. Its sanity and tranquillity terrified Faustaff. He turned his back on it and began to walk with effort towards the door.

As he neared it a figure stepped out from the shadows of the arches and touched his arm.

'Orelli does not only die for you, professor,' Klosterheim said smiling. 'He dies because of you. You began the activation. I compliment you on your strength of will. I should have expected you to have succumbed by now. All the others have.'

'Succumbed to what exactly, Klosterheim?'

'To the Ritual – the Activation Ritual. Every new planet must undergo it. Under normal circumstances the entire population of a fresh simulation must play out its myth rôles before it awakes. "The work before the dream and the dream before the wakening", as some writer of yours once put it. You people have some reasonable insights into your situation from time to time, you know. Come.' Klosterheim led Faustaff from the cathedral, 'I can take you to see more. The show is about to start in earnest. I can't guarantee that you will survive it.'

A sun now shone in the sky, bringing bright light and heavy shade to the world, though it still did not live. The sun was swollen and a glowing red; Faustaff blinked and reached into his pocket to get his sunglasses. He put them on.

'That's right,' grinned Klosterheim. 'Gird on your armour and prepare for an interesting battle.'

'Where are we going?' Faustaff asked vaguely.

'Out into the world. You will see it naked. Every man has his rôle to play today. You have defeated me, Faustaff – perhaps you had not realised that. You have set E-Zero in motion by your ignorant actions. I can only hope that E-Zero will defeat you in turn, though I am not sure.'

'Why aren't you sure?' Faustaff asked, still only half-interested.

'There are levels that even I had not prepared for,' Klosterheim answered. 'Perhaps you will not find your rôle on E-Zero. Perhaps you have resisted and retained your personality because you are already living your rôle. Could it be that we have all underestimated you?'

Chapter Fifteen
The Revels of E-Zero

FAUSTAFF COULD NOT understand the full implication of Klosterheim's statement but he allowed the man to lead him out of the cathedral grounds and into a wooded park behind it.

'You know there is little left of E-1 now,' Klosterheim said casually as they walked. 'The war was very brief. I think a few survivors are lingering on, by all accounts.'

Faustaff knew that Klosterheim had deliberately chosen this moment to tell him, probably hoping to demoralise him. He controlled the feelings of loss and despair that came to him and tried to answer as casually.

'It was only to be expected, I suppose.'

Klosterheim smiled. 'You might be pleased to know that many people from the other simulations have been transferred to E-Zero. Not an act of mercy on the part of the principals, of course. Merely a selection of the most likely specimens for populating this Earth.'

Faustaff paused. Ahead he could make out a number of figures. He peered through the trees at them, frowning. Most of them were naked. Like Orelli's men, they were moving in a ritualistic, puppetlike manner, their faces blank. There was an approximately equal number of men and women.

Klosterheim waved a hand. 'They will not see us – we are invisible to them while they are in this state.'

Faustaff was fascinated. 'What are they doing?'

'Oh, working out their positions in the world. We'll go a little closer, if you like.'

Klosterheim led Faustaff towards the group.

Faustaff felt he was witnessing an ancient and primitive ceremony. People seemed to be imitating animals of various kinds. One man had branches tied to his head in a familiar representation of a stag. A combination of man, beast and plant which was significant to Faustaff without his understanding quite why. A woman stooped and picked up the skin of a lioness draping it around her naked body. There was a pile of animal skins in the centre of the posturing group. Some of the people already wore skins or masks. Here were representations of bears, owls, hares, wolves, snakes, eagles, bats, foxes, badgers and many other animals. A fire burned to one side of the glade.

Soon the whole group had clothed itself in pelts or masks.

In the centre now stood a woman. She wore a dog's skin around her shoulders and a crudely painted dog's mask on her face. She had long black hair that escaped from behind the mask and fell down her back. The dance around her became increasingly formal, but much faster than previously.

Faustaff grew tense as he watched.

The circle drew tighter and tighter around the dog-woman. She stood there impassively until the group suddenly stopped and faced her. Then she began to cringe, raising her head in a long-drawn-out canine howl, her arms stretched in front of her with the palms outwards.

With a roar they closed on her.

Faustaff began to run forward bent on trying to help the girl. Klosterheim pulled at his arm.

'Too late,' he said. 'It never takes long.'

The group was already backing away. Faustaff glimpsed the mangled corpse of the girl lying on the ground, the dogskin draped across her.

Bloody-mouthed, the horned man ran towards the fire and pulled a brand from it. Others brought wood that had already been gathered, heaping it around the girl. The wood was ignited and the pyre began to burn.

A wordless, ululating song began to come from the lips of the group and another dance began; this time it seemed to symbolise exaltation of some kind.

Faustaff turned away. 'That is nothing but magic, Klosterheim – primitive superstition. What kind of perverse minds have your principals if they can produce scientific miracles and – permit *that*!'

'Permit? They encourage it. It is necessary to every simulation.'

'How can ritual sacrifice be necessary to a modern society?'

'You ask that, after your own simulation has just destroyed itself? There was little difference, you know – only the scale and the complexity. The woman died quickly. She might have died more slowly of radiation sickness on E-1 if that was where she came from.'

'But what purpose does a thing like that serve?'

Klosterheim shrugged. 'Ah, purpose, Faustaff. You think there is purpose?'

'I must think so, Klosterheim.'

'It is supposed to serve a limited purpose, that sort of ritual. Even in your terms, it should be obvious that primitive peoples symbolise their fears and wishes in ritual. The cowardly dog, the malevolent woman – both were destroyed in that rite you witnessed.'

'Yet in reality, they continue to exist. That kind of ritual achieves nothing.'

'Only a temporary feeling of security. You are right. You are a rational man, Faustaff. I still fail to understand why you would not join forces with me – for I am also a rational man. You cling to primitive instincts, naïve ideals. You refuse to let your reason have full reign over you. Then you are shocked by what you have just seen. It is within the power of neither of us to change those people, but we could have taken advantage of their weaknesses and at least benefited ourselves.'

Faustaff could think of no reply, but he remained deeply unconvinced by Klosterheim's argument. He shook his head slowly.

Klosterheim made an impatient movement. 'Still? I had hoped that you would join me in defeat!' He laughed.

They left the park and walked along a street. On lawns, in the streets, on vacant lots and in gardens, the ritualistic revels of E-Zero were taking place. Klosterheim and Faustaff were unnoticed and undisturbed. It was more than a reversion to the primitive, Faustaff thought as they wandered through the scenes of dark carnival, it was a total adoption of the identities of psychological-mythical archetypes. As Klosterheim had said, every man and woman had their rôle. These rôles fell into a few definite categories. The more outstanding ones dominated the rest. He saw men and women in cowled cloaks, their faces hidden, driving dozens of naked acolytes before them with flails or tree branches; he saw a man copulating with a woman dressed as an ape; another woman, taking no part herself, seemed to be ordering an orgy. Everywhere were scenes of bloodshed and bestiality. It reminded Faustaff of the Roman Games, of the Dark Ages, of the Nazis. But there were other rituals that did not seem to fit in; they were quieter, less frenetic rituals that reminded Faustaff strongly of the few church services he had attended as a child.

Some kind of attitude was beginning to dawn in his confused mind, some realisation of why he had refused to agree with Klosterheim in spite of everything he had discovered since their first meeting.

If he were witnessing magical ceremonies, then they were of two distinct kinds. He knew little about anthropology or superstition, mistrusted Jung and found mysticism boring – yet he had heard of Black Magic and White Magic, without understanding the differences that people claimed for them. Perhaps what had horrified him was the black variety. Were the other scenes he had noticed the manifestations of white magic?

The very idea of thinking in terms of magic or superstition appalled him. He was a scientist and to him magic meant ignorance and the encouragement of ignorance. It meant senseless murder, fatalism, suicide, hysteria. Suddenly the idea came to him that it also meant the Hydrogen Bomb and World War. In short, it meant the rejection of the human factor in one's nature – the total acceptance of the beast. But what was white magic? Ignorance, also, probably. The black variety encouraged the bestial side of Man's nature, so perhaps the white variety encouraged – what? – the 'godly' side? The will to evil and the will to good.

Nothing wrong with that as an idea. But Man was not a beast and he was not a god; he was Man. Intellect was what distinguished him from other species of animal. Magic, as far as Faustaff knew, rejected reason. Religion accepted it, of course, but hardly encouraged it. Only science accepted it and encouraged it. Faustaff suddenly saw mankind's social and psychological evolution in a clear, simple light. Science alone accepted Man as he was and sought to exploit his full potential.

Yet this planet he stood on was the creation of a superb understanding of science – and at the same time these dreadful magical rituals were allowed to take place.

For the first time Faustaff felt that the creators of the simulations had gone wrong somewhere – gone wrong in their own terms.

With a shock he acknowledged the possibility that not even they understood what they were doing.

He turned to suggest this to Klosterheim, whom he had assumed was following just behind him.

But Klosterheim had gone.

Chapter Sixteen
The Black Ritual

THEN FAUSTAFF GLIMPSED Klosterheim just before the man turned a corner of the street. He began to run after him, pushing through the revellers who did not see him.

Klosterheim was climbing into a car when Faustaff next saw him. Faustaff shouted but Klosterheim did not reply. He started the car and was soon speeding away.

Another car was parked nearby. Faustaff climbed into it and gave chase.

More than once he was forced to swerve to avoid groups of people who were, like the others, completely oblivious of him, but he kept on Klosterheim's trail without too much difficulty.

Klosterheim was on the Long Beach road. Soon the sea was visible ahead. Klosterheim began to follow the coast and Faustaff noticed that even the seashore was not free of its rituals. There was a big, old hacienda-style house visible ahead and Faustaff saw Klosterheim turn his car into its drive.

Faustaff wasn't sure that Klosterheim had realised he was being followed. Out of caution he stopped his own car a short distance before he reached the house. He got out and began to walk towards it.

By the time Faustaff had walked warily up the drive, he found Klosterheim's car empty. Evidently the man had gone inside.

The front door of the house was locked. He walked around it until he came to a window. He looked in. The window opened into a large room that seemed to take up most of the ground floor.

Klosterheim was in there and so were a great many others. Faustaff saw Maggy White there. She was glowering at Klosterheim who wore his familiar mocking grin. Maggy White was dressed in a loose black robe. Its hood was thrown back over her shoulders. Apart from her, only Klosterheim wore any kind of conventional clothing.

The others all wore black hoods and nothing else. The women knelt in the centre, their bowed heads towards Maggy White. The men stood around the walls. Some of them held large, black candles. One of them gripped a huge medieval sword.

Maggy White seated herself in a thronelike chair at one end of the room. She was speaking to Klosterheim who gestured at her and left the room for a moment to reappear wearing a similar robe to the one she wore.

Maggy White disapproved but seemed to be able to do nothing to stop Klosterheim.

Faustaff wondered why she should be involving herself in a ritual. It was, even to him, evidently a black magic ritual, with Maggy representing the Queen of Darkness or whatever it was. Klosterheim now seated himself at the other end of the room and arranged his robe, smiling at Maggy and saying something which caused her to frown even more heavily.

From what he knew of such things, Faustaff supposed that Klosterheim was representing the Prince of Darkness. He seemed to remember that the woman usually had a male lieutenant.

Two of the men went out and came back with a very beautiful young girl. She was certainly under twenty and probably much younger. She seemed totally dazed, but not in the same trancelike state as the others. Faustaff got the impression that she had not undergone the psychological reversal that the rest had suffered. Her blonde hair was piled on her head and her body looked as if it had been oiled.

The kneeling women rose as she entered and they stepped back towards the wall to line it like the men.

Rather reluctantly, Maggy signed to Klosterheim who rose and walked jauntily towards the girl, parodying the ritualistic movements of the people. The two men forced the girl down so that she was lying on her back in front of Klosterheim who stared smilingly down at her. He half-turned to Maggy and spoke. The woman pursed her lips and her eyes were angry.

To Faustaff it seemed that Maggy White might be going through with something she did not like, but doing it conscientiously. Klosterheim, on the other hand, was enjoying himself, plainly taking a delight in his power over the others.

He knelt in front of the girl and began to caress her body. Faustaff saw the girl's head jerk suddenly and her eyes flare into awareness. He saw her begin to struggle. The two men stepped forward and held her.

Faustaff looked down and saw a large flat stone, used as part of the garden's decoration. He picked it up and flung it through the window.

He had expected the people to be startled by his action, but as he clambered through the window he saw that only Maggy White and Klosterheim were staring at him.

'Leave her alone, Klosterheim,' Faustaff said.

'Someone has to do it, professor.' Klosterheim said calmly. 'Besides which, we are the best people for the job, Miss White and myself. We do not act from any kind of instinct. There is no lust in us – is there, Miss White?'

Maggy White simply shook her head, her lips tight.

'We have no instincts whatsoever, professor,' Klosterheim went on. 'It is a source of regret to Miss White, I think, but not to me. After all, you are an example of how certain instincts can be harmful to a man.'

'I've seen you angry and frightened,' Faustaff reminded him.

'Certainly I might have expressed anger and fear but these were mental states, not emotional ones, or is there no difference in your terms, professor?'

'Why are you taking part in these things?' Faustaff ignored Klosterheim's question and addressed them both.

'For amusement in my case,' Klosterheim said. 'I am equipped to experience sensual pleasure, also – though I do not spend a lifetime seeking it as you seem to.'

'There could be more to it,' Maggy White said quietly. 'I've already said this to you – maybe they can experience more pleasure.'

'I'm aware of your obsession, Miss White,' Klosterheim smiled. 'But I am sure you're wrong. Everything they do is on a puny scale.' He looked at Faustaff. 'You see, professor, Miss White feels that by taking part in these rites it will somehow confirm on her a mysterious ecstasy. She thinks you have something we do not.'

'Perhaps we have,' Faustaff said.

'Perhaps it is not worth having,' Klosterheim suggested.

'I'm not sure,' Faustaff looked at the people around him. The two men were still holding the girl, though now she seemed to have lapsed into a similar state to their own. 'It doesn't have to be this.'

'No indeed.' Klosterheim's tone was sardonic. 'It could be something else. I think your friends Nancy Hunt and Gordon Ogg are involved in something you would prefer.'

'Are they all right?'

'Perfectly at this stage. They have come to no physical harm.' Klosterheim grinned.

'Where are they?'

'They ought to be somewhere nearby.'

'Hollywood,' Maggy White said. 'One of the film company lots.'

'Which one?'

'Simone-Dane-Keene, I think. It's almost an hour's drive.'

Faustaff pushed the two men aside and picked up the girl.

'Where do you think you're taking her?' Klosterheim mocked. 'She won't know anything after the activation.'

'Call me a dog in the manger,' Faustaff said as he carried the girl towards the front door and unlatched it.

He walked out to the street, reached his car, dumped the girl in the back seat and began to drive towards Hollywood.

Chapter Seventeen
The White Ritual

THE CAR WAS fast and the freeways clear. As he drove, Faustaff wondered about the pair he had left. From what Klosterheim had said, it was fairly obvious that they weren't human; were probably, as he'd suspected, near-human androids, more advanced versions of the robot D-squaders.

He hadn't asked the nature of the ritual in which, he assumed, Nancy and Gordon had become involved. He simply wanted to reach them as soon as possible so that he could be of help to them if they needed it.

He knew the S-D-K lot. S-D-K had been the biggest of the old-style motion picture makers on E-1. He had once visited the lot from curiosity on one of his occasional trips to E-1 Los Angeles.

Every so often he found it necessary to slow the car and steer through or around a throng of people performing what were to him obscure rites. They were not all obscene or violent, but the sight of the blank faces was sufficient to disturb him.

He had noticed a change, however. The buildings seemed in slightly sharper focus than when he had first arrived on E-Zero. The impression of newness, too, was beginning to wear off a little. Evidently these pre-activation rites had some link with the altering nature of the new planet. From his own experience he knew that it was this world's influence which produced the inability to associate properly, the quite rapid loss of personal identity, the slip back into the rôle of whatever psychological archetype was strongest in the particular psyche of the individual; but there also seemed to be a kind of feedback where the people somehow helped to give the planet a more positive atmosphere of reality. Faustaff found the idea hard to grasp in any terms familiar to him.

He was nearing Hollywood now. He could see the big illuminated S-D-K sign ahead. Soon, he was turning into the lot. It was silent, apparently empty. He got out of the car, leaving the girl where she was. He locked the doors and began to walk in the direction of a notice which said *NO. 1 STAGE*.

A door was set in the concrete wall. It was covered with cautionary signs. Faustaff pushed it open and looked inside. The jungle of cameras and electronic equipment partially hid a set. It looked like a set for an historical film. There was nobody in sight.

Faustaff tried the next stage. He walked in. There were no cameras about and all the equipment seemed neatly stowed. A set was up, however. It was probably being used for the same film. It showed the interior of a medieval castle. For a moment Faustaff wondered at the craftsmen who had built the set so that it looked so convincing.

There was a ritual being enacted on the set. Nancy Hunt was wearing a white, diaphanous shift and her red hair had been combed out and arranged to flow over her back and shoulders. Beside her was a man dressed in black armour that looked real. Either the costume was from the film, or else it had come from the same source as all the other costumes that Faustaff had seen. The man in black armour was drawing down his visor. He had a huge broadsword in his right hand.

With a measured tread another figure came clumping from the wings. It was Gordon Ogg, also in full armour of bright steel with a plain white surcoat over it. He held a large sword in his right hand.

Faustaff shouted: 'Nancy! Gordon! What are you doing?'

They didn't hear. Evidently they were as much in a dreamlike state as the rest.

With peculiar movements which resembled, to Faustaff, the highly mannered motions of a traditional Japanese mime-play, Ogg approached Nancy and the black-armoured man. His lips moved in speech, but Faustaff could tell that no words sounded.

In an equally formal way the black-armoured man gripped Nancy's arm and pulled her back, away from Ogg. Ogg now lowered his visor and seemed to challenge the other man with a movement of his sword.

Faustaff didn't think that Ogg was in any danger. He watched as Nancy stepped to one side and Ogg and his opponent touched swords. Shortly the black-armoured man dropped his sword and knelt in front of Gordon Ogg. Ogg then threw away his sword. The man rose and began to strip off his armour. Nancy came forward and also knelt before Ogg. Then she got up and left the set, returning with a large golden cup which she offered to Ogg. He took it and drank from it – or pretended to, since Faustaff could see it was actually empty. Ogg picked up his sword and sheathed it.

Faustaff realised that he had only witnessed a small part of the ceremony and it now seemed over. What would Nancy and Gordon do?

There was a little more mime, with Nancy appearing to offer herself to Ogg and being sympathetically rejected. Then Ogg turned and began to move off the set, followed by everyone else. He held the golden cup high. It was obviously a symbol that meant something to him and the others.

Faustaff wondered if it represented the Holy Grail, and then wondered what the Holy Grail represented in Christian mythology and mysticism. Didn't it have a much older origin? Hadn't he read about a similar bowl appearing in Celtic mythology? He couldn't be sure.

Ogg, Nancy and the rest were now walking past him. He decided to follow them. At least he would be able to keep a watchful eye on his friends to make sure they didn't come to harm. It was, he reflected, like trying to deal with a somnambulist. It was probably even more dangerous to attempt to wake them up. Sleepwalkers, he now remembered, were said to perform rituals of this kind sometimes – usually simpler, but occasionally quite complex. There must surely be a link.

The procession left the set and walked out into the arena-like compound. Tall concrete walls rose on every side.

They paused here and turned their faces to the sun, Gordon raising the bowl towards it, as if to catch its rays. A subdued chanting could now be heard coming from them all. It was a wordless chant – or at least in a language completely unfamiliar to Faustaff. It had vague affinities with Greek, but it was more like the Voice of Tongues which Faustaff had heard on a V-cast once in the South. How had it been described by a psychologist? The language of the unconscious. It was the kind of sound people used in their sleep sometimes, Faustaff found it slightly unnerving as he listened to the chant.

They were still chanting as Klosterheim made his appearance. He had found a sword from somewhere and was gleefully leading the black-hooded acolytes into the arena. Maggy White, looking rather uncertain, followed behind. She seemed to be almost as much in Klosterheim's power as the men who were with him.

Gordon Ogg turned as Klosterheim shouted something in the same strange language they had been chanting in. From Klosterheim the words seemed halting, as if he had learned them with difficulty.

Faustaff knew that Klosterheim was shouting a challenge.

Gordon Ogg handed the cup to Nancy and drew his sword.

Watching the scene, Faustaff was suddenly struck by its ludicrousness. He began to laugh aloud. It was his old laugh, rich and warm, totally without tension. The laughter was picked up by the high walls and amplified, its echoes rolling around the arena. For a moment everyone seemed to hear it and hesitated. Then, with a yell, Klosterheim leaped at Ogg.

This action only caused Faustaff to laugh the more.

Chapter Eighteen
The Encounter

KLOSTERHEIM SEEMED BENT on killing Ogg, but he was such an inept swordsman that the Englishman, plainly trained in fencing, defended himself easily, in spite of the fact that his movements were so formal.

Faustaff snorted with laughter and stepped forward to grasp Klosterheim's arm. The android was startled. Faustaff removed the sword from his hand.

'This is all part of the ritual!' Klosterheim said seriously. 'You're breaking the rules again.'

'Calm down, Klosterheim,' Faustaff chuckled and wiped his eyes. 'No need to get emotional.'

Gordon was still going through the motions of defence. He looked so much like Don Quixote in his armour and long moustache that his behaviour seemed funnier than ever to Faustaff who started to roar with laughter again.

Ogg began to look bewildered. His movements became more hesitant and less formal. Faustaff placed himself in front of him. Ogg blinked and lowered his sword. He frowned at Faustaff for a moment and then snapped down his visor and stood there rigidly, like a statue.

Faustaff raised his fist and tapped on the helmet. 'Come out of there, Gordon – you don't need the armour any more. Wake up, Gordon!'

He saw that the others were beginning to stir. He went up to Nancy and stroked her face. 'Nancy?'

She smiled vaguely, without looking at him.

'Nancy – it's Faustaff.'

'Faustaff,' she murmured distantly. 'Fusty?'

He grinned. 'The same.'

She looked up at him, still smiling. He chuckled and she looked into his eyes. Her smile broadened. 'Hi, Fusty. What's new?'

'You'd be surprised,' he said. 'Have you ever seen anything so funny?' He waved his hand to indicate the costumed figures about them. He pointed at the suit of armour. 'Gordon's in there,' he told her.

'I know,' she said. 'I really thought I was dreaming – you know, one of those dreams where you know you're dreaming but can't do anything about it. It was quite a nice dream.'

'Nothing wrong with dreams, I guess,' Faustaff said, putting his arm round her and hugging her. 'They serve their purpose, but...'

'This dream was serving a purpose until you interrupted it,' Maggy White said.

'But did you agree with the purpose?' Faustaff asked her.

'Well – yes. The whole thing is necessary. I told you.'

'I still don't know the original purposes for the simulations,' Faustaff admitted. 'But it seems to me that nothing can be achieved by this sort of thing.'

'I'm not sure,' Maggy White replied thoughtfully. 'I don't know... I'm still loyal to the principals, but I wonder... They don't seem very successful.'

'You're not kidding,' Faustaff agreed feelingly. 'What have they scrapped? A thousand simulations?'

'They'll never succeed,' Klosterheim sneered. 'They've lost touch completely. Forget them.'

Maggy White turned on him angrily. 'This whole fiasco is your work, Klosterheim. If you hadn't disobeyed your orders E-Zero would now be well on the way to normal activation. I don't know what's going to happen now. This will be the first time that anything has gone wrong *before* full activation!'

'You should have listened to me. We need never have allowed full activation if we had been careful. We could have ruled this world easily. We could have defied the principals. At best all they could have done would have been to start afresh.'

'There isn't time to start afresh. It would be tantamount to destroying their whole project, what you would have done!' Maggy glowered at him. 'You tried to defeat the principals!'

Klosterheim turned his back on her with a sigh.

'You're too idealistic. Forget them. They are failures.'

Gordon Ogg's armour creaked. His arm moved towards his visor and slowly began to raise it. He looked out at them, blinking.

'By God,' he said wonderingly. 'Am I really dressed up in this stuff? I thought I was...'

'Dreaming? You must be hot in there, Gordon,' Faustaff said. 'Can you get it off?'

Ogg tugged at the helmet. 'I think it screws off,' he said. Faustaff grasped the helmet and with some difficulty eased it round. Ogg took it off. They began to unstrap the rest of the armour, Nancy helping. A murmur of voices around them showed that both the people who had been with Klosterheim and the people who had followed Gordon and Nancy were now waking up, confused.

Faustaff saw Maggy White stoop towards the sword and jumped up from where he was trying to unbuckle Gordon's left greave.

She had brought the sword down on Klosterheim's skull before he could reach her. He turned towards her with a smile, reached out for her, and then toppled. The top of his head had caved in completely, showing the brain. No blood came. Maggy began to hack at his body until Faustaff stopped her. She became impassive, looking down at Klosterheim's corpse. 'A work of art,' she said. 'Like me.'

'What are you going to do now?' Faustaff asked her.

'I don't know,' she said. 'Everything's gone wrong. All the rites you've seen are only the beginning. There's a series of huge assemblies later on – the final pre-activation rituals. You've broken the pattern.'

'Surely what's happened can't make much difference on a world scale.'

'You don't understand. Every symbol means something. Every

individual has a rôle. It's all connected together. It's like a complicated electronic circuit – break it in one place and the whole thing seizes up. These rituals may seem horrifying and primitive to you – but they were inspired by a deeper knowledge of scientific principles than anything you're likely to have. The rituals establish the basic pattern of every individual's life. His inner drives are expressed and given form in the pre-activation rituals. This means that when he "wakes up" and begins to lead his ordinary life, the code is imprinted in him and he will exist according to that code. Only a few, comparatively speaking, find new codes – new symbols – new lives. You're one of them – the most successful.

'Circumstances and your own integrity have enabled you to do what you have done. What the result will be, I can't think. There seems to be no division between your inner life and your outer personality. It's as if you are playing a rôle whose influence goes beyond the bounds of the principals' experiments and affects them directly. I don't think they intended to produce a type like you.'

'Will you tell me now who these "principals" are?' Faustaff asked her quietly.

'I can't,' she said. 'I obey them and I have been instructed to reveal as little about them as possible. Klosterheim said far too much and by that action, among others, helped to create this situation. Perhaps we should have killed you straight away. We had a number of opportunities. But we were both curious and delayed things for too long. We were both, in our ways, fascinated by you. As you can see, we let your personality assume too much control over us.'

'We must do something,' Faustaff told her gently.

'I agree. Let's go back to the house first and talk it over.'

'What about all these others?'

'We can't do much for them – they're confused, but they'll be all right for a while.'

Outside the movie lot stood the small truck in which Klosterheim had obviously brought his followers. Faustaff's car stood near it. In it a naked girl tugged at the doors and hammered on the window. Seeing them, she began to wind the window down.

'What the hell's going on?' she asked in a harsh, Brooklyn accent. 'Is this a kidnapping or something? Where am I?'

Faustaff unlocked the door and let her out.

'Jesus!' she said. 'What is it – a nudist camp? I want my clothes.'

Faustaff pointed back at the main gate of the lot. 'You'll find some in there,' he told her.

She looked up at the S-D-K sign. 'You're making a movie? Or is this one of those Hollywood parties I've heard about?'

Faustaff chuckled. 'With a figure like that you *ought* to be in pictures. Go and see if anyone spots you.'

She sniffed and began to walk towards the gate.

Gordon Ogg and Nancy got into the back seats and Maggy White climbed in beside Faustaff as he started the car, turned it neatly in the street and drove towards downtown LA.

People were wandering about everywhere, many of them still in their ritual costumes. They looked puzzled and a bit dazed. They were arguing and talking among themselves. There didn't seem to be much trouble; nobody looked afraid. There were a few cars on the road and sometimes a group of people would wave to him to stop as he passed, but he just waved back with a grin.

Everything seemed funny to him now. He realised that he was his old self again and wondered how and where he had started to lose his sense of humour.

Faustaff noticed, as he passed the spot, that the Time Dump had vanished and the anachronisms were gone too. Everything looked fairly normal.

He asked Maggy White about it.

'Those things are automatically eradicated,' she told him. 'If they don't fit the pattern then the simulation can't work smoothly until everything is rationalised. The pre-activation process gets rid of anything like that. Since it's been interrupted, perhaps a few anachronisms will continue to exit. I don't know. It hasn't happened before on any large scale. It's like anything else, you see. The apparatus can't be tested thoroughly until it is tried out on whatever it was designed for. This is another function of the pre-activation process.'

The house, in which they travelled from E-3 to E-Zero, was still there and so was the cathedral, visible behind it.

Faustaff had a thought. He dropped the other three at the house and drove round to the cathedral. Even before he opened the door he heard shouting echoing around inside the building.

There was Orelli, still nailed to the cross. But he was far from tranquil. His face was twisted in pain.

'Faustaff!' he said hoarsely as the professor approached. 'What happened to me? What am I doing here?'

Faustaff found a candlestick that could probably be used to get the nails out.

'This is going to be painful, Orelli,' he said.

'Get me down. It couldn't be any more painful.'

Faustaff began to lever the nails from Orelli's flesh. He took the man in his arms and laid him on the altar. He moaned in agony.

'I'll get you back to the house,' Faustaff said, picking up the ex-cardinal. 'There'll probably be dressings of some kind there.'

Orelli was weeping as Faustaff carried him out to the car. Faustaff felt that it wasn't the pain that was making Orelli weep, it was probably the memory of the dream he had only recently awakened from.

Driving away from the cathedral, Faustaff decided that it would be better to go to the nearest hospital. Presumably it would be equipped with antibiotics and medicated gauze.

It took him a quarter of an hour to find a hospital. He went into its empty hall and through to the emergency rooms. In a big medical chest he found everything he wanted and began to treat Orelli.

By the time he had finished, the ex-cardinal was asleep from the sedative he had administered.

Faustaff took him to a bed and tucked him in.

Orelli would be all right for a while, he decided.

He drove back to the house, parked the car and went inside. Maggy White, Gordon Ogg and Nancy were sitting in the living room, drinking coffee and eating sandwiches.

The scene seemed so normal as to be incongruous. Faustaff

told them what he had done with Orelli and sat down to have some food and coffee.

As they finished and Faustaff lit cigarettes for himself and Nancy, Maggy White seemed to come to a decision.

'We could use the machinery in this house to get to the principals,' she said thoughtfully. 'Would you like me to take you to them, Faustaff?'

'Wouldn't that be going against your instructions?'

'It is the best thing I can think of. I can't do anything else now.'

'Naturally I'd like to contact your principals,' Faustaff nodded. He now began to feel excited. 'Though at this stage I can't see any way of sorting out the mess that everything's in. Do you know how many of the other simulations still exist?'

'No. Perhaps they have all been destroyed by now.'

Faustaff sighed. 'Their efforts and mine both appear to have been wasted.'

'I'm not sure,' she said. 'Let's see. We'd have to leave your friends behind.'

'Do you mind?' Faustaff asked them. They shook their heads. 'Perhaps you could go and make sure Orelli's all right,' Faustaff suggested. He told them where the hospital was. 'I know how we all felt towards him, but he's paid a big enough price, I think. I don't think you'll hate him when you see him. I'm not sure his sanity will survive even now.'

'Okay,' Nancy said, getting up. 'I hope you'll get back soon, Fusty. I want to see more of you.'

'It's mutual,' he smiled. 'Don't worry. Goodbye, Gordon.' He shook hands with Ogg. 'See you!'

They left the house.

Faustaff followed Maggy White into the other room where the equipment was.

'There's just one button to press,' she told him. 'But it only works for Klosterheim or me. I'd have used it before if I could have got the house to myself, but I got diverted – I had to stay to see what you did.' She reached out and pressed the button.

The walls of the house seemed to change colour, rapidly going through the whole spectrum; they seemed to flow in on Faustaff, covering him with soft light, then they flattened out.

They stood on a vast plateau roofed by a huge, dark dome. Light came from all sides, the colours merging to become a white that was not really white, but a visible combination of all colours.

And giants looked down on them. They were human, with calm, ascetic features, completely naked and hairless. They were seated in simple chairs that did not appear to have any real substance and yet supported them perfectly.

They were about thirty feet high, Faustaff judged.

'My principals,' Maggy White said.

'I'm glad to meet you at last,' Faustaff told them. 'You seem to be in some sort of dilemma.'

'Why have you come here?' One of the giants spoke. His voice did not seem in proportion to his size. It was quiet and well-modulated, without emotion.

'To make a complaint, among other things,' said Faustaff. He felt that he should be overawed by the giants, but perhaps all the experiences that had led up to this meeting had destroyed any sense of wonder he might have had otherwise. And he felt the giants had bungled too much to deserve a great deal of respect from him.

Maggy White was explaining everything that had happened. When she finished, the giants got up and walked through the walls of light. Faustaff sat down on the floor. It felt hard and cold and it made the parts of his body that touched it feel as if they had received a slight local anaesthetic. Its perpetual changing of colour didn't help him to feel any more comfortable.

'Where have they gone?' he asked Maggy.

'To debate what I have told them,' she said. 'They shouldn't be long.'

'Are you ready to tell me who they actually are?'

'Let them tell you,' she said. 'I'm sure they will.'

Chapter Nineteen
Conversation with the Principals

THE PRINCIPALS SOON returned. When they had seated themselves one of them spoke.

'There is a pattern to everything,' he said. 'But everything makes the pattern. The human failing is to make patterns out of parts of the whole and call it the whole. Time and Space has a pattern, but you see only a few elements on your simulations. Our science reveals the full dimensions and enables us to create the simulations.'

'I understand that,' said Faustaff. 'But why do you create the simulations in the first place?'

'Our ancestors evolved on the original planet many millions of years ago. When their society had developed to the necessary point, they set off to explore the multiverse and understand it. Approximately ten thousand of your years ago we returned to the planet of our origin, having mapped and studied the multiverse and learned all its fundamental principles. We found that the society that had produced us had decayed. We expected that of course. But what we had scarcely realised was the extent to which we ourselves had been physically changed by our journeyings. We are immortals, in the sense that we shall exist until the end of the current phase of the multiverse. This knowledge has altered our psychology, naturally. In your terms we have become superhuman but we feel this as a loss rather than as an accomplishment. We decided to attempt to reproduce the civilisation that had produced us.

'There were a few primitive inhabitants left on the Earth, which had long since begun a metamorphosis into an altered chemical state. We revitalised the planet, giving it an identical nature to the one it had had when civilisation first began to exist in any real form. We expected the inhabitants to react to this. We expected – and there was no cause then to expect otherwise – to develop a race which would rapidly achieve an identical civilisation to the one which had created us. But the first experiment failed – the inhabitants stayed on the same level of barbarism that they had been on when we first found them, but they began to fight one another. We decided to create an entirely new planet and try again. So as not to alter the balance of the multiverse, we extended a kind of "well" into what you call, I believe, "subspace", and built our new planet there. This proved a failure, but we learned from it. Since then we have built more than a thousand simulations of the original Earth and have gradually been adding to our understanding of the complexity of the project we undertook. Everything on every planet has a part to play. A building, a tree, an animal, a man. All link in as essentials to the structure. They have a physical rôle to play in the ecological and sociological nature of the planet, and they have a psychological rôle – a symbolic nature. That is why we find it useful to have the populace of every new simulation (which is drawn from previous abandoned simulations) externalise and dramatise its symbolic and psychological rôle before full activation. To some extent it is also therapeutic and in many ways has the effect of simulating the birth and childhood of the adults we use. You doubtless noticed that there were no children on the new simulation. We find children very difficult to use on a freshly activated world.'

'But why all those simulations?' Faustaff said. 'Why not one planet which you could – judging by what you do anyway – brainwash en masse and channel it the way you want to?'

'We are trying to produce an identical evolutionary pattern to the one which produced us. It would be impractical to do as you suggest. The psychological accretions would build up too rapidly. We need a fresh environment every time. All this was considered before we began work on the first simulation.'

'And why don't you interfere directly with the worlds? Surely you could destroy them as easily as you create them.'

'They are not easily created and are not easily destroyed. We dare not let a hint of our presence get to the simulations. We did not exist when our ancestors evolved, therefore no-one should guess we exist now. We use our androids for destroying the failed simulations, or, for more sophisticated work, we use near-humans like the one who brought you here. They seem to be human and the natural assumption, if their activities are discovered and their missions fail, is that they are employed by other human beings. It is a very delicate kind of experiment, since it involves complicated entities like yourself, and we cannot afford, normally, to interfere directly. We do not want to become gods. Religion has a function in a society's earliest stages, but that function is soon replaced by the sciences. To provide what would be to your people "proof" of supernatural beings would be completely against our interest.'

'What of the people you kill? Have you no moral attitude to that?'

'We kill very few. Normally the population of one simulation is transferred to another. Only the children are destroyed in any quantity.'

'*Only* the children!'

'I understand your horror. I understand your feelings towards children. It is necessary that you should have them – it is a virtue when you have these feelings in any strength – in your terms. In our terms, the whole race is our children. Compare our destruction of your immature offspring to your own destruction of male sperm and female ova in preventing birth. Your feelings are valid. We have no use for such feelings. Therefore, to us they are invalid.'

Faustaff nodded. 'I can see that. But I *have* these feelings. Besides which, I think there is a flaw in your argument. We feel that it is wrong to expect our children to develop as duplicates of ourselves. This defeats progress in any sense.'

'We are not seeking progress. There is no progress to be made. We know the fundamental principles of everything. We are immortal, we are secure.'

Faustaff frowned for a moment and then asked, 'What are your pleasures?'

'Pleasures?'

'What makes you laugh, for instance?'

'We do not laugh. We would know joy – fulfilment – if our experiment were to be successful.'

'So, currently, you have no pleasures. Nothing sensual or intellectual?'

'Nothing.'

'Then you are dead, in my terms,' Faustaff said. 'Forget about the simulations. Can't you see that all your energies have been diverted into a ridiculous, useless experiment? Let us develop as we will – or destroy ourselves if we must. Let me take the knowledge you have given me back to E-Zero and tell everyone of your existence. You have kept them in fear, you have allowed them to despair, you have, in certain directions, kept them in ignorance. Turn your attention to yourselves – look for pleasure, create things to give you pleasure. Perhaps in time you would succeed in reproducing this Golden Age you speak of – but I doubt it. Even if you did, it would be a meaningless achievement, particularly if the eventual result was a race like yourselves. You have logic. Use it to find enjoyment in subjective pursuits. A thing does not have to have meaning to be enjoyed. Where are your arts, your amusements, your entertainments?'

'We have none. We have no use for them.'

'Find a use.'

The giant rose. His companions got up at the same time.

Once again they left the place and Faustaff waited, assuming they were debating what he had said.

They returned eventually.

'There is a possibility that you have helped us,' said the giant as he and his companions seated themselves.

'Will you agree to let E-Zero develop without interference?' Faustaff asked.

'Yes. And we shall allow the remaining subspacial simulations to exist. There is one condition.'

'What's that?'

'Our first illogical act – our first – joke – will be to have all the thirteen remaining simulations existing together in ordinary space-time. What influence this will in time have on the structure of the multiverse we cannot guess, but it will bring an element of uncertainty into our lives and thus will help us in our quest for pleasures. We shall have to enlarge your sun and replace the other planets in your system, for the thirteen worlds will constitute a much larger mass since we visualise them as being close together and easily accessible to one another. We feel that we shall be creating something that has no great practical use, within the limited sense of the word, but which will be pleasing and unusual to the eye. It will be the first thing of its kind in this universe.'

'You certainly work fast,' Faustaff smiled. 'I'm looking forward to the result.'

'No physical danger will result from what we do. It will be – spectacular, we feel.'

'So it's over – you're abandoning the experiment altogether. I didn't think you'd be so easily convinced.'

'You have released something in us. We are proud of you. By accident we helped create you. We are not abandoning the experiment, strictly speaking. We are going to let it run its own course from now on. Thank you.'

'And thank you, gentlemen. How do I get back?'

'We will return you to E-Zero by the usual method.'

'What about Maggy White?' Faustaff said, turning towards the girl.

'She will stay with us. She might be able to help us.'

'Goodbye, then, Maggy,' Faustaff kissed her on the cheek and squeezed her arm.

'Goodbye,' she smiled.

The walls of light began to flow inwards, enfolding Faustaff. Soon they took on the shape of the room in the house.

He was back on E-Zero. The only difference was that the equipment had vanished. The room looked completely normal.

He went to the front door. Gordon Ogg and Nancy were coming up the path.

'Good news,' he grinned, walking towards them. 'I'll tell you all about it. We've got a lot of work to do to help everybody organise themselves.'

Chapter Twenty
The Golden Roads

BY THE TIME the principals were ready to create their 'joke', the populations of the subspacial worlds had been informed of everything Faustaff could tell them. He had been interviewed for the Press, given V and radio time, and there had been no questioning voices. Somehow, all he said struck the worlds' populations as being true. It explained what they saw around them, what they felt within them.

The time came, and everyone was ready for it, when the thirteen planets began to phase into ordinary space-time.

Faustaff and Nancy were back in Los Angeles when it happened, standing in the garden of the house which had first brought them to E-Zero and where they now lived. It was night when the twelve other simulations made their appearance. The dark sky seemed to ripple gently and they were there; a cluster of worlds moving in unison through space, with E-Zero in the centre, like so many gigantic moons.

Faustaff recognised the green jungle world of E-12; the desert-sea world of E-3. There was the vast continental atoll that was the only land area on E-7; the more normal-seeming worlds of E-2 and E-4; the mountainous world of E-11.

Now Faustaff received the impression that the sky was *flowing* and he realised that, miraculously, the atmospheres of the Earth simulations were merging to form a complete envelope around the world-cluster. Now the jungle world could supply oxygen to the worlds with less vegetation, and moisture would come from the worlds predominantly of water.

He saw E-1, as he craned his neck to see them all. It seemed covered by black and scarlet clouds. It was right, he felt, that it should have been included; a symbol of ignorance and fear, a symbol of what the idea of hell actually meant in physical terms. The atmosphere did not seem to extend to E-1, for though its presence was necessary, it had been isolated.

Faustaff realised that though the principals had made a joke, it was a joke with many points to it.

'I hope they don't get too earnest about this now,' Nancy said, hugging Faustaff's arm.

'I don't think they're going to be earnest for long,' he smiled. 'Just serious maybe. A good joke needs a spot of everything.' He shook his head in wonderment. 'Look at it all. It's impossible in our scientific terms, but they've done it. I've got to hand it to them; when they decide to be illogical, they go the whole hog!'

Nancy pointed into the sky. 'Look,' she said. 'What's happening now?'

There was a further movement in the sky. Other objects began to appear; great golden structures whose reflected light turned the night to near-day; arcs of flame, roads of light between the worlds. Faustaff shielded his eyes to peer at them. They ran from world to world, spanning the distances like fiery rainbows. Only E-1 was not touched by them.

'That's what they are,' Faustaff said in realisation. 'They're roads – roads that we can travel to reach the other simulations. See –' he pointed to an object that hung in the sky above their heads, rapidly passing as the world turned on its axis – 'there's one end of ours. We could reach it in a plane, then we could walk across, if we had a lifetime to spare! But we can build transport that will travel the roads in a few days! These worlds are like islands in the same lake, and those roads link us all together.'

'They're very beautiful,' said Nancy quietly.

'Aren't they!'

Faustaff laughed in pleasure at the sight and Nancy joined in.

They were still laughing when the sun rose, a massive, splendid sun that made Faustaff realise that he had never really known daylight until that moment.

The giant sun's rays caught the gold of the roads so that they flamed even more brilliantly.

Used now to the code in which the principals had tried to write the history of his race, Faustaff looked at the roads and understood the many things they meant; to him, to the worlds and to the men, women and children who must now all be looking up at them.

And in its isolation, E-1 glared luridly in the new daylight.

Faustaff and Nancy turned to look at it. 'There's no need to fear that now, Nancy,' he said to her. 'We can start getting somewhere at last, as long as we remember to relax a bit. Those roads mean understanding; communication…'

Nancy nodded seriously. Then she looked up at Faustaff and her expression turned into a spreading grin. She winked at him. He grinned and winked back.

They went into the house and were soon rolling about in bed together.

The Ice Schooner

For Keith Roberts – master steersman

Chapter One
Konrad Arflane

When Konrad Arflane found himself without an ice ship to command, he left the city-crevasse of Brershill and set off on skis across the great ice plateau; he went with the intention of deciding whether he should live or die.

In order to allow himself no compromise, he took a small supply of food and equipment, reckoning that if he had not made up his mind within eight days he would die anyway of starvation and exposure.

As he saw it, his reason for doing this was a good one. Although only thirty-five and one of the best-known skippers on the plateau, he had little chance of obtaining a new captaincy in Brershill and refused to consider serving as a first or second officer under another master even if it were possible to get such a berth. Only fifteen years before, Brershill had had a fleet of over fifty ships. Now she had twenty-three. While he was not a morbid man, Arflane had decided that there was only one alternative to taking a command with some foreign city, and that was to die.

So he set off, heading south across the plateau. There would be few ships in that direction and little to disturb him.

Arflane was a tall, heavy man with a full, red beard that sparkled with rime. He was dressed in the black fur of the seal and the white fur of the bear. To protect his head from the cut of the cold wind he wore a thick bearskin hood; to protect his eyes from the reflected glare of the sun on the ice, he wore a visor of thin cloth stretched on a sealbone frame. At his hip he had a short cutlass in a sealskin scabbard, and in either hand he held eight-foot harpoons, which served him both as weapons and as ski-poles. His skis were long strips cut from the bone of the great land whale.

On these he was able to make good speed and soon found himself well beyond the normal shipping routes.

As his distant ancestors had been men of the sea, Konrad Arflane was a man of the ice. He had the same solitary habits, the same air of self-sufficiency, the same distant expression in his grey eyes. The only great difference between Arflane and his ancestors was that they had been forced at times to desert the sea, whereas he was never away from the ice; for in these days it encircled the world.

As Arflane knew, at all points of the compass lay ice of one sort or another; cliffs of ice, plains of ice, valleys of ice and even, though he had only heard of them, whole cities of ice. Ice that constantly changed its colour as the sky changed colour; ice of pale blue, purple and ultramarine, ice of crimson, of yellow and emerald green. In summer crevasses, glaciers and grottoes were made even more beautiful by the deep, rich, glittering shades they reflected, and in winter the bleak ice mountains and plateaux possessed overpowering grandeur as they rose white, grey and black beneath the grim, snow-filled skies. At all seasons there was no scenery that was not ice in its many varieties and colourings and Arflane was deeply aware that the landscape would never change. There would be ice for eternity.

The great ice plateau, which was the territory best known to Arflane, occupied and entirely covered the part of the world once known as the Matto Grosso. The original mountains and valleys had long since been engulfed and the present plateau was several hundred miles in diameter, gradually sloping at its furthest points and joining with the rougher ice surrounding it. Arflane knew the plateau better than most men, for he had first sailed it with his father before his second birthday and had been master of a staysail schooner before he was twenty-one. His father had been called Konrad Arflane, as had all in the male line for hundreds of years, and they had been masters of ships. Only a few generations back, members of the Arflane family had owned several vessels.

The ice ships – trading vessels and hunting craft for the most part – were sailing ships mounted on runners like giant skis which bore them across the ice at speed. Centuries old, the ships were the principal source of communication, sustenance and trade for the inhabitants of the Eight Cities of the plateau. These settlements, situated in crevasses below the level of the ice, owned sailing craft and their power depended on the size and quality of their fleets.

Arflane's home city, Brershill, had once been the most powerful of them all, but her fleet was diminishing rapidly and there were now more masters than ships; for Friesgalt, always Brershill's greatest rival, had risen to become the pre-eminent city of the plateau, dictating the terms of trade, monopolising the hunting grounds, and buying, as with Arflane's barquentine, ships from the men of other cities who were unable to compete.

When he was six days out of Brershill and still undecided as to his fate, Konrad Arflane saw a dark object moving slowly towards him over the frozen white plain. He stopped and stared ahead, trying to distinguish the nature of the object. There was nothing by which he could judge its size. It could be anything from a wounded land whale, dragging itself on its huge, muscular flippers, to a wild dog that had lost its way far from the warm ponds where it preyed on the seals.

Arflane's normal expression was remote and insouciant, but at this moment there was a hint of curiosity in his eyes as he stood watching the object's slow progress. He considered what he should do.

Moody skies, immense, grey, and heavy with snow, rolled above his head, blotting out the sun. Lifting his visor, Arflane peered at the moving thing, wondering if he should approach it or ignore it. He had not come out onto the ice to hunt, but if the thing were a whale and he could finish it and cut his mark on it he would become comparatively rich and his future would be that much easier to decide.

Frowning, he dug his harpoons into the ice and pushed himself forward on his skis. His muscles rolled beneath his fur jacket and the pack on his back was jostled as he went skimming swiftly towards the thing. His movements were economical, almost nervous. He leaned forward on the skis, riding the ice with ease.

For a moment the red sun broke through the layers of cold cloud and ice sparkled like diamonds from horizon to horizon. Arflane saw that it was a man who lay on the ice. Then the sun was obscured again.

Arflane felt resentful. A whale, or even a seal, could have been killed and put to good use, but a man was of no use at all. What was even more annoying was that he had deliberately chosen this way so that he would avoid contact with men or ships.

Even as he sped across the silent ice towards the man, Arflane considered ignoring him. The ethics of the icelands put him under no obligation to help; he would feel no pang of conscience if he left the man to die. For some reason, though he was taciturn by nature, Arflane found himself continuing to approach. It was difficult to arouse his curiosity, but, once aroused, it had to be satisfied. The presence of men was very rare in this region.

When he was close enough to be able to make out details of the figure on the ice, he brought himself to a gradual halt and watched.

There was certainly little life left in the man. The exposed face, feet and hands were purple with cold and covered with frostbite swellings. Blood had frozen on the head and arms. One leg was completely useless, either broken or numb. Inadequate tatters of rich furs were tied around the body with strips of gut and leather; the head was bare and the grey hair shone with frost. This was an old man, but the body, though wasted, was big, and the shoulders were wide. The man continued to crawl with extraordinary animal tenacity. The red, half-blind eyes stared ahead; the great, gaunt skull, with its blue lips frozen in a grin, rolled as the figure moved on elbows and belly over the frozen plain. Arflane was unnoticed.

Konrad Arflane stared moodily at the figure for a moment, then he turned to go back. He felt an obscure admiration for the dying old man. He thought that it would be wrong to intrude on such a private ordeal. He poised his harpoons, ready to push himself across the ice in the direction from which he had come, but, hearing a sound behind him, he glanced back and saw that the creature had collapsed and now lay completely still on the white ice. It would not be long before he died.

On impulse, Arflane pushed himself around again and slid forward on the skis until he was able to crouch beside the body. Laying down a harpoon and steadying himself with the other, he grasped one of the shoulders in his thickly gloved hand. The grip was gentle, virtually a caress. 'You are a determined old man,' he murmured.

The great head moved so that Arflane could now see the frozen face beneath the ice-matted mane of hair. The eyes opened slowly; they were full of an introverted madness. The blue, swollen lips parted and a guttural sound came from the throat. Arflane looked broodingly into the insane eyes for a moment; then he unslung his bulky pack and opened it, taking out a flask of spirit. He clumsily removed the cap from the flask and put the neck to the puffy, twisted mouth, pouring a little of the spirit between the lips. The old man swallowed, coughed, and gasped, then, quite levelly, he said: 'I feel as if I burn, yet that's impossible. Before you go, sir, tell me if it is far to Friesgalt...'

The eyes closed and the head dropped. Arflane looked at him indecisively. He could tell, both from the remains of the clothing and from the accent, that the dying man was a Friesgaltian aristocrat. How had he come to be alone on the ice without retainers? Once again, Arflane considered leaving him to die. He had nothing to gain from trying to save him; he was as good as dead. Arflane had only contempt and hatred for the grand lords of Friesgalt, whose tall ice schooners these days dominated the frozen plains. Compared to the men of other cities the Friesgaltian nobility was soft-living and godless. It openly mocked the doctrine of the Ice Mother; it heated its houses to excess; it was often thriftless. It refused to make its women do the simplest manual work; it even gave some of them equality with men.

Arflane sighed and then frowned again, looking down at the old aristocrat, judging him. He balanced his own prejudice and his sense of self-preservation against his grudging admiration for the man's tenacity and courage. If he were the survivor of a shipwreck, then plainly he had crawled many miles to get this far. A wreck could be the only explanation for his presence on the ice. Arflane made up his mind. He took a fur-lined sleeping sack from his pack, unrolled it and spread it out. Walking clumsily on his skis, he went to the man's feet and got them into the neck of the sack and began to wrestle the rest of the body down into it until he could tie the sack's hood tightly around the man's head, leaving only the smallest aperture through which he could breathe. Then he shifted his pack so that it hung forward on his chest by its straps and hauled the sleeping sack onto his back until the muffled face was just above the level of his own broad shoulders. From a pouch at his belt, he took two lengths of leather and strapped the fur-swathed old man in place. Then, with difficulty even for someone of his strength, he heaved on his harpoons and began the long ski trek to Friesgalt.

The wind was rising at his back. Above him it had cut the clouds into swirling grey streamers and revealed the sun, which threw the shadows of the clouds onto the ice. The ice seemed alive, like a racing tide, black in the shadow and red in the sunlight, sparkling like clear water. The plateau seemed infinite, having no projections, no landmarks, no indication of horizon save for the clouds which appeared to touch the ice far away. The sun was setting and he had only two hours or so in which to travel, for it was unwise to travel at night. He was heading towards the west, towards Friesgalt, chasing the great red globe as it sank. Light snow and tiny pieces of ice whirled over the plateau, moved, as he was moved, by the cold wind. Arflane's powerful arms pumped the tall harpoons up and down as he leaned forward, partly for speed, partly because of the burden on his back, his legs spread slightly on the tough whalebone skis.

He sped on, until the dusk faded into the darkness of night and the moon and stars could occasionally be seen through the thickening clouds. Then he slowed himself and stopped. The wind was falling, its sound now like a distant sigh; even that faded as Arflane removed the body from his back and the pack from his chest and pitched his tent, driving in the bone spikes at an angle to the ice.

When the tent was ready he got the old man inside it and started his heating unit; a precious possession but one which he mistrusted almost as much as naked fire, which he had seen only twice in his life. The unit was powered by small solar batteries, and Arflane, like everyone else, did not understand how it worked. Even the explanations in the old books meant nothing to him. The batteries were supposed to be almost everlasting, but good ones were becoming scarcer.

He prepared broth for them both, and with some more spirit from his flask revived the old man, loosening the thongs around the sack's neck.

The moon shone through the worn fabric of the tent and gave Arflane just enough light to work by.

The Friesgaltian coughed and groaned. Arflane felt him shudder.

'Do you want some broth?' Arflane asked him.

'A little, if you can spare it.' The exhausted voice, still containing the traces of an earlier strength, had a puzzled note.

Arflane put a beaker of warm broth to the broken lips. The Friesgaltian swallowed and grunted. 'Enough for the meantime; I thank you.' Arflane replaced the beaker on the heater and squatted in silence for a while. It was the Friesgaltian who spoke first.

'How far are we from Friesgalt?'

'Not far. Perhaps ten hours' journey on skis. We could move on while the moon is up, but I'm not following a properly mapped route. I shan't risk travelling until dawn.'

'Of course. I had thought it was closer, but...' The old man coughed again, weakly, and a thin sigh followed. 'One misjudges distances easily. I was lucky. You saved me. I am grateful. You are from Brershill, I can tell by your accent. Why...?'

'I don't know,' said Arflane.

Silence followed and Arflane prepared to lie down on the groundsheet. The old man had his sleeping sack but it would not be too cold if, against his normal instincts, he left the heating unit on. The weak voice spoke again. 'It is unusual for a man to travel the unmapped ice alone, even in summer.'

'True,' Arflane replied.

After a pause, the Friesgaltian said hoarsely, evidently tiring: 'I am the Lord Pyotr Rorsefne. Most men would have left me to die on the ice – even the men of my own city.'

Arflane grunted impatiently.

'You are a generous man,' added the principal Ship Lord of Friesgalt before he slept at last.

'Possibly just a fool,' said Arflane, shaking his head. He lay back on the groundsheet, his hands behind his head. He pursed his lips for a moment, frowning lightly. Then he smiled a little ironically. The smile faded as he, too, fell asleep.

Chapter Two
Ulsenn's Wife

SCARCELY MORE THAN eight hours after dawn Konrad Arflane sighted Friesgalt. Like all the Eight Cities it lay beneath the surface of the ice, carved into the faces of a wide natural crevasse almost a mile deep. Its main chambers and passages were hollowed from the rock that began several hundred feet below, though many of its storehouses and upper chambers had been cut from the ice itself. Little of Friesgalt was visible above the surface; the only feature to be seen clearly was the wall of ice blocks that surrounded the crevasse and protected the entrance to the city both from the elements and from human enemies.

It was, however, the field of high ships' masts that really indicated the city's location. At first sight it seemed that a forest sprouted from the ice, with every tree symmetrical and every branch straight and horizontal; a dense, still, even menacing forest that defied nature and seemed like an ancient geometrician's dream of ideally ordered landscape.

When he was close enough to make out more detail, Arflane saw that fifty or sixty good-sized ice ships lay anchored to the ice by means of mooring lines attached to bone spikes hammered into the hard surface. Their weathered fibreglass hulls were scarred by centuries of use and most of their accessories were not the original parts, but copies made from natural materials. Belaying pins had been carved from walrus ivory, booms had been fashioned of whalebone, and the rigging was a mixture of precious nylon, gut and strips of sealskin. Many of their runners were also fashioned of whalebone, as were the spars that joined them to the hulls.

The sails, like the hulls, were of the original synthetic material. There were great stocks of nylon sailcloth in every city; indeed, their very economy was heavily based on the amount of fabric existing in their store chambers. Every ship but one, which was preparing to get under way, had its sails tightly furled.

Twenty ships long and three deep, Friesgalt's docks were impressive. There were no new ships here. There was no means, in Arflane's world, of building new ones. All the ships were worn by age, but were nonetheless sturdy and powerful; and every ship had an individual line, partly due to the various embellishments made by generations of crews and skippers, partly because of the cuts of rigging favoured by different captains and owners.

The yards of the masts, the riggings, the decks and the surrounding ice were thick with working, fur-clad sailors, their breath white in the cold air. They were loading and unloading the vessels, making repairs and putting their craft in order. Stacks of baled pelts, barrels and boxes stood near the ships. Cargo booms jutted over the sides of the vessels, being used to winch the goods up to deck level and then swing over the hatches where they dropped the bales and barrels into the waiting hands of the men whose job it was to stow the cargo. Other cargoes were being piled on sledges that were either pulled by dogs or dragged by hand towards the city.

Beneath the lowering sky, from which a little light snow fluttered, dogs barked, men shouted, and the indefinable smell of shipping mingled with the more easily distinguished smells of oil and skins and whale flesh.

Some distance off along the line a whaler was crewing up. The whaling men generally kept themselves apart from other sailors, disdaining their company, and the crews of the trading vessels were relieved that they did so; for both the North Ice and the South Ice whalers were more than boisterous in their methods of entertaining themselves. They were nearly all large men, swaggering along with their ten-foot harpoons on their shoulders, careless of where they swung them. They wore full, thick beards; their hair was also thick and much longer than the norm. It was often, like their beards, plaited, fashioned into strange barbaric styles, and held in place by whale grease. Their furs were rich, of a kind normally worn only by aristocrats, for whale men could afford anything they pleased to purchase if they were successful; but the furs were stained and worn casually. Arflane had been a whaling skipper through much of his career, and felt a comradeship for these coarse-voiced North Ice whaling men as they swung aboard their ship.

Aside from the few whalers, which were mainly three-masted barques or barquentines, there were all kinds of boats and ships on the oil-slippery ice. There were the little yachts and ketches used for work around the dock, and brigs, brigantines, two-mast two-topsail schooners, cutters and sloops. Most of the trading ships were three-mast square-rigged ships, but there was a fair scattering of two-mast brigs and two-mast schooners. Their colours for the most part were dull weather-beaten browns, blacks, greens.

The hunting ships of the whaling men were invariably black-hulled, stained by the blood of generations of slaughtered land whales.

Arflane could now make out the names of the nearer craft. He recognised most of them without needing to read the characters carved into their sides. A heavy three-master, the *Land Whale*, was nearest him; it was from the city of Djobhabn, southernmost of the Eight, and had a strong resemblance to the one-time sea mammal which, many centuries earlier, had left the oceans as the ice had gradually covered them, returning once again to the land it had left in favour of the sea. The *Land Whale* was heavy and powerful, with a broad prow that tapered gradually towards the stern. Her runners were short and she squatted on them, close to the ice.

A two-masted brig, the *Heurfrast*, named for the Ice Mother's mythical son, lay nearby, unloading a cargo of sealskins and bear pelts, evidently just back from a successful hunting expedition. Another two-master – a brigantine – was taking on tubs of whale oil, preparatory, Arflane guessed, to making a trading voyage among the other cities; this was the *Good Wind*, christened in the hope that the name would bring luck to the ship. Arflane knew her for an unreliable vessel, ironically subject to getting herself becalmed at crucial times; she had had many owners. Other two-masted brigs and two- or three-masted schooners, as well as barques, were there, and Arflane knew every ship by its name; he could see the barquentine *Katarina Ulsenn* and its sister ships, the *Nastasya Ulsenn* and the *Ingrid Ulsenn*, all owned by the powerful Ulsenn family of Friesgalt and named after Ulsenn matrons. There was the Brershillian square-rigger, the *Leaper*, and another three-master from Brershill, the slender hunting barque *Bear Scenter*. Two trading brigs, small and bulky, were from Chaddersgalt, the city closest to Brershill, and others were from Djobhabn, Abersgalt, Fyorsgep and Keltshill, the rest of the Eight Cities.

The whale-hunting craft lay away from the main gathering of ships. They were battered-looking vessels, with a spirit of pride and defiance about them. Traditionally, whaling ships were called by paradoxical names, and Arflane recognised whalers called *Sweet Girl*, *Truelove*, *Smiling Lady*, *Gentle Touch*, *Soft Heart*, *Kindness* and similar names, while others were called *Good Fortune*, *Hopeful*, *Lucky Lance* and the like. From them came the reek of their trade: blood and animal flesh.

Also to one side, but at the other end of the line to the whaling ships, stood the ice clippers, their masts towering well above those of all the surrounding craft, their whole appearance one of cruel arrogance. These were the fast-running, slim-prowed and stately queens of the plateau that, at their best, could travel at more than twice the speed of any other ship. Their hulls, supported on slender runners, dwarfed everything nearby, and from their decks one could look down on the poop deck of any other ship.

Tallest and most graceful of all these four-masted clippers was the principal ship of the Friesgaltian fleet, the *Ice Spirit*, with her sails trimly furled and every inch of her gleaming with polished bone, fibreglass, soft gold, silver, copper and even iron. An elegant craft, with very clean lines, she would have surprised her ancient designer if he could have seen her now, for she bore embellishments.

Her bow, bowsprit and forecastle were decorated with the

huge elongated skulls of the adapted sperm whale. The beak-like mouths bristled with savage teeth, grinning out disdainfully on the other shipping, witnesses to the skill, bravery and power of the ship's owners, the Rorsefne family. Though she was known as a schooner, the *Ice Spirit* was really a square-rigged barque in the old terminology of the sea. Originally all the big clippers had been fore-and-aft schooner-rigged, but this rig had been proven impracticable soon after ice navigation had become fully understood and square rig had been substituted; but the old name of schooner had stuck. The Rorsefne flag flew from above her royals; all four flags were large. Painted in black, white, gold and red by some half-barbaric artist, the Rorsefne standard showed the symbolic white hands of the Ice Mother, flanked by a bear and a whale, symbols of courage and vitality, while cupped in the hands was an ice ship. A grandiose flag, thought Arflane, hefting his near-dead burden on his back and skimming closer to the great concourse of craft.

As Arflane approached the ships, the schooner he had noticed preparing to leave let go its moorings and its huge sails bulged as the wind filled them. Only the mainsail and two forestay sails had been unfurled, enough to take the ship out slowly until it was clear of the others.

It turned into the wind and slid gracefully towards him on its great runners. He stopped and saluted cheerfully as the ship sailed by. It was the *Snow Girl* out of Brershill. The runners squealed on the smooth ice as the helmsman swung his wheel and steered a course between the few irregularities worn by the constant passage of ships. One or two of the sailors recognised him and waved back from where they hung in the rigging, but most were busy with the sails. Through the clear, freezing air, Arflane heard the voice of the skipper shouting his orders into a megaphone. Then the ship had passed him, letting down more sail and gathering speed.

Arflane felt a pang as he turned and watched the ship skim over the ice towards the east. It was a good craft, one he would be pleased to command. The wind caught more sail and the *Snow*

Girl leaped suddenly, like an animal. Startled by the sudden burst of speed, the black and white snow-kites that had been circling above her squawked wildly and flapped upwards, before diving back to the main gathering of ships to drift expectantly above them or perch in the top trees in the hope of snatching titbits of whale meat or seal blubber from the carcasses being unloaded.

Arflane dug his lances deep into the ice and pushed his overloaded skis forward, sliding now between the lines and hulls of the ships, avoiding the curious sailors who glanced at him as they worked, and making his way towards the high wall of ice blocks sheltering the city-crevasse of Friesgalt.

At the main gate, which was barely large enough to let through a sledge, a guard stood squarely in the entrance, an arrow nocked to his ivory bow. The guard was a fair-haired youngster with his fur hood flung back from his head and an anxious expression on his face which made Arflane believe that the lad had only recently been appointed to guard the gate.

'You are not of Friesgalt and you are plainly not a trader from the ships,' said the youth. 'What do you want?'

'I carry your Lord Rorsefne on my back,' said Arflane. 'Where shall I take him?'

'The Lord Rorsefne!' The guard stepped forward, lowering his bow and pulling back the headpiece of the sleeping sack so that he could make out the face of Arflane's burden. 'Are there no others? Is he dead?'

'Almost.'

'They left months ago – on a secret expedition. Where did you find him?'

'A day's journey or so east of here.' Arflane loosened the straps and began lowering the old man to the ice. 'I'll leave him with you.'

The young man looked hesitant and then said: 'No – stay until my relief arrives. He is due now. You must tell all you know. They might want to send out a rescue party.'

'I can't help them,' Arflane said impatiently.

'Please stay – just to tell them exactly how you found him. It will be easier for me.'

Arflane shrugged. 'There is nothing to tell.' He bent and began dragging the body inside the gate. 'But I'll wait, if you like, until they give me back my sleeping sack.'

Beyond the gate was a second wall of ice blocks, at chest height. Peering over it, Arflane saw the steep path that led down to the first level of the city. There were other levels at intervals, going down as far as the eye could see. On the far side of the crevasse Arflane made out some of the doorways and windows of the residential levels. Many of them were embellished with ornate carvings and bas-reliefs chiselled from the living rock. More elaborate than any cave dwellings of millennia ago, these troglodytic chambers had from the outside much of the appearance of the first permanent shelters mankind's ancestors had possessed. The reversion to this mode of existence had been made necessary centuries earlier when it had become impossible to build surface houses as the temperature decreased and the level of the ice rose. The first crevasse-dwellers had shown forethought in anticipating the conditions to come and had built their living quarters as far below ground as possible in order to retain as much heat as they could. These same men had built the ice ships, knowing that, with the impossibility of sustaining supplies of fuel, these were the most practical form of transportation.

Arflane could now see the young guard's relief on the nearside ramp leading to the second level to the top. He was dressed in white bearskins and armed with a bow and a quiver of arrows. He toiled up the slope in the spiked boots that it was best to wear when ascending or descending the levels, for there was only a single leather rope to stop a man from falling off the comparatively narrow ramp into the gorge.

When the relief came the young guard explained what had happened. The relief, an old man with an expressionless face, nodded and went to take up his position on the gate.

Arflane squatted and unlaced his skis while the young guard

fetched him a pair of spiked boots. When Arflane had got these on, they lifted the faintly stirring bundle between them and began carefully to descend the ramp.

The light from the surface grew fainter as they descended, passing a number of men and women busy with trade goods being taken to the surface and supplies of food and hides being brought down. Some of the people realised the identity of the Lord Rorsefne. Arflane and the guard refused to answer their incredulous and anxious questions but stumbled on into the ever-increasing darkness.

It took a long time to get the Lord Rorsefne to a level lying mid-way on the face of the crevasse. The level was lighted dimly by bulbs powered by the same source that heated the residential sections of the cavern city. This source lay at the very bottom of the crevasse and was regarded, even by the myth-mocking Friesgaltian aristocracy, with superstition. To the ice-dwellers, cold was the natural condition of everything and heat was an evil necessity for their survival, but it did not make it any the less unnatural. In the Ice Mother's land there was no heat and none was needed to sustain the eternal life of all those who joined Her when they died and became cold. Heat could destroy the ice, and this was sure proof of its evil. Down at the bottom of the crevasse, the heat, it was rumoured, reached an impossible temperature and it was here that those who had offended the Ice Mother went in spirit after they had died.

The Lord Rorsefne's family inhabited a whole level of the city on both sides of the crevasse. A bridge spanned the gorge and the two men had to cross it to reach the main chambers of the Rorsefne household. The bridge, made of hide, swayed and sagged as they crossed. Waiting for them on the other side was a square-faced middle-aged man in the yellow indoor livery of the Rorsefnes.

'What have you got there?' he asked impatiently, thinking that Arflane and the guard were traders trying to sell something.

'Your master,' Arflane said with a slight smile. He had the satisfaction of seeing the servant's face fall as he recognised the half-hidden features of the man in the sleeping sack.

Hurriedly, the servant helped them through a low door which had the Rorsefne arms carved into the rock above it. They went through two more doors before reaching the entrance hall.

The big hall was well lit by light tubes embedded in the wall. It was overheated also, and Arflane began to sweat in mental and physical discomfort. He pushed back his hood and loosened the thongs of his coat. The hall was richly furnished; Arflane had seen nothing like it. Painted hangings of the softest leather covered the rock walls; and even here, in the entrance hall, there were chairs made of wood, some with upholstery of real cloth. Arflane had only seen sailcloth and one wooden artefact in his life. Leather, no matter how finely it could be tanned, was never so delicate as the silk and linen he looked at now. It was hundreds of years old, preserved in the cold of the store chambers, no doubt, and must date back to a time before his ancestors had come to live in the ravines of the south, when there was still vegetation on the land and not just in the warm ponds and the ocean of blasphemous legend. Arflane knew that the world, like the stars and the moon, was comprised almost wholly of ice and that one day at the will of the Ice Mother even the warm ponds and the rock-caverns that sustained animal and human life would be turned into the ice which was the natural state of all matter.

The yellow-clad servant had disappeared but now returned with a man almost as tall as Arflane. He was thin-faced, with pursed lips and pale blue eyes. His skin was white, as if it had never been exposed above ground, and he wore a wine-red jacket and tight black trousers of soft leather. His clothing seemed effete to Arflane.

He stopped near the unconscious body of Rorsefne and looked down at it thoughtfully; and then he raised his head and glanced distastefully at Arflane and the guard.

'Very well,' he said. 'You may go.'

The man could not help his voice – perhaps not his tone either – but both irritated Arflane. He turned to leave. He had expected, without desiring it, at least some formal statement of thanks.

'Not you, stranger,' said the tall man. 'I meant the guard.'

The guard left and Arflane watched the servants carry the old man away. He said: 'I'd like my sleeping sack back later,' then looked into the face of the tall man.

'How is the Lord Rorsefne?' said the other distantly.

'Dying, perhaps. Another would be – but he could live. He'll lose some fingers and toes at the very least.'

Expressionlessly, the other man nodded. 'I am Janek Ulsenn,' he said, 'the Lord Rorsefne's son-in-law. Naturally we are grateful to you. How did you find the lord?'

Arflane explained briefly.

Ulsenn frowned. 'He told you nothing else?'

'It's a marvel he had the strength to tell me as much.' Arflane could have liked the old man, but he knew he could never like Ulsenn.

'Indeed?' Ulsenn thought for a moment. 'Well, I will see you have your reward. A thousand good bearskins should satisfy you, eh?'

It was a fortune.

'I helped the old man because I admired his courage,' Arflane said brusquely. 'I do not want your skins.'

Ulsenn seemed momentarily surprised. 'What *do* you want? I see you're,' he paused, 'from another city. You are not a nobleman. What...?' He was plainly puzzled. 'It is unheard of that a man – without a code – would bother to do what you did. Even one of us would hesitate to save a stranger.' His final sentence held a note of belligerence, as if he resented the idea of a foreigner and commoner making the gesture Arflane had made, as if selfless action were the prerogative of the rich and powerful.

Arflane shrugged. 'I liked the old man's courage.' He made to leave, but as he did so a door opened on his right and a black-haired woman wearing a heavy dress of fawn and blue entered the hall. Her pale face was long and firm-jawed, and she walked with natural grace. Her hair flowed over her shoulders, and she had gold-flecked brown eyes. She glanced at Ulsenn with a slight interrogatory frown.

Arflane inclined his head slightly and reached for the door handle.

The woman's voice was soft, perhaps a trifle hesitant. 'Are you the man who saved my father's life?'

Unwillingly, Arflane turned back and stood facing her with his legs spread apart as if on the deck of a ship. 'I am, madam – if he survives,' he said shortly.

'This is my wife,' said Ulsenn with equally poor grace. 'The Lady Ulrica.'

She smiled pleasantly. 'He wanted me to thank you and wants to express his gratitude himself when he feels stronger. He would like you to stay here until then – as his guest.'

Arflane had not looked directly at her until now and when he raised his head to stare for a moment into her golden eyes she appeared to give a faint start, but at once was composed again.

'Thank you,' he said, looking with some amusement in Ulsenn's direction, 'but your husband might not feel so hospitable.'

Ulsenn's wife gave her husband a glance of vexed surprise. Either she was genuinely upset by Ulsenn's treatment of Arflane, or she was acting for Arflane's benefit. If she were acting, Arflane was still at a loss to understand her motives; for all he knew, she was merely using this opportunity to embarrass her husband in front of a stranger of lower rank than himself.

Ulsenn sighed. 'Nonsense. He must stay if your father desires it. The Lord Rorsefne, after all, is head of the house. I'll have Onvald bring him something.'

'Perhaps our guest would prefer to eat with us,' she said sharply. There was definitely animosity between the two.

'Ah, yes,' muttered Ulsenn bleakly.

Wearying of this, Arflane said with as much politeness as he could muster: 'With your permission I'll eat at a traders' lodging and rest there, too. I have heard you have a good travellers' hostel on the sixteenth level.' The guard had told him that as they had passed the place earlier.

She said quietly, 'Please stay with us. After what –'

Arflane bowed and again looked directly at her, trying to judge her sincerity. This woman was not of the same stuff as her husband, he decided. She resembled her father in features to some extent and he thought he saw the qualities in her that he had admired in the old man; but he would not stay now.

She avoided his glance. 'Very well. What name shall be asked at the travellers' lodging?'

'Captain Konrad Arflane,' he said gruffly, as if reluctantly confiding a secret, 'of Brershill. Ice Mother protect you.'

Then, with a curt nod to them both, he left the hall, passing through the triple doors and slamming the last heavily and fiercely behind him.

Chapter Three
The Ice Spirit

Against his normal instincts, Konrad Arflane decided to wait in Friesgalt until the old man could talk to him. He was not sure why he waited; if asked, he would have said it was because he did not want to lose a good sleeping sack and besides, he had nothing better to do. He would not have admitted that it was Ulrica Ulsenn who kept him in the city.

He spent most of his time wandering around on the surface among the big ships. He deliberately did not call at the Rorsefne household, being too stubborn. He waited for them to contact him.

In spite of his strong dislike of the man, Arflane thought he understood Janek Ulsenn better than other Friesgaltians he had encountered. Ulsenn was not typical of the modern aristocracy of Friesgalt, who belittled the rigid and haughty code of their ancestors. In the other poorer cities the old traditions were still respected, though the merchant princes there had never had the power of families like the Rorsefnes and Ulsenns. Arflane could admire Ulsenn at least for refusing to soften his attitudes. In that respect he and Ulsenn had something in common. Arflane hated the signs of gradual change in his environment that he had half-consciously noted. Thinking was looser; the softening of the harsh but sensible laws of survival in the icelands was even illustrated by his own recent action in helping the old man. Only disaster could come of this trend towards decadence and more like Ulsenn were needed in positions of influence where they could stop the gradual rejection of traditional social behaviour, traditional religion and traditional thinking. There was no other way to ensure their ability to stay alive in an environment where animal life was not meant to exist. Let the rot set in, Arflane thought, and the Ice Mother would lose no time in sweeping away the last surviving members of the race.

It was a sign of the times that Arflane had become something of a hero in the city. A century earlier they would have sneered at his weakness. Now they congratulated him and he in turn despised them, understanding that they patronised him as they might have honoured a brave animal, that they had contempt for his values and, indeed, his very poverty. He wandered alone, his face stern, his manner surly, avoiding everyone and knowing without caring that he was reinforcing their opinion that all not of Friesgalt were uncouth and barbaric.

On the third day of his stay he went to look, with grudging admiration, at the *Ice Spirit*.

As he came up to the ship, ducking under her taut mooring lines, someone shouted down at him.

'Captain Arflane!'

He looked up reluctantly. A fair, bearded face peered over the rail. 'Would you like to come aboard and look around the ship, sir?'

Arflane shook his head; but a leather ladder was already bouncing down the side, its bottom striking the ice near his feet. He frowned, desiring no unnecessary involvement with the Friesgaltians, but deeply curious to set foot on the deck of a vessel that was almost a myth in the icelands.

He made up his mind quickly, grasped the ladder and began to climb towards the ivory-inlaid rail far above.

Swinging his leg over the rail, he was greeted with a smile by the bearded man, dressed in a rich jerkin of white bear cub's fur and tight, grey sealskin trousers, almost a uniform among Friesgaltian ships' officers.

'I thought you might like to inspect the ship, captain, as a fellow sailor.' The man's smile was frank and his tone did not have the hint of condescension Arflane half expected. 'My name's Petchnyoff, second officer of the *Ice Spirit*.' He was a comparatively young man for a second officer. His beard and hair were soft and blond, tending to give him a foolish look, but his voice was strong and steady. 'Can I show you around?'

'Thanks,' said Arflane. 'Shouldn't you ask your captain first?' He, when commanding his own ship, was firm about such courtesies.

Petchnyoff smiled. 'The *Ice Spirit* has no captain, as such. She's captained by the Lord Rorsefne under normal conditions, or by someone he has appointed when he's unable to be aboard. In your case, I'm sure he'd want me to show you over the ship.'

Arflane disapproved of this system, which he had heard about; in his opinion a ship should have a permanent captain, a man who spent most of his life aboard her. It was the only way to get the full feel of a ship and learn what she could do and what she could not.

The ship had three decks, main, middle and poop, each of diminishing area, with the two upper decks aft of them as they stood there. The decks were of pitted fibreglass, like the hull, and spread with ground-up bone to give the feet better purchase. Most of the ship's superstructure was of the same fibreglass, worn, scratched and battered from countless voyages over countless years. Some doors and hatch covers had been replaced by facsimiles fashioned of large pieces of ivory glued together and carved elaborately in contrast to the unadorned fibreglass. The ivory was yellowed and old in many places and looked almost as ancient as the originals. Lines – a mixture of nylon, gut and leather – stretched from the rails into the top trees.

Arflane looked up, getting the best impression of the ship's size he had had yet. The masts were so high they seemed almost to disappear from sight. The ship was well kept, he noted, with every yard and inch of rigging so straight and true that he would not have been surprised to have seen men crawling about in the top trees, measuring the angle of the gaffs. The sails were furled tight, with every fold of identical depth; and Arflane saw that the ivory booms, too, were carved with intricate pictorial designs. This was a show ship and he was filled with resentment that she was so rarely sailed on a working trip.

Petchnyoff stood patiently at his side, looking up also. The light had turned grey and cold, giving an unreal quality to the day.

'It'll snow soon,' said the second officer.

Arflane nodded. He liked nothing better than a snowstorm. 'She's very tidily kept,' he said.

Petchnyoff noted his tone and grinned. 'Too tidy, you think. You could be right. We have to keep the crew occupied. We get precious little chance of sailing her, particularly since the Lord Rorsefne's been away.' He led Arflane towards an ivory door let into the side of the middle deck. 'I'll show you below first.'

The cabin they entered held two bunks and was more luxuriously furnished than any cabin Arflane had seen. There were heavy chests, furs, a table of whalebone and chairs of skins slung on bone frames. A door led off this into a narrow companionway.

'These are the cabins of the captain and any guests he happens to have with him,' Petchnyoff explained, pointing out doors as they passed them. 'The cabin we came through was mine. I share it with the third officer, Kristoff Hinsen. He's on duty, but he wants to meet you.'

Petchnyoff showed Arflane the vast holds of the ship. They seemed to go on for ever. Arflane began to think that he was lost in a maze the size of a city, the ship was so big. The crew's quarters were clean and spacious. They were under-occupied since only a skeleton crew was aboard, primarily to keep the ship looking at her best and ready to sail at the whim of her owner-captain. Most of the ship's ports were of the original thick, unbreakable glass. As he went by one, Arflane noticed that it was darker outside and that snow was falling in great sheets onto the ice, limiting visibility to a few yards.

Arflane could not help being impressed by the capacity of the ship and envied Petchnyoff his command. If Brershill had one vessel like this, he thought, the city would work her to good advantage and soon regain her status. Perhaps he should be thankful that the Friesgaltians did not make better use of her, otherwise they might have captured an even bigger portion of the trade.

They climbed up eventually to the poop deck. It was occupied by an old man who appeared not to notice them. He was staring intently at the dimly seen wheel positioned below on the middle deck. It had been lashed fast so that the runners which it steered would not shift and strain the ship's moorings. Though the old man's eyes were focused on the wheel he seemed to be contemplating some inner thought. He turned as they joined him at the rail. His beard was white and he wore his coarse fur hood up, shadowing his eyes. He had his jerkin tightly laced and there were mittens on his hands. Snow had settled on his shoulders; the snow was still heavy, darkening the air and drifting through the rigging to heap itself on the decks. Arflane heard it pattering on the canvas high above.

'This is our third officer, Kristoff Hinsen,' Petchnyoff said, slapping the old man's arm. 'Meet the Lord Rorsefne's saviour, Kristoff.'

Kristoff regarded Arflane thoughtfully. He had a face like an old snow-kite, with knowing beady black eyes and a hooked nose.

'You're Captain Arflane. You commanded the *North Wind*, eh?'

'I'm surprised you should know about that,' Arflane replied. 'I left her five years ago.'

'Aye. Remember a ship you nosed into an ice break south of here? The *Tanya Ulsenn*?'

Arflane laughed. 'I do. We were racing for a whale herd that had been sighted. The others dropped out until there was only us and the *Tanya*. It was a profitable trip once we'd put the *Tanya* into the ice break. Were you aboard her?'

'I was the captain. I lost my commission through your trick.'

Arflane had acted according to the accepted code of the ice sailors, but he studied Kristoff's face for signs of resentment. There seemed to be none.

'They were better times for me,' said Arflane.

'And for me,' Kristoff said. He chuckled. 'So our victories and defeats come to the same thing in the end. You've no ship to captain now – and I'm third officer aboard a fancy hussy who lies in bed all day.'

'She should sail,' Arflane said, looking around him. 'She's worth ten of any other ship.'

'The day this old whore sails on a working trip – that's the day the world will end!' Kristoff kicked at the deck in disgust. 'I tried your tactic once, you know, Captain Arflane, when I was second officer aboard the *Heurfrast*. The captain was hurt – tangled up in a harpoon line of all things – and I was in command. You know that old hunter, the *Heurfrast*?'

Arflane nodded.

'Well, she's hard to handle until you get the feel of her and then she's easy. It was a year or so later when we were racing two brigs from Abersgalt. One overturned in our path and we had to go round her, which gave the other a good start on us. We managed to get up behind her and then we saw this ice break ahead. I decided to try nosing her in.'

'What happened?' Arflane asked, smiling.

'We *both* went in – I didn't have your sense of timing. For that, they pensioned me off on this petrified cow-whale. I realise now that your trick was harder than I thought.'

'I was lucky,' Arflane said.

'But you'd used that tactic before – and since. You were a good captain. We Friesgaltians don't usually admit there are any better sailors than our own.'

'Thanks,' said Arflane, unable to resist the old man's flattery and beginning to feel more comfortable now that he was in the company of men of his own trade. 'You nearly pulled yourself out of my trap, I remember.'

'Nearly,' Hinsen sighed. 'The sailing isn't what it was, Captain Arflane.'

Arflane grunted agreement.

Petchnyoff smiled and pulled up his hood against the weather. The snow fell so thickly that it was impossible to make out more than the faint outlines of the nearer ships.

Standing there in relaxed silence, Arflane fancied that they could be the only three men in all the world; for everything was still beneath the falling snow that muffled any sound.

'We'll see less of this weather as time goes on,' said Petchnyoff thankfully. 'Snow comes only once in ten or fifteen days now. My father remembers it falling so often it seemed to last the whole summer. And the winds were harsher in the winter too.'

Hinsen dusted snow off his jerkin. 'You're right, lad. The world has changed since I was young – she's warming up. In a few generations we'll be skipping about on the surface naked.' He laughed at his own joke.

Arflane felt uneasy. He did not want to spoil the pleasant mood, but he had to speak. 'Not talk the Ice Mother should hear, friends,' he said awkwardly. 'Besides, what you say is untrue. The climate alters a little one way or another from year to year, but over a lifetime it grows steadily colder. That must be so. The world is dying.'

'So our ancestors thought, and symbolised their ideas in the creed of the Ice Mother,' Petchnyoff said, smiling. 'But what if there were no Ice Mother? Suppose the sun were getting hotter and the world changing back to what it was before the ice came? What if the idea were true that this is only one of several ages when the ice has covered the world? Certain old books say as much, captain.'

'I would call that blasphemous nonsense,' Arflane said sharply. 'You know yourself that those books contain many strange notions which we know to be false. The only book I believe is the Book of the Ice Mother. She came from the centre of the universe, bringing cleansing ice; one day Her purpose will be fulfilled and all will be ice, all will be purified. Read what you will into that, say that the Ice Mother does not exist – that Her story only represents the truth – but you must admit that even some of the old books said the same, that all heat must disappear.'

Hinsen glanced at him sardonically. 'There are signs that the old ideas are false,' he murmured. 'Followers of the Ice Mother say "All must grow cold"; but you know that we have scholars in Friesgalt who make it their business to measure the weather. We got our power through their knowledge. The scholars say the level of the ice has dropped a few degrees in the last two or three years, and one day the sun will burn yellow-hot again and it will melt the ice away. They say that the sun is hotter already and the beasts move south, anticipating the change. They smell a new sort of life, Arflane. Life like the weed-plants we find in the warm ponds, but growing on land out of stuff that is like little bits of crumbled rock – out of earth. They believe that these must already exist somewhere – that they have always existed, perhaps on islands in the sea…'

'There is no *sea*!'

'The scholars think we could not have survived if there were not a sea somewhere, and these plants growing on islands.'

'No!' Arflane turned his back on Hinsen.

'You say not? But reason says it is the truth.'

'Reason?' Arflane sneered. 'Or some twist of mind that passes for reason? There's no true logic in what you say. You only prattle a warped idea you would *rather* believe. Your kind of thinking will bring disaster to us all!'

Hinsen shook his head. 'I see this as a fact, Captain Arflane – the ice is softening as we grow soft. Just as the beasts scent the new life, so do we – that is why our ideas are changing. I *desire* no change. I am only sorry, for I could love no other world than the one I know. I'll die in my own world, but what will our descendants miss? The wind, the snow, and the swift ice – the sight of a herd of whales speeding in flight before your fleet, the harpoon's leap, the fight under a red, round sun hanging frozen in the blue sky; the spout of black whale blood, brave as the men who let it… Where will all that be when the icelands become dirty, unfirm earth and brittle green? What will men become? All we love and admire will be belittled and then forgotten in that clogged, hot, unhealthy place. What a tangled, untidy world it will be. But it *will* be!'

Arflane slapped the rail, scattering the snow. 'You are insane! How can all this change?'

'You could be right,' Hinsen replied softly. 'But what I see, sane or not, is what I see, straight and definite – inevitable.'

'You'd deny every rule of nature?' Arflane asked mockingly. 'Even a fool must admit that nothing becomes hot of its own accord after it has become cold. See what is about you, not what you *think* is here! I understand your reasoning. But it is soft reasoning, wishful reasoning. Death, Kristoff Hinsen, *death* is all that is inevitable! Once there was this dirt, this green, this life – I accept that. But it died. Does a man die, become cold, and then suddenly grow warm again, springing up saying "I died, but now I live!"? Can't you see how your logic deceives you? Whether the Ice Mother is real or only a symbol of what is real, She must be honoured. Lose sight of that, as you in Friesgalt have done, and our people will die sooner than they need. You think me a superstitious barbarian, I know, for holding the views I hold – but there is good sense in what I say.'

'I envy you for being able to stay so certain,' Kristoff Hinsen said calmly.

'And I pity you for your unnecessary sorrow!'

Embarrassed, Petchnyoff took Arflane's arm. 'Can I show you the rest of the ship, captain?'

'Thank you,' said Arflane brusquely, 'but I have seen all I want. She is a good ship. Don't let her rot, also.'

His face troubled, Hinsen started to say something, but Arflane turned away. He left the poop and descended to the lower deck, clambered over the side, climbed down the ladder and marched back towards the underground city, his boots crunching in the snow.

Chapter Four

The Shipsmasher Hostel

After his visit to the ice schooner Konrad Arflane became increasingly impatient with his wait in Friesgalt. He had still had no word from the Ulsenns about the old man's condition and he was disturbed by the atmosphere he found in the city. He had come to no decision regarding his own affairs; but he resolved to try to get a berth, even as a petty officer for the time being, on the next Brershill ship that came in.

He took to haunting the fringes of the great dock, avoiding contact with all the ships and in particular the *Ice Spirit*, and looking out for a Brershill craft.

On the fourth morning of his wait a three-masted barque was sighted. She was gliding in under full sail, flying a Brershill flag and travelling faster than was wise for a vessel so close to the dock. Arflane smiled as she came nearer, recognising her as the *Tender Maiden*, a whaler skippered by his old friend Captain Jarhan Brenn. She seemed to be sailing straight for the part of the dock where ships were thickest, and the men working there began to scatter in panic, doubtless fearing that she was out of control. When she was only a short distance from the dock she turned smoothly and rapidly in a narrow arc, reefed sails and slid towards the far end of the line where other whaling vessels were already moored. Arflane began to run across the ice, his ridged boots giving him good purchase.

Panting, he reached the *Tender Maiden* just as she was throwing down her anchor ropes to the mooring hands who stood by with their spikes and mallets.

Arflane grinned a little as he seized the bone spikes and heavy iron mallet from a surprised mooring hand and began driving a spike into the ice. He reached out for a nearby line and tautened it, lashing it fast to the spike. The ship stirred for a moment, resisting the lines, and then was still.

From above him on the deck he heard someone laughing. Looking up, he saw that the ship's captain, Jarhan Brenn, was standing at the rail.

'Arflane! Are you down to working as a mooring hand? Where's your ship?'

Arflane shrugged and spread his hands ironically, then grabbed hold of the mooring line and began to swing himself up it until he was able to grasp the rail and climb over it to stand beside his old friend.

'No ship,' he told Brenn. 'She was given up to honour a bad debt of the owner's. Sold to a Friesgalt merchant.'

Brenn nodded sympathetically. 'Not the last, I'd guess. You should have stayed at the whaling. There's always work for us whalers, whatever happens. And you didn't even marry the woman in the end.' He chuckled.

Brenn was referring to a time, six years since, when Arflane had taken a trading command as a favour to a girl he had wished to marry. It was only after he had done this that he had realised that he wanted no part of a girl who could demand such terms. By then it had been too late to get back his command of the whaler.

He smiled ruefully at Brenn and shrugged again. 'With my poor luck, Brenn, I doubt I'd have sighted a whale in all these six years.'

His friend was a short, stocky man, with a round, ruddy face and a fringe beard. He was dressed in heavy black fur, but his head and hands were bare. His greying hair was cropped close, for a whaler, but his rough, strong hands showed the calluses that only a harpoon could make. Brenn was respected as a skipper in both the South Ice and North Ice hunting fields. Currently, by the look of his rig, he was hunting the North Ice.

'Poor luck isn't yours alone,' Brenn grunted in disgust. 'Our holds are just about empty. Two calves and an old cow are all we have aboard. We ran out of provisions and plan to trade our cargo for more supplies, then we'll try the South Ice and hope the hunting's better. Whales are getting hard to find in the north.'

Brenn was unusual in that he hunted both south and north. Most whaling men preferred one type of field or the other (for their characteristics were very different) but Brenn did not mind.

'Aren't all the hunting fields poor this season?' Arflane asked. 'I heard that even seal and bear are scarcer, and no walrus have been seen for two seasons.'

Brenn pursed his lips. 'The patch will pass, with the Ice Mother's help.' He slapped Arflane's arm and began to move down the deck to supervise the unloading of the cargo from the central hold. The ship stank of whale blood and blubber. 'Look at our catch,' he said, as Arflane followed him. 'There was no need for flenching. We just hauled 'em in and stowed 'em whole.' Flenching was the whaling man's term for cutting up the whale. This was normally done on the ice, and then the pieces were winched aboard for stowing. If there had been no need to do this, then the catch must be small indeed.

Balancing himself by gripping a ratline, Arflane peered into the hold. It was dark, but he could make out the stiff bodies of two small calves and a cow-whale which did not look much bigger. He shook his head in sympathy. There was hardly enough there to reprovision the ship for the long haul to the South Ice. Brenn must be in a gloomier mood than he seemed.

Brenn shouted orders and his hands began to lower themselves into the hold as derricks were swung across and tackles dropped. The whaling men worked slowly and were plainly depressed. They had every reason to be in poor spirits, since the proceeds of a catch were always divided up at the end of a hunting voyage, and every man's share depended on the number and size of the whales caught. Brenn must have asked his crew to forgo its share in this small catch in the hope that the South Ice would yield a better one. Whaling men normally came into a dock with plenty of credit and they liked to spend it. Whalers with no credit were surly and quick-tempered. Arflane realised that Brenn would be aware of this and must be worrying how he would be able to control his crew during their stay in Friesgalt.

'Where are you berthing?' he asked quietly, watching as the first of the calves was swung up out of the hold. The dead calf had the marks of four or five harpoons in its hide. Its four great flippers, front and back, waved as it turned in the tackle. Like all young land whales, there was only sparse hair on its body. Land whales normally grew their full covering of wiry hair at maturity, after three years. As it was, this calf was twelve feet long and must have weighed only a few tons.

Brenn sighed. 'Well, I've good credit at the Shipsmasher hostel. I always pay in a certain amount of my profit there every time we dock in Friesgalt. My men will be looked after all right, for a few days at least, and by that time we should be ready to sail again. It depends on the sort of bargain I can make with the merchants – and how soon I can make it. I'll be out looking for the best offer tomorrow.'

The Shipsmasher, named, like all whaling men's hostels, after a famous whale, was not the best hostel in Friesgalt. It had claims, in fact, for being the worst. It was a 'top-deck' hostel on the third level from the top, cut from ice and not from rock. Arflane realised that this was a bad time to ask his friend for a berth. Brenn must be cutting all possible corners to provision and re-equip his ship on the gamble that the South Ice would yield a better catch.

The derricks creaked as the calf was swung towards the side.

'We're getting 'em out as soon as possible,' Brenn said. 'There's a chance that someone will want the catch right away. The faster the better.'

Brenn shouted to his first officer, a tall, thin man by the name of Olaf Bergsenn. 'Take over, Olaf, I'm going to the Shipsmasher. Bring the men there when you're finished. You know who to put on watch.'

Bergsenn's lugubrious face did not change expression as he nodded once and moved along the stained deck to supervise the unloading.

A gangplank had been lowered and Arflane and Brenn walked

down it in short, jerky steps, watched by a knot of gloomy harpooners who lounged, harpoons across their shoulders, near the mainmast. It was a tradition that only the captain could leave the ship before the cargo had been unloaded.

When they got to the city wall, the guard recognised Arflane and let him and Brenn through. They began to descend the ramp. The ice of the ramp and the wall beside it was ingrained with powdered rock that had itself worn so it now resembled stone. The rope rail on the other side of the ramp also showed signs of constant wear. On the far wall of the crevasse, for some distance down, Arflane could see people moving up and down the ramps, or working on the ledges. At almost every level the chasm was criss-crossed by rope bridges, and some way up the crevasse, above their heads now, was the single permanent bridge, which was only used when especially needed.

As they stumbled down the ramps towards the third level Brenn smiled once or twice at Arflane, but was silent. Arflane wondered if he were intruding and asked his friend if he would like him to leave him at the Shipsmasher, but Brenn shook his head.

'I wouldn't miss a chance of seeing you, Arflane. Let me talk to Flatch, then we'll have a barrel of beer and I'll tell you all my troubles and listen to yours.'

There were three whaling hostels on the third level. They walked past the first two – the King Herdarda and the Killer Pers – and came to the Shipsmasher. Like the other two, the Shipsmasher had a huge whale jawbone for a doorway and a small whale skull hanging as a sign outside.

They opened the battered door and walked straight into the hostel's main room.

It was dark, large and high-roofed, though it gave the impression of being cramped. Its walls were covered with crudely tanned whale hides. Faulty lighting strips flickered at odd places on ceiling and walls and the place smelled strongly of ale, whale meat and human sweat. Crude pictures of whales, whaling men and whaling ships were hung on the hides, as were harpoons, lances and the three-foot broad-bladed cutlasses, similar to the one Arflane wore, that were used mainly for flenching. Some of the harpoons had been twisted into fantastic shapes, telling of the death struggles of particular whales. None of these whaling tools was crossed, for the whale men regarded it as unlucky to cross harpoons or flenching cutlasses.

Groups of whaling men lounged at the closely packed tables, sitting on hard benches and drinking a beer that was brewed from one of the many kinds of weed found in the warm ponds. This ale was extremely bitter and few but whaling men would drink it.

Arflane and Brenn walked through the clusters of tables up to the small counter. Behind it, in a cubbyhole, sat a shadowy figure who rose as they approached.

Flatch, the owner of the Shipsmasher, had been a whaling man years before. He was taller than Arflane but almost unbelievably obese, with a great belly and enormously fat arm and leg. He had only one eye, one ear, one arm and one leg, as if a huge knife had been used to sheer off everything down one side of him. He had lost these various organs and limbs in an encounter with the whale called Shipsmasher, a huge bull that he had been the first to harpoon. The whale had been killed, but Flatch had been unable to carry on whaling and had bought the hostel out of his share of the proceeds. As a tribute to his kill he had named the hostel after it. As recompense he had used the whale's ivory to replace his arm and leg, and a triangle of its hide was used as a patch for his missing eye.

Flatch's remaining eye peered through the layers of fat surrounding it and he raised his whalebone arm in greeting.

'Captain Arflane. Captain Brenn.' His voice was high and unpleasant, but at the same time barely audible, as if it was forced to travel up through all the fat around his throat. His many chins moved slightly as he spoke, but it was impossible to tell if he greeted them with any particular feeling.

'Good morning, Flatch,' Brenn said cordially. 'You'll remember the beer and provisions I've supplied you with all these past seasons?'

'I do, Captain Brenn.'

'I've need of the credit for a few days. My men must be fed, boozed and whored here until I'm ready to sail for the South Ice. I've had bad luck in the north. I ask you only fair return for what I've invested, no more.'

Flatch parted his fat lips and his jowls moved up and down. 'You'll get it, Captain Brenn. Your help saw me through a bad time for two seasons. Your men will be looked after.'

Brenn grinned, as if in relief. He seemed to have been expecting an argument. 'I'll want a room for myself,' he said. He turned to Arflane. 'Where are you staying, Arflane?'

'I have a room in a hostel some levels down,' Konrad Arflane told him.

'How many in your crew, captain?' Flatch asked.

Brenn told him, and answered the few other questions Flatch asked him. He began to relax more, glancing around the hostel's main room, looking at some of the pictures on the walls.

As he was finishing with Flatch a man got up from a nearby table and took several steps towards them before stopping and confronting them.

He cradled a long, heavy harpoon in one massive arm and the other hand was on his hip. His face, even in the poor, flickering light, could be seen to be red, mottled and ravaged by wind, sun and frostbite. It was a near-fleshless head and the bones jutted like the ribs of a ship. His nose was long and narrow, like the inverted prow of a clipper, and there was a deep scar under his right eye and another on his left cheek. His hair was black, piled and plaited on his head in a kind of coiled pyramid that broke at the top into two stiff pieces resembling the fins of a whale or a seal. This strange hairstyle was held in place by clotted blubber and its smell was strong. His furs were of fine quality, but matted with whale blood and blubber, smelling rancid; the jacket was open to the neck, revealing a whale-tooth necklace. From both earlobes were suspended pieces of flat, carved ivory. He wore boots of soft leather, drawn up to the knee and fastened against his fur breeches by means of bone pins. Around his waist was a broad belt, from which hung a scabbarded cutlass and a large pouch. He seemed a savage, even among whaling men, but he had a powerful presence, partially due to his narrow eyes, which were cold, glinting blue.

'You're sailing to the South Ice, did I hear you say, skipper?' His voice was deep and harsh. 'To the south?'

'Aye.' Brenn looked the man up and down. 'And I'm fully crewed – or as fully crewed as I can afford.'

The huge man nodded and moved his tongue inside his mouth before spitting into a spittoon near the counter.

The spittoon had been made from a whale's cranium. 'I'm not asking for a berth, skipper. I'm my own man. Captains ask me to sail with them, not the other way about. I'm Urquart.'

Arflane had already recognised the man, but Brenn by some fluke could never have seen him. Brenn's expression changed. 'Urquart – Long Lance Urquart. I'm honoured to meet you.' Urquart was known as the greatest harpooner in the history of the icelands. He was rumoured to have killed more than twenty bull-whales single-handed.

Urquart moved his head slightly, as if acknowledging Brenn's compliment. 'Aye.' He spat again and looked broodingly at the cranium spittoon. 'I'm a South Ice man myself. You hunt the North Ice mainly, I hear.'

'Mainly,' Brenn agreed, 'but I know the South Ice well enough.' His tone was puzzled, though he was too polite, or too overawed, to ask Urquart directly why he had addressed him.

Urquart leaned on his harpoon, clutching it with both big, bony hands and sucking in his lips. The harpoon was ten feet long, and its many barbs were six inches or more across, curving down for nearly two feet of its length, with a big metal ring fixed beneath them where tackle was tied.

'There's a great many North Ice men have turned to the South Ice this season as well as last,' said Urquart. 'They've found few fish, Captain Brenn.'

Whaling men – particularly harpooners – invariably called whales 'fish' in a spirit of studied disdain for the huge mammals.

'You mean the hunting's poor there, too.' Brenn's face clouded.

'Not so poor as on the North Ice from what I hear,' Urquart said slowly. 'But I only tell you because you seem about to take a risk. I've seen many skippers – good ones like yourself – do the same. I speak friendly, Captain Brenn. The luck is bad, both north and south. A decent herd's not been sighted all season. The fish are moving south, beyond our range. Our ships follow them further and further. Soon it'll not be possible to provision for long enough voyages.' Urquart paused, and then he added, 'The fish are leaving.'

'Why tell me this?' Brenn said, half angry with Urquart in his disappointment.

'Because you're Konrad Arflane's friend,' Urquart said without looking at Arflane, who had never met him in his life before, had only seen him at a distance.

Arflane was astonished. 'You don't know me, man…'

'I know your actions,' Urquart murmured, then drew in a deep breath as if talking had winded him. He turned slowly on his heel and walked with a long, loping stride towards the door, ducked his head beneath the top of the frame and was gone.

Brenn snorted and shifted his feet. He slapped his leg several times and then frowned at Arflane. 'What was he talking about?'

Arflane leaned back against the counter. 'I don't know, Brenn. But if Urquart warned you that the fishing is poor on the South Ice, you should heed that.'

Brenn laughed briefly and bitterly. 'I can't afford to heed it, Arflane. I'll just pray all night to the Ice Mother and hope She gives me better luck. It's all I can do, man!' His voice had risen almost to a shout.

Flatch had reseated himself in his cubbyhole behind the counter, but he rose, looking like some monstrous beast himself, and glanced enquiringly with his single eye as Brenn faced him again and ordered whale steaks with seka weed and a barrel of beer to be brought to them at their table.

Later, after Brenn's men had come in and been cheered by the discovery that Flatch was willing to provide them with everything they needed, Arflane and Brenn sat opposite each other at a side table with the beer barrel against the wall. Every so often they would turn the spigot and replenish their cups. The cups were unbreakable, fashioned of some ancient plastic substance. The beer did not, as they had hoped, improve their spirits, although Brenn managed to look confident enough whenever any of his men addressed him through the shadowy gloom of the hostel room.

The beer had in fact succeeded in turning Brenn in on himself and he was uncommunicative, constantly twisting his head around to look at the door, which had now been closed. Arflane knew that Brenn was expecting no-one.

At last he leaned over the table and said, 'Urquart seemed a gloomy individual, Brenn – perhaps even mad. He sees the bad luck of everything. I've been here for some days, and I've seen the catches unloaded. They're smaller than usual, certainly, but not that small. We've both had as poor catches and they've done us no harm in the long term. It happened to me for several seasons running and then I had plenty of luck for another three. The owners were worried, but...'

Brenn looked up from his cup. 'There you have it, Arflane. I'm my own master now. The *Tender Maiden*'s mine. I bought her two seasons back.' Again he laughed bitterly. 'I thought I was doing a sensible thing, seeing that so many of us have had our ships sold over our heads in past years. It looks as if I'll be selling my own craft over my own head at this rate, or hiring out to some Friesgaltian merchant. I'll have no choice. And there's my crew – willing to gamble with me. Do I tell them Urquart's news? They've wives and children, as I have. Shall I tell them?'

'It would do no good,' Arflane said quietly.

'And where are the fish going?' Brenn continued. He put his cup down heavily. 'What's happening to the herds?'

'Urquart said they're going south. Perhaps the clever man will be the one who learns how to follow them – how to live off what provisions he can find on the ice. There are more warm ponds to the south – possibly a means of tracking the herds could be devised...'

'Will that help me this season?'

'I don't know,' Arflane admitted. He was thinking now about his conversation aboard the *Ice Spirit* and he began to feel even more depressed.

Flatch's whores came down to the main room of the hostel. Flatch had done nothing by halves. There was a girl for every man, including Arflane and Brenn. Katarina, Flatch's youngest daughter, a girl of eighteen, approached them, holding the hand of another girl who was as dark and pretty as Flatch's daughter was fair and plain. Katarina introduced the other girl as Maji.

Arflane attempted to sound jovial. 'Here,' he said to Brenn, 'here's someone to cheer you up.'

Leaning back, with the drunken, dark-haired girl Maji cuddled against his chest, Brenn roared with laughter at his own joke. The girl giggled. On the other side of the table Arflane smiled and stroked Katarina's hair. She was a warm-hearted girl and able instinctively to make men relax. Maji winked up at Brenn. The women had succeeded, where Arflane had failed, in restoring Brenn's natural optimism.

It was very late. The air was stale and hot and the hostel room was noisy with the drunken voices of the whalers. Through the poor, flickering light Arflane could see their fur-clad silhouettes reeling from table to table or sitting slumped on the benches. Brenn's crew was not the only one in the Shipsmasher. There were men from two other ships there, a Friesgaltian North Ice whaler and another North Icer from Abersgalt. If South Ice men had been there there might have been trouble, but these crews seemed to be mingling well with Brenn's men. Out of the press of bulky bodies rose the long lances of the harpooners, swaying like slender masts in a high wind, their barbed tips casting distorted shadows in the shuddering light from the faulty strips. There were thumps as men fell or knocked over barrels. There was the smell of spilled bitter beer which ran over the tables and swamped the floor. Arflane heard the giggles of the girls and the harsh laughter of the men and, though the temperature was too warm for his own comfort, he felt himself begin to relax now that he was in the company of men whom he understood. Off-ship, crews had more or less equal status with the officers, and this contributed to the free and easy atmosphere in the Shipsmasher.

Arflane poured himself another cup of beer as Brenn began a fresh story.

The outer door opened suddenly and cold air blew in, making Arflane shiver, though he was grateful for it. Silence fell as the men turned. The door slammed shut and a man of medium height, swathed in a heavy sealskin cloak, began to walk between the tables.

He was not a whaling man.

That could be judged from the cut of his cloak, the way he walked, the texture of his skin. His hair was short and dark, cut in a fringe over his eyes and scarcely reaching to the nape of his neck. There was a gold bracelet curving up his right forearm and a silver ring on the second finger of his right hand. He moved casually, but somewhat deliberately, and had a slight, ironic smile on his lips. He was handsome and fairly young. He nodded a greeting to the men, who still stared at him suspiciously.

One heavily built harpooner opened his mouth and laughed at the young man, and others began to laugh too. The young man raised his eyebrows and put his head to one side, looking at them coolly.

'I am seeking Captain Arflane.' His voice was melodious and aristocratic, with a Friesgalt accent. 'I heard he was here.'

'I'm Arflane. What do you want?' Konrad Arflane looked with some hostility at the young man.

'I'm Manfred Rorsefne. May I join you?'

Arflane shrugged and Rorsefne came and sat on the bench next to Katarina Flatch.

'Have a drink,' said Arflane, pushing his full cup towards Rorsefne. He realised, as he made the movement, that he was quite drunk. This realisation caused him to pause and rub his forehead. When he looked up at Manfred Rorsefne, he was glowering.

Rorsefne shook his head. 'No, thank you, captain. I'm not in a drinking mood. I wanted to speak with you alone if that is possible.'

Suddenly petulant, Arflane said, 'It is not. I'm enjoying the company of my friends. What is a Rorsefne doing in a top-deck hostel anyway?'

'Looking for you, obviously.' Manfred Rorsefne sighed theatrically. 'And looking for you at this hour because it is important. However,' he began to rise, 'I will come to your hostel in the morning. I am sorry for intruding, captain.' He glanced at Katarina Flatch a trifle cynically.

As Rorsefne made his way towards the door, one of the men thrust a harpoon shaft in front of his legs and he tripped and stumbled. He tried to recover his balance, but another shaft took him in the back and sent him sprawling. He fell as the whalers laughed raucously.

Arflane watched expressionlessly. Even an aristocrat was not safe in a whaling hostel if he had no connection with whaling. Manfred Rorsefne was simply paying for his folly.

The big harpooner who had first laughed at Rorsefne now stood up and grabbed the young man by the collar of his cloak. The cloak came away and the harpooner staggered back, laughing drunkenly. Another joined him, a stocky, red-headed man, and reached down to grab Rorsefne's jacket. But Rorsefne rolled over to face the man, his smile still ironic, and tried to get to his feet.

Brenn leaned forward to see what was going on. He glanced at Arflane. 'D'you want me to stop them?'

Arflane shook his head. 'It's his own fault. He's a fool for coming here.'

'I've never heard of an intrusion like it,' Brenn agreed, settling back.

Rorsefne was now on his feet, reaching past the red-headed whale man towards the sealskin cloak held by the big harpooner. 'I'll thank you for my cloak,' he said, his tone light, but shaking slightly.

'That's our payment for your entertainment,' grinned the harpooner. 'You can go now.'

Rorsefne's eyes were hooded as he folded his arms across his chest. Arflane admired him for taking a stand.

'It would seem,' said Rorsefne quietly, 'that I have given you more entertainment than you have given me.' His voice was now firm.

Arflane got up on impulse and squeezed past Flatch's daughter to stand to the left of the harpooner. Arflane was so drunk that he had to lean for a moment against the edge of a table.

'Give him the cloak, lad,' he said, his voice slurring. 'And let's get on with our drinking. The boy's not worth our trouble.'

The big harpooner ignored Arflane and continued to grin at the young aristocrat, dangling the rich cloak in one hand, teasing him. Arflane lurched forward and grabbed the cloak out of the man's hand. The harpooner turned, grunting, and hit Arflane across the face. Brenn stood up from his corner, shouting at his man, but the harpooner ignored him and bent to pick up the cloak from where it had fallen. Perhaps encouraged by Arflane's action, Manfred Rorsefne also stooped forward towards the cloak. The red-headed whale man hit him. Rorsefne reeled and then struck back.

Arflane, sobered somewhat by the blow, took hold of the harpooner by the shoulder, swung him round, and punched him in the face. Brenn came scrambling over the table, shouting incoherently and trying to stop the fight before it went too far. He attempted to pull Arflane and the harpooner apart.

The Friesgalt whale men were now yelling angrily, siding, perhaps for the sake of the fight, with Manfred Rorsefne, who was wrestling with the red-headed whaler.

The fight became confused. Screaming girls gathered their skirts about them and made for the back room of the hostel. Harpoons were used like quarterstaves to batter at heads and bodies.

Arflane saw Brenn go down with a blow on the head and tried to reach his friend. Every whale man in the hostel seemed to be against him. He struck out in all directions but was soon overcome by their numbers. Even as he fell to the floor, still fighting, he felt the cold air come through the door again and wondered who had entered.

Then a great roaring voice, like the noise of the north wind at its height, sounded over the din of the fight. Arflane felt the whale man's hands leave him and got up, wiping blood from his eyes. His ears were ringing as the voice he had heard roared again.

'Fish, you cave-bound fools! Fish, I tell you! Fish, you dog-hunters! Fish, you beer-swillers! Fish to take the rust off your lances! A herd of a hundred or more, not fifty miles distant at sou'-sou'-west!'

Blinking through the blood, which came from a shallow cut on his forehead, Arflane saw that the speaker was the man he and Brenn had encountered earlier – Long Lance Urquart.

Urquart had one arm curled around his great harpoon and the other around the shoulders of a half-grown boy who looked both excited and embarrassed. The lad wore a single plait, coated with whale grease, and a white bearskin coat that showed by its richness that he was a whaling hand, probably a cabin boy.

'Tell them, Stefan,' Urquart said, more softly now that he could be heard.

The boy spoke in a stutter, pointing back through the still-open doorway into the light. 'Our ship passed them coming in at dusk. We were loaded up and could not stop, for we had to make Friesgalt by nightfall. But we saw them. Heading from north to south, on a line roughly twenty degrees west. A big herd. My father – our skipper – says there hasn't been a bigger herd in twenty seasons.'

Arflane bent to help Brenn who was staggering to his feet, clutching his head.

'Did you hear that, Brenn?'

'I did.' Brenn smiled in spite of his bruised, swollen lips. 'The Ice Mother's good to us.'

'There's enough out there for every ship in the dock,' Urquart continued, 'and more besides. They're travelling fast, from what the lad's father says, but good sailing should catch 'em.'

Arflane looked around the room, trying to find Manfred Rorsefne. He saw him leaning against a wall, a flenching cutlass, that had obviously been one of the wall's ornaments, clutched in his right hand. He still wore his ironic smile. Arflane looked at him thoughtfully.

Urquart also turned his attention from the men and seemed surprised when he saw Rorsefne there. The expression passed quickly and his gaunt features became frozen again. He took his arm from the boy's shoulders and shifted his harpoon to cradle it in his other arm. He walked towards Manfred Rorsefne and took the cutlass from him.

'Thanks,' said Rorsefne, grinning, 'it was becoming heavy.'

'What were you doing in this place?' Urquart asked brusquely. Arflane was surprised by his familiarity with the youth.

Rorsefne nodded his head in Arflane's direction. 'I came to give a message to Captain Arflane, but he was busy with his friends. Some others decided I should provide entertainment since I was here. Captain Arflane and I seemed agreed that they had had enough…'

Urquart's narrow, blue eyes turned to look carefully at Arflane. 'You helped him, captain?'

Arflane let his face show his disgust. 'He was a fool to come alone to a place like this. If you know him take him home, Urquart.'

The men were beginning to leave the hostel, pulling their hoods about their heads, picking up their harpoons as they hurried back to their ships, knowing that their skippers would want to sail with the first light.

Brenn clapped Arflane on the shoulder. 'I must go. We've enough provisions for a short haul. It was good to see you, Arflane.'

In the company of two of his harpooners, Brenn left the hostel. Save for Urquart, Rorsefne and Arflane, the place was now empty.

Flatch came stumping down between the overturned tables, his gross body swaying from side to side. He was followed by three of his daughters who began to clean up the mess. They appeared to take it for granted. Flatch watched them work and did not approach the three men.

Urquart's strangely arranged hair threw a huge shadow on the far wall, by the door. Arflane had not noticed before how closely it resembled the tail of a land whale.

'So you helped another Rorsefne,' Urquart murmured, 'though once again you had no need to.'

Arflane rubbed his damaged forehead. 'I was drunk. I didn't interfere for his sake.'

'It was a good fight, however,' Manfred Rorsefne said lightly. 'I did not realise I could fight so well.'

'They were playing.' Arflane's tone was weary and contemptuous.

Gravely, Urquart nodded in agreement. He shifted his grip on his harpoon and looked directly at Rorsefne. 'They were playing with you,' he repeated.

'Then it was a good game, cousin,' Rorsefne said, looking up into Urquart's bleak eyes. 'Eh?' The Long Lance's tall, gaunt figure was immobile, the features composed. His eyes looked towards the door. Arflane wondered why Rorsefne called Urquart 'cousin', for it was unlikely that there was a true blood link between the aristocrat and the savage harpooner.

'I will escort you both back to the deeper levels,' said Urquart slowly.

'What's the danger now?' Manfred Rorsefne asked him. 'None. We'll go alone, cousin, and then perhaps I'll be able to deliver my message to Captain Arflane after all.'

Urquart shrugged, turned and left the hostel without a word.

Manfred grinned at Arflane who merely scowled in return. 'A moody man, cousin Long Lance. Now, captain, would you be willing to listen while I tell you what I came to say?'

Arflane spat into the whale cranium nearby. 'It can do no harm,' he said.

As they walked carefully down the sloping ramps to the lower levels, avoiding the drunken whalers who staggered past them on their way up, Manfred Rorsefne said nothing and Arflane was too bored and tired to ask him directly what his message was. The effects of the beer had worn off, and the pains in his bruised body were beginning to make themselves felt. The shadowy figures of the whalers, hurrying back to their ships through the dim light, could be seen in front of them and behind them. Occasionally a man shouted, but for the most part the whalers moved in comparative silence, though the constant shuffle of their ridged boots on the causeways echoed around the crevasse. Here and there a man clung to the swaying guard ropes, having staggered too close to the edge. It was not unusual for drunken sailors to lose their footing and fall to the mysterious bottom of the gorge.

Only when Arflane stopped at the entrance to his hostel and the last of the whalers had gone by did Rorsefne speak.

'My uncle's better. He seems eager to see you.'

'Your uncle?'

'Pyotr Rorsefne. He is better.'

'When does he want to see me?'

'Now, if it is convenient.'

'I'm too tired. Your fight…'

'I apologise, but I had no intention of involving you…'

'You should not have gone to the Shipsmasher. You knew that.'

'True. The mistake was mine, captain. In fact, if cousin Long Lance had not brought his good news, I could have your death on my conscience now…'

'Don't be stupid,' Arflane said disdainfully. 'Why d'you call Urquart your cousin?'

'It embarrasses him. It's a family secret. I'm not supposed to tell anyone that Urquart is my uncle's natural son. Are you coming to our quarters? You could sleep there, if you're so tired, and see my uncle first thing in the morning.'

Arflane shrugged and followed Manfred Rorsefne down the ramp. He was half asleep and half drunk and the memory which kept recurring as he walked was not that of Pyotr Rorsefne, but of his daughter.

Chapter Five
The Rorsefne Household

WAKING IN A bed that was too soft and too hot, Konrad Arflane looked dazedly about the small room. It was lined with rich wall hangings of painted canvas depicting famous Rorsefne ships on their voyages and hunts. Here a four-masted schooner was attacked by gigantic land whales, there a whale was slain by a captain with poised harpoon; elsewhere ships floundered in ice breaks or approached cities across the panorama of the ice; old wars were fought, old victories glorified; valiant Rorsefne men were at all times in the forefront, usually managing to bear the Rorsefne flag. Action and violence were on all sides.

There was a trace of humour in Arflane's expression as he stared round at the paintings. He sat up, pushing the furs away from his naked body. His clothes lay on a bench against the wall nearest the door. He swung his legs to the floor and stood up, walking across the carpet of fur to where a washstand had been prepared for him. As he washed, dousing himself in cold water, he realised that his memory of how he had arrived here was vague. He must have been very drunk to have agreed to Manfred Rorsefne's suggestion that he stay the night. He could not understand how he had come to accept the invitation. As he dressed, pulling on the tight undergarments of soft leather and struggling into his jacket and trousers, he wondered if he would see Ulrica Ulsenn that day.

Someone knocked and then Manfred Rorsefne entered, wearing a fur cloak dyed in red and blue squares. He smiled quizzically at Arflane.

'Well, captain? Are you feeling any ill effects?'

'I was drunk, I suppose,' Arflane said resentfully, as if blaming the young man. 'Do we see old Rorsefne now?'

'Breakfast first, I think.' Manfred led him into a wide passage also covered in dark, painted wall hangings. They passed through a door at the end and entered a large room in the centre of which was a square table made of beautifully carved whale ivory. On the table were several loaves of a kind of bread made from warm-pond weed, dishes of whale, seal and bear meat, a full tureen containing a stew, and a large jug of *hess*, which had a taste similar to tea.

Already seated at the table was Ulrica Ulsenn, wearing a simple dress of black and red leather. She glanced up as Arflane entered, gave him a shy smile and looked down at her plate.

'Good morning,' Arflane said gruffly.

'Good morning.' Her voice was almost inaudible. Manfred Rorsefne pulled back the chair next to hers.

'Would you care to sit here, captain?'

Uneasily, Arflane went to sit down. As he pulled his chair in to the table, his knee brushed hers. They both recoiled at once. On the opposite side of the table Manfred Rorsefne was helping himself to seal meat and bread. He glanced humorously at his cousin and Arflane. Two female servants came into the room. They were dressed in long brown dresses, with Rorsefne insignia on the sleeves.

One of them remained in the background; the other stepped forward and curtseyed. Ulrica Ulsenn smiled at her. 'Some more *hess*, please, Mirayn.'

The girl took the half-empty jug from the table. 'Is everything else in order, my lady?'

'Yes, thank you.' Ulrica glanced at Arflane. 'Is there anything you lack, captain?'

Arflane shook his head.

As the servants were leaving, Janek Ulsenn pushed in past them. He saw Arflane beside his wife and nodded brusquely, then sat down and began to serve himself from the dishes.

There was an unmistakeable atmosphere of tension in the room. Arflane and Ulrica Ulsenn avoided looking at one another. Janek Ulsenn glowered, but did not lift his eyes from his food;

Manfred Rorsefne looked amusedly at all of them, adding, it would seem deliberately, to their discomfort.

'I hear a big herd's been sighted,' Janek Ulsenn said at last, addressing Manfred and ignoring his wife and Arflane.

'I was one of the first to hear the news,' Manfred smiled. 'Wasn't I, Captain Arflane?'

Arflane made a noise through his nose and continued to eat. He was embarrassingly aware of Ulrica Ulsenn's presence so close to him.

'Are we sending a ship?' Manfred asked Janek Ulsenn. 'We ought to. There's plenty of fish for all, by the sound of it. We ought to go ourselves – we could take the two-mast schooner and enjoy the hunt for as long as it lasted.'

Ulrica seemed to welcome the suggestion. 'A splendid idea, Manfred. Father's better, so he won't need me. I'll come too.' Her eyes sparkled. 'I haven't seen a hunt for three seasons!'

Janek Ulsenn rubbed his nose and frowned. 'I've no time to spare for a foolhardy pleasure voyage.'

'We could be back within a day.' Manfred's tone was eager. 'We'll go, Ulrica, if Janek hasn't the spirit for it. Captain Arflane can take command...'

Arflane scowled. 'Lord Ulsenn chose the right word – foolhardy. A yacht – with a woman on board – whale hunting! I'd take no such responsibility. I'd advise you to forget the idea. All it would need would be for one bull to turn and your boat would be smashed in seconds.'

'Don't be dull, captain,' Manfred admonished. 'Ulrica will come anyway. Won't you, Ulrica?'

Ulrica Ulsenn shrugged slightly. 'If Janek has no objection.'

'I have,' Ulsenn muttered.

'You are right to advise her against a trip like that,' Arflane said. He was unwilling to join forces with Ulsenn, but in this case he knew it was his duty. There was a good chance that a yacht would be destroyed in the hunt.

Ulsenn straightened up, his eyes resentful. 'But if you wish to go, Ulrica,' he said firmly, staring hard at Arflane, 'you may do so.'

Arflane shifted his own gaze so that he looked directly into Ulsenn's eyes. 'In which case, I feel that you must have an experienced man in command. I'll skipper the craft.'

'You must come too, cousin Janek,' Manfred put in banteringly. 'You have a duty to our people. They will respect you the more if they see that you are willing to face danger.'

'I do not care what they think,' Ulsenn said, glaring at Manfred Rorsefne. 'I am not afraid of danger. I am busy. Someone has to run your father's affairs while he is ill!'

'One day is all you would lose.' Manfred was plainly taunting the man.

Ulsenn paused, evidently torn between decisions. He got up from the table, his breakfast unfinished.

'I'll consider it,' he said as he left the room.

Ulrica Ulsenn rose.

'You deliberately upset him, Manfred. You have offended him and embarrassed Captain Arflane. You must apologise.'

Manfred made a mock bow to Arflane. 'I am sorry, captain.'

Arflane looked thoughtfully up into Ulrica Ulsenn's beautiful face. She flushed and left the room in the direction her husband had taken.

As the door closed, Manfred burst into laughter. 'Forgive me, captain. Janek is so pompous and Ulrica hates him as much as I do. But Ulrica is so *loyal*!'

'A rare quality,' Arflane said dryly.

'Oh, indeed!' Manfred got up from the table. 'Now. We'll go to see the only one of them who is worth any loyalty.'

Heads of bear, walrus, whale and wolf decorated the skin-covered walls of the large bedroom. At the far end was the high, wide bed and in it, propped against folded furs, lay Pyotr Rorsefne. His bandaged hands lay on the bed covers; apart from some faint scars on his face, these were the only sign that he had been so close to death. His face was red and healthy, his eyes bright, and his movements alert as he turned his head to look towards Arflane and Manfred Rorsefne. His great mane of grey hair was combed and fell to his shoulders. He now had a heavy moustache and beard; both were nearly snow white. His body, what Arflane could see of it, had filled out and it was hard to believe that such a recovery could have been possible. Arflane credited the miracle to the old man's natural vitality and love of life, rather than to any care he had received. Momentarily, he wondered why Rorsefne was still in bed.

'Hello, Arflane. I recognise you, you see!' His voice was rich and vibrant, with all trace of weakness gone. 'I'm well again – or as well as I'll ever be. Forgive this manner of meeting, but those milksops think I won't be able to get my balance. Lost the feet – but the rest I kept.'

Arflane nodded, responding against his will to the old man's friendliness.

Manfred brought up a chair from a corner of the room.

'Sit down,' Pyotr Rorsefne said. 'We'll talk. You can leave us now, Manfred.'

Arflane seated himself beside the bed and Manfred, reluctantly it seemed, left the room.

'You and I thwarted the Ice Mother,' Rorsefne smiled, looking closely at Arflane. 'What do you feel about that, captain?'

'A man has a right to try to preserve his life for as long as possible,' Arflane replied. 'The Ice Mother surely does not resent having to wait a little longer.'

'It used to be thought that no man should interfere in another man's life – or his death. It used to be said that if a man was about to be taken by the Ice Mother then it was no-one's right to thwart her. That was the old philosophy.'

'I know. Perhaps I'm as soft as some of the others I've condemned while I've been here.'

'You've condemned us, have you?'

'I see a turning away from the Ice Mother. I see disaster resulting from that, sir.'

'You hold with the old ideas, not the new ones. You do not believe the ice is melting?'

'I do not, sir.'

A small table stood beside the bed. On it was a large chart box, writing materials, a jug of *hess* and a cup. Pyotr Rorsefne reached towards the cup. Arflane forestalled him, poured some *hess* from the jug, and handed him the drink. Rorsefne grunted his thanks. His expression was thoughtful and calculating as he looked into Arflane's face.

Konrad Arflane stared back, boldly enough. This man was one he believed he could understand. Unlike the rest of his family, he did not make Arflane feel uncomfortable.

'I own many ships,' Rorsefne murmured.

'I know. Many more than actually sail.'

'Something else you disapprove of, captain? The big clippers not at work. Yet you're aware, I'm sure, that if I set them to hunting and trading, we should reduce all the other cities to poverty within a decade.'

'You're generous.' Arflane found it surprising that Rorsefne should boast about his charity; it did not seem to fit with the rest of his character.

'I'm wise.' Rorsefne gesticulated with one bandaged hand. 'Friesgalt needs the competition as much as your city and its like need the trade. Already we're too fat, soft, complacent. You agree, I think.'

Arflane nodded.

'It's the way of things,' Rorsefne sighed. 'Once a city becomes so powerful, it begins to decline. It lacks stimulus. We are reaching the point, here on the plateau of the Eight Cities, where we have nothing left to spur us on. What's more, the game is leaving. I see death for all in not too short a time, Arflane.'

Arflane shrugged. 'It's the Ice Mother's will. It must happen sooner or later. I'm not sure that I follow all your reasoning, but I do know that the softer people become, the less chance they have of survival…'

'If the natural conditions are softer, then the people can afford to become so,' Rorsefne said quietly. 'And our scientists tell us that the level of the ice is dropping, that the weather is improving, season by season.'

'I once saw a great line of ice cliffs on the horizon,' Arflane interrupted. 'I was astonished. There'd never been cliffs there before – particularly ones that stood on their peaks, with their bases in the clouds. I began to doubt all I knew about the world. I went home and told them what I had seen. They laughed at me. They said that what I had seen was an illusion – something to do with light – and that if I went to look the next day the cliffs would be gone. I went the next day. The cliffs were gone. I knew then that I could not always trust my senses, but that I could trust what I knew to be right within me. I know that the ice is not melting. I know that your scientists have been deceived, as I was, by illusions.'

Rorsefne sighed. 'I would like to agree with you, Arflane…'

'But you do not. I have had this argument already.'

'No, I meant it. I want to agree with you. It is simply that I need proof, one way or the other.'

'Proof surrounds you. The natural course is towards utter coldness and death. The sun must die and the wind must blow us into the night.'

'I've read that there were other ages when ice covered the world and then disappeared.' Rorsefne straightened his back and leaned forward. 'What of those?'

'They were only the beginning. Two or three times, the Ice Mother was driven back. But She was stronger, and had patience. You know the answers. They are in the creed.'

'The scientists say that again Her power is waning.'

'That cannot be. Her total domination of all matter is inevitable.'

'You quote the creed. Have you no doubts?'

Arflane got up from his seat. 'None.'

'I envy you.'

'That, too, has already been said to me. There is nothing to envy. Perhaps it is better to believe in an illusion.'

'I cannot believe in it, Arflane.' Rorsefne leaned forward, his bandaged hands reaching for Arflane's arm. 'Wait. I told you I needed proof. I know, I think, where that proof may be found.'

'Where?'

'Where I went with my ship and my crew. Where I returned from. A city – many months' travel from here, to the distant north. New York. Have you heard of it?'

Arflane laughed. 'A myth. I spoke of illusions…'

'I've seen it – from a distance, true, but there was no doubting its existence. My men saw it. We were short of provisions and under attack from barbarians. We were forced to turn before we could get closer. I planned to go back with a fleet. I saw New York, where the Ice Ghosts have their court. The city of the Ice Mother. A city of marvels. I saw its buildings rising tier upon tier into the sky.'

'I know the tale. The city was drowned by water and then frozen, preserved complete beneath the ice. An impossible legend. I may believe in the doctrines of the Ice Mother, my lord, but I am not so superstitious…'

'It is true. I have seen New York. Its towers thrust upwards from a gleaming field of smooth ice. There is no telling how deep they go. Perhaps the Ice Mother's court is there, perhaps that part is a myth… But if the city has been preserved, then its knowledge has been preserved too. One way or the other, Arflane, the proof I spoke of is in New York.'

Arflane was perplexed, wondering if the old man's fever was still with him.

Rorsefne seemed to guess his thoughts. He laughed, tapping the chart box. 'I'm sane, captain. Everything is in here. With a good ship – better than the one I took – New York can be reached and the truth discovered.'

Arflane sat down again. 'How was the first ship wrecked?'

Rorsefne sighed. 'A series of misfortunes – ice breaks, shifting cliffs, land whale attacks, the attacks of the barbarians. Finally, ascending to the plateau up the Great North Course, the ship could stand no more and fell apart, killing most of us. The rest set off to walk to Friesgalt, the boats being crushed, hoping we should meet a ship. We did not. Soon, only I remained alive.'

'So bad luck was the cause of the wreck?'

'Essentially. A better ship would not suffer such luck.'

'You know this city's location?'

'More – I have the whole course plotted.'

'How did you know where to go?'

'It wasn't difficult. I read the old books, compared the locations they gave.'

'And now you want to take a fleet there?'

'No.' Rorsefne sank back on the furs. 'I would be a hindrance on such a voyage. I went secretly the first time, because I wanted no rumours spreading to disturb the people. At a time of stress, such news could destroy the stability of our entire society. I think it best to keep the city a secret until one ship has been to New York and discovered what knowledge the city actually does hold. I intend to send the *Ice Spirit*.'

'She's the best ship in the Eight Cities.'

'They say a ship's as good as her master,' Rorsefne murmured. His strength was beginning to fail him. 'I know of no better master than yourself, Captain Arflane. I trust you – and your reputation is good.'

Arflane did not refuse immediately, as he had expected he would. He had half anticipated the old man's suggestion, but he was not sure that Rorsefne was completely sane. Perhaps he, too, had seen a mirage of some kind, or a line of mountains that had looked like a city from a distance. Yet the idea of New York, the thought of discovering the mythical palace of the Ice Mother and of verifying his own instinctive knowledge of the inevitability of the ice's rule, appealed to him and excited his imagination. He had, after all, nothing to keep him on the plateau; the quest was a noble one, almost a holy one. To go north towards the home of the Ice Mother, to sail, like the mariners of ancient times, on a great voyage of many months, seeking knowledge that might change the world, suited his essentially romantic nature. What was more, he would command the finest ship in the world, sailing across unknown seas of ice, discovering new races of men if Rorsefne's talk of barbarians were true. New York, the fabled city, whose tall towers jutted from a plain of smooth ice… What if after all it did not exist? He would sail on and on, farther and farther north, while everything else travelled south.

Rorsefne's eyes were half closed now. His appearance of health had been deceptive; he had exhausted himself.

Arflane got up for the second time.

'I have agreed – against my better judgement – to captain a yacht in which your family intend to follow a whale hunt today.'

Rorsefne smiled weakly. 'Ulrica's idea?'

'Manfred's. He has somehow committed Lord Janek Ulsenn, your daughter and myself to the scheme. Your daughter supported Manfred. As head of the family you should...'

'It is not your affair, captain. I know you speak from good will, but Manfred and Ulrica know what is right for them. Rorsefne stock breeds best encountering danger – it needs to seek it out.' Rorsefne paused, studying Arflane's face again, frowning a little curiously. 'I should not have thought it like you to offer unasked-for advice, captain...'

'It is not my way, normally.' Arflane himself was now perplexed. 'I don't know why I mentioned this. I apologise.' He was not acting in a normal fashion at all, he realised. What was causing the change?

For a moment he saw the whole Rorsefne family as representing danger for him, but the danger was nebulous. He felt a faint stirring of panic and rubbed his bearded chin rapidly. Looking down into Rorsefne's face, he saw that the man was smiling very slightly. The smile seemed sympathetic.

'Is Janek going, did you say?' Rorsefne asked suddenly, breaking the mood.

'It seems so.'

Rorsefne laughed quietly. 'I wonder how he was convinced. No matter. With luck he'll be the one killed and she'll find herself a man to marry, though they're scarce enough. You'll skipper the yacht?'

'I said I would, though I don't know why. I am doing many things I would not do elsewhere. I am in something of a quandary, Lord Rorsefne.'

'Don't worry,' Rorsefne chuckled. 'You're simply not adjusted to our way of doing things.'

'Your nephew puzzles me. Somehow he managed to talk me into agreeing with him, when everything I feel disagrees with him. He is a subtle young man.'

'He has his own kind of strength,' Rorsefne said affectionately. 'Do not underestimate Manfred, captain. He appears weak, both in character and in physique, but he likes to give that appearance.'

'You make him seem very mysterious,' Arflane said half jokingly.

'He is more complicated than us, I think,' Rorsefne replied. 'He represents something new – possibly just a new generation. You dislike him, I can see. You may come to like him as much as you like my daughter.'

'Now you are being mysterious, sir. I expressed no liking for anyone in particular.'

Rorsefne ignored this remark. 'See me after the hunt,' he said in his failing voice. 'I'll show you the charts. You can tell me then if you accept the commission.'

'Very well. Goodbye, sir.'

Leaving the room, Arflane realised that he had been drawn irrevocably into the affairs of the Rorsefne household and that, ever since he had saved the man's life, his fate had been linked with theirs. They had somehow seduced him, made him their man. He knew that he would take the command offered by Pyotr Rorsefne just as he had taken the command of the yacht offered by Manfred Rorsefne. Without appearing to have lost any of his integrity, he was no longer his own master. Pyotr Rorsefne's strength of character, Ulrica Ulsenn's beauty and grace, Manfred Rorsefne's subtlety, even Janek Ulsenn's belligerence, had combined to trap him. Disturbed, Arflane walked back towards the breakfast room.

Chapter Six
The Whale Hunt

DIVIDED FROM THE main fleet by a low wall of ice blocks, the yacht, slim-prowed and handsome, lay in her anchor lines in the private Rorsefne yard.

Tramping across the ice in the cold morning, with the sky a smoky yellow, broken by streaks of orange and a dark pink that the ice reflected, Arflane followed Manfred Rorsefne as he made his way towards the yacht through the still-soft layers of snow. Behind Arflane came Janek and Ulrica Ulsenn, sitting on a small, ornate sleigh drawn by servants. Man and wife sat side by side, swathed in rich furs, their hands buried in huge muffs, their faces almost wholly hidden by their hoods.

The yacht had already been crewed, and the men were preparing to sail. A bulky, spring-operated harpoon gun, rather like a giant crossbow, had been loaded and set up in the bow. The big harpoon with its half-score of tapering barbs jutted out over the bowsprit, a savage phallus.

Arflane smiled as he looked at the heavy harpoon. It seemed too big for the slender yacht that carried it. It dominated the boat – a fore-and-aft-rigged schooner – it drew all attention to itself. It was a fine, cruel harpoon.

He followed Manfred up the gangplank and was surprised to see Urquart standing there, watching them from sharp, sardonic eyes, his own harpoon cradled as always in his left arm, his gaunt features and tall body immobile until he turned his back on them suddenly and walked aft up the deck towards the wheelhouse.

Janek Ulsenn, his lips pursed and his expression one of thinly disguised anxiety, was helping his wife on board. Arflane thought that perhaps she should be helping her husband.

A ship's officer in white and grey fur came along the deck

towards the new arrivals. He spoke to Manfred Rorsefne, though protocol demanded that he address the senior member of the family, Janek Ulsenn.

'We're ready to sail, sir. Will you be taking command?'

Manfred shook his head slowly and smiled, stepping aside so that he no longer stood between Arflane and the officer.

'This is Captain Arflane. He will be master on this trip. He has all powers of captain.'

The officer, a stocky man in his thirties with a black, rimed beard, nodded to Arflane in recognition. 'I know of you, sir. Proud to sail with you. Can I show you the ship before we loose lines?'

'Thanks.' Arflane left the rest of the party and accompanied the officer towards the wheelhouse. 'What's your name?'

'Haeber, sir. First officer. We have a second officer, a bosun and the usual small complement. Not a bad crew, sir.'

'Used to whale hunting?'

A shadow passed across Haeber's face. He said quietly: 'No, sir.'

'Any of the men whaling hands?'

'Very few, sir. We have Mr Urquart aboard, as you know, but he's a harpooner of course.'

'Then your men will have to learn quickly, won't they?'

'I suppose so, sir.' Haeber's tone was carefully noncommittal. For a moment it was in Arflane's mind to echo Haeber's doubt; then he spoke briskly.

'If your crew's as good as you say, Mr Haeber, then we'll have no trouble on the hunt. I know whales. Make sure you listen carefully to every order I give and there'll be no great problems.'

'Aye, aye, sir.' Haeber's voice became more confident.

The yacht was small and neat. She was a fine craft of her class, but Arflane could see at once that his suspicions as to her usefulness as a whaler were justified. She would be fast – faster than the ordinary whaling vessels – but she had no strength to her. She was a brittle boat. Her runners and struts were too thin for heavy work and her hull was liable to crack on collision with an outcrop of ice, another ship, or a fully grown whale.

Arflane decided he would take the wheel himself. This would give the crew confidence, for his helmsmanship was well known and highly regarded. But first he would let one of the officers take the ship onto the open ice while he got the feel of her. Her sails were ready for letting out and men stood by the anchor capstans along both sides of the deck.

After testing the wheel, Arflane took the megaphone Haeber handed him and climbed the companionway to the bridge above the wheelhouse.

Ahead he could see the distant outlines of ships sailing under full canvas towards the South Ice. The professional whalers were well ahead and Arflane was satisfied that at least the yacht would not get in their way before the main hunting began and the whale herd scattered. It was always at this time that the greatest confusion arose, with danger of collision as the ships set off after their individual prey. The yacht should come in after the whalers had divided and be able to select a small whale to chase – preferably some half-grown calf. Arflane sighed, annoyed at having to hunt such unmanly prey just for the sport of the aristocrats who were now traipsing along the deck towards the bridge. They were evidently planning to join him and, since the craft was theirs, they had a right to be on the bridge so long as they did not interfere with the captain's efficient command of the ship.

Arflane lifted the megaphone.

'All hands to their posts!'

The few crewmen who were not at their posts hastened to them. The others tensed, ready to obey Arflane's orders.

'Cast off anchors!'

As one, the anchor men let go the anchor lines and the ship began to slide towards the gap in the ice wall. Her runners scraped and bumped rhythmically as she gained speed down the slight incline and passed between the blocks, making for the open ice.

'Ready the mains'l!'

The men in the yards of the mainmast placed their hands on their halyards.

'Let go the mains'l!'

The sail cracked open, its boom swinging as it filled out. The boat's speed doubled almost at once. At regular intervals Arflane ordered more sail on and soon the yacht was gliding over the ice under full canvas. Air slapped Arflane's face, making it tingle with cold. He breathed in deeply, savouring the sharp chill of it in his nostrils and lungs, clearing the stale city air from his system. He gripped the bridge rail as the boat rode the faint undulations of the ice, carving her way through the thin layer of snow, crossing the black scars left by the runners of the ships who had gone ahead of her.

The sun was almost at zenith, a dull, deep red in the torn sky. Clouds swept before them, their colours changing gradually from pale yellow to white against the clear blue; the colour of the ice changed to match the clouds, now pure white and sparkling. The other ships were hull-down below the distant horizon. Save for the slight sounds that the ship made, the creak of yards and the bump of the runners, there was silence.

Tossed by the tearing skids, a fine spray of snow rose on both sides of the boat as she plunged towards the South Ice.

Arflane was conscious of the three members of the Friesgalt ruling family standing behind him. He did not turn. Instead he looked curiously at the figure who could be seen leaning in the bow by the harpoon gun, his gloved fingers gripping a line, his bizarre, strangely dressed hair streaming behind him, his lance cradled in the crook of his arm. Urquart, either from pride or from a wish for privacy, had spoken to no-one since he had come aboard. Indeed, he had boarded the craft of his own accord and his right to be there had not been questioned.

'Will we catch the whalers, captain?' Manfred Rorsefne spoke as quietly as ever; there was no need to raise his voice in the near-tangible silence of the icelands.

Arflane shook his head. 'No.'

He knew in fact there was every chance of catching the professional whalers; but he had no intention of doing so and fouling their hunting. As soon as they were well under way, he planned to take in sail on some pretext and cut his speed.

*

An hour later the excuse occurred to him. They were leaving the clean ice and entering a region sparsely occupied by ridges of ice standing alone and fashioned into strange shapes by the action of the wind. He deliberately allowed the boat to pass close by one of these, to emphasise the danger of hitting it.

When they were past the spur, he half-turned to Rorsefne, who was standing behind him. 'I'm cutting speed until we're through the ridges. If I don't, there's every chance of our hitting one and breaking up – then we'll never see the whale herd.'

Rorsefne gave him a cynical smile, doubtless guessing the real reason for the decision, but made no comment.

Sail was taken in, under Arflane's instructions, and the boat's speed decreased by almost half. The atmosphere on board became less tense. Urquart, still in his self-appointed place in the bow, turned to glance up at the bridge. Then as if he had satisfied himself on some point, he shrugged slightly and turned back to look out towards the horizon.

The Ulsenns were sitting on a bench under the awning behind Arflane. Manfred Rorsefne leaned on the rail, staring up at the streamers of clouds above them.

The ridges they were now passing were carved into impossible shapes by the elements.

Some were like half-finished bridges, curving over the ice and ending suddenly in jagged outline. Others were squat, a mixture of rounded surfaces and sharp angles; and still others were tall and slender, like gigantic harpoons stuck butt-foremost into the ice. Most of them were in clumps set far enough apart to afford easy passage for the yacht as she glided on her course, but every so often Haeber, at the wheel, would steer a turn or two to one side or another to avoid a ridge.

The ice under the runners was rougher than it had been, for this ground was not travelled as much as the smoother terrain surrounding the cities. The boat's motion was still easy, but the undulation was more marked than before.

In spite of the lack of canvas, the yacht continued to make good speed, sails swelling with the steady following wind.

Knowing there was as yet little for him to do, Arflane agreed to Rorsefne's suggestion that they go below and eat. He left Haeber in charge of the bridge and the bosun at the wheel.

The cabins below were surprisingly large, since no space was used for carrying cargo of any kind other than ordinary supplies. The main cabin was as luxuriously furnished, by Arflane's standards, as the *Ice Spirit*'s had been, with chairs of canvas stretched on bone frames, an ivory table and ivory shelves and lockers lining the bulkhead. The floor was carpeted in the tawny summer coat of the wolf (a beast becoming increasingly rare) and the ports were large, letting in a great deal more light than was usual in a boat of her size.

The four of them sat around the carved ivory table while the cook served their midday meal of broth made from the meat of the snow-kite, seal steaks and a mess of the lichen that grew on the surface of the ice in certain parts of the plateau. There was hardly any conversation during the meal, which suited Arflane. He sat at one end of the table, while Ulrica Ulsenn sat at the other. Janek Ulsenn and Manfred Rorsefne sat on his right and left. Occasionally Arflane would look up from his food at the same time as Ulrica Ulsenn and their eyes would meet. For him, it was another uncomfortable meal.

By the early afternoon the boat was nearing the region where the whales had been sighted. Arflane, glad to be away from the company of the Ulsenns and Manfred Rorsefne, took over the wheel from the bosun.

The masts of some of the whalers were now visible in the distance. The whaling fleet had not, it appeared, divided yet. All the ships seemed to be following much the same course, which meant that the whales were still out of sight.

As they drew nearer, Arflane saw the masts of the ships begin to separate; it could only mean that the herd had been sighted. The whalers were spreading out, each ship chasing its individual quarry.

Arflane blew into the bridge speaking tube. Manfred Rorsefne answered.

'The herd's been spotted,' Arflane told him. 'It's splitting up. The big ones will be what the whalers are after. I suppose we'll find a little whale for ourselves.'

'How long to go, captain?' Rorsefne's voice now held a trace of excitement.

'About an hour,' Arflane answered tersely, and replaced the stopper of the speaking tube.

On the horizon to starboard was a great cliff of ice rising hundreds of feet into the deep purple of the sky. To port were small sharp ridges of ice running parallel to the cliffs. The yacht was sailing between them now towards the slaughtering grounds where ships could be discerned already engaged in hunting down and killing the great beasts.

Standing on the bridge, Arflane prepared to go down and take the wheel again as he saw the prey that the yacht would hunt: a few bewildered calves about half a mile ahead of them, almost directly in line with the boat's present course. Rorsefne and the Ulsenns came up to the rail, craning their necks as they stared at the quarry.

They were soon passing close enough to be able to see individual ships at work.

With both hands firmly on the wheel and Haeber beside him with his megaphone ready to relay orders, Arflane guided the boat surely on her course, often steering in a wide arc to avoid the working ships.

Dark red whale blood ran over the churned whiteness of the ice; small boats, with harpooners ready in their bows, sped after the huge mammals or elsewhere were hauled at breakneck pace in the wake of skewered leviathans, towed by taut harpoon lines wound around the small capstans in the bows. One boat passed quite close, seeming hardly to touch the ground as it bounced over the ice, drawn by a pain-enraged cow who was four times the length and twice the height of the boat itself. She was opening and shutting her massive, tooth-filled jaws as she moved, using front and back flippers to push herself at almost unbelievable speed away from the source of her agony. The boat's runners, sprung on a matrix of bone, came close to breaking as she was hurled into the air and crashed down again. Her crew were sweating and clinging grimly to her sides to avoid being flung out; those who could doused the running lines with water to stop them burning. The cow's hide, scarred, ripped and bleeding from the wounds of a dozen harpoons, was a brown-grey colour and covered in wiry hair. Like most of her kind, it did not occur to her to turn on the boat which she could have snapped in two in an instant with her fifteen-foot jaws.

She was soon past, and beginning to falter as Arflane watched.

In another place a bull had been turned over onto his back and was waving his massive flippers feebly in his death throes. Around him, several boatloads of hunters had disembarked onto the ice and were warily approaching with lances and flenching cutlasses at the ready. The men were dwarfed by the monster who lay dying on his back, his mouth opening and shutting, gasping for breath.

Beyond, Arflane saw a cow writhing and shuddering as her blood spouted from a score of wounds.

The yacht was almost on the calves now.

Arflane's eyes were attracted by a movement to starboard. A huge bull-whale was rushing across the ice directly in the path of the yacht, towing a longboat behind him. A collision was imminent.

Desperately, he swung his wheel hard over. The yacht's runners squealed as she began to turn, narrowly missing the snorting whale, but still in danger of fouling the boat's lines and wrecking them both. Arflane leaned with all his strength on the wheel and barely succeeded in steering the yacht onto a parallel course. Now he could see the occupants of the boat. Standing by the prow, a harpoon ready in one hand, the other gripping the side, was Captain Brenn. His face was twisted in hatred for the beast as it dragged his longboat after it. The whale, startled by the sudden appearance of the yacht, now turned round until its tiny eyes glimpsed Brenn's boat. Instantly it rushed down on Brenn and his crew. Arflane heard the captain scream as the huge jaws opened to their full extent and crunched over the longboat.

A great cry went up from the whalers as the bull shook the broken boat. Arflane saw his friend flung to the ice and attempt to crawl away, but now the whale saw him and its jaws opened again, closing on Brenn's body.

For a moment the whaling captain's legs kicked, then they too disappeared. Arflane had automatically turned the wheel again, to go to the rescue of his friend, but it was too late.

As they bore down on the towering bulk of the bull, he saw that Urquart was no longer at the bow. Manfred Rorsefne stood in his place, swinging the great harpoon gun into line.

Arflane grabbed his megaphone and yelled through it.

'Rorsefne! Fool! Don't shoot it!'

The other evidently heard him, waved a one-handed acknowledgement, then bent back over the gun.

Arflane tried to turn the boat's runners in time, but it was too late. There was a thudding concussion that ran all along the boat as the massive harpoon left the gun and, its line racing behind it, buried itself deep in the whale's side.

The monster rose on its hind flippers, its front limbs waving. A high screaming sound came from its open jaws and its shadow completely covered the yacht. The boat lurched forward, dragged by the harpoon line, its forward runners rising off the ice. Then the line came free. Rorsefne had not secured it properly. The boat thudded down.

The bull lowered his bulk to the ice and began to move rapidly towards the yacht, its jaws snapping. Arflane managed to turn again; the jaws missed the prow, but the gigantic body smashed against the starboard side. The yacht rocked, nearly toppled, then righted herself.

Manfred Rorsefne was fumbling with the gun, trying to load another harpoon. Then the starboard runners, strained beyond endurance by the jolt they had taken, cracked and broke. The yacht collapsed onto her starboard side, the deck sloping at a steep

angle. Arflane was sent flying against the bulkhead as the yacht skidded sideways across the ice, colliding with the rear quarters of the whale as it turned to attack.

Arflane reached out and grabbed the rail of the companionway. He began with great difficulty to crawl up to the bridge. His only thoughts now were for the safety of Ulrica Ulsenn.

As he clambered up, he stared into the terrified face of Janek Ulsenn. He swung aside to let the man push past him. When he reached the bridge, he saw Ulrica lying crumpled against the rail.v

Arflane slithered across the sloping deck, and crouched to turn her over. She was not dead, but there was a livid bruise on her forehead.

Arflane paused, staring at the beautiful face; then he swung her across his shoulder and began to fight his way back to the companionway as the whale bellowed and returned to the attack.

When he reached the deck the crewmen were clambering desperately over the port rail, dropping to the ice and running for their lives. Manfred Rorsefne, Urquart and Haeber were nowhere to be seen; but Arflane made out the figure of Janek Ulsenn being helped away from the wrecked boat by two of the crew.

Climbing across the sloping deck by means of the tangle of rigging, Arflane had almost reached the rail when the whale crashed down on the boat's bow. He fell backwards against the wheelhouse, seeing the vast bulk of the creature's head a few feet away from him.

He lost his hold on Ulrica and she rolled away from him towards the stern. He crawled after her, grabbing at the trailing fabric of her long skirt. Again the boat listed, this time towards the bow; he barely managed to stop himself from being catapulted into the gaping jaws by clinging to the mainmast shrouds. Supporting the woman with one arm, he glanced around for a means of escape.

As the whale's head turned, the cold, pain-glazed eyes of the monster regarding him, he grabbed the starboard rail and flung himself and the girl towards and over it, careless of any consideration other than escaping the beast for a few moments.

They fell heavily to the snow. He dragged himself upright,

once again got Ulrica Ulsenn over his shoulder and began to stumble away, his boots sliding on the ice beneath the thin covering of snow. Ahead of him lay a harpoon that must have been shaken from the ship. He paused to pick it up, then staggered on. Behind him the whale snorted; he heard the thump of its flippers, felt them shaking the ground as the beast lumbered in pursuit.

He turned, saw the creature bearing down on him, threw Ulrica's body as far away from him as possible and poised the harpoon. His only chance was to strike one of the eyes and pierce the brain, killing the beast before it killed him; then he might save Ulrica.

He flung the harpoon at the whale's glaring right eye. The barbs struck true, pierced, but did not reach the brain. The whale stopped in its tracks, turning as it attempted to shake the lance from its blinded eye.

The left eye saw Arflane.

The creature paused, snorting and squealing in a curiously high-pitched tone.

Then, before it could come at him again, Arflane glimpsed a movement to his right. The whale also saw the movement and it lifted its head, opening its jaws.

Urquart, with his huge harpoon held in one hand, came running at the beast, hurled himself without stopping at its body, his fingers grasping its hair.

The whale reared again, but could not dislodge the harpooner. Urquart began relentlessly to climb up onto its back. The whale, instinctively aware that once it rolled over and exposed its belly it would be lost, bucked and threshed, but could not rid itself of the small creature that had now reached its back and, on hands and knees, was moving up to its head.

The whale saw Arflane again and snorted.

Cautiously, it pushed itself forward on its flippers, forgetting its burden. Arflane was transfixed, watching in fascination as Urquart slowly rose to a standing position, planting his feet firmly on the whale's back and raising his harpoon in both hands.

The whale quivered, as if anticipating its death. Then Urquart's

muscles strained as, with all his strength, he drove the mighty harpoon deep into the creature's vertebrae, dragged it clear and plunged it in again.

A great column of blood gouted from the whale's back obscuring all sight of Urquart and spattering down on Arflane. He turned towards Ulrica Ulsenn as she stirred and moaned.

The hot black blood rained down on her too, drenching them both.

She stood up dazedly and opened her arms, her golden eyes looking into Arflane's.

He stepped forward and embraced her, holding her tightly against his blood-slippery body while behind them the monster screamed, shuddered and died. For minutes its pungent, salty blood gushed out in huge spurts, drenching them, but they were hardly aware of it.

Arflane held the woman to him. Her hands clutched at his back as she shivered and whimpered. She had begun to weep.

He stood there holding her for several minutes at the very

least, his own eyes tightly shut, before he became aware of the presence of others.

He opened his eyes and looked about him.

Urquart lounged nearby, his body relaxed, his eyes hooded, his face as sternly set as ever. Near him was Manfred Rorsefne. The young man's left arm hung limply at his side and his face was white with pain, but when he spoke it was in the same light, insouciant tone he always used.

'Forgive me this interruption, captain. But I think we are about to see the noble Lord Janek…'

Reluctantly Arflane released Ulrica; she wiped blood from her face and looked about her vaguely. For a second she held his arm, then released it as she recognised her cousin.

Arflane turned and saw the dead bulk of the monster towering over them only a few feet away. Rounding it, aided by two of his men, came Janek Ulsenn. He had broken at least one leg, probably both.

'Haeber is dead,' Manfred said. 'And half the crew.'

'We all deserve to be dead,' grunted Arflane. 'I knew that boat was too brittle – and you were a fool to use the harpoon. It might have avoided us if you hadn't provoked it.'

'And then we should have missed the excitement!' Rorsefne exclaimed. 'Don't be ungrateful, captain.'

Janek Ulsenn looked at his wife and saw something in her expression which made him frown. He glanced at Arflane questioningly. Manfred Rorsefne stepped forward and gave Ulsenn a mock salute.

'Your wife is still in one piece, Janek, if that's what concerns you. Doubtless you're curious as to her fate after you left her on the bridge…'

Arflane looked at Rorsefne. 'How did you know he did that?'

Manfred smiled. 'I, captain, climbed the rigging. I had a splendid view. I saw everything. No-one saw me.' He turned his attention back to Janek Ulsenn. 'Ulrica's life was saved by Captain Arflane and later, when he killed the whale, by cousin Urquart. Will you thank them, my lord?'

Janek Ulsenn said: 'I have broken both my legs.'

Ulrica Ulsenn spoke for the first time. Her voice was as vibrant as ever, though a little distant, as if she had not entirely recovered from her shock.

'Thank you, Captain Arflane. I am very grateful. You seem to make it your business saving Rorsefnes.' She smiled weakly and looked round at Urquart. 'Thank you, Long Lance. You are a brave man. You are both brave.'

The glance she then turned on her husband was one of pure contempt. His own expression, already drawn by the pain from his broken legs, became increasingly tense. He spoke sharply. 'There is a ship which will take us back.' He motioned with his head. 'It is over there. We will go to it, Ulrica.'

When Ulrica obediently followed her departing husband as he was helped away by his men, Arflane made to step forward; but Manfred Rorsefne's hand gripped his shoulder.

'She is his wife,' Manfred said softly and quite seriously.

Arflane tried to shake off the young man's grip. In a lighter tone Manfred added: 'Surely you, of all people, respect our old laws and customs most, Captain Arflane?'

Arflane spat on the ice.

Chapter Seven

The Funeral on the Ice

LORD PYOTR RORSEFNE had died in their absence; two days later his funeral took place.

Also to be buried that day were Brenn of the *Tender Maiden* and Haeber, first officer of the ice yacht. There were three separate funerals being held beyond the city, but only Rorsefne's was splendid.

Looking across the white ice, with its surface snow whipped into eddying movement by the frigid wind, Arflane could see all three burial parties. He reflected that it was the Rorsefnes who had killed his old friend Brenn, and Haeber too; their jaunt to the whaling grounds had caused both deaths. But he could not feel much bitterness.

On his distant left and right were black sledges bearing the plain coffins of Brenn and Haeber, while ahead of him moved the funeral procession of Pyotr Rorsefne, of which he was part, coming behind the relatives and before the servants and other mourners. His face was solemn but Arflane felt very little emotion at all, although initially he had been shocked to learn of Rorsefne's death.

Wearing the black sealskin mourning cloak stitched with the red insignia of the Rorsefne clan, Arflane sat in a sleigh drawn by wolves with black-dyed coats. He held the reins himself. Also in heavy black cloaks, Manfred Rorsefne and the dead man's daughter, Ulrica, sat together on another sleigh drawn by black wolves, and behind them were miscellaneous members of the Rorsefne and Ulsenn families. Janek Ulsenn was too ill to attend. At the head of the procession, moving slowly, was the black funeral sleigh, with its high prow and stern, bearing the ornate ivory coffin in which lay the dead Lord Rorsefne.

Ponderously, the dark procession crossed the ice. Above it, heavy white clouds gathered and the sun was obscured. Light snow was falling.

At length the burial pit came into sight. It had been carved from the ice and gleaming blocks of ice stood piled to one side. Near this pile stood a large loading boom which had been used to haul up the blocks. The boom with its struts and hanging tackle resembled a gallows, silhouetted against the cold sky.

The air was very quiet, save for the slow scrape of the runners and the faint moan of the wind.

A motionless figure stood near the piled ice blocks. It was Urquart, face frozen as usual, bearing his long lance as usual, come to witness his father's burial. Snow had settled on his piled hair and his shoulders, increasing his resemblance to a member of the Ice Mother's hierarchy.

They came nearer and Arflane was able to hear the creak of the loading beam as it swung in the wind; he saw that Urquart's face was not quite without expression. There was a peculiar look of disappointment there, as well as a trace of anger.

The procession gradually came to a halt near the black hole in the ice. Snow pattered on the coffin and the wind caught their cloaks and ripped the hood from Ulrica Ulsenn's head. Arflane glimpsed her tear-streaked face as she pulled the fabric back into place. Manfred Rorsefne, his broken arm in a sling beneath his cloak, turned to nod at Arflane. They got down from their sleighs and, with four of the male relatives, approached the coffin.

Manfred, helped by a boy of about fifteen, cut loose the black wolves and handed their harness to two servants who stood ready. Then, three men on either side, they pushed the heavy sleigh to the pit.

It balanced on the edge for a moment, as if in reluctance, then slid over and fell into the darkness. They heard it crash at the bottom; then they walked to the pile of ice blocks to throw them into the pit and seal it. But Urquart had already taken the first block in both hands, his harpoon for once lying on the ice where he had placed it. He lifted the block high and flung it down with great force, his lips drawn back from his teeth, his eyes full of fire. He paused, looking into the pit, wiping his hands on his greasy coat, then, picking up his harpoon, he walked away as Arflane and the others began to push the rest of the blocks towards the edge.

It took an hour to fill the pit and erect the flag bearing the Rorsefne arms. The flag fluttered in the wind. Gathered around it now were the mourners, their heads bowed as Manfred Rorsefne used his good hand to climb clumsily to the top of the heaped ice to begin the funeral oration.

'The Ice Mother's son returns to her cold womb,' he began in the traditional way. 'As She gave him life, She takes it; but he will exist now for eternity in the halls of ice where the Mother holds court. Imperishable, She rules the world. Imperishable are those who join Her now. Imperishable, She will make the world one thing, without age or movement; without desire or frustration; without anger or joy; perfect and whole and silent. Let us join Her soon.'

He had spoken well and clearly, with some emotion.

Arflane dropped to one knee and repeated the final sentence. 'Let us join Her soon.'

Behind him, responding with less fervour, the others followed his example, muttering the words where he had spoken them boldly.

Chapter Eight
Rorsefne's Will

Arflane, possibly more than anyone, sensed the guilt Ulrica Ulsenn felt over her father's death. Very little guilt, or indeed grief now, showed on her features, but her manner was at once remote and tense. It was at her instigation, as well as Manfred's, that the disastrous expedition had set off on the very day her father had died.

Arflane realised that she was not to blame for thinking him almost completely recovered; in fact there seemed no logical reason why he should have weakened so rapidly. It appeared that his heart, always considered healthy, had given out soon after he had dictated a will which was to be read later that afternoon to Arflane and the close relatives. Pyotr Rorsefne had died at about the same time the whale had attacked and destroyed the yacht, a few hours after he had spoken to Arflane of New York.

Sitting stiffly upright in a chair, hands clasped in her lap, Ulrica Ulsenn waited with Arflane, Manfred Rorsefne and her husband, who lay on a raised stretcher, in the anteroom adjoining what had been her father's study. The room was small, its walls crowded with hunting trophies from Pyotr Rorsefne's youth. Arflane found unpleasant the musty smell that came from the heads of the beasts.

The door of the study opened and Strom, the wizened old man who had been Pyotr Rorsefne's general retainer, beckoned them wordlessly into the room.

Arflane and Manfred Rorsefne stooped to pick up Ulsenn's stretcher and followed Ulrica Ulsenn into the study.

The study was reminiscent of a ship's cabin, though the light came from dim lighting strips instead of portholes. Its walls were lined from floor to ceiling with lockers. A large desk of yellow ivory stood in the centre; on it rested a single sheet of thin plastic.

The sheet was large and covered in brown writing, as if it had been inscribed in blood. It curled at the ends; evidently it had been unrolled only recently.

The old man took Manfred Rorsefne to the desk and sat him down in front of the paper; then he left the room.

Manfred sighed and tapped his fingers on the desk as he read the will. Normally Janek Ulsenn should have fulfilled this function, but the fever which had followed his accident had left him weak and only now was he pushing himself into a sitting position so that he could look over the top of the desk and regard his wife's cousin through baleful, disturbed eyes.

'What does it say?' he asked, weakly but impatiently.

'Little that we did not expect,' Manfred told him, still reading. There was a slight smile on his lips now.

'Why is this man here?' Ulsenn motioned with his hand towards Arflane.

'He is mentioned in the will, cousin.'

Arflane glanced over Ulsenn's head at Ulrica, but she refused to look in his direction.

'Read it out,' said Ulsenn, sinking back onto one arm. 'Read it out, Manfred.'

Manfred shrugged and began to read.

'"The Will of Pyotr Rorsefne, Chief Ship Lord of Friesgalt",' he began. '"The Rorsefne is dead. The Ulsenn rules."' He glanced sardonically at the reclining figure. '"Save all my fortune and estates and ships, which I hereby will to be divided equally between my daughter and my nephew, I hereby present the command of my schooner the *Ice Spirit* to Captain Konrad Arflane of Brershill, so that he may take her to New York on the course charted on the maps I also leave to him. If Captain Arflane should find the city of New York and live to return to Friesgalt, he shall become whole owner of the *Ice Spirit*, and any cargo she may then carry. To benefit from my will, my daughter Ulrica and my nephew Manfred must accompany Captain Arflane upon his voyage. Captain Arflane shall have complete power over all who sail with him. Pyotr Rorsefne of Friesgalt."'

Ulsenn was raising himself to a sitting position again. He glowered at Arflane. 'The old man was full of fever. He was insane. Forget this condition. Dismiss Captain Arflane, divide the property as the will stipulates. Would you embark upon another crazy voyage so soon after the first? Be warned; the first voyage anticipates the second, should you take it!'

'By the Ice Mother, cousin, how superstitious you have become,' Manfred Rorsefne murmured. 'You know very well that should we ignore one part of the will, then the other becomes invalid. And think how you would benefit if we did perish! Your wife's share and mine would make you the most powerful man to have ruled in all the Eight Cities.'

'I care nothing for the wealth. I am wealthy enough. It is my wife I wish to protect!'

Again Manfred Rorsefne smiled sardonically, recalling Ulsenn's desertion of his wife aboard the yacht. Ulsenn scowled at him, then relapsed, gasping, onto his pillows.

Stony-faced, Ulrica rose. 'He had best be taken to his bed,' she said.

Arflane and Manfred picked up the stretcher between them, and Ulrica led the way through dark passages to Ulsenn's bedroom, where servants took him and helped him into the large bed. His face was white with pain and he was almost fainting, but he continued to mutter about the stupidity of the old man's will.

'I wonder if he will decide to accompany us when we sail,' Manfred said as they left. He smiled ironically. 'Probably he will find that his health and his duties as the new lord will keep him in the crevasse.'

The three of them walked back to one of the main living rooms. It was furnished with brightly painted wall hangings and chairs and couches of wood-and-fibreglass frames padded and covered in animal skins. Arflane threw himself onto one of the couches and Ulrica sat opposite him, her eyes downcast. Only her long-fingered hands moved slightly in her lap.

Manfred did not sit.

'I must go to proclaim my uncle's will – or rather most of it,' he said. He had to go to the top of the crevasse-city and use a megaphone to repeat the words of the will to all the citizens. Friesgalt was acknowledging Pyotr Rorsefne's death in the traditional way. All work had ceased and the citizens had retired to their cavern homes for the three days of mourning.

When Manfred left, Ulrica did not, as Arflane had expected, make some excuse to follow. Instead she ordered a servant to bring them some hot *hess*. 'You will have some, captain?' she asked faintly.

Arflane nodded, looking at her curiously. She got up and moved about the room for a moment, pretending to inspect scenes on the wall hangings; they must have been more than familiar to her.

Arflane said at length, 'You should not feel that you did any wrong, Lady Ulsenn.'

She turned, raising her eyebrows. 'Wrong? What do you mean?'

'You did not desert your father. We all thought he was completely recovered. He said so himself. You are not guilty.'

'Thank you,' she said. She bowed her head, a trace of irony in her tone. 'I was not aware that I felt guilt.'

'I'm sorry that I should have thought so,' he said.

When she next looked at him, it was with a more candid expression as she studied his face. Gradually despair and quiet agony came into her eyes.

He rose awkwardly and went towards her, taking her hands in his, holding them firmly.

'You are strong, Captain Arflane,' she murmured. 'I am weak.'

'Not so,' he said heavily. 'Not so, ma'am.'

She gently removed her hands from his and went to sit on a couch. The servant returned, placed the *hess* on a small table near the couch and left again. She reached forward and poured a goblet of the stuff, handing it up to him. He took it, standing over her with his legs slightly apart, looking down at her sympathetically.

'I was thinking that there is much of your father in you,' he said. 'The strength is there.'

'You did not know my father well,' she reminded him quietly.

'Well enough, I think. You forget that I saw him when he thought he was alone and dying. It was what I felt was in him, then, that I see in you now. I would not have saved his life if I had not seen that quality.'

She gave a great sigh and her golden eyes glistened with tears. 'Perhaps you were wrong,' she said.

He sat beside her on the couch, shaking his head. 'All the strength of the family went into you for this generation. Your weakness is probably his, too.'

'What weakness?'

'A wild imagination. It took him to New York – or so he said – and it took you on the whale hunt.'

She smiled gratefully, her features softening as she looked directly at him. 'If you are trying to comfort me, captain, I think you are succeeding.'

'I'd comfort you more if –' He had not meant to speak. He had not meant to take her hands again as he did; but she did not resist and though her expression became serious and thoughtful, she did not seem offended.

Now Arflane breathed rapidly, remembering when he had embraced her on the ice. She flushed, but still she let him grip her hands.

'I love you,' said Arflane, almost miserably.

Then she burst into tears, took her hands away, and flung herself against him. He held her tightly while she wept, stroking her long, fine hair, kissing her forehead, caressing her shoulders. He felt the tears in his own eyes as he responded to her grief. Only barely aware of what he did next, he picked her up in his arms and carried her from the room. The passages were deserted as he took her towards her bedroom, where he still believed he intended to lay her on the bed and let her sleep. He kicked open the door – it was across the corridor from Ulsenn's – and kicked it shut behind him when he had entered.

The room was furnished with chairs, lockers and a dressing table of softly tinted ivory. White furs were heaped on the wide bed and also lined the walls.

He stopped and placed her on the bed, but he did not straighten up.

Now he knew that, in spite of the dreadful guilt he felt, he could do nothing to control his actions. He kissed her mouth. Her arms went around his neck as she responded, and he lowered his massive body onto hers, feeling the warmth and the contours of her flesh through the fabric of the dress, feeling her writhe and tremble beneath him like a frightened bird.

She shuddered under his touch and told him that she was a virgin, that she had never allowed Janek to consummate their marriage. Then she reached over to him and kissed him.

Chapter Nine
Ulrica Ulsenn's Conscience

Early in the morning, looking down on her as she slept with her face just visible above the furs and her black hair spread out on the pillow, Arflane felt remorse. No remorse, he knew, would be sufficient to make him part with Ulrica now, but he had broken the law he respected; the law he regarded as just and vital to the existence of his world. This morning he saw himself as a hypocrite, as a deceiver, and as a thief. While he was reconciled to these new rôles, the fact that he had assumed them depressed him; and he was further depressed by the knowledge that he had taken advantage of the woman's vulnerability at a time when her own guilt and grief had combined to weaken her moral strength.

Arflane did not regret his actions. He considered regret a useless emotion. What was done was done, and now he must decide what to do next.

He sighed as he clothed himself, unwilling to leave her but aware of what the law would do to her if she were discovered as an adulteress. At worst, she would be exposed on the ice to die. At the very least both he and she would be ostracised in all the Eight Cities; this in itself was effectually a lingering death sentence.

She opened her eyes and smiled at him sweetly; then the smile faltered.

'I'm leaving,' he whispered. 'We'll talk later.'

She sat up in the bed, the furs falling away from her breasts. He bent forward to kiss her, gently pulling her arms from his neck as she tried to embrace him.

'What are you going to do?' she asked.

'I don't know. I'd thought of going away – to Brershill.'

'Janek would break your city apart to find us. Many would die.'

'I know. Would he divorce you?'

'He owns me because I have the highest rank of any woman in Friesgalt; because I am beautiful and well mannered and rich.' She shrugged. 'He is not particularly interested in demanding his rights. He would divorce me because I refused to entertain his guests, not because I refused to make love to him.'

'Then what can we do? I shall deceive him only while I must protect you. I doubt in any case if I would be able to deceive him for long.'

She nodded. 'I doubt it, also.' She smiled up at him again. 'But if you took me away, where could we go?'

He shook his head. 'I don't know. To New York, perhaps. Remember the will?'

'Yes – New York.'

'We will talk later today, when we have an opportunity,' he said. 'I must go before the servants come.'

It had not occurred to either of them to question the fact that she was Janek Ulsenn's property, no matter how little he deserved her; but now, as he made to leave, she grasped his arm and spoke earnestly.

'I am yours,' she said. 'I am rightfully yours, despite my marriage vows. Remember that.'

He muttered something and went to the door, opening it cautiously and slipping into the corridor.

From Ulsenn's room, as Arflane passed it, there came a groan of pain as the new Lord of Friesgalt turned in his bed and twisted his useless legs.

At breakfast they were as shy as ever of exchanging glances. They sat at opposite ends of the table, with Manfred Rorsefne between them. His arm was still strapped in splints to his chest, but he appeared to be in as light-hearted a mood as ever.

'I gather my uncle had already told you he wanted you to command the *Ice Spirit* and take her to New York?' he said to Arflane.

Arflane nodded.

'And did you agree?' Manfred asked.

'I half agreed,' Arflane replied, pretending a greater interest in his meal than he felt, resentful of Manfred's presence in the room.

'What do you say now?'

'I'll skipper the ship,' Arflane said. 'She'll take time to crew and provision. She may need to be refitted. Also I'll want a careful look at those charts.'

'I'll get them for you,' Manfred promised. He glanced sideways at Ulrica. 'How do you feel about the proposed voyage, cousin?'

She flushed. 'It was my father's wish,' she said flatly.

'Good.' Manfred sat back in his chair, evidently in no hurry to leave. Arflane resisted the temptation to frown.

He tried to prolong the meal, hoping that Manfred would lose patience, but finally he was forced to let the servants take away his plate. Manfred made light conversation, seemingly oblivious of Arflane's reluctance to talk to him. At length, evidently unable to bear this, Ulrica got up from the table and left the room. Arflane controlled his desire to follow her immediately.

Almost as soon as she had gone, Manfred Rorsefne pushed back his chair and stood up. 'Wait here, captain. I'll bring the charts.'

Arflane wondered if Manfred guessed anything of what had happened during the night. He was almost sure that, if he did guess, the young man would say nothing to Janek Ulsenn, whom he despised. Yet three days before, on the ice, Manfred had restrained him from following Ulrica and had seemed resolved to make sure that Arflane would not interfere between Ulsenn and his wife. Arflane found the young man an enigma. At some times he seemed cynical and contemptuous of tradition; at others he seemed anxious to preserve it.

Rorsefne returned with the maps tucked under his good arm. Arflane took them from him and spread them out on the table that had been cleared of the remains of the meal.

The largest chart was drawn to the smallest scale, showing an area of several thousand miles. Superimposed on it in outline were what Arflane recognised as the buried continents of North and South America. Old Pyotr Rorsefne must have gone to considerable trouble with his charts, if this were his work.

Clearly marked was the plateau occupying what had once been the Matto Grosso territory and where the Eight Cities now lay; also clearly marked, about two-thirds up the eastern coastline of the northern continent, was New York. From the Matto Grosso to New York a line had been drawn. In Rorsefne's handwriting were the words 'Direct Course (Impossible)'. A dotted line showed another route that roughly followed the ancient land masses, angling approximately north-west by north before swinging gradually to east by north. This was marked 'Likely Course'. Here and there it had been corrected in a different coloured ink; it was obvious that these were the changes made on the actual voyage, but there were only a few scribbled indications of what the ship had been avoiding. There were several references to ice breaks, mountains, barbarian camps, but no details of their precise positions.

'These charts were amended from memory,' Manfred said. 'The log and the original charts were lost in the wreck.'

'Couldn't we look for the wreck?' Arflane asked.

'We could – but it would hardly be worth it. The ship broke up completely. Anything like the log or the charts would have been destroyed or buried by now.'

Arflane spread the other charts out. They were of little help, merely giving a clearer idea of the region a few hundred miles beyond the plateau.

Arflane spoke rather petulantly. 'All we know is where to look when we get there,' he said. 'And we know that it's possible to get there. We can follow this course and hope for the best – but I'd expected more detailed information. I wonder if the old man really did find New York.'

'We'll know in a few months, with any luck.' Manfred smiled.

'I'm still unhappy with the maps.' Arflane began to roll up the big chart.

'We'll have a better ship, a better crew – and a better captain than my uncle took.' Manfred spoke reassuringly.

Arflane tidied the other charts. 'I'll pick every member of my crew myself. I'll check every inch of rigging and every ounce of provisions we take aboard. It will be at least two weeks before we're ready to sail.'

Manfred was about to speak when the door opened. Four servants walked in, carrying Janek Ulsenn's stretcher. The new ruler of Friesgalt seemed in better health than he had the previous evening. He sat up in the stretcher.

'There you are, Manfred. Have you seen Strom this morning?'

Manfred shook his head. 'I was in my uncle's quarters earlier. I didn't see him.'

Ulsenn signalled abruptly for the servants to lower the stretcher to the floor. They did so carefully.

'Why were you in those quarters? They are mine now, you know.' Ulsenn's haughty voice rose.

Manfred indicated the rolled charts on the table.

'I had to get these to show Captain Arflane. They are the charts we need to plan the *Ice Spirit*'s voyage.'

'You mean to follow the letter of the will, then?' Janek Ulsenn said acidly. 'I still object to the venture. Pyotr Rorsefne was mad when he wrote it. He has made a common foreign sailor one of his heirs! He might just as well have left his wealth to Urquart, who is, after all, his kin. I could declare the will void...'

Manfred pursed his lips and shook his head slowly. 'You could not, cousin. Not the will of the old lord. I have declared it publicly. Everyone will know if you do not adhere to its instructions...'

A thought occurred to Arflane. 'You told the whole crevasse about New York? The old man didn't want the knowledge made general –'

'I didn't mention New York by name, but only as a "distant city below the plateau",' Manfred assured him.

Ulsenn smiled. 'Then there you are. You merely said to the most distant of the Eight Cities...'

Manfred sneered very slightly. 'Below the plateau? Besides, if it were one of the Eight that the will referred to, then it would have been making what was virtually a declaration of war. Your pain clouds your intelligence, cousin.'

Ulsenn coughed and glared up at Manfred. 'You are impertinent, Manfred. I am Lord now. I could order you both put to death...'

'With no trial? These are empty threats, cousin. Would the people accept such an action?'

In spite of the great personal authority of the Chief Ship Lord, the real power still rested in the hands of the mass of citizens, who had been known in the past to depose an unwelcome or tyrannical owner of the title. Ulsenn could not afford to take drastic action against any member of the much-respected Rorsefne family. As it was, his own standing in the city was comparatively slight. He had risen to the title by marriage, not by direct blood line or by any other means. If he were to imprison Manfred or someone whom Manfred protected, Ulsenn might easily find himself with a civil war on his hands, and he knew what the result of such a war would be.

Ulsenn, therefore, remained silent.

'It is Pyotr Rorsefne's *will*, cousin,' Manfred reminded him firmly. 'Whatever you may feel about it, Captain Arflane commands the *Ice Spirit*. Don't worry. Ulrica and I will go along to represent the family.'

Ulsenn darted a sharp, enigmatic look at Arflane. He signalled for his servants to pick up the stretcher. 'If Ulrica goes – I will go!' The servants carried him from the room.

Arflane realised that Manfred Rorsefne was looking with amused interest at his face. The young man must have read the expression there. Arflane had not been prepared for this declaration. He had been confident that Ulsenn would have been too involved with his new power, too ill and too cowardly to join the expedition. He had been confident in his anticipation of Ulrica's company on the proposed voyage. Now he could anticipate nothing.

Manfred laughed.

'Cheer up, captain. Janek won't bother us on the voyage. He's an accountant, a stay-at-home merchant who knows nothing of sailing. He could not interfere if he wished to. He won't help us find the Ice Mother's lair – but he won't hinder us, either.'

Although Manfred's reassurance seemed genuine, Arflane still could not tell if the young man had actually guessed the real reason for his disappointment. For that matter, he wondered if Janek Ulsenn had guessed what had happened in his wife's bedroom that night. The look he had given Arflane seemed to indicate that he suspected something, though it seemed impossible that he could know what had actually taken place.

Arflane was disturbed by the turn of events. He wanted to see Ulrica at once and talk to her about what had happened. He had a sudden feeling of deep apprehension.

'When will you begin inspecting the ship and picking the crew, captain?' Manfred was asking.

'Tomorrow,' Arflane told him ungraciously. 'I'll see you before I get out there.'

He made a curt farewell gesture with his hand and left the room. He began to walk through the low corridors, searching for Ulrica.

He found her in the main living room where, on the previous night, he had first caressed her. She rose hurriedly when he entered. She was pale; she held her body rigidly, her hands gripped tightly together at her waist. She had bound up her hair, drawing it back tightly from her face. She was wearing the black dress of fine sealskin which she had worn the day before at the funeral. Arflane closed the door, but she moved towards it, attempting to pass him. He barred the way with one arm and tried to look into her eyes, but she averted her head.

'Ulrica, what is it?' The sense of foreboding was now even stronger. 'What is it? Did you hear that your husband intends to come with us on the voyage? Is that why…?'

She looked at him coolly and he dropped his arm away from the door.

'I am sorry, Captain Arflane,' she said formally. 'But it would be best if you forgot what passed between us. We were both in unusual states of mind. I realise now that it is my duty to remain faithful to my –'

Her whole manner was artificially polite.

'Ulrica!' He gripped her shoulders tightly. 'Did he tell you to say this? Has he threatened you…?'

She shook her head. 'Let me go, captain.'

'Ulrica…' His voice had broken. He spoke weakly, dropping his hands from her shoulders. 'Ulrica, why…?'

'I seem to remember you speaking quite passionately in favour of the old traditions,' she said. 'More than once I've heard you say that to let slip our code will mean our perishing as a people. You mentioned that you admired my father's strength of mind and that you saw the same quality in me. Perhaps you did, captain. I intend to stay faithful to my husband.'

'You aren't saying what you mean. I can tell that. You love me. This mood is just a reaction – because things seem too complicated now. You told me that you were rightfully mine. You *meant* what you said this morning.' He hated the tone of desperation in his own voice, but he could not control it.

'I mean what I am saying now, captain; and if you respect the old way of life, then you will respect my request that you see as little of me as possible from now on.'

'No!' He roared in anger and lurched towards her. She stepped back, face frozen and eyes cold. He reached out to touch her and then slowly withdrew his hands and stepped aside to let her pass.

She opened the door. He understood now that no outside event had caused this change in her. The cause was her own conscience. He could not argue with her decision. Morally, it was right. There was nothing he could do; there was no hope he could hold. He watched her walk slowly away from him down the corridor. Then he slammed the door, his face twisted in an expression of agonised despair. There was a snapping sound and the door swung back. He had broken its lock. It would no longer close properly.

He hurried to his room and began to bundle his belongings together. He would make sure that he obeyed her request. He would not see her again, at least until the ship was ready to sail. He would go out to the *Ice Spirit* at once and begin his work.

He slung the sack over his shoulder and hurried through the

winding corridors to the outer entrance. Bloody thoughts were in his mind and he wanted to get into the open, hoping that the clean air of the surface would blow them away.

As he reached the outer door, he met Manfred Rorsefne in the hall. The young man looked amused.

'Where are you off to, captain?'

Arflane glared at him, wanting to strangle the supercilious expression from Rorsefne's face.

'I see you're leaving, captain. Off to the *Ice Spirit* so soon? I thought you were going tomorrow...'

'Today,' Arflane growled. He recovered some of his self-assurance. 'Today. I'll get started at once. I'll sleep on board until we sail. It will be best...'

'Perhaps it will,' Rorsefne agreed, speaking half to himself as he watched the big, red-bearded sailor stride rapidly from the house.

Chapter Ten

Konrad Arflane's Mood

Of the newly discovered facts about his own character that obsessed Konrad Arflane, the most startling was that he had never suspected himself capable of renouncing all his principles in order to possess another man's wife. He also found it difficult to equate with his own idea of himself the knowledge that, having been stopped from seeing the woman, he should not become reconciled, or indeed grateful.

He was far from being either. He slept badly, his attention turned constantly to thoughts of Ulrica Ulsenn. He waited without hope for her to come to him and when she did not he was angry. He stalked about the big ship, bawling out the men over quibbling details, dismissing hands he had hired the day before, muttering offensively to his officers in front of the men, demanding that he should be made aware of all problems aboard, then swearing furiously when some unnecessary matter was brought to him.

He had had the reputation of being a particularly good skipper; stern and remote, but fair. The whaling hands, whom he preferred for his crewmen, had been eager to sign with the *Ice Spirit*, in spite of the mysterious voyage she was to make. Now many were regretting it.

Arflane had appointed three officers – or rather he had let two appointments stand and had signed on Long Lance Urquart as third officer, below Petchnyoff and old Kristoff Hinsen. Urquart seemed oblivious to Arflane's irrational moods, but the two other men were puzzled and upset by the change in their new skipper. Whenever Urquart was not in their quarters – which was often – they would take the opportunity to discuss the problem. Both had liked Arflane when they had first met him.

Petchnyoff had had a high regard for his integrity and strength of will; Kristoff Hinsen felt a more intimate relationship with him, based on memories of the days when they had been rival skippers. Neither was capable of analysing the cause of the change in Arflane's temperament; yet so much did they trust their earlier impressions of him that they were prepared for a while to put up with his moods in the hope that, once under way, he would become the man they had first encountered. Petchnyoff's patience as the days passed was increasingly strained and he began to think of resigning his command, but Hinsen persuaded him to wait a little longer.

The huge vessel was being fitted with completely new canvas and rigging. Arflane personally inspected every pin, every knot, and every line. He climbed over the ship inch by inch, checking the set of the yards, the tension of the rigging, the snugness of the hatch covers, the feel of the bulkheads, until he was satisfied. He tested the wheel time after time, turning the runners this way and that to get to know their exact responses. Normally the steering runners and their turntable were immovably locked in relation with each other. On the foredeck, though, immediately above the great gland of the steering pin, was housed the emergency bolt, with a heavy mallet secured beside it. Dropping the bolt would release the skids, allowing them to turn in towards each other creating in effect a huge ploughshare that dug into the ice, bringing the vessel to a squealing and frequently destructive halt. Arflane tested this apparatus for hours. He also dropped the heavy anchors once or twice. These were on either side of the ship, beneath her bilges. They consisted of two great blades. Above them, through guides let into the hull, rods reached to the upper deck. Pins driven through the rods kept the blades clear of ice; beside each stanchion, mallets were kept ready to knock the pegs clear in case of danger or emergency. The heavy anchors were seldom used, and never by a good skipper; contact with racing ice would wear them rapidly away, and replacements were now nearly unobtainable.

At first men and officers had called out cheerfully to him as he went about the ship; but they soon learned to avoid him, and the superstitious whaling hands began to speak of curses and of a foredoomed voyage; yet very few disembarked of their own accord.

Arflane would watch moodily from the bridge as bale after bale and barrel after barrel of provisions was swung aboard, packing every inch of available space. With each fresh ton that was taken into the holds, he would again test the wheel and the heavy anchors to see how the *Ice Spirit* responded.

One day on deck Arflane saw Petchnyoff inspecting the work of a sailor who had been one of a party securing the mainmast ratlines. He strode up to the pair and pulled at the lines, checking the knots. One of them was not as firm as it could be.

'Call that a knot, do you, Mr Petchnyoff ?' he said offensively. 'I thought you were supposed to be inspecting this work!'

'I am, sir.'

'I'd like to be able to trust my officers,' Arflane said with a sneer. 'Try to see that I can in future.'

He marched off along the deck. Petchnyoff slammed a belaying pin he had been holding down onto the deck, narrowly missing the surprised hand.

That evening, Petchnyoff had got half his kit packed before Hinsen could convince him to stay on board.

The weeks went by. There were four floggings for minor offences. It was as if Arflane were deliberately trying to get his crew to leave him before the ship set sail. Yet many of the men were fascinated by him, and the fact that Urquart had thrown in his lot with Arflane must have had something to do with the whaling hands staying.

Manfred Rorsefne would occasionally come aboard to confer with Arflane. Originally Arflane had said that it would take a fortnight to ready the ship, but he had put off the sailing date further and further on one excuse and another, telling Rorsefne that he was still not happy that everything had been done that could be done, reminding him that a voyage of this kind demanded a ship that was as perfect as possible.

'True, but we'll miss the summer at this rate,' Manfred Rorsefne reminded him gently. Arflane scowled in reply, saying he could sail in any weather. His carefulness on one hand, and his apparent recklessness on the other, did little to reassure Rorsefne; but he said nothing.

Finally there was absolutely no more to be done aboard the ice schooner. She was in superb trim; all her ivory was polished and shining, her decks were scrubbed and freshly boned. Her four masts gleamed with white, furled canvas; her rigging was straight and taut; the boats, swinging in davits fashioned from the jawbones of whales, hung true and firm; every pin was in place and every piece of gear was where it should be. The barbaric whale skulls at her prow glared towards the north as if defying all the dangers that might be awaiting them. The *Ice Spirit* was ready to sail.

Still reluctant to send for his passengers, Arflane stood in silence on the bridge and looked at the ship. For a moment it occurred to him that he could take her out now, leaving the Ulsenns and Manfred Rorsefne behind. The ice ahead was obscured by clouds of snow that were lifted by the wind and sent drifting across the bow; the sky was grey and heavy. Gripping the rail in his gauntleted hands, Arflane knew it would not be difficult to slip out to the open ice in weather like this.

He sighed and turned to Kristoff Hinsen who stood beside him.

'Send a man to the Rorsefne place, Mr Hinsen. Tell them if the wind holds we'll sail tomorrow morning.'

'Aye, aye, sir.' Hinsen paused, his weather-beaten features creased in doubt. 'Tomorrow morning, sir?'

Arflane turned his brooding eyes on Hinsen. 'I said tomorrow. That's the message, Mr Hinsen.'

'Aye, aye, sir.' Hinsen left the bridge hurriedly.

Arflane knew why Hinsen queried his orders. The weather was bad and obviously getting worse. By morning they would have a heavy snowstorm; visibility would be poor, and the men would find it difficult to set the canvas. But Arflane had made up his mind; he looked away, back towards the bow.

Two hours later he saw a covered sleigh being drawn across the ice from the city. Tawny wolves pulled it, their paws slipping on the ice.

A strong gust of wind blew suddenly from the west and buffeted the side of the ship so that it moved slightly to starboard in its mooring cables. Arflane did not need to order the cables checked. Several hands instantly ran to see to them. It was a larger crew than he normally liked to handle, but he had to admit, even in his poor temper, that their discipline was very good.

The wolves came to an untidy stop close to the ship's side. Arflane cursed and swung down from the bridge, moving to the rail and leaning over it. The driver had brought the carriage in too close for his own safety.

'Get that thing back!' Arflane yelled. 'Get beyond the mooring pegs. Don't you know better than to come so close to a ship of this size while there's a heavy wind blowing? If we slip one cable you'll be crushed.'

A muffled head poked itself from the carriage window. 'We are here, Captain Arflane. Manfred Rorsefne and the Ulsenns.'

'Tell your driver to get back! He ought to –' A fresh gust of wind slammed against the ship's side and sent it skidding several feet closer to the carriage until the slack of the mooring cables on the other side was taken up. The driver looked startled and whipped his wolves into a steep turn. They strained in their harness and loped across the ice with the carriage in tow.

Arflane smiled unpleasantly.

With a wind as erratic as this, few captains would allow their ships out of their moorings, but he intended to sail anyway. It might be dangerous, but it would seem worse to Ulsenn and his relatives.

Manfred Rorsefne and the Ulsenns had got out of the carriage and were standing uncertainly, looking up at the ship, searching for Arflane.

Arflane turned away from them and went back to the bridge.

Fydur, the ship's bosun, saluted him as he began to climb the companionway. 'Shall I send out a party to take the passengers aboard, sir?'

Arflane shook his head. 'Let them make their own way on board,' he told the bosun. 'You can lower a gangplank if you like.'

A little later he watched Janek Ulsenn being helped up the gangplank and along the deck. He saw Ulrica, completely swathed in her furs, moving beside her husband. Once she looked up at the bridge and he caught a glimpse of her eyes – the only part of her face not hidden by her hood. Manfred strolled along after them, waving cheerfully up at Arflane, but he was forced to clutch a line as the ship moved again in her moorings.

Within a quarter of an hour he had joined Arflane on the bridge.

'I've seen my cousin and her husband into their respective cabins, captain,' he said. 'I'm settled in myself. At last we're ready, eh?'

Arflane grunted and moved down the rail to starboard, plainly trying to avoid the young man. Manfred seemed unaware of this; he followed, slapping his gloved hands together and looking about him. 'You certainly know your ships, captain. I thought the *Spirit* was as neat as she could be until you took over. We should have little trouble on the voyage, I'm sure.'

Arflane looked around at Rorsefne.

'We should have no trouble at all,' he said grimly. 'I hope you'll remind your relatives that I'm in sole command of this ship from the moment she sails. I'm empowered to take any measure I think fit to ensure the smooth running of the vessel…'

'All this is unnecessary, captain.' Rorsefne smiled. 'We accept that, of course. That is the law of the ice. No need for details; you are the skipper, we do as you tell us to do.'

Arflane grunted. 'Are you certain Janek Ulsenn understands that?'

'I'm sure he does. He'll do nothing to offend you – save perhaps scowl at you a little. Besides, his legs are still bothering him. He's not entirely fit; I doubt if he'll be seen above deck for a while.' Manfred paused and then stepped much closer to Arflane. 'Captain – you haven't seemed yourself since you took this command. Is something wrong? Are you disturbed by the idea of the voyage? It occurred to me that you might think there was – um – sacrilege involved.'

Arflane shook his head, looking full into Manfred Rorsefne's face. 'You know I don't think that.'

Rorsefne appeared to be disconcerted for a moment. He pursed his lips. 'It's no wish of mine to intrude on your personal…'

'Thank you.'

'It would seem to me that the safety of the ship depends almost wholly upon yourself. If you are in poor spirits, captain, perhaps it would be better to delay the voyage longer?'

The wind was whining through the top trees. Automatically, Arflane looked up to make sure that the yards were firm. 'I'm not in poor spirits,' he said distantly.

'I think I could help…'

Arflane raised the megaphone to his lips and bawled at Hinsen as he crossed the quarter-deck.

'Mr Hinsen! Get some men into the mizzen to'g'l'nt yards and secure that flapping canvas!'

Manfred Rorsefne said nothing more. He left the bridge.

Arflane folded his arms across his chest, his features set in a scowl.

Chapter Eleven

Under Sail

AT DAWN THE next morning a blizzard blew in a great white sheet across the city and the forest of ships, heaping snow on the decks of the *Ice Spirit* till the schooner strained at her anchor lines. Sky and land were indistinguishable and only occasionally were the masts of the other vessels to be seen, outlined in black against the sweeping wall of snow. The temperature had fallen below zero. Ice had formed on the rigging and in the folds of the sails. Particles of ice, whipped by the wind, flew in the air like bullets; it was almost impossible to move against the blustering pressure of the storm. Loose canvas flapped like the broken flippers of seals; the wind shrilled and moaned through the tall masts and boats swung and creaked in their davits.

As a muffled tolling proclaimed two bells in the morning watch, Konrad Arflane, wearing a bandage over his mouth and nose and a snow visor over his eyes, stepped from his cabin below the bridge. Through a mist of driving snow he made his way forward to the bow and peered ahead; it was impossible to see anything in the swirling wall of whiteness. He returned to his cabin, passing Petchnyoff, the officer of the watch, without a word.

Petchnyoff stared after his skipper as the door of the cabin closed. There was a strange, resentful look in the first officer's eyes.

By six-thirty in the morning, as the bell rang five, the driving snow had eased and weak sunshine was filtering through the clouds. Hinsen stood beside Arflane on the bridge, a megaphone in his hand. The crew were climbing into the shrouds, their thickly clad bodies moving slowly up the ratlines. On the deck by the mainmast stood Urquart, his head covered by a tall hood, in charge of the men in the yards. The anchor men stood by their mooring lines, watching the bridge and ready to let go.

Arflane glanced at Hinsen. 'All prepared, Mr Hinsen?'

Hinsen nodded.

Aware that Rorsefne and the Ulsenns were still sleeping below, Arflane said, 'Let go the anchor lines.'

'Let go the anchor lines!' Hinsen's voice boomed over the ship and the men sprang to release the cables. The taut lines whipped away and the schooner lurched forward.

'Set upper and lower fore to'g'l'nts.'

The order was repeated and obeyed.

'Set stays'ls.'

The staysails blossomed out.

'Set upper and lower main to'g'l'nts and upper tops'l.'

The sails billowed and swelled as they caught the wind, curving like the wings of monstrous birds, pulling the ship gradually away. Snow sprayed as the runners sliced through the surface and the schooner began to move from the port, passing the still-anchored ships near her, dipping her bowsprit as she descended a slight incline in the ice, surging as she felt the rise on the other side. Kites squawked, swooping and circling excitedly around the top trees where the grandiose standard of the Rorsefne stood straight in the breeze. In her wake the ship left deep twin scars in the churned snow and ice. A huge, graceful creature, making her stately way out of port in the early morning under only a fraction of her sail, the ice in the rigging melting and falling off like a shower of diamonds, the *Ice Spirit* left Friesgalt behind and moved north beneath the lowering sky.

'All plain sail, Mr Hinsen.'

Sheet by sheet the sails were set until the ship sped over the ice under full canvas. Hinsen glanced at Arflane questioningly; it was unusual to set so much canvas while leaving port. But then he noticed Arflane's face as the ship began to gain speed. The captain was relaxing visibly. His expression was softening, there seemed to be a trace of a smile on his lips and his eyes were beginning to brighten.

Arflane breathed heavily and pushed back his visor, exhilarated by the wind on his face, the rolling of the deck beneath his feet. For the first time since Ulrica Ulsenn had rejected him he felt a lifting of the weight that had descended on him. He half smiled at Hinsen. 'She's a real ship, Mr Hinsen.'

Old Kristoff, overjoyed at the change in his master, grinned broadly, more in relief than in agreement. 'Aye, sir. She can move.'

Arflane stretched his body as the ship lunged forward over the seemingly endless plateau of ice, piercing the thinning curtain of snow. Below him on the decks, and above in the rigging, sailors moved like dark ghosts through the drifting whiteness, working under the calm, fixed eye of Long Lance Urquart as he strode up and down the deck, his harpoon resting in its usual place in the crook of his arm. Sometimes Urquart would jump up into the lower shrouds to help a man in difficulties with a piece of tackle. The cold and the snow, combined with the need to wear particularly thick gloves, made it difficult for even the whale men to work, though they were better used to the conditions than were the merchant sailors.

Arflane had hardly spoken to Urquart since the man had come aboard to sign on. Arflane had been happy to accept the harpooner, offering him the berth of third officer. It had vaguely occurred to him to wonder why Urquart should want to sail with him, since the tall harpooner could have no idea of where the ship was bound; but his own obsessions had driven the question out of his head. Now, as he relaxed, he glanced curiously at Urquart. The man caught his eye as he turned from giving instructions to a sailor. He nodded gravely to Arflane.

Arflane had instinctively trusted Urquart's ability to command, knowing that the harpooner had great prestige among the whalers; he had no doubts about his decision, but now he wondered again why Urquart had joined the ship. He had come, uninvited, on the whale hunt. That was understandable maybe; but there was no logical reason why a professional harpooner should wish to sail on a mysterious voyage of exploration. Perhaps Urquart felt protective towards his dead father's daughter and nephew, had decided to come with them to be sure of their safety on the trip; the image of the Long Lance at old Rorsefne's graveside suddenly came back to Arflane. Perhaps, though, Urquart felt friendship towards him personally. After all, only Urquart had seemed instinctively to respect Arflane's troubled state of mind over the past weeks and to understand his need for solitude. Of all the ship's complement, Arflane felt comradeship only towards Urquart, who was still a stranger to him. Hinsen he liked and admired, but since their original disagreement on the *Ice Spirit* over two months earlier, he had not been able to feel quite the same warmth towards him as he might have done.

Arflane leaned on the rail, watching the men at work. The ship was in no real danger until she had to descend the plateau, and they would not reach the edge for several days sailing at full speed; he gave himself the pleasure of forgetting everything but the motion of the ship beneath him, the sight of the snow spray spurting from the runners, the long streamers of clouds above him breaking up now and letting through the early-morning sunlight and glimpses of a pale red and yellow sky reflected by the ice.

There was an old saying among sailors that a ship beneath a man was as good as a woman, and Arflane began to feel that he could agree. Once the schooner had gotten under way, his mood had lifted. He was still concerned about Ulrica; but he did not feel the same despair, the same hatred for all humanity that had possessed him while the ship was being readied for the voyage. He began to feel guilty, now he thought back, that he had been so ill-mannered towards his officers and so irrational in his dealings with the crew. Manfred Rorsefne had been concerned that his mood would continue. Arflane had rejected the idea that he was in any kind of abnormal mood, but now he realised the truth of Rorsefne's statement of the night before; he would have been in no state to command the ship if his temper had not changed. It puzzled him that mere physical sensation, like the ship's passage over the ice, could so alter a man's mental attitudes within the space of an hour. Admittedly in the past he had always been restless and ill-tempered when not on board ship, but he had never gone so far as to behave unfairly towards the men serving under him. His self-possession was his pride. He had lost it; now he had found it again.

Perhaps he did not realise at that point that it would take only a glimpse or two of Ulrica Ulsenn to make him once more lose that self-possession in a different way. Even when he looked around to see Janek Ulsenn being helped up to the bridge by Petchnyoff, his spirits were unimpaired; he smiled at Ulsenn in sardonic good humour.

'Well, we're under way, Lord Ulsenn. Hope we didn't wake you.'

Petchnyoff looked surprised. He had become so used to the skipper's surly manner that any sign of joviality was bound to set him back.

'You did wake us,' Ulsenn began, but Arflane interrupted him to address Petchnyoff.

'You took the middle watch and half the morning watch, I believe, Mr Petchnyoff.'

Petchnyoff nodded. 'Yes, sir.'

'I would have thought it would have suited you to be in your bunk by now,' Arflane said as pleasantly as he could. He did not want an officer who was going to be half asleep when his watch came round again.

Petchnyoff shrugged. 'I'd planned to get some rest in, sir, after I'd eaten. Then I met Lord Ulsenn coming out of his cabin…'

Arflane gestured with his hand. 'I see. You'd better go to your bunk now, Mr Petchnyoff.'

'Aye, aye, sir.'

Petchnyoff backed down the companionway and disappeared. Ulsenn was left alone. Arflane had deliberately ignored him and Ulsenn was aware of it; he stared balefully at Arflane.

'You may have complete command of this ship, captain, but it would seem to me that you could show courtesy both to your officers and your passengers. Petchnyoff has told me how you have behaved since you took charge. Your boorishness is a watchword in all Friesgalt. Because you have been given a responsibility that elevates you above your fellows, it is no excuse for taking the opportunity to…'

Arflane sighed. 'I have made sure that the ship is in the best possible order, if that's what Petchnyoff means,' he commented reasonably. He was surprised that Petchnyoff should show such disloyalty; but perhaps the man's ties were, after all, closer to the ruling class of Friesgalt than to a foreign skipper. His own surliness over the past weeks must in any case have helped turn Petchnyoff against him. He shrugged. If the first officer was offended then he could remain so, as long as he performed his duties efficiently.

Ulsenn had seen the slight shrug and misinterpreted it. 'You are not aware of what your men are saying about you, captain?'

Arflane leaned casually with his back against the rail, pretending an interest with the racing ice to starboard. 'The men always grumble about the skipper. It's the extent of their grumbling and how it affects their work that's the thing to worry about. I've hired whaling men for this voyage, Lord Ulsenn – wild whaling men. I'd expect them to complain.'

'They're saying that you carry a curse,' Ulsenn murmured, looking cunningly at Arflane.

Arflane laughed. 'They're a superstitious lot. It gives them satisfaction to believe in curses. They wouldn't follow a skipper unless they could colour his character in some way. It appeals to their sense of drama. Calm down, Lord Ulsenn. Go back to your cabin and rest your legs.'

Ulsenn's lean face twitched in anger. 'You are an impertinent boor, captain!'

'I am also adamant, Lord Ulsenn. I'm in full command of this expedition and any attempt to oust my authority will be dealt with in the normal manner.' Arflane relished the opportunity to threaten the man. 'Have the goodness to leave the bridge!'

'What if the officers and crew aren't satisfied with your command? What if they feel you are mishandling the ship?' Ulsenn leaned forward, his voice high-pitched.

Having so recently regained his own self-control, Arflane felt a somewhat ignoble enjoyment in witnessing Ulsenn losing his. He smiled again. 'Calm yourself, my lord. There is an accepted procedure they may take if they are dissatisfied with my command. They could mutiny, which would be unwise; or they could vote for a temporary command and appeal to me to relinquish my post. In which case they must abandon the expedition, return immediately to a friendly city and make a formal report.' Arflane gestured impatiently. 'Really, sir, you must accept my command once and for all. Our journey will be a long one and conflicts of this kind are best avoided.'

'You have produced the conflict, captain.'

Arflane shrugged in contempt and did not bother to reply.

'I reserve the right to countermand your orders if I feel they are not in keeping with the best interests of this expedition,' Ulsenn continued.

'And I reserve the right, sir, to hang you if you try. I'll have to warn the crew that they're to accept only my orders. That would embarrass you, I think.'

Ulsenn snorted. 'You're aware, surely, that most of your crew, including your officers, are Friesgaltians? *I* am the man they will listen to before they take such orders from – a foreign –'

'Possibly,' Arflane said equably. 'In which case, my rights as commander of this ship entitle me, as I believe I've pointed out, to punish any attempt to usurp my authority, whether in word or deed.'

'You know your rights, captain,' Ulsenn retaliated with attempted sarcasm, 'but they are artificial. Mine are the rights of blood – to command the men of Friesgalt.'

Beside Arflane, Hinsen chuckled. The sound was totally unexpected; both men turned to stare. Hinsen looked away, covering his mouth a trifle ostentatiously with one gloved hand.

The interruption had, however, produced its effect. Ulsenn was completely deflated. Arflane moved forward and took his arm, helping him towards the companionway.

'Possibly all our rights are artificial, Lord Ulsenn, but mine are designed to keep discipline on a ship and make sure that it is run as smoothly as possible.'

Ulsenn began to clamber down the companionway. Arflane motioned Hinsen forward to help him; but when the older man attempted to take his arm, Ulsenn shook him off and made something of a show of controlling his pain as he limped unaided across the deck.

Hinsen grinned at Arflane. The captain pursed his lips in disapproval. The sky was lightening now, turning to a bright, pale blue that was reflected in the flat ice to either side, as the last shreds of clouds disappeared.

The ship moved smoothly, sharply outlined against a mirror amalgam of sky and ice. Looking forward, Arflane saw the men relaxing, gathering in knots and groups on the deck. Through them, moving purposefully, Urquart was shouldering his way towards the bridge.

Chapter Twelve

Over the Edge

VAGUELY SURPRISED, ARFLANE watched the harpooner climb to the poop deck. Perhaps Urquart sensed that his mood had changed now and that he would be ready to see him. The harpooner nodded curtly to Hinsen and presented himself before Arflane, stamping the butt of his great weapon down on the deck and leaning on it broodingly. He pushed back the hood of his coat, revealing his heap of matted black hair. The clear blue eyes regarded Arflane steadily; the gaunt, red face was as immobile as ever. From him came a faint stink of whale blood and blubber.

'Well, sir.' His voice was harsh but low. 'We are under way.' There was a note of expectancy in his tone.

'You want to know where we're bound, Mr Urquart?' Arflane said on impulse. 'We're bound for New York.'

Hinsen, standing behind Urquart, raised his eyebrows in surprise. 'New York!'

'This is confidential,' Arflane warned him. 'I don't propose to tell the men just yet. Only the officers.'

Over Urquart's grim features there spread a slow smile. When he spun his lance and drove it point first into the deck it seemed to be a gesture of approval. The smile quickly disappeared, but the blue eyes were brighter. 'So we sail to the Ice Mother, captain.' He did not question the existence of the mythical city; quite plainly he believed firmly in its reality. But Hinsen's old, rugged face bore a look of heavy scepticism.

'Why do we sail to New York, sir? Or is the voyage simply to discover if such a place does exist?'

Arflane, more absorbed in studying Urquart's reaction, answered abstractedly. 'The Lord Pyotr Rorsefne discovered the city, but was forced to turn back before he could explore it. We have charts. I think the city exists.'

'And the Ice Mother's in residence?' Hinsen could not avoid the hint of irony in his question.

'We'll know that when we get there, Mr Hinsen.' For a moment Arflane turned his full attention to his second officer.

'She'll be there,' Urquart said with conviction.

Arflane looked curiously at the tall harpooner, then addressed Kristoff Hinsen again. 'Remember, Mr Hinsen, I've told you this in confidence.'

'Aye, sir.' Hinsen paused. Then he said tactfully, 'I'll take a tour about the ship, sir, if Mr Urquart wants a word with you. Better have someone keeping an eye on the men.'

'Quite right, Mr Hinsen. Thank you.'

When Hinsen had left the bridge, the two men stood there in silence for a while, neither feeling the need to speak. Urquart wrested his harpoon from the deck and walked towards the rail. Arflane joined him.

'Happy with the voyage, Mr Urquart?' he asked at length.

'Yes, sir.'

'You really think we'll find the Ice Mother?'

'Don't you, captain?'

Arflane gestured uncertainly. 'Three months ago, Mr Urquart – three months ago I would have said yes, there would be evidence in New York to support the doctrine. Now…' He paused helplessly. 'They say that the scientists have disproved the doctrine. The Ice Mother is dying.'

Urquart shifted his weight. 'Then She'll need our help, sir. Maybe that's why we're sailing. Maybe it's fate. Maybe She's calling for us.'

'Maybe.' Arflane sounded doubtful.

'I think so, captain. Pyotr Rorsefne was Her messenger, you see. He was sent to you – that's why you found him on the ice – and when he had delivered his message to us, he died. Don't you see, sir?'

'It could be true,' Arflane agreed.

Urquart's mysticism was disconcerting, even to Arflane. He looked directly at the harpooner and saw the fanaticism in the face, the utter conviction in his eyes. Not so long ago he had had a similar conviction. He shook his head sadly.

'I am not the man I was, Mr Urquart.'

'No, sir.' Urquart seemed to share Arflane's sadness. 'But you'll find yourself on this voyage. You'll recover your faith, sir.'

Offended for the moment by the intimacy of Urquart's remark, Arflane drew back. 'Perhaps I don't need that faith any more, Mr Urquart.'

'Perhaps you need it most of all now, captain.'

Arflane's anger passed. 'I wonder what has happened to me,' he said thoughtfully. 'Three months ago…'

'Three months ago you had not met the Rorsefne family, captain.' Urquart spoke grimly, but with a certain sympathy. 'You've become infected with their weakness.'

'I understood you to feel a certain loyalty – a certain protective responsibility to the family,' Arflane said in surprise. He realised that this understanding had been conjecture on his part, but he had been convinced that he was right.

'I want them kept alive, if that's what you mean,' Urquart said noncommittally.

'I'm not sure I understand you…' Arflane began, but was cut short by Urquart turning away from him and looking distantly towards the horizon.

The silence became uncomfortable and Arflane felt disturbed by the loss of Urquart's confidence. The half-savage harpooner did not elaborate on his remark, but eventually turned back to look at Arflane, his expression softening by a degree.

'It's the Ice Mother's will,' he said. 'You needed to use the family so that you could get the ship. Avoid our passengers all you can from now on, captain. They are weak. Even the old man was too indulgent, and he was better than any that still live…'

'You say it was the Ice Mother,' Arflane replied gloomily. 'I think it was a different kind of force, just as mysterious, that involved me with the family.'

'Think what you like,' Urquart said impatiently, 'but I know what is true. I know your destiny. Avoid the Rorsefne family.'

'What of Lord Ulsenn?'

'Ulsenn is nothing.' Urquart sneered.

Impressed by Urquart's warning, Arflane was careful to say nothing more of the Rorsefne family. He had already noted how much involved with the three people he had become. Yet surely, he thought, there were certain strengths in all of them. They were not as soft as Urquart thought. Even Ulsenn, though a physical coward, had his own kind of integrity, if it was only a belief in his absolute right to rule. It was true that his association with the family had caused him to forsake many of his old convictions, yet surely that was his weakness, not theirs? Urquart doubtless blamed their influence. Perhaps he was right.

He sighed and dusted at the rail with his gloved hand. 'I hope we find the Ice Mother,' he said eventually. 'I need to be reassured, Mr Urquart.'

'She'll be there, captain. Soon you'll know it, too.' Urquart reached out and gripped Arflane's shoulder. Arflane was startled, but he did not resent the gesture. The harpooner peered into his face. The blue eyes were alight with the certainty of his own ideas. He shook his harpoon. 'This is true,' he said passionately. He pointed out to the ice. 'That is true.' He dropped his arm. 'Find your strength again, captain. You'll need it on this voyage.'

The harpooner clambered down from the bridge and disappeared, leaving Arflane feeling at the same time uneasy and more optimistic than he had felt for many months.

From that time on, Urquart would frequently appear on the bridge. He would say little; would simply stand by the rail or lean against the wheelhouse, as if by his presence he sought to transmit his own strength of will to Arflane. He was at once both silent mentor and support to the captain as the ship moved rapidly towards the edge of the plateau.

A few days later Manfred Rorsefne and Arflane stood in Arflane's cabin, consulting the charts spread on the table before them.

'We'll reach the edge tomorrow,' Rorsefne indicated the chart of the plateau (the only detailed map they had). 'The descent should be difficult, eh, captain?'

Arflane shook his head. 'Not necessarily. By the look of it, there's a clear run down at this point.' He put a finger on the chart. 'If we steer a course north-east by north by three-quarters north we should reach this spot where the incline is fairly smooth and gradual and no hills in our way. The ice only gets rough at the bottom, and we should have lost enough momentum by then to be able to cross without much difficulty. I can take her down, I think.'

Rorsefne smiled. 'You seem to have recovered your old self-confidence, captain.'

Arflane resented the suggestion. 'We'd best set the course,' he said coldly.

As they left his cabin and came out on deck they almost bumped into Janek and Ulrica Ulsenn. She was helping him towards the entrance to the gangway that led to their quarters. Rorsefne bowed and grinned at them, but Arflane scowled. It was the first time since the voyage began that he had come so close to the woman. She avoided his glance, murmuring a greeting as she passed. Ulsenn, however, directed a poisonous glare at Arflane.

His legs very slightly weak, Arflane clambered up the companionway to the bridge. Urquart was standing there, nursing his harpoon and looking to starboard. He nodded to Arflane as the two men entered the wheelhouse.

The helmsman saluted Arflane as they came in. The heavy wheel moved very slightly and the man corrected it.

Arflane went over to the big, crude compass. The chronometer next to it was centuries old and failing, but the equipment was still sufficient to steer a fairly accurate course. Arflane unrolled the chart and spread it on the table next to the compass, making a few calculations, then he nodded to himself, satisfied that he had been right.

'We'd better have an extra man on that wheel,' he decided. He put his head around the door of the wheelhouse and spoke to Urquart. 'Mr Urquart – we need another hand on the wheel. Will you get a man up here?'

Urquart moved towards the companionway.

'And put a couple more hands aloft, Mr Urquart,' Arflane called. 'We need plenty of lookouts. The edge's coming up.'

Arflane went back to the wheel and took it over from the helmsman. He gripped the spokes in both hands, letting the wheel turn a little of its own accord as its chains felt the great pull of the runners. Then, his eye on the compass, he turned the *Ice Spirit* several points to starboard.

When he was satisfied that they were established on their new course, he handed the wheel back to the helmsman as the second man came in.

'You've got an easy berth for a while, sailor,' Arflane told the new man. 'I want you to stand by to help with the wheel if it becomes necessary.'

Rorsefne followed Arflane out onto the bridge again. He looked towards the quarter-deck and saw Urquart speaking to a small group of hands. He pointed towards the harpooner. 'Urquart seems to have attached himself to you, too, captain. He must regard you as one of the family.' There was no sarcasm in his voice, but Arflane glanced at him suspiciously.

'I'm not sure of that.'

The young man laughed. 'Janek certainly isn't, that's certain. Did you see how he glared at you as we went by? I don't know why he came on this trip at all. He hates sailing. He has responsibilities in Friesgalt. Maybe it was to protect Ulrica from the attentions of a lot of hairy sailors!'

Again Arflane felt uncomfortable, not sure how to interpret Rorsefne's words. 'She's safe enough on this ship,' he growled.

'I'm sure she is,' Manfred agreed. 'But Janek doesn't know that. He treats her jealously. She might be a whole storehouse full of canvas, the value he puts on her!'

Arflane shrugged.

Manfred lounged against the rail, staring vacantly up into the shrouds where one of the lookouts appointed by Urquart was already climbing towards the crow's nest in the mainmast royals.

'I suppose this will be our last day on safe ice,' he said. 'It's been too uneventful for me so far, this voyage. I'm looking forward to some excitement when we reach the edge.'

Arflane smiled. 'I doubt if you'll be disappointed.'

The sky was still clear, blue and cloudless. The ice scintillated with the mirrored glare of the sun and the white, straining sails of the ship seemed to shimmer, reflecting in turn the brilliance of the ice. The runners could be heard faintly, bumping over the slightly uneven terrain, and sometimes a yard creaked above them. The mainmast lookout had reached his post and was settling himself into the crow's nest.

Rorsefne grinned. 'I hope I won't be. And neither will you, I suspect. I thought you enjoyed a little adventure yourself. This kind of voyage can't be much pleasure for you, either.'

The next day, the edge came into sight. It seemed that the horizon had drawn nearer, or had been cut off short, and Arflane, who had only passed close to the edge once in his life, felt himself shiver as he looked ahead.

The slope was actually fairly gradual, but from where he was positioned it looked as if the ground ended and the ship would plunge to destruction. It was as if he had come to the end of the world. In a sense he had; the world beyond the edge was completely unknown to him. Now he felt a peculiar kind of fear as the prow dipped and the ship began her descent.

On the bridge, Arflane put a megaphone to his lips.

'Get some grappling lines over the side, Mr Petchnyoff!' He shouted to his first officer on the quarter-deck: 'Jump to it!'

Petchnyoff hurried towards the lower deck to get a party together. Arflane watched as they began to throw out the grappling lines. The barbed prongs would slow their progress since all but the minimum sail had been taken in.

The grapples bit into the ice with a harsh shrieking and the ship began to lose speed. Then she began to wobble dangerously.

Hinsen was shouting from the wheelhouse. 'Sir!'

Arflane strode into the wheelhouse. 'What is it, Mr Hinsen?'

The two hands at the wheel were sweating, clinging to the wheel as they desperately tried to keep the *Ice Spirit* on course.

'The runners keep turning, sir,' Hinsen said in alarm. 'Just a little this way and that, but we're having difficulty holding them. We could go over at this rate. They're catching in the channels in the ice, sir.'

Arflane positioned himself between the two hands and took hold of the wheel. He realised at once what Hinsen meant. The runners were moving along shallow, iron-hard grooves in the ice caused by the gradual descent of ice flows over the centuries. There was a real danger of the ship's turning side-on, toppling over on the slope.

'We'll need two more hands on this,' Arflane said. 'Find two of the best helmsmen we've got, Mr Hinsen – and make sure they've got muscles!'

Kristoff Hinsen hurried from the wheelhouse while Arflane and the hands hung on to the wheel, steering as best they could. The ship had begun to bump noticeably now and her whole deck was vibrating.

Hinsen brought the two sailors back with him and they took over. Even with the extra hands the ship continued to bump and veer dangerously on the slope, threatening to go completely out of control. Arflane looked to the bow. The bottom of the incline was out of sight. The slope seemed to go on for ever.

'Stay in charge here, Mr Hinsen,' Arflane said. 'I'll go forward and see if I can make out what kind of ice is lying ahead of us.'

Arflane left the bridge and made his way along the shivering deck until he reached the forecastle. The ice ahead seemed the same as the kind they were on at the moment. The ship bumped, veered and then swung back on course again. The angle of the incline seemed to have increased and the deck sloped forward noticeably. As he turned back, Arflane saw Ulrica Ulsenn standing quite close to him. Janek Ulsenn was a little further behind her, clinging to the port rail, his eyes wide with alarm.

'Nothing to worry about, ma'am,' Arflane said as he approached her. 'We'll get her out of this.'

Janek Ulsenn had looked up and was calling his wife to him. With a hint of misery in her eyes, she turned back to her husband, gathered up her skirts and moved away from Arflane across the swaying deck.

It was the first time he had seen any emotion at all in her face since they had parted. He felt a certain amount of surprise. His concern for the safety of the ship had made him forget his feelings for her and he had spoken to her as he might have spoken to reassure any passenger.

He was tempted to follow her then, but the ship lurched suddenly off course again and seemed in danger of sliding sideways.

Arflane ran rapidly back towards the bridge, clambered up and dashed into the wheelhouse. Hinsen and the four sailors were wrestling with the wheel, their faces streaming with sweat and their muscles straining. Arflane grabbed a spoke and joined them as they tried to get the ship back on course.

'We're travelling too damned slowly,' he grunted. 'If we could make better speed there might be a chance of bouncing over the channels or even slicing through them.'

The ship lurched again and they grappled with the wheel. Arflane gritted his teeth as they forced the wheel to turn.

'Drop the bolts, sir!' Hinsen begged him. 'Drop the heavy anchors!'

Arflane scowled at him. A captain never dropped the heavy anchors unless the situation was insoluble.

'What's the point of slowing down, Mr Hinsen?' he said acidly. 'It's extra speed we need – not less.'

'Stop the ship altogether, sir – knock out the emergency bolt as well. It's our only chance.'

Arflane spat on the deck. 'Heavy anchors – emergency bolts – we're as likely to be wrecked using them as not! No, Mr Hinsen – we'll go down under full canvas!'

Hinsen almost lost control of the wheel again in his astonishment. He stared unbelievingly at his skipper.

'Full canvas, sir?'

The wheel jumped again and the ship's runners squealed jarringly as she began to lurch sideways. For several moments they strained at the wheel in silence until they had turned her back onto course.

'Two or three more like that, we'll lose her,' the hand nearest Arflane said with conviction.

'Aye,' Arflane grunted, glaring at Hinsen. 'Set all sail, Mr Hinsen.'

When Hinsen hesitated once more, Arflane impatiently left the wheel, grabbed a megaphone from the wall and went out onto the bridge.

He saw Petchnyoff on the quarter-deck. The man looked frightened. There was an atmosphere of silent panic on the ship.

'Mr Petchnyoff!' Arflane bellowed through the megaphone. 'Get the men into the yards! Full canvas!'

The shocked faces of the crew stared back at him. Petchnyoff's face was incredulous. 'What was that, sir?'

'Set all sails, Mr Petchnyoff. We need some speed so we can steer this craft!'

The ship shuddered violently and began to turn again.

'All hands into the shrouds!' Arflane yelled, dropped the megaphone and ran back into the wheelhouse to join the men on the wheel. Hinsen avoided his eye, evidently convinced that the captain was insane.

Through the wheelhouse port, Arflane saw the men scrambling aloft. Once again they barely succeeded in turning the ship back on her course. Everywhere the sails began to crack down and billow out as they caught the wind. The ship began to move even faster down the steepening slope.

Arflane felt a strong sense of satisfaction as the wheel became less hard to handle. It still needed plenty of control, but they were having no great difficulty in holding their course. Now the danger was that they would find an obstruction on the slope and crash into it at full speed.

'Get onto the deck, Mr Hinsen,' he ordered the frightened second officer. 'Tell Mr Urquart to go aloft with a megaphone and keep an eye out ahead!'

The ice on both sides of the ship was now a blur as the ship gathered speed. Arflane glanced through the port and saw Urquart climbing into the lower yards of the foremast.

The huge ship leaped from the surface and came down again hard with her runners creaking, but she had become increasingly easier to handle and there were no immediate obstacles in sight.

Urquart's face was calm as he glanced back at the wheelhouse, but the crew looked very frightened still. Arflane enjoyed their discomfort. He grinned broadly, his exhilaration tinged with some of their panic as he guided the ship down.

For an hour the schooner continued her rapid descent; it seemed that she sped down a slope that had no top and no bottom, for both were completely out of sight. The ship was handling easily, the runners hardly seeming to touch the ice. Arflane decided he could give the wheel to Hinsen. The second officer did not seem to relish the responsibility.

Going forward, Arflane climbed into the rigging to hang in the ratlines beside Urquart.

The harpooner smiled slightly. 'You're in a wild mood, skipper,' he said approvingly.

Arflane grinned back at him.

Before them, the ice sloped sharply, seeming to stretch on for ever. On both sides it raced past, the spray of ice from the runners falling on deck. Once a chip of ice caught Arflane on the mouth, drawing blood, but he hardly felt it.

Soon the slope began to level out and the ice became rougher, but the ship's speed hardly slowed at all. Instead the great craft bounced over the ice, rising and falling as if carried on a series of huge waves.

The sensation added to Arflane's good spirits. He began to relax. The danger was as good as past. Swinging in the ratlines, he hummed a tune, sensing the tension decrease throughout the ship.

Some time later Urquart's voice said quietly: 'Captain.' Arflane glanced at the man and saw that his eyes had widened. He was pointing ahead.

Arflane peered beyond the low ridges of ice and saw what looked like a greenish-black streak cutting across their path in the distance. He could not believe what it was. Urquart spoke the word.

'Crevasse, captain. Looks like a wide one, too. We'll never cross it.'

Since the last chart had been made, a crack must have appeared in the surface of the ice at the bottom of the slope. Arflane cursed himself for not having anticipated something like it, for new crevasses were common enough, particularly in terrain like this.

'And we'll never stop in time at this speed.' Arflane began to climb down the ratlines to the deck, trying to appear calm, hoping that the men would not see the crevasse. 'Even the heavy anchors couldn't stop us – we'd just flip right over and tumble into it wrong side up.'

Arflane reached the deck, trying to force himself to take some action when he was full of a deeply apathetic knowledge that there was no action to be taken.

Now the men saw the crevasse as the ship sped closer. A great shout of horror went up from them as they, too, realised that there was no chance of stopping.

As Arflane reached the companionway leading to the bridge, Manfred Rorsefne and the Ulsenns hurried onto the deck. Manfred shouted to Arflane as he began to climb the ladder.

'What's happening, captain?'

Arflane laughed bitterly. 'Take a look ahead!'

He reached the bridge and ran across to the wheelhouse, taking over the wheel from the ashen-faced Hinsen.

'Can you turn her, sir?'

Arflane shook his head.

The ship was almost on the crevasse now. Arflane made no attempt to alter course.

Hinsen was almost weeping with fear. 'Please, sir – try to turn her!'

The huge, yawning abyss rushed closer, the deep green ice of its sides flashing in the sunlight.

Arflane felt the wheel swing loose in his grasp; the front runners left firm ground and reached out over the crevasse as the ship hurtled into it.

Arflane sensed a peculiar feeling, almost of relief, as he anticipated the plunge downward. Then, suddenly, he began to smile. The schooner was travelling at such speed that she might just reach the other side. The far edge of the crevasse was still on the incline, lower than the opposite edge.

Then the schooner had leaped through the air and smashed down on the other side. She rolled, threatening to capsize. Arflane staggered, but managed to cling to the wheel and swing her hard over. She began to slow under her impact, the runners scraping and bumping.

'We're all right, sir!' Hinsen was grinning broadly. 'You got us across, sir!'

'Something did, Mr Hinsen. Here – take the wheel again.'

When Hinsen had taken over, Arflane went slowly out onto the bridge.

Men were picking themselves up from where they had fallen. One man lay still on the deck. Arflane left the bridge and made his way to where the hand was sprawled. He bent down beside him, turning him over. Half the bones in the body were broken. Blood crawled from the mouth. The man opened his eyes and smiled faintly at Arflane.

'I thought I'd had it that time, sir,' he said. The eyes closed and the smile faded. The man was dead.

Arflane got up with a sigh, rubbing his forehead. His whole body was aching from handling the wheel. There was a scuffle of movement as the hands moved to the rails to look back at the crevasse, but not one of them spoke.

From the foremast, where he still clung, Urquart was roaring with laughter. The harsh sound echoed through the ship and broke the silence. Some of the men began to cheer and shout, turning away from the rails and waving at Arflane. Stern-faced, the skipper made his way to the bridge and stood there for a moment while his men continued to cheer. Then he picked up his megaphone from where he had dropped it earlier and put it to his lips.

'All hands back aloft! Take in all sail! Jump to it!'

In spite of their excitement, the crew leaped readily to obey him and the yards were soon alive with scurrying men reefing the sails.

Petchnyoff appeared on the quarter-deck. He looked up at his skipper and gave him a strange, dark look. He wiped his sleeve across his forehead and moved down towards the lower deck.

'Better get those grapples in, Mr Petchnyoff,' Arflane shouted at him. 'We're out of danger now.'

He looked aft at the disappearing crevasse, congratulating himself on his good fortune. If he had not decided to go down at full speed they would have reached the crevasse and been swallowed by it. The ship had leaped forty feet.

He went back to the wheel to test and judge if the runners were in good order. They seemed to be working well, so far as their responses were concerned, but he wanted to satisfy himself that they had sustained no damage of any kind.

As the ship bumped to a gradual halt, all her sail furled, Arflane prepared to go over the side. He climbed down a rope ladder to the ice. The big runners were scratched and indented in places but were otherwise undamaged. He looked up admiringly at the ship, running his hand along one of her struts. He was convinced that no other vessel could have taken the impact after leaping the crevasse.

Clambering back to the deck, he encountered Janek Ulsenn. The man's lugubrious features were dark with anger. Ulrica stood just behind him, her own face flushed. Beside her, Manfred Rorsefne looked as amusedly insouciant as ever. 'Congratulations, captain,' he murmured. 'Great foresight.'

Ulsenn began to bluster. 'You are a reckless fool, Arflane! We were almost destroyed, every one of us! The men may think you anticipated that crevasse – but I know you did not. You have lost all their confidence!'

The statement was patently false. Arflane laughed and glanced about the ship.

'The men seem in good spirits to me.'

'Mere reaction, now that the danger's past. Wait until they start to think what you nearly did to them!'

'I'm inclined to think, cousin,' Manfred said, 'that this incident will simply restore their faith in their captain's good luck. The hands place great store on a skipper's luck, you know.'

Arflane was looking at Ulrica Ulsenn. She tried to glance away, but then she returned his look and Arflane thought that her expression might be one of admiration; then her eyes became cold and he shivered.

Manfred Rorsefne took Ulrica's arm and helped her back towards the gangway to her cabin, but Ulsenn continued to confront Arflane.

'You will kill us all, Brershillian!' He was apparently unaware that Arflane was paying little attention to him. His fear had caused him to forget his humiliation of a few days before. Arflane looked at him calmly.

'I will certainly kill somebody one day.' He smiled, and strode towards the foredeck under the admiring eyes of his crew and the enraged glare of Lord Janek Ulsenn.

With the plateau left behind, the ice became rough but easier to negotiate as long as the ship maintained a fair speed. The outline of the plateau was visible behind them for several days, a vast wall of ice rising into the clouds. The air was warmer now and there was less snow. Arflane felt uncomfortable as the heat increased and the air wavered, sometimes seeming to form odd shapes out of nothing. There were glaciers to be seen to all points ahead and, in the heat, Arflane became afraid that they would hit an ice break. Ice breaks occurred where the crust of the ice became thin over an underground river. A ship floundering in an ice break, since it had not been built for any kind of water, often had little chance of getting out and could easily sink.

As the ship moved on, travelling north-west by north, and nearing the equator, the crew and officers settled into a more orderly routine. Arflane's previous moods were forgotten; his luck was highly respected, and he had become very popular with the men.

Only Petchnyoff surprised Arflane in his refusal to forgive him for his earlier attitude. He spent most of his spare time with Janek Ulsenn; the two men could often be seen walking along the deck together. Their friendliness irritated Arflane to some extent. He felt that in a sense Petchnyoff was betraying him, but it was no business of his what company the young first officer chose, and he performed his duties well enough. Arflane even began to feel a slight sympathy for Ulsenn; he felt he should allow the man one friend on the voyage.

Urquart still had the habit of standing near him on the bridge and the gaunt harpooner had become a comfort to Arflane. They rarely talked, but the sense of comradeship between them had become very strong.

It was even possible for Arflane to see Ulrica Ulsenn without attempting to force some reaction from her, and he had come to tolerate Manfred Rorsefne's sardonic, bantering manner.

It was only the heat that bothered him now. The temperature had risen to several degrees above zero and the crew were working stripped to the waist. Arflane, against his will, had been forced to remove his heavy fur jacket. Urquart, however, had refused to take off any of his clothing and stoically bore his discomfort.

Arflane kept two lookouts permanently on watch for signs of thin ice. At night, he took in all sail and threw out grappling hooks so that the ship drifted very slowly.

The wind was poor and progress was slow enough during the day. From time to time mirages were observed, usually in the form of inverted glaciers, and Arflane had a great deal of difficulty explaining them to the men, who superstitiously regarded them as omens that had to be interpreted.

Until one day the wind dropped altogether, and they were becalmed.

Chapter Thirteen
The Harpoon

THEY WERE BECALMED for a week in the heat. The sky and ice glared shimmering copper under the sun. Men sat around in bunches, disconsolately playing simple games, or talking in low, miserable voices. Though stripped of most of their clothes, they still wore their snow visors. From a distance they looked like so many ungainly birds clustered on the deck. The officers kept them as busy as they could, but there was little to do. When Arflane gave a command the men obeyed less readily than before; morale was becoming bad.

Arflane was frustrated and his own temper was starting to fray again. His movements became nervous and his tone brusque.

Walking along the lower deck, he was approached by Fydur, the ship's bosun, a hairy individual with great dark beetling eyebrows.

'Excuse me, sir, sorry to bother you, but any idea how long we'll...'

'Ask the Ice Mother, not me.' Arflane pushed Fydur to one side, leaving the man sour-faced and angry.

There were no clouds to be seen; there was no sign of the weather changing. Arflane, brooding again on Ulrica Ulsenn, stalked about the ship with his face set in a scowl.

On the bridge one day he looked down and saw Janek Ulsenn and Petchnyoff talking with some animation to Fydur and a group of the hands. By the way in which some of them glanced at the bridge, Arflane could guess the import of the conversation. He glanced questioningly at Urquart, who was leaning against the wheelhouse; the harpooner shrugged.

'We've got to give them something to do,' Arflane muttered.

'Or tell them something to improve their spirits. There's the beginnings of a mutiny in that little party, Mr Urquart.'

'Aye, sir.' Urquart sounded almost smug.

Arflane frowned, then made up his mind. He called to the second officer, at his post on the quarter-deck.

'Get the men together, Mr Hinsen. I want to talk to them.'

'All hands in line!' Hinsen shouted through his megaphone. 'All hands before the bridge. Captain talking.'

Sullenly the hands began to assemble, many of them scowling openly at Arflane. The little group with Ulsenn and Petchnyoff straggled up and stood behind the main press of men.

'Mr Petchnyoff. Will you come up here!' Arflane looked sharply at his first officer. 'You too, please, Mr Hinsen. Bosun – to your post.'

Slowly Petchnyoff obeyed the command and Fydur, with equally poor grace, took up his position facing the men.

When all the officers were behind him on the bridge, Arflane cleared his throat and gripped the rail, leaning forward to look down at the crew.

'You're in a bad mood, lads, I can see. The sun's too hot and the wind's too absent. There isn't a damned thing I can do about getting rid of the first or finding the second. We're becalmed and that's all there is to it. I've seen you through one or two bad scrapes already – so maybe you'll help me sweat this one out. Sooner or later the wind will come.'

'But *when*, sir?' A hand spoke up; one of those who had been conversing with Ulsenn.

Arflane glanced grimly at Fydur. The bosun pointed a finger at the hand. 'Hold your tongue.'

Arflane was in no mood to answer the remark directly. He paused, then continued.

'Perhaps we'll get a bit of wind when discipline aboard this ship tightens up. But I can't predict the weather. If some of you are so damned eager to be on the move, then I suggest you get out onto the ice and pull this tub to her destination!'

Another man muttered something. Fydur silenced him.

Arflane leaned down. 'What was that, bosun?'

'Wanted to know just what our destination was, sir,' Fydur replied. 'I think a lot of us...'

'That's why I called you together,' Arflane went on. 'We're bound for New York.'

Some of the men laughed. To go to New York was a metaphor meaning to die – to join the Ice Mother.

'New York,' Arflane repeated, glaring at them. 'We've charts that show the city's position. We're going north to New York. Questions?'

'Aye, sir – they say New York doesn't exist on this world, sir. They say it's in the sky – or – somewhere...' The tall sailor who spoke had a poor grasp of metaphysics.

'New York's as solid as you and on firm ice,' Arflane assured him. 'The Lord Pyotr Rorsefne saw it. That was where he came from when I found him. It was in his will that we should go there. You remember the will? It was read out soon after the lord died.'

The men nodded, murmuring to one another.

'Does that mean we'll see the Ice Mother's court?' another sailor asked.

'Possibly,' Arflane said gravely.

The babble that broke out among the men rose higher and higher. Arflane let them talk for a while. Most of them had received the news dubiously at first, but now some of them were beginning to grin with excitement, their imagination captured.

After a while Arflane told the bosun to quiet them down. As the babble died, and before Arflane could speak, the clear, haughty tones of Janek Ulsenn came over the heads of the sailors. He was leaning against the mizzen mast, toying with a piece of rope. 'Perhaps that is why we are becalmed, captain?'

Arflane frowned. 'What do you mean by that, Lord Ulsenn?'

'It occurred to me to wonder that the reason we are getting no wind is because the Ice Mother isn't sending us any. She does not want us to visit Her in New York!' Ulsenn was deliberately playing on the superstition of the hands. This new idea set them babbling again.

This time Arflane roared to them to stop talking. He glowered at Ulsenn, unable to think of a reply that would satisfy his men.

Urquart stepped forward then and leaned his harpoon against the rail. Still dressed in all his matted furs, his blue eyes cold and steady, he seemed, himself, to be some demigod of the ice. The men fell silent.

'What do we suffer from?' he called harshly. 'From cold impossible to bear? No! We suffer from *heat*! Is that the Ice Mother's weapon? Would She use Her enemy to stop us? No! You're fools if you think She's against us. When has the Ice Mother decreed that men should not sail to Her in New York? Never! I know the doctrine better than any man aboard. I am the Ice Mother's pledged servant; my faith in Her is stronger than anything you could feel. I *know* what the Ice Mother wishes; She wishes us to sail to New York. She wishes us to pay Her court so that when we return to the Eight Cities we may silence all who doubt Her! Through Captain Arflane She fulfils Her will; that's why I sail with him. That's why we all sail with him. It's our destiny.'

The harsh, impassioned tones of Urquart brought complete silence to the crew, but they had no apparent effect on Ulsenn.

'You're listening to a madman talk,' he called. 'And another madman's in command. If we follow these two our only destiny is a lonely death on the ice.'

There was a blur of movement, a thud; Urquart's great harpoon flew across the deck over the heads of the sailors to bury itself in the mast, an inch from Ulsenn's head. The man's face went white and he staggered back, eyes wide. He began to sputter something, but Urquart vaulted over the bridge rail to the deck and pushed his way through the crowd to confront the aristocrat.

'You speak glibly of death, Lord Ulsenn,' Urquart said savagely. 'But you had best speak quietly or perhaps the Ice Mother may see fit to take you to Her bosom sooner than you might wish.' He began to tug the harpoon from the mast. 'It is for the sake of your kind that we sail. Best let a little of your blood tonight, my tame little lord, to console the Ice Mother – lest all your blood be let before this voyage ends.'

With tears of rage in his eyes, Ulsenn hurled himself at the massive harpooner. Urquart smiled quietly and picked the man up to throw him, almost gently, to the deck. Ulsenn landed on his face and rolled over, his nose bleeding. He crawled back, away from the smiling giant. The men were laughing now, almost in relief.

Arflane's lips quirked in a half smile, too; then all his humour vanished as Ulrica Ulsenn ran over the deck to her injured husband, knelt beside him and wiped the blood from his face.

Manfred Rorsefne joined them on the bridge.

'Shouldn't you have a little better control over your officers, captain?' he suggested blandly.

Arflane wheeled to face him. 'Urquart knows my will,' he said.

Hinsen was pointing to the south. 'Captain – big clouds coming up aft!'

Within an hour the sails were filled with a wind that also brought chilling sleet, forcing them to huddle back into their furs.

They were soon under way through the grey morning. The crew were Arflane's men again. Ulsenn and his wife had disappeared below and Manfred Rorsefne had joined them; but, for the moment, Arflane insisted that all his officers stay with him on the bridge while he ordered full canvas set and sent the lookouts aloft.

Hinsen and Petchnyoff waited expectantly until he turned his attention back to them. He looked at Petchnyoff sombrely for a time; tension grew between them before he turned away, shrugging. 'All right, you're dismissed.'

With Urquart a silent companion beside him, Arflane laughed quietly as the ship gathered speed.

Two nights later Arflane lay in his bunk unable to sleep. He listened to the slight bumping of the runners over the uneven surface of the ice, to the sleet-laden wind in the rigging and the creak of the yards. All the sounds were normal; yet some sixth sense insisted that something was wrong. Eventually he swung from his bunk, climbed into his clothes, buckled his flenching cutlass around his waist and went on deck. He had been ready for trouble of some kind ever since he had watched Petchnyoff, Ulsenn and Fydur talking together. Urquart's oratory would have had little effect on them, he was certain. Fydur might be loyal again, but Ulsenn certainly wasn't; on the few occasions when he had showed himself above decks it had been invariably with Petchnyoff.

Arflane looked up at the sky. It was still overcast and there were few stars visible. The only light came from the moon and the lights that burned dimly in the wheelhouse. He could just make out the silhouettes of the lookouts in the crosstrees, high above, the bulky forms of the lookouts forward and aft. He looked back at the wheelhouse. Petchnyoff should be on watch; he could see no-one but the helmsman on the bridge.

He climbed up and strode into the wheelhouse. The helmsman gave him a short nod of recognition. 'Sir.'

'Where's the officer of the watch, helmsman?'

'He went forward, sir, I believe.'

Arflane pursed his lips. He had seen no-one forward but the man on watch. Idly he walked over to the compass, comparing it with a chart.

They were a full three degrees off course. Arflane looked up sharply at the helmsman. 'Three degrees off course, man! Have you been sleeping?'

'No, sir!' The helmsman looked aggrieved. 'Mr Petchnyoff said our course was true, sir.'

'Did he?' Arflane's face clouded. 'Alter your course, helmsman. Three degrees starboard.'

He left the bridge and began to search the ship for Petchnyoff. The man could not be found. Arflane went below to the lower deck where the hands lay in their hammocks. He slapped the shoulder of the nearest man. The sailor grunted and cursed.

'What's up?'

'Captain here. Get on deck with the helmsman. Know any navigation?'

'A bit, sir,' the man mumbled as he swung out of his hammock, scratching his head.

'Then get above to the bridge. Helmsman'll tell you what to do.'

Arflane stamped back through the dark gangways until he reached the passengers' quarters. Janek Ulsenn's cabin faced his wife's. Arflane hesitated and then knocked heavily on Ulsenn's door. There was no reply. He turned the handle. The door was not locked. He went in.

The cabin was empty. Arflane had expected to find Petchnyoff there. The pair must be somewhere on the ship. No lights shone in any of the other cabins.

His rage increasing with every pace, Arflane returned to the quarter-deck, listening carefully for any murmur of conversation which would tell him where the two men were.

A voice from the bridge called to him.

'Any trouble, sir?'

It was Petchnyoff.

'Why did you desert your watch, Mr Petchnyoff?' Arflane shouted. 'Come down here!'

Petchnyoff joined him in a few moments. 'Sorry, sir, I –'

'How long were you gone from your post?'

'A little while, sir. I had to relieve myself.'

'Come with me to the bridge, Mr Petchnyoff.' Arflane clambered up the companionway and pushed on into the wheelhouse. He stood by the compass as Petchnyoff entered. The two men by the wheel looked curiously at the first officer.

'Why did you tell this man that we were on course when we were three degrees off?' Arflane thundered.

'Three degrees, sir?' Petchnyoff sounded offended. 'We weren't off course, sir.'

'Weren't we, Mr Petchnyoff? Would you like to consult the charts?'

Petchnyoff went to the chart table and unrolled one of the maps. His voice sounded triumphant as he said, 'What's wrong, sir? This is the course we're following.'

Arflane frowned and came over to look at the chart. Peering at it closely, he could see where a line had been erased and another one drawn in. He looked at the chart he had consulted earlier. That showed the original course. Why should someone tamper with the charts? And if they did, why make such a small alteration that was bound to be discovered? It could be Ulsenn making mischief, Arflane supposed. Or even Petchnyoff trying to cause trouble.

'Can you suggest how this chart came to be changed, Mr Petchnyoff?'

'No, sir. I didn't know it had been. Who could have…?'

'Has anyone been here tonight – a passenger, perhaps? Any member of the crew who had no business here?'

'Only Manfred Rorsefne earlier, sir. No-one else.'

'Were you here the whole time?'

'No, sir. I went to inspect the watch.'

Petchnyoff could easily be lying. He was in the best position to alter the chart. There again, the helmsman could have been bribed by Manfred Rorsefne to let him look at the charts. There was no way of knowing who might be to blame.

Arflane tapped his gloved fingers on the chart table.

'We'll look into this in the morning, Mr Petchnyoff.'

'Aye, aye, sir.'

As he left the wheelhouse, Arflane heard the lookout shouting. The man's voice was thin against the sounds of the wind-blown sleet. The words, however, were quite clear.

'*Ice break! Ice break!*'

Arflane ran to the rail, trying to peer ahead. An ice break at night was even worse than an ice break in the day. The ship was moving slowly; there might be time to throw out grapples. He shouted up to the bridge. 'All hands on deck. All hands on deck, Mr Petchnyoff!'

Petchnyoff's voice began to bellow through a megaphone, repeating Arflane's orders.

In the darkness, men began to surge about in confusion. Then the whole ship lurched to one side and Arflane was thrown off his feet. He slid forward, grabbing the rail and hauling himself up, struggling for a footing on the sloping deck as men yelled in panic.

Over the sound of their voices, Arflane heard the creaking and cracking as more ice gave way under the weight of the ship. The vessel dipped further to port.

Arflane swore violently as he staggered back towards the wheelhouse. It was too late to drop the heavy anchors; now they might easily help push the ship through the ice.

Around him in the night, pieces of ice were tossed high into the air to smash down on the deck. There was a hissing and gurgling of disturbed water, a further creaking as new ice gave way.

Arflane rushed into the wheelhouse, grabbed a megaphone from the wall and ran back to the bridge.

'All hands to the lines! All hands over the starboard side! Ice break! Ice break!'

Elsewhere Petchnyoff shouted specific orders to hands as they grabbed mooring cables and ran to the side. They knew their drill. They had to get over the rail with the cables and try to drag the ship back off the thin ice by hand. It was the only chance of saving her.

Again the ice creaked and collapsed. Spray gushed; slabs of ice began to groan upwards and press against the vessel's sides. Water began to creep along the deck.

Arflane swung his leg over the bridge rail and leaped down to the deck. The starboard runners were now lifting into the air; the *Ice Spirit* was in imminent danger of capsizing.

Hinsen, half dressed, appeared beside Arflane. 'This is a bad one, sir – we're too deep in by the looks of it. If the ice directly beneath us goes, we don't stand a chance…'

Arflane nodded curtly. 'Get over the side and help them haul. Is someone looking after the passengers?'

'I think so, sir.'

'I'll check. Do your best, Mr Hinsen.'

Arflane slid down towards the door below the bridge, pushing it open and stumbling down the gangway towards the passengers' cabins.

He passed both Manfred Rorsefne's cabin and Ulsenn's. When he reached Ulrica Ulsenn's cabin he kicked the door open and rushed in.

There was no-one there.

Arflane wondered grimly whether his passengers had somehow left the ship before the ice break had come.

Chapter Fourteen
The Ice Break

THE MONSTROUS SHIP lurched heavily again, swinging Arflane backwards into the doorframe of Ulrica Ulsenn's cabin.

Manfred Rorsefne's door opened. The young man was dishevelled and gasping; blood from a head wound ran down his face. He tried to grin at Arflane, staggered into the gangway and fell against the far wall.

'Where are the others?' Arflane yelled above the sound of creaking and shattering ice. Rorsefne shook his head.

Arflane stumbled along the gangway until he could grab the handle of the door to Janek Ulsenn's cabin. The ship listed, this time to port, as he opened the door and saw Ulsenn and his wife lying against the far bulkhead. Ulsenn was whimpering and Ulrica was trying to get him to his feet. 'I can't make him move,' she said. 'What has happened?'

'Ice break,' Arflane replied tersely. 'The ship's half in the water already. You've all got to get overboard at once. Tell him that.' Then he grunted impatiently and grabbed Ulsenn by the front of his jacket, hauling the terrified man over his shoulder. He gestured towards the gangway. 'Can you help your cousin, Ulrica – he's hurt.'

She nodded and pulled herself to her feet, following him out of the cabin.

Manfred managed to smile at them as they came out, but his face was grey and he was hardly able to stand. Ulrica took his arm.

As they fought their way out to the swaying deck, Urquart joined them; the harpooner shouldered his lance and helped Ulrica with Manfred, who seemed close to fainting.

Around them in the black night, slabs of ice still rose and fell, crashing onto the deck, but the ship slipped no further into the break.

Arflane led them to the rail, grasped a dangling line and swung himself and his burden down the side, jumping the last few feet to the firm ice. Dimly seen figures milled around; over his head, the mooring lines running from the rail strummed in the darkness. Urquart and Ulrica Ulsenn were somehow managing between them to lower Rorsefne down. Arflane waited until they were all together and then jerked the trembling form of Janek Ulsenn from his shoulder and let the man fall to the ice. 'Get up,' he said curtly. 'If you want to live you'll help the men with the lines. Once the ship goes, we're as good as dead.'

Janek Ulsenn climbed to his feet; he scowled at Arflane and looked around him angrily until he saw Ulrica and Manfred standing with Urquart. 'This man,' he said, pointing at Arflane, 'this man has once again put our lives in jeopardy by his senseless –'

'Do as he says, Janek,' Ulrica said impatiently. 'Come. We'll both help with the lines.'

She walked off into the darkness. Ulsenn scowled back at Arflane for a second and then followed her. Manfred swayed, looking faintly apologetic. 'I'm sorry, captain, I seem…'

'Stay out of the way until we've done what we can,' Arflane instructed him. 'Urquart – let's get on with it.'

With the harpooner beside him he pushed through the lines of men heaving on the ropes until he found Hinsen in the process of hammering home a mooring spike.

'What are our chances?' Arflane asked.

'We've stopped the slide, sir. There's firm ice here and we've got a few pegs in. We might do it.' The bearded second officer straightened up. He pointed to the next gang who were struggling to keep their purchase on their line. 'Excuse me, sir. I must attend to that.'

Arflane strode along, inspecting the gangs of sailors as they slipped and slithered on the ice, sometimes dragged forward by the weight of the ship; but now her angle of list was less than forty-five degrees and Arflane saw that there was a reasonable chance of saving the *Ice Spirit*. He stopped to help haul on a line and Urquart moved up to the next team to do the same.

Slowly the ship wallowed upright. The men cheered; then the sound died as the *Ice Spirit*, drawn by the mooring lines, continued to slide towards them under the momentum. The ship began to loom down.

'Get back!' Arflane cried. 'Run for it!'

The crew panicked, skidding and sliding on the ice as they ran. Arflane heard a scream as a man slipped and fell beneath the side-turned runners. Others died in the same way before the ship slowed and bumped to a stop.

Arflane began to walk forward, calling back over his shoulder. 'Mr Urquart, will you attend to the burial of those men?'

'Aye, aye, sir,' Urquart replied from the darkness.

Arflane moved around to the port side of the great ship, inspecting the damage. It did not seem to be very bad. One runner was slightly askew, but that could be rectified by a little routine repair work. The ship could easily continue her journey.

'All right,' he shouted. 'Everybody except the burial gang on board. There's a runner out of kilter and we'll need a working party on it right away. Mr Hinsen, will you do what's necessary?'

Arflane clambered up a loose mooring line and returned to the poop deck. He took a megaphone from its place in the wheelhouse and shouted through it: 'Mr Petchnyoff. Come up to the bridge, please.'

Petchnyoff joined him within a few minutes. He looked enquiringly at Arflane. His deceptively foolish expression had increased and, seeing him through the darkness, Arflane thought he had the face of an imbecile. He wondered vaguely if, in fact, Petchnyoff were unstable. If that were the case, then it was just possible that the first officer had himself altered the course and for no reason but petty spite and a wish to create trouble for a captain he disliked.

'See that the ship's firmly moored while the men make the repairs, Mr Petchnyoff.'

'Aye, aye, sir.' Petchnyoff turned away to obey the order.

'And when that's done, Mr Petchnyoff, I want all officers and passengers to assemble in my cabin.'

Petchnyoff glanced back at him questioningly.

'See to it, please,' Arflane said.

'Aye, aye, sir.' Petchnyoff left the bridge.

Shortly before dawn the three officers, Petchnyoff, Hinsen and Urquart, together with the Ulsenns and Manfred Rorsefne, stood in Arflane's cabin while the captain sat at his table and studied the charts he had brought with him from the wheelhouse.

Manfred Rorsefne's injury had not been as bad as it had looked; his head was now bandaged and his colour had returned. Ulrica Ulsenn stood apart from her husband who leaned against the bulkhead beside Petchnyoff. Urquart and Hinsen stood together, their arms folded across their chests, waiting patiently for their captain to speak.

At length Arflane, who had remained deliberately silent for longer than he needed to, looked up, his expression bleak. 'You know why I have these charts here, Mr Petchnyoff,' he said. 'We've already discussed the matter. But most of you others won't understand.' He drew a long breath. 'One of the charts was tampered with in the night. The helmsman was misled by it and altered course by a full three points. As a result we landed in the ice break and we were almost killed. I don't believe anyone could have known we were heading for the break, so it's plain that the impulse to spoil the chart came from some irresponsible desire to irritate and inconvenience me – or maybe to delay us for some reason I can't guess. Manfred Rorsefne was seen in the wheelhouse and...'

'Really, captain!' Manfred's voice was mockingly offended. 'I was in the wheelhouse, but I hardly know one point of the compass from another. I certainly could not have been the one.'

Arflane nodded. 'I didn't say I suspected you, but there's no doubt in my mind that one of you must have made the alteration. No-one else has access to the wheelhouse. For that reason, I've asked you all here so that the one who did change the chart can tell me. I'll take no disciplinary action in this case. I'm asking this so I can punish the helmsman on duty if he was bribed or threatened into letting the chart be changed. In the interests of all our safety it is up to me to find out who it was.'

There was a pause. Then one of them spoke. 'It was I. And I did not bribe the helmsman. I altered the chart days ago while it was still in your cabin.'

'It was a foolish thing to do,' Arflane said wearily. 'But I thought it would have been you. Presumably this was when you were trying to get us to turn back.'

'I still think we should turn back,' Ulsenn said. 'Just as I altered the chart, I'll use any means in my power to convince either you or the men of the folly of this venture.'

Arflane stood up, his expression suddenly murderous. Then he controlled himself and leaned forward over the table, resting his weight on his palms. 'If there's any more trouble aboard of that kind, Lord Ulsenn,' he said icily, 'I will not hold an inquiry. Neither will I ignore it. I will make no attempt to be just. I will simply put you in irons for the rest of the voyage.'

Ulsenn shrugged and scratched ostentatiously at the side of his face.

'Very well,' Arflane told them. 'You may all leave. I expect the officers to pay attention to any suspicious action Lord Janek Ulsenn might make in future, and I want it reported. I'd also appreciate the co-operation of the other passengers. In future I will treat Ulsenn as an irresponsible fool – but he can remain free so long as he doesn't endanger us again.'

Angered by the slight, Ulsenn stamped from the cabin and slammed the door in the faces of his wife and Manfred Rorsefne as they attempted to follow him.

Hinsen was smiling as he left, but the faces of Petchnyoff and Urquart were expressionless, doubtless for very different reasons.

Chapter Fifteen
Urquart's Fear

THE SHIP SAILED on, with the crew convinced of their skipper's outstanding luck. The weather was good, the wind strong and steady, and they made excellent speed. The ice was clear of glaciers or other obstructions as long as they followed old Rorsefne's chart closely and thus they were able to sail both day and night.

One day, as Arflane stood with Urquart on the bridge, they saw a glow on the horizon that resembled the first signs of dawn. Arflane checked the big old chronometer in the wheelhouse. The time was a few minutes before six bells in the middle watch – three in the morning.

Arflane rejoined Urquart on the bridge. The harpooner's face was troubled. He sniffed the air, turning his head this way and that, his flat bone earrings swinging. Arflane could smell nothing.

'Do you know what it means?' he asked Urquart.

Urquart grunted and rubbed at his chin. As the ship sped closer to the source of the reddish light Arflane himself began to notice a slight difference in the smell of the air, but he could not define it.

Without a word Urquart left the bridge and began to walk forward, hefting his harpoon up and down in his right hand. He seemed unusually nervous.

Within an hour the glow on the horizon filled half the sky and illuminated the ice with blood-red light. It was a bizarre sight; the smell on the breeze had become much stronger, an acrid, musty odour that was entirely unfamiliar to Arflane. He, too, began to feel troubled. The air seemed to be warmer, the whole deck awash with the strange light. Ivory beams, belaying pins, hatch covers and the whale skulls in the prow all reflected it; the face of the helmsman in the wheelhouse was stained red, as were the features of the men on watch who looked questioningly up at him. Night was virtually turned to day, though overhead the sky was pitch-black – blacker than it normally seemed now that it contrasted with the lurid glare ahead.

Hinsen came out on deck and climbed the companionway to stand beside Arflane. 'What is it, sir?' He shuddered violently and moistened his lips.

Arflane ignored him, re-entered the wheelhouse and consulted Rorsefne's map. He had not been using the old man's original, but a clearer copy. Now he unrolled the original and peered at it in the red, shifting light from the horizon. Hinsen joined him, staring over his shoulder at the chart.

'Damn,' Arflane murmured. 'It's here and we ignored it. The writing's so hard to read. Can you see what it says, Mr Hinsen?'

Hinsen's lips moved as he tried to make out the tiny printed words that Rorsefne had inscribed in his failing hand before he died. He shook his head and gave a weak smile of apology. 'Sorry, sir.'

Arflane tapped two fingers on the chart. 'We need a scholar for this.'

'Manfred Rorsefne, sir? I think he might be something of a scholar.'

'Fetch him, please, Mr Hinsen.'

Hinsen nodded and left the wheelhouse. The air bore an unmistakeable stink now. Arflane found it hard to breath, for it carried dust that clogged his mouth and throat.

The light, now tinged with yellow, was unstable. It flickered over the ice and the swiftly travelling ship. Sometimes part of the schooner was in shadow, sometimes it was illuminated completely. Arflane was reminded of something that had frightened him long ago. He was beginning to guess the meaning of old Rorsefne's script well before Manfred Rorsefne, rubbing at his eyes with one finger, appeared in the wheelhouse.

'It's like a great fire,' he said, and glanced down at the chart Arflane was trying to show him. Arflane pointed to the word.

'Can you make that out? Can you read your uncle's writing better than us?'

Manfred frowned for a moment and then his face cleared. 'Fire mountains,' he said. He looked at Arflane with some anxiety, his air of insouciance gone completely.

'Fire...' Arflane, too, made no attempt to disguise the horror he felt. Fire, in the mythology of the ice, was the arch-enemy of the Ice Mother. Fire was evil. Fire destroyed. It melted the ice. It warmed things that should naturally be cold.

'We'd better throw out the grapples, captain,' Hinsen said thickly.

But Arflane was consulting the chart. He shook his head. 'We'll be all right, Mr Hinsen, I hope. This course takes us through the fire mountains, as far as I can tell. We don't get close to them at all – not enough to endanger ourselves at any rate. Rorsefne's chart's been good up to now. We'll hold our course.'

Hinsen looked at him nervously but said nothing.

Manfred Rorsefne's initial anxiety seemed over. He was looking at the horizon with a certain curiosity. 'Flaming mountains,' he exclaimed. 'What wonders we're finding, captain!'

'I'll be happier when this particular wonder's past,' Arflane said with an attempt at humour. He cleared his throat twice, slapped his hand against his leg and paced about the wheelhouse. The helmsman's face caught his attention; it was a parody of fear. Arflane forgot his own nervousness in his laughter at the sight. He slapped the helmsman on the shoulder. 'Cheer up, man. We'll sail miles to starboard of the nearest if that chart's accurate!' Rorsefne joined in his laughter and even Hinsen began to smile.

'I'll take the wheel, sir, if you like,' Hinsen said. Arflane nodded and tapped the helmsman's arm.

'All right, lad,' Arflane told him as Hinsen took over. 'You get below. You don't want to be blinded.'

He went out onto the bridge, his face tense as he looked towards the horizon.

Soon they could see the individual mountains silhouetted in the distance. Red and yellow flames and rolling black smoke spouted from their craters and luminous crimson lava streamed down their sides; the heat was appalling and the poisoned air stung and clogged their lungs. From time to time a cloud of smoke would drift across the ship, making strange patterns of light and shadow on the decks and sails. The earth shook slightly and across the ice came the distant rumble of the volcanoes.

The scene was so unfamiliar to them that they could hardly believe in its reality; it was like a nightmare landscape. Though the night was turned almost as bright as day and they could see for miles in all directions, the light was lurid and shifted constantly, and when not obscured by the smoke they could make out the dark sky with the stars and the moon clearly visible.

Arflane noticed that the others were sweating as much as he. He looked for Urquart and saw the outline of the harpooner forward, unmistakeable with his barbed lance held close to his body. He left the bridge and moved through the weird light towards Urquart, his shadow huge and distorted.

Before he reached the harpooner, he saw him fall to both knees on the deck near the prow. The harpoon was allowed to fall in front of him. Arflane hurried forward and saw, even in that light, that Urquart's face was as pale as the ice. The man was muttering to himself and his body was racked by violent shuddering; his eyes were firmly shut. Perhaps it was the nature of the light, but on his knees Urquart looked impossibly small, as if the fire had melted him. Arflane touched his shoulder, astounded by this change in a man whom he regarded as the soul of courage and self-control.

'Urquart? Are you ill?'

The lids opened, revealing prominent whites and rolling orbs. The savage features, scarred by wind, snow and frostbite, twitched.

To Arflane the display was almost a betrayal; he had looked to Urquart as his model. He reached out and grasped the man's broad shoulders, shaking him ferociously. 'Urquart! Come on, man! Pull yourself out of this!'

The eyes fell shut and the strange muttering continued; Arflane furiously smacked the harpooner across the face with the back of his hand. 'Urquart!'

Urquart flinched at the blow but did nothing; then he flung

himself face forward on the deck, spreadeagled as if in cringing obeisance to the fire. Arflane turned, wondering why so many emotions in him should be disturbed. He strode rapidly back to the bridge, saying nothing to Manfred Rorsefne as he rejoined him. Men were coming out on deck now; they looked both frightened and fascinated as they recognised the source of the light and the stink.

Arflane raised the megaphone to his lips.

'Back to your berths, lads. We're sailing well away from the mountains and we'll be through them by dawn. Back below. I want you fresh for your duties in the morning.'

Reluctantly, muttering among themselves, the sailors began to drift back below decks. As the last little knot of men climbed the companionway to their quarters, Janek Ulsenn emerged from below the bridge. He glanced quickly at Arflane and then moved along the deck to stand by the mizzen mast. Petchnyoff came out a few seconds later and also began to make his way towards the mizzen. Arflane bawled at him through the megaphone.

'To your berth, Mr Petchnyoff! It's not your turn on watch. The passengers can do what they want – but you've your duty to remember.'

Petchnyoff paused, then glared at Arflane defiantly. Arflane motioned with the megaphone. 'We don't need your help, thanks. Get back to your cabin.'

Petchnyoff now turned towards Ulsenn, as if expecting orders. Ulsenn signed with his hand and in poor grace Petchnyoff went back below. Shortly afterwards Ulsenn followed him. Arflane reflected that they were probably nursing their imagined wrongs together, but as long as there were no more incidents to affect the voyage he did not care what the two men said to each other.

A little while later he ordered the watch changed and gave orders to the new lookouts to keep a special eye open for any sign of an ice break or the steam that would indicate one of the small warm lakes fed by underground geysers that would doubtless occur in this region. That done, he decided to get some sleep himself. Hinsen had been roused well before his turn on watch was due to begin, so Manfred Rorsefne agreed to share the morning watch with him.

Before he opened the door of his cabin, Arflane glanced back along the deck. The red, shadowy light played over Urquart's still-prone figure as if in a victory dance. Arflane rubbed at his beard, hesitated, then went into his cabin and closed the door firmly behind him. He stripped off his coat and laid it on the lid of his chest, then went to the water barrel in one corner and poured water into a bowl, washing himself clean of the sweat and dust that covered him. The image of Urquart preyed on his mind; he could not understand why the man should be so affected by the fire mountains. Naturally, since fire was their ancient enemy, they were all disturbed by it, but Urquart's fear was hysterical.

Arflane drew off his boots and leggings and washed the rest of his body. Then he lay down on the wide bunk, finding it difficult to sleep. Finally he fell into a fitful doze, rising as soon as the cook knocked on the door with his breakfast. He ate little, washed again and dressed, then went out on deck, noticing at once that Urquart was no longer there.

The morning was overcast and in the distance the fire mountains could still be seen; in the daylight they did not look so alarming. He saw that the sails had been blackened by the smoke and that the whole deck was smothered in a light, clinging grey ash.

The ship was moving slowly, the runners hampered by the ash that also covered the ice for miles around, but the fire mountains were well behind them. Arflane dragged his body up to the bridge, feeling tired and ill. The men on deck and in the yards were also moving with apparent lethargy. Doubtless they were all suffering from the effects of the fumes they had inhaled the night before.

Petchnyoff met him on the bridge. The first officer was taking his turn on watch and made no attempt to greet him; Arflane ignored him, went into the wheelhouse and took a megaphone from the wall. He returned to the bridge and called to the bosun who was on duty on the middle deck. 'Lets get this craft shipshape, bosun. I want this filth cleaned off every surface and every inch of sail as soon as you like.'

Fydur acknowledged Arflane's order with a movement of his hand. 'Aye, aye, sir.'

'You'd better get the grappling anchors over the side,' Arflane continued. 'We'll rest in our lines for today while she's cleaned. There must be warm ponds somewhere. We'll send out a party to find them and bring us back some seal meat.'

Fydur brightened up at the prospect of fresh meat. 'Aye, aye, sir,' he said emphatically.

Since they had been becalmed Fydur seemed to have avoided the company of Ulsenn and Petchnyoff, and Arflane was sure the bosun was no longer in league with them.

At Fydur's instructions the sails were taken in and the grappling anchors heaved over the side so that their sharp barbs dug into the ice, gradually slowing the ship to a stop. Then a party of mooring hands was sent over to drive in the pegs and secure the *Ice Spirit* until she was ready to sail.

As soon as the men were working on cleaning the schooner and volunteers had been called to form an expedition to look for the warm ponds and the seals that would inevitably be there, Arflane went below and knocked on the door of Urquart's small cabin. There was a stirring sound and a heavy thump from within, but no reply.

'Urquart,' Arflane said hesitantly. 'May I enter? It's Arflane.'

Another noise from the cabin and the door was flung open, revealing Urquart standing, glaring. The harpooner was stripped to the waist. His long, sinewy arms were covered in tiny tattoos and his muscled torso seemed to be a mass of white scars. But it was the fresh wound across his upper arm that Arflane noticed. He frowned and pointed to it.

'How did this happen?'

Urquart grunted and stepped backwards into the crowded cabin that was little bigger than a cupboard. His chest of belongings filled one bulkhead and the other was occupied by the bunk. Furs were scattered over the bunk and on the floor.

Urquart's harpoon stood against the opposite bulkhead, dominating the tiny cabin. A knife lay on top of the chest and beside it was a bowl of blood.

Then Arflane realised the truth, that Urquart had been letting his blood for the Ice Mother. It was a custom that had almost died out in recent generations. When a man had blasphemed or otherwise offended the Ice Mother, he let his blood and poured it into the ice, giving the deity some of his warmth and life. Arflane wondered what particular blasphemy Urquart felt he had committed; though doubtless it was something to do with his hysteria of the previous night.

Arflane nodded enquiringly at the bowl. Urquart shrugged. He seemed to have regained his composure.

Arflane leaned against the bunk. 'What happened last night?' he asked as casually as he could. 'Did you offend against the Mother?'

Urquart turned his back and began to pull on his matted furs. 'I was weak,' he grunted. 'I lay down in fear of the enemy.'

'It offered us no harm,' Arflane told him.

'I know the harm it offered,' Urquart said. 'I have done what I think I should do. I hope it is enough.' He tied the thongs of his coat and went to the porthole, opening it; then he picked up the bowl and flung the blood through the opening to the ice beyond.

Closing the porthole, he threw the bowl back on top of the chest, crossed to grasp his harpoon and then paused, his face as rigid as ever, waiting for Arflane to let him pass.

Arflane remained where he was.

'I ask only in a spirit of comradeship, Urquart,' he said. 'If you could tell me about last night...'

'You should *know*,' Urquart growled. 'You are Her chosen one, not I.' The harpooner was referring to the Ice Mother, but Arflane was still puzzled. However, it was evident that Urquart did not intend to say anything more. Arflane turned and walked into the gangway. Urquart followed him, stooping a little to avoid striking his head on the beams. They went out on deck. Urquart strode forward without a word and began to climb the rigging of the foremast. Arflane watched him until he reached the upper yards, his harpoon still cradled in his arm, to hang in the rigging and stare back at the fire mountains that were now so far away.

Arflane gestured impatiently, feeling offended at the other's surliness, and went back to the bridge.

By evening the ship had been cleaned of every sign of the ash that had fouled her, but the hunting party had not returned. Arflane wished that he had given them more explicit instructions and told them to return before dusk, but he had not expected any difficulty locating a pond. They had taken a small sailboat and should have made good speed; now the *Ice Spirit* would have to wait until they returned and it was unlikely that they would travel at night, which meant that the next morning would doubtless be wasted as well. Arflane was to take the middle watch again and would need to be on duty at midnight. He decided, as the watch rang the four bells terminating the first dog-watch, that he would try to sleep to catch up on the rest he had been unable to get the previous night.

The evening was quiet as he took one quick tour around the deck before going to his cabin. There were a few muffled sounds of men working, a little subdued conversation, but nothing to disturb the air of peace about the ship.

Arflane glanced up as he reached the foredeck. Urquart was still there, hanging as if frozen in the rigging. It was more difficult to understand the strange harpooner than Arflane had thought. Now he was too tired to bother. He walked back towards the bridge and entered his cabin. He was soon asleep.

Chapter Sixteen
The Attack

Automatically, Arflane awoke as seven bells were struck above, giving him half an hour before his spell on watch. He washed and dressed and prepared to leave his cabin by the outer door; then a knock came on the door that opened on the gangway between decks.

'Enter,' he said brusquely.

The handle turned and Ulrica Ulsenn stood facing him. Her face was slightly flushed but she looked at him squarely. He began to smile, opening his arms to take her, but she shook her head as she closed the door behind her.

'My husband is planning – with Petchnyoff – to – murder you, Konrad.' She pressed her hand against her forehead. 'I overheard him talking with Petchnyoff in his cabin. Their idea is to kill you and bury your body in the ice tonight.' She looked at him steadily. 'I came to tell you,' she said, almost defiantly.

Arflane folded his arms across his chest and smiled. 'Thanks. Petchnyoff knows it's my turn on watch soon. They'll doubtless try to do it when I'm taking my tour around the deck. I wondered if they had that in mind. Well...' He went over to his chest, took out the belt that held his scabbarded flenching cutlass and buckled it on. 'Perhaps this will end it, at last.'

'You'll kill him?' she asked quietly.

'There'll be two of them. It's fair.'

He stepped towards her and she drew away. He put out a hand and gripped the back of her neck, drawing her to him. She came reluctantly, then slid her arms around his waist as he stroked her hair. He heard her give a deep, racking sigh.

'I really didn't expect him to go this far,' Arflane said after a moment. 'I thought he had some sense of honour.'

She looked up at him, tears in her eyes. 'You've taken it all away from him,' she said. 'You have humiliated him too much…'

'From no malice,' he said. 'Self-protection.'

'So you say, Konrad.'

He shrugged. 'Maybe. But if he'd challenged me openly I would have refused. I can easily kill him. I would have refused the chance. But now…'

She moaned and flung herself away from him onto the bunk, covering her face. 'Either way it would be murder, Konrad. You've driven him to this!'

'He's driven himself to it. Stay here.'

He left the cabin and stepped lightly on deck; his manner was apparently casual as he glanced around him. He turned and ascended the companionway to the bridge. Manfred Rorsefne was there. He nodded agreeably to Arflane. 'I sent Hinsen below an hour ago. He seemed tired.'

'It was good of you,' Arflane said. 'Do you know if the hunting party's returned yet?'

"They're not back.'

Arflane muttered abstractedly, looking up into the rigging.

'I'll get to my own bunk now, I think,' Rorsefne said. 'Goodnight, captain.'

'Goodnight.' Arflane watched Rorsefne descend to the middle deck and disappear below.

The night was very still. The wind was light and made little sound. Arflane heard the man on the upper foredeck stamp his feet to get the stiffness from them.

It would be an hour before he took his second tour. He guessed that it would be then that Ulsenn and Petchnyoff would attempt to stage their attack. He went into the wheelhouse. As they were at anchor, there was no helmsman on duty; doubtless this was why the two men had chosen this night to try to kill him; there would be no witness.

Arflane climbed down to the middle deck, looking aft at the distant but still visible glow from the fire mountains. It reminded him of Urquart; he looked up to see the harpooner still hanging high above in the rigging of the foremast. He could expect no help from Urquart that night.

There was a commotion in the distance; he ran to the rail to peer into the night, seeing a few figures running desperately towards the ship. As they came closer he recognised some of the men from the hunting party. They were shouting incoherently. He dashed to the nearest tackle locker and wrenched it open, pulling out a rope ladder. He rushed back to the rail and lowered the ladder down the side; he cupped his hands and yelled over the ice.

'This way aboard!'

The first of the sailors ran up and grabbed the ladder, beginning to climb. Arflane heard him panting heavily. He reached down and helped the man aboard; he was exhausted, his furs torn and his right hand bleeding from a deep cut.

'What happened?' Arflane asked urgently.

'Barbarians, sir. I've never seen anything like them. They're not like true men at all. They've got a camp near the warm ponds. They saw us before we saw them... They use – *fire*, sir.'

Arflane tightened his lips and slapped the man on the back. 'Get below and alert all hands.'

As he spoke, a streak of flame flew out of the night and took the man on lower foredeck watch in the throat. Arflane saw it was a burning arrow. The man shrieked and beat at the flames with his gloved hands, then toppled backwards and fell dead on the deck.

All at once the night was alive with blazing arrows. The sailors on deck flung themselves flat in sheer terror, reacting with a fear born of centuries of conditioning. The arrows landing on the deck burned out harmlessly, but some struck the canvas and here and there a furled sail was beginning to flare. Sailors screamed as arrows struck them and their furs caught light. A man went thrashing past Arflane, his whole body a mass of flame. There were small fires all over the ship.

Arflane rushed for the bridge and began to ring the alarm bell furiously, yelling through the megaphone: 'All hands on deck! Break out the weapons! Stand by to defend ship!'

From the bridge he could see the leading barbarians. In shape they were human, but were completely covered in silvery white hair; otherwise they seemed to be naked. Some carried flaming brands; all had quivers of arrows slung over their shoulders and powerful-looking bone bows in their hands.

As armed sailors began to hurry on deck, holding bows of their own and harpoons and cutlasses, Arflane called to the archers to aim for the barbarians with the brands. Further down the deck, Petchnyoff commanded a gang forming a bucket chain to douse the burning sails.

Arflane leaned over the bridge rail, shouting to Fydur as he ran past with an armful of bows and half a dozen quivers of arrows. 'Let's have one of those up here, bosun!'

The bosun paused to select a weapon and a quiver and throw it up to Arflane, who caught it deftly, slung the quiver over his shoulder, nocked an arrow to the string and drew it back. He let fly at one of the brand-holding barbarians and saw the man fall to the ice with the arrow protruding from his mouth.

A fire arrow flashed towards him. He felt a slight shock as the thing buried itself in his left shoulder, but if there was pain he did not notice it in his panic. The flames unnerved him. With a shaking hand he dragged out the shaft and flung it from him, slapping at his blazing coat until the flames were gone. Then he was forced to grip the rail with his right hand and steady himself; he felt sick.

After a moment he picked up the bow and fitted another arrow to the string. There were only two or three brands to be seen on the ice now and the barbarians seemed to be backing off. Arflane took aim at one of the brands and missed, but another arrow from somewhere killed the man. Arrows were still coming out of the night; most of them were not on fire. The silvery coats of the barbarians made them excellent targets and they were beginning to fall in great numbers before the retaliating shafts of Arflane's archers.

The attack had come on the port side; now some premonition made Arflane turn and look to starboard.

Unnoticed, nearly a dozen white-furred barbarians had managed to climb to the deck. They rushed across the deck, their red eyes blazing and their mouths snarling. Arflane shot one and stooped to grasp the megaphone to bellow a warning. He dropped the bow, drew his cutlass and vaulted over the bridge rail to the deck.

One of the barbarians shot at him and missed. Arflane slammed the hilt of his sword into the man's face and swung at another, feeling the sharp blade bite into his neck. Other sailors had joined him and were attacking the barbarians, whose bows were useless at such close quarters. Arflane saw Manfred Rorsefne beside him; the man grinned at him.

'This is more like it, eh, captain?'

Arflane threw himself at the barbarians, stabbing one clumsily in the chest and hacking him down. Elsewhere the sailors were butchering the remaining barbarians who were hopelessly outnumbered.

The noise of the battle died away and there were no more barbarians to kill. On Arflane's right a man was screaming.

It was Petchnyoff. There were two fire arrows in him, one in his groin and the other near his heart. A few little flames burned on his clothes and his face was blackened by fire. By the time Arflane reached him, he was dead.

Arflane went back to the bridge. 'Set all sail! Let's move away from here.'

Men began to scramble eagerly up the masts to let out the sails that were undamaged. Others let go the anchor lines and the ship began to move. A few last arrows rattled on the deck. They glimpsed the white forms of the barbarians disappearing behind them as the huge ship gathered speed.

Arflane looked back, breathing heavily and clutching his wounded shoulder. Still there was little pain. Nonetheless it would be reasonable to attend to it. Hinsen came along the deck. 'Take charge, Mr Hinsen,' he said. 'I'm going below.'

At his cabin door Arflane hesitated, then changed his mind and moved along to pass through the main door into the gangway where the passengers had their cabins. The gangway joined the one which led to his cabin, but he did not want to see Ulrica for the moment. He walked along the dark passage until he reached Ulsenn's door.

He tried the handle. It was locked. He leaned back and smashed his foot into it; the exertion made his wounded shoulder begin to throb painfully. He realised that the wound was worse than he had thought.

Ulsenn wheeled as Arflane entered. The man had been standing looking out of the port.

'What do you mean by…?'

'I'm arresting you,' Arflane said, his voice slurred by the pain.

'For what?' Ulsenn drew himself up. 'I…'

'For plotting to murder me.'

'You're lying.'

Arflane had no intention of mentioning Ulrica's name. Instead he said: 'Petchnyoff told me.'

'Petchnyoff is dead.'

'He told me as he died.'

Ulsenn tried to shrug but the gesture was pathetic. 'Then Petchnyoff was lying. You've no evidence.'

'I need none. I'm captain.'

Ulsenn's face crumpled as if he were about to weep. He looked utterly defeated. This time his shrug was one of despair. 'What more do you want from me, Arflane?' he said wearily.

For a moment Arflane regarded Ulsenn and pitied him, the pity tinged with his own guilt. The man looked up at him almost pleadingly. 'Where's my wife?' he said.

'She's safe.'

'I want to see her.'

'No.'

Ulsenn sat down on the edge of his bunk and put his face in his hands.

Arflane left the cabin and closed the door. He went to the door that led out to the deck and called two sailors over. 'Lord Ulsenn's cabin is the third on the right. He's under arrest. I want you to put a bar across the door and guard it until you're relieved. I'll wait while you get the materials you need.'

When Arflane had supervised the work and the bar was in place with the door chained to it to his satisfaction, he walked down the gangway to his own cabin.

Ulrica had fallen asleep in his bunk. He left her where she lay and went to her cabin, packing her things into her chest and dragging it up the gangway under the curious eyes of the sailors on guard outside Ulsenn's door. He got the chest into his cabin and heaved it into place beside his; then he took off his clothes and inspected the shoulder. It had bled quite badly but had now stopped. It would be all right until morning.

He lay down beside Ulrica.

Chapter Seventeen

The Pain

IN THE MORNING the pain in his shoulder had increased; he winced and opened his eyes.

Ulrica was already up, turning the spigot of the big water barrel, soaking a piece of cloth. She came back to the bunk, face pale and set, and began to bathe the inflamed shoulder. It only seemed to make the pain worse.

'You'd better find Hinsen,' he told her. 'He'll know how to treat the wound.'

She nodded silently and began to rise. He grasped her arm with his right hand.

'Ulrica. Do you know what happened last night?'

'A barbarian raid, wasn't it?' she said tonelessly. 'I saw fire.'

'I meant your husband – what I did.'

'You killed him.' Again the statement was flat.

'No. He didn't attack me as he'd planned. The raid came too soon. He's in his cabin – confined there until the voyage is over.'

She smiled a little ironically then. 'You're merciful,' she said finally, then turned and left the cabin.

A little while later she came back with Hinsen and the second officer did what was necessary. She helped him bind Arflane's shoulder. Infection was rare on the ice plains, but the wound would take some time to heal.

'Thirty men died last night, sir,' Hinsen told him, 'and we've six wounded. The going will be harder with us so undermanned.'

Arflane grunted agreement. 'I'll talk to you later, Mr Hinsen. We'll need Fydur's advice.'

'He's one of the dead, sir, along with Mr Petchnyoff.'

'I see. Then you're now first officer and Urquart second. You'd better find a good man to promote to bosun.'

'I've got one in mind, sir – Rorchenof. He was bosun on the *Ildiko Ulsenn.*'

'Fine. Where's Mr Urquart?'

'In the fore rigging, sir. He was there during the fight and he's been there ever since. He wouldn't answer when I called to him, sir. If I hadn't noticed his breathing I'd have thought he was frozen.'

'See if you can get him down. If not, I'll attend to it later.'

'Aye, aye, sir.' Hinsen went out.

Ulrica was standing near her trunk, looking down at it thoughtfully.

'Why are you so depressed?' he said, turning his head on the pillow and looking directly at her.

She shrugged, sighed and sat down on the trunk, folding her arms under her breasts. 'I wonder how much of this we have engineered between us,' she said.

'What do you mean?'

'Janek – the way he has behaved. Couldn't we have forced him to do what he did, so that we could then feel we'd acted righteously? Couldn't this whole situation have been brought about by us?'

'I didn't want him aboard in the first place. You know that.'

'But he had no choice. He was forced to join us by the manner of *our* actions.'

'I didn't ask him to plan to kill me.'

'Possibly you forced him to that point.' She clasped her hands together tightly. 'I don't know.'

'What do you want me to do, Ulrica?'

'I expect you to do no more.'

'We are together.'

'Yes.'

Arflane sat up in his bunk. 'This is what has happened,' he said, almost defensively. 'How can we change it now?'

Outside, the wind howled and snow was flung against the porthole. The ship rocked slightly to the motion of the runners over the rough ice; Arflane's shoulder throbbed in pain. Later she came and lay beside him and together they listened as the storm grew worse outside.

Feeling the force of the driving snow against his face and body, Arflane felt better as he left the cabin in the late afternoon and, with some difficulty, climbed the slippery companionway to the bridge where Manfred Rorsefne stood.

'How are you, captain?' Rorsefne asked. His voice was at once distant and agreeable.

'I'm fine. Where are the officers?'

'Mr Hinsen's aloft and Mr Urquart went below. I'm keeping an eye on the bridge. I'm feeling quite professional.'

'How's she handling?'

'Well, under the circumstances.' Rorsefne pointed upwards, through the rigging, partially obscured by the wall of falling snow. Dark shapes, bundled in furs, moved among the crosstrees. Sails were being reefed. 'You picked a good crew, Captain Arflane. How is my cousin?' The question was thrown in casually, but Arflane did not miss the implication.

The ship began to slow. Arflane cast a glance towards the wheelhouse before he answered Rorsefne. 'She's all right. You know what's happened?'

'I anticipated it.' Rorsefne smiled quietly and raised his head to stare directly aloft.

'You...' Arflane was unable to frame the question. 'How...?'

'It's not my concern, captain,' Rorsefne interrupted. 'After all, you've full command over all who sail in this schooner.' The irony was plain. Rorsefne nodded to Arflane and left the bridge, climbing carefully down the companionway.

Arflane shrugged, watching Rorsefne walk through the snow that was settling on the middle deck. The weather was getting worse and would not improve; winter was coming and they were heading north. With a third of their complement short they were going to be in serious trouble unless they could make the best possible speed to New York. He shrugged again; he felt mentally and physically exhausted and was past the point where he could feel even simple anxiety.

As the last light faded Urquart emerged from below the bridge and looked up at him. The harpooner seemed to have recovered himself; he hefted his lance in the crook of his arm and swung up the companionway to stand by the rail next to Arflane. He seemed to be taking an almost sensual pleasure in the bite of the wind and snow against his face and body. 'You are with that woman now, captain?' he said remotely.

'Yes.'

'She will destroy you.' Urquart spat into the wind and turned away. 'I will see to clearing the hatch covers.'

Watching Urquart as he supervised the work on the deck, Arflane wondered suddenly if the harpooner's warnings were inspired by simple jealousy of Arflane's relationship with the woman who was, after all, Urquart's half-sister. That would also explain the man's strong dislike of Ulsenn.

Arflane remained needlessly on deck for another hour before eventually going below.

Chapter Eighteen

The Fog

Autumn rapidly became winter as the ship moved northwards. The following weeks saw a worsening of the weather, the overworked crew of the ice schooner finding it harder and harder to manage the vessel efficiently. Only Urquart seemed grimly determined to ensure that she stayed on course and made the best speed she could. Because of the almost constant snowstorms, the ship travelled slowly; New York was still several hundred miles distant.

Most of the time it was impossible to see ahead; when the snow was not falling, fogs and mists would engulf the great ship, often so thick that visibility extended for less than two yards. In Arflane's cabin the lovers huddled together, united as much by their misery as their passion. Manfred Rorsefne had been the only one who bothered to visit Janek Ulsenn; he reported to Arflane that the man seemed to be bearing his imprisonment with fortitude if not with good humour. Arflane received the news without comment. His native taciturnity had increased to the point where on certain days he would not speak at all and would lie motionless in his bunk from morning to night. In such a mood he would not eat and Ulrica would lie with him, her head on his shoulder, listening to the slow bump of the runners on the ice and the creak of the yards, the sound of the snow falling on the deck above their heads. When these sounds were muffled by the fog it seemed that the cabin floated apart from the rest of the ship. In these moments Arflane and Ulrica would feel their passion return and would make violent love as if there were no time left to them. Afterwards Arflane would go out to the fog-shrouded bridge to stand there and learn from Hinsen, Urquart or Manfred Rorsefne the distance they had travelled. He had become a sinister figure to the men, and even the officers, with the exception of Urquart, seemed uneasy in his presence. They noticed how Arflane had appeared to age; his face was lined and his shoulders stooped. He rarely looked at them directly but stared abstractedly out into the falling snow or fog. Every so often, apparently without realising it, Arflane would give a long sigh and he would make some nervous movement, brushing rime from his beard or tapping at the rail. While Hinsen and Rorsefne felt concerned for their skipper, Urquart appeared disdainful and tended to ignore him. For his part, Arflane did not care whether he saw Hinsen and Rorsefne or not, but made evident efforts to avoid Urquart whenever he could. On several occasions when he was standing on the bridge and saw Urquart advancing, he hastily descended the companionway before the second officer could reach him. Generally Urquart did not appear to notice this retreat, but once he was seen to smile a trifle grimly when the door of Arflane's cabin closed with a bang as the harpooner climbed to the bridge.

Hinsen and Rorsefne talked often. Rorsefne was the only man aboard in whom Hinsen could confide his own anxiety. The atmosphere among the men was not so much one of tension as of an apathy reflected in the sporadic progress of the ship.

'It often seems to me that we'll stop altogether,' Hinsen said, 'and live out the rest of our lives in a timeless shroud of fog. Everything's gotten so hazy...'

Rorsefne nodded sympathetically. The young man did not seem so much depressed as careless about their fate.

'Cheer up, Mr Hinsen. We'll be all right. Listen to Mr Urquart. It's our destiny to reach New York...'

'I wish the captain would tell the men that,' Hinsen said gloomily. 'I wish he'd tell them something – anything.'

Rorsefne nodded, his face for once thoughtful.

Chapter Nineteen
The Light

THE MORNING AFTER Hinsen's and Rorsefne's conversation Arflane was awakened by the sound of knocking on the outer door of his cabin. He rose slowly, pushing the furs back over Ulrica's sleeping body. He pulled on his coat and leggings and unbolted the door.

Manfred Rorsefne stood there; behind him the fog swirled, creeping into the cabin. The young man's arms were folded over his chest; his head was cocked superciliously to one side. 'May I speak to you, captain?'

'Later,' Arflane grunted, casting a glance at the bunk where Ulrica was stirring.

'It's important,' Manfred said, advancing.

Arflane shrugged and stepped back to let Rorsefne enter as Ulrica opened her eyes and saw them both. She frowned. 'Manfred…'

'Good morning, cousin,' Rorsefne said. His voice had a touch of humour in it which neither Arflane nor Ulrica could understand. They looked at him warily.

'I spoke to Mr Hinsen this morning,' Rorsefne said, walking over to where Arflane's chest stood next to Ulrica's. 'He thinks the weather will be clearing soon.' He sat down on the chest. 'If he's right we'll be making better speed shortly.'

'Why should he think that?' Arflane asked without real interest.

'The fog seems to be dispersing. There's been little snow for some days. The air is drier. I think Mr Hinsen's experienced enough to make the right judgement by these signs.'

Arflane nodded, wondering what was Rorsefne's real reason for the visit. Ulrica had turned over, burying her face in the fur of the pillows and drawing the coverings over her neck.

'How's your shoulder?' Rorsefne asked casually.

'All right,' Arflane grunted.

'You don't appear well, captain.'

'There's nothing wrong with me,' Arflane said defensively. He straightened his stooped back a little and walked slowly to the bowl by the water barrel. He turned the spigot and filled the bowl, beginning to wash his lined face.

'Morale is bad on board,' Rorsefne continued.

'So it seems.'

'Urquart is keeping the men moving, but they need someone with more experience to make them do their best,' Rorsefne said meaningly.

'Urquart seems to be managing very well,' Arflane said.

'So he is – but that's not my point.'

Surprised by the directness of Rorsefne's implication, Arflane turned, drying his face on his sleeve. 'It's not your business,' he said.

'Indeed, you're right. It's the captain's business, surely, to deal with the problems of his own ship. My uncle gave you this command because he thought you were the only man who could be sure of getting the *Ice Spirit* to New York.'

'That was long ago,' said Arflane obliquely.

'I'm refreshing your memory, captain.'

'Is that all your uncle wanted? It would seem to me that he envisaged very well what would happen on the voyage. He all but offered me his daughter, Rorsefne, just before he died.' In the bunk Ulrica buried her head deeper in the pillows.

'I know. But I don't think he completely understood either your character or hers. He saw something as happening naturally. He didn't think Janek would come with us. I doubt if my uncle knew the meaning of conscience in the personal sense. He did not understand how guilt could lead to apathy and self-destruction.'

Arflane's tone was defensive when he replied, 'First you discuss the condition of morale on board, and now you tell me what Ulrica and myself feel. What did you come here for?'

'All these things are connected. You know that very well, captain.'

Rorsefne stood up. Although actually the smaller he seemed to dominate Arflane. 'You're ill and your sickness is mental and emotional. The men understand this, even if they're too inarticulate to voice it. We're desperately short-handed. Where we need a man doing the work of two, we find he'll scarcely perform what were his normal duties before the attack. They respect Urquart, but they fear him too. He's alien. They need a man with whom they feel some kinship. You were that man. Now they begin to think you're as strange as Urquart.'

Arflane rubbed his forehead. 'What does it matter now? The ship can hardly move with the weather as it is. What do you expect me to do, go out there and fill them full of confidence so they can then sit around on deck singing songs instead of mumbling while they wait for the fog to lift? What good will it do? What action's *needed*? None.'

'I told you that Hinsen feels the weather's clearing,' Rorsefne said patiently. 'Besides, you know yourself how important a skipper's manner is, whatever the situation. You should not reveal so much of yourself out there, captain.'

Arflane began to tie the thongs of his coat, his fingers moving slowly. He shook his head and sighed again.

Rorsefne took a step closer. 'Go around the ship, Captain Arflane. See if the sailor in you is happy with her condition. The sails are slackly furled, the decks are piled with dirty snow, hatch covers left unfastened, rigging badly lashed. The ship's as sick as you yourself. She's about ready to rot!'

'Leave me,' Arflane said, turning his back on Rorsefne. 'I don't need moral advice from you. If you realised the problem…'

'I don't care. My concern's for the ship, those she carries, and her mission. My cousin loved you because you were a better man than Ulsenn. You had the strength she knew Ulsenn didn't possess. Now you're no better than Ulsenn. You've forfeited the right to her love. Don't you sense it?'

Rorsefne went to the cabin door, pulled it open and stalked out, slamming it behind him.

Ulrica sat in the bunk and looked up at Arflane, her expression questioning.

'You think what he thinks, eh?' Arflane said.

'I don't know. It's more complicated…'

'That's true,' Arflane murmured bitterly. His anger was rising; it seemed to lend new vitality to his movements as he stalked about the cabin gathering his outer garments.

'He's right,' she said reflectively, 'to remind you of your duties as captain.'

'He's a passenger – a useless piece of cargo – he has no right to tell me anything!'

'My cousin's an intelligent man. What's more he likes you, feels sympathetic towards you…'

'That's not apparent. He criticises without understanding…'

'He does what he thinks he should – for your benefit. He does not care for himself. He's never cared. Life is a game for him that he feels he must play to the finish. The game must be endured, but he doesn't expect to enjoy it.'

'I'm not interested in your cousin's character. I want him to lose interest in mine.'

'He sees you destroying yourself – and me,' she said with a certain force. 'It is more than you see.'

Arflane paused, disconcerted. 'You think the same, then?'

'I do.'

He sat down suddenly on the edge of the bunk. He looked at her; she stared back, her eyes full of tears. He put out a hand and stroked her face. She took his hand in both of hers and kissed it.

'Oh, Arflane, what has happened…?'

He said nothing, but leaned across her and kissed her on the lips, pulling her to him.

An hour later he got up again and stood by the bunk, looking thoughtfully at the floor.

'Why should your cousin be so concerned about me?' he said.

'I don't know. He's always liked you.' She smiled. 'Besides – he may be concerned for his own safety if he thinks you're not running the ship properly.'

He nodded. 'He was right to come here,' he said finally. 'I was wrong to be so angry. I've been weak. I don't know what to do, Ulrica. Should I have accepted this commission? Should I have let my feelings towards you rule me so much? Should I have imprisoned your husband?'

'These are personal questions,' she said gently, 'which do not involve the ship or anyone aboard save ourselves.'

'Don't they?' He pursed his lips. 'They seem to.' He straightened his shoulders. 'Nonetheless, Manfred was right. You're right. I should be ashamed...'

She pointed to the porthole. 'Look,' she said. 'It's getting lighter. Let's go on deck.'

There were only wisps of fog in the air now and thin sunlight was beginning to pierce the clouds above them. The ship was moving slowly under a third of her canvas.

Arflane and Ulrica walked hand in hand along the deck.

The browns and whites of the ship's masts and rigging, the yellow of her ivory, all were mellowed by the sunlight. There was an occasional thud as her runners crossed an irregularity in the ice, the distant voice of a man in the rigging calling to a mate, a warm smell on the air. Even the slovenliness of the decks seemed to give the ship a battered, rakish appearance and did not offend Arflane as much as he had expected. The sunlight began to break rapidly through the clouds, dispersing them, until the far horizon could be made out from the rail. They were crossing an expanse of ice bordered in the distance by unbroken ranges of glaciers of a kind Arflane had never seen before. They were tall and jagged and black. The ice in all directions was dappled with yellow light as the clouds broke up and pale blue sky could be seen above.

Ulrica gripped his arm and pointed to starboard. Sweeping down from the clearing sky, as if released by the breaking up of the clouds, came a flock of birds, their dark shapes wheeling and diving as they came closer.

'Look at their colour!' she exclaimed in surprise.

Arflane saw the light catch the shimmering plumage of the leading birds and he, too, was astonished. The predominant colour was gaudy green. He had seen nothing like it in his life; all the animals he knew had muted colours necessary for survival in the icelands. The colour of these birds disturbed him. The glinting flock soon passed, heading towards the dark glaciers on the horizon. Arflane stared after them, wondering why they affected him so much, wondering where they came from.

Behind him a voice sounded from the bridge. 'Get those sails set. All hands aloft.' It belonged to Urquart.

Arflane gently removed Ulrica's hand from his arm and walked briskly along the deck towards the bridge. He climbed the companionway and took the megaphone from the hands of the surprised harpooner. 'All right, Mr Urquart. I'll take over.' He spoke with some effort.

Urquart made a little grunting sound in his throat and picked up his harpoon from where he had rested it against the wheelhouse. He stumped down the companionway and took a position on the quarter-deck, his back squarely to Arflane.

'Mr Hinsen!' Arflane tried to put strength and confidence into his voice as he called to the first officer, who was standing by one of the forward hatches. 'Will you bring the bosun up?'

Hinsen acknowledged the order with a wave of his hand and shouted to a man who was in the upper shrouds of the mainmast. The man began to swing down to the deck; together he and Hinsen crossed to the bridge. The man was tall and heavily built, with a neatly trimmed beard as red as Arflane's.

'You're Rorchenof, bosun on the *Ildiko Ulsenn*, eh?' Arflane said as they presented themselves below him on the quarter-deck.

'That's right, sir – before I went to the whaling.' There was character in Rorchenof's voice and he spoke almost challengingly, with a trace of pride.

'Good. So when I say to set all sail you'll know what I mean. We've a chance to make up our speed. I want those yards crammed with every ounce of canvas you can get on them.'

'Aye, aye, sir.' Rorchenof nodded.

Hinsen clapped the man on the shoulder and the bosun moved to take up his position. Then the first officer glanced up at Arflane doubtfully, as if he did not place much faith in Arflane's new decisiveness.

'Stand by, Mr Hinsen.' Arflane watched Rorchenof assemble the men and send them into the rigging. The ratlines were soon full of climbing sailors. When he could see that they were ready, Arflane raised the megaphone to his lips.

'Set all sail!' he called. 'Top to bottom, stem to stern.'

Soon the whole ship was dominated by a vast cloud of swelling canvas and the ship doubled, quadrupled her speed in a matter of minutes, leaping over the gleaming ice.

Hinsen plodded along the deck and began to retie a poorly spliced line. Now that the fog had cleared he could see that there were many bad splicings about the ship; they would have to be attended to before nightfall.

A little later, as he worked on a second knot, Urquart came and stood near him, watching.

'Well, Mr Urquart – skipper's himself again, eh?' Hinsen studied Urquart's reaction closely.

A slight smile crossed the gaunt harpooner's face. He glanced up at the purple and yellow sky. The huge sails interrupted his view; they stretched out, full and sleek as a gorged cow-whale's belly. The ship was racing as she had not raced since the descent of the plateau. Her ivory shone, as did her metal, and her sails reflected the light. But she was not the proud ship she was when she had first set sail. She carried too many piles of dirty snow for that, her hatches did not fit as snugly as they had, and her boats did not hang as straight and true in their davits.

Urquart reached up with one ungloved hand and his red, bony fingers caressed the barbs of his harpoon. The mysterious smile was still on his lips but he made no attempt to answer Hinsen. He jerked his head towards the bridge and Hinsen saw that Manfred Rorsefne stood beside the captain. Rorsefne had evidently only just arrived; they saw him slap Arflane's shoulder and lean casually on the rail, turning his head from left to right as he surveyed the ship.

Hinsen frowned, unable to guess what Urquart was trying to tell him. 'What's Rorsefne to do with this?' he asked. 'If you ask me, we've him to thank for the captain's revival of spirit.'

Urquart spat at a melting pile of snow close by. 'They're skippering this craft now, between them,' he said. 'He's like one of those toys they make for children out of seal cubs. You put a string through the muscles of the mouth and pull it and the creature smiles and frowns. Each of them has a line. One pulls his lips up, the other pulls them down. Sometimes they change lines.'

'You mean Ulrica Ulsenn and Manfred Rorsefne?'

Urquart ran his hand thoughtfully down the heavy shaft of his harpoon. 'With the Ice Mother's help he'll escape them yet,' he said. 'We've a duty to do what we can.'

Hinsen scratched his head. 'I wish I could follow you better, Mr Urquart. You mean you think the skipper will keep his good mood from now on?'

Urquart shrugged and walked away, his stride long and loping as ever.

Chapter Twenty
The Green Birds

In spite of the uneasy atmosphere aboard, the ship made excellent speed, sailing closer and closer to the glacier range. Beyond that range lay New York; they were now swinging onto a course east by north, and this meant the end of their journey was in sight. The good weather held, though Arflane felt it unreasonable to expect it to remain so fine all the way to New York.

Across the blue ice plains, beneath a calm, clear sky, the *Ice Spirit* sailed, safely skirting several ice breaks and sometimes sighting barbarians in the distance. The silver-furred nomads offered them no danger and were passed quickly.

Urquart began to take up his old position on the bridge beside the skipper, though the relationship between the two men was not what it had been; too much had happened to allow either to feel quite the same spirit of comradeship.

Leaving twin black scars in the snow and ice behind her, her sails bulging, her ivory-decorated hull newly polished and her battered decks tidied and cleaned of snow, the ice schooner made her way towards the distant glaciers.

It was Urquart who first sighted the herd. It was a long way off on their starboard bow, but there was no mistaking what it was. Urquart jabbed his lance in the direction of the whales and Arflane, by shielding his eyes, could just make them out, black shapes against the light blue of the ice.

'It's not a breed I know,' Arflane said, and Urquart shook his head in agreement. 'We could do with the meat,' the captain added.

'Aye,' grunted Urquart, fingering one of his bone earrings. 'Shall I tell the helmsman to alter course, skipper?'

Arflane decided that, practical reasons aside, it would be worth stopping in order to provide a diversion for the men. He nodded to Urquart, who strode into the wheelhouse to take over the great wheel from the man on duty.

Ulrica came up on deck and glanced at Arflane. He smiled down at her and signed for her to join him. She sensed Urquart's antipathy and for that reason rarely went to the bridge; she came up a little reluctantly and hesitated when she saw that the harpooner was in the wheelhousc. She glanced aft and then approached Arflane. 'It's Janek, Konrad,' she said. 'He seems to be ill. I spoke to the guards today. They said he wasn't eating.'

Arflane laughed. 'Probably starving himself out of spite,' he said. Then he noticed her expression of concern. 'All right. I'll see him when I get the chance.'

The ship was turning now, closing with the land whale herd. They were of a much smaller variety than any Arflane knew, with shorter heads in relation to their bodies, and their colour was a yellow-brown. Many were leaping across the ice, propelling themselves by unusually large back flippers. They did not look dangerous, though; he could see that before long they would have fresh meat.

Urquart gave the wheel back to the helmsman and moved along the deck towards the prow, taking a coil of rope from a tackle locker and tying one end to the ring of his harpoon, winding the rest of the rope around his waist. Other sailors were gathering around him, and he pointed towards the herd. They disappeared below to get their own weapons.

Urquart crossed to the rail and carefully climbed over it, his feet gripping the tiny ridge on the outer hull below the rail. Once the ship lurched and he was almost flung off.

The strange-looking whales were beginning to scatter before the skull-decorated prow of the huge schooner as, with runners squealing, it pursued the main herd.

Urquart hung, grinning, on the outside rail, an arm wrapped around it, the other poising the harpoon. One slip, a sudden motion of the ship, and he could easily lose his grip and be plunged under the runners.

Now the ship was pacing a large bull-whale which leaped frantically along, veering off as its tiny eyes caught sight of the *Ice Spirit* close by. Urquart drew back his harpoon, flung the lance at an angle, caught the beast in the back of its neck. Then the ship was past the creature. The line attached to the harpoon whipped out; the beast reared, leaping on its hind flippers, rolling over and over with its mouth snapping. The whale's teeth were much larger than Arflane had suspected.

The rope was running out rapidly and threatened to yank Urquart from his precarious position as the ship began to turn.

Other whaling hands were now hanging by one arm from the rail, drawing back their own harpoons as the ship approached the herd again. The chase continued in silence save for the noises of the ship and the thump of flippers over the ice.

Just as Arflane was certain Urquart was about to be tugged from the rail by the rope, the harpooner removed the last of the line from his waist and lashed it to the nearest stanchion. Looking back, Arflane saw the dying whale dragged, struggling, behind the ship by Urquart's harpoon. The other harpooners were flinging their weapons out, though most lacked the uncanny accuracy of Urquart. A few whales were speared and soon there were more than a dozen being dragged along the ice in the wake of the ship, their bodies smashing and bleeding as they were bounced to death on the ice.

Now the ship turned again, slowing; hands came forward, ready to haul in the catches. Ice anchors were thrown out. The schooner lurched to a halt, the sailors descended to the ice with flenching cutlasses to slice up the catch.

Urquart went with them, borrowing a cutlass from one of the hands. Arflane and Ulrica stood by the rail, looking at the men hacking at the corpses, arms rising and falling as they butchered the catch, spilling their blood on the ice as the setting sun, red as the blood, sent long, leaping shadows of the men across the white expanse. The pungent smell of the blood drifted on the evening air, reminding them of the time when they had first embraced.

Manfred Rorsefne joined them, smiling at the working, fur-clad sailors as one might smile at children playing. There was not a man there who was not covered from hand to shoulder with the thick blood; many of them were drenched in the stuff, licking it from their mouths with relish.

Rorsefne pointed to the tall figure of Urquart as the man yanked the harpoon from his kill and made with his right hand some mysterious sign in the air.

'Your Urquart seems in his element, Captain Arflane,' he said. 'And the rest of them are elated, aren't they? We were lucky to sight the herd.'

Arflane nodded, watching as Urquart set to work flenching his whale. There was something so primitive, so elemental, about the way the harpooner slashed at the dead creature that Arflane thought once again how much Urquart resembled a demigod of the ice, an old-time member of the Ice Mother's pantheon.

Rorsefne watched for a few minutes more before turning away with a murmured apology. Glancing at him, Arflane guessed that the young man was not enjoying the scene.

Before nightfall the meat had been sliced from the bones and the blubber and oil stored in barrels that were being swung aboard on the tips of the lower yards. Only the skeletons of the slaughtered whales remained on the stained ice, their shadows throwing strange patterns in the light from the setting sun.

As they prepared to go below, Arflane caught a movement from the corner of his eye. He stared up into the darkening scarlet sky to see a score of shapes flying towards them. They flew rapidly; they were the same green birds they had encountered several days earlier. They were like albatrosses in appearance, with large, curved beaks and long wings; they came circling in to land on the bones of the whales, their beady eyes searching the bloody ice before they hopped down to gobble the offal and scraps of meat and blubber left behind by the sailors.

Ulrica gripped Arflane's hand tightly, evidently as unsettled by the sight as he. One of the scavengers, a piece of gut hanging from its beak, turned its head and seemed to stare knowingly at them, then spread its wings and flapped across the ice.

The birds had come from the north this time. When Arflane had first seen them they were flying from south to north. He wondered where their nests were. Perhaps in the range of glaciers ahead of them; the range they would have to sail through before they could reach New York.

Thought of the mountains depressed him; it was not going to be easy to negotiate the narrow pass inscribed on Rorsefne's chart.

When the sun set, the green birds were still feeding, their silhouettes stalking among the bones of the whales like the figures of some conquering army inspecting the corpses of the vanquished.

Chapter Twenty-One
The Wreck

THERE WAS A collision at dawn. Konrad Arflane was leaving his cabin with the intention of seeing Janek Ulsenn and deciding if the man really was ill when a great shock ran through the length of the ship and he was thrown forward on his face.

He picked himself up, blood running from his nose, and hurried back to Ulrica in his cabin. She was sitting up in the bunk, her face alarmed.

'What is it, Konrad?'

'I'm going to see.'

He ran out on deck. There were men sprawled everywhere. Some had fallen from the rigging and were obviously dead; the rest were simply dazed and already climbing to their feet.

In the pale sunlight he looked towards the prow, but could see no obstruction. He ran forward to peer over the skull-decorated bowsprit. He saw that the forward runners had been trapped in a shallow crevasse that could not be seen from above. It was no fault of the lookouts that the obstruction had not been sighted. It was perhaps ten feet wide and only a yard or so deep, but it had succeeded in nearly wrecking the ship. Arflane swung down a loose line to stand on the edge of the opening and inspect the runners.

They did not seem too badly damaged. The edge of one had been cracked and a small section had broken away and could be seen lying at the bottom of the crevasse, but it was not sufficient to impair their function.

Arflane saw that the crevasse ended only a few yards to starboard. It was simply bad luck that they had crossed at this point. The ice schooner could be hauled back, the runners turned and she would be on her way again, hardly the worse for the collision.

Hinsen was peering over the forward rail. 'What is it, sir?'

'Nothing to worry about, Mr Hinsen. The men will have some hard work to do this morning, though. We'll have to haul the ship out. Get the bosun to back the courses. That'll give them some help if we can catch enough wind.'

'Aye, aye, sir.' Hinsen's face disappeared.

As Arflane began to clamber hand over hand up the rope, Urquart came to the rail and helped him over it. The gaunt harpooner pointed silently to the north-west. Arflane looked and cursed.

There were some fifty barbarians riding rapidly towards them. They appeared to be mounted on animals very much like bears; they sat on the broad backs of the beasts with their legs stretched in front of them, holding the reins attached to the animals' heads. Their weapons were bone javelins and swords. They were clad in furs but otherwise seemed like ordinary men, not the creatures they had encountered earlier.

Arflane dashed to the bridge, bellowed through his megaphone for all hands to arm themselves and stand by to meet the attack.

The leading barbarians were almost upon the ship. One of them shouted in a strange accent, repeating the words over and over again. Arflane realised, eventually, what the man was shouting.

'You killed the last whales! You killed the last whales!'

The riders spread out as they neared the ship, evidently planning an approach from all sides. Arflane caught a glimpse of thin, aquiline faces under the hoods; then the javelins began to clatter onto the deck.

The first wave of spears hurt no-one. Arflane picked one of the finely carved javelins up in either hand and flung them back at the fast-riding barbarians. He in turn missed both his targets. The javelins were not designed for this kind of fighting and the barbarians were so far proving a nuisance more than a positive danger.

But soon they began to ride in closer and Arflane saw a sailor fall before he could shoot the arrow from the bow he carried.

Two more of the crew were killed by well-aimed javelins, but the more sophisticated retaliation from the decks of the ship was taking its toll of the attackers. More than half the barbarians fell from their mounts with arrow wounds before the remainder withdrew, massing for a renewed attack on the port side.

Arflane now had a bow and he, Hinsen and Manfred Rorsefne stood together, waiting for the next assault. A little further along the rail stood Urquart. He had half a dozen of the bone javelins ranged beside him on the rail and had temporarily abandoned his own harpoon, which was more than twice the size and weight of the barbarian weapons.

The powerful legs of the bearlike creatures began to move swiftly as, yelling wildly, the barbarians rushed at the ship. A cloud of javelins whistled upwards; a cloud of arrows rushed back. Two barbarians died from Urquart's well-aimed shafts and four more were badly wounded. Most of the others fell beneath the arrows. Arflane turned to grin at Hinsen but the man was dead, impaled by a carved bone javelin that had gone completely through his body. The first officer's eyes were open and glazed as the grip on the rail that had kept him upright gradually relaxed and he toppled to the deck.

Rorsefne murmured in Arflane's ear, 'Urquart is hurt, it seems.'

Arflane glanced along the rail, expecting to see Urquart prone, but instead the harpooner was tearing a javelin from his arm and leaping over the rail, followed by a group of yelling sailors.

The barbarians were regrouping again, but only five remained unwounded. A few more hung in their saddles, several of them with half a dozen arrows sticking in them.

Urquart led his band across the ice, screaming at the few survivors. His huge harpoon was held menacingly in his right hand while his left gripped a pair of javelins. The barbarians hesitated; one drew his sword. Then they turned their strange mounts and rushed away across the ice before the triumphant figure of Urquart shouting and gesticulating behind them.

The raid was over, with less than ten men wounded and only four, including Hinsen, dead. Arflane looked down at the older man's body and sighed. He felt no rancour towards the barbarians. If he had heard the man who had shouted correctly, their whale hunt had destroyed the barbarians' means of staying alive.

Arflane saw the new bosun Rorchenof coming along the deck and signed for him to approach. The bosun saw the corpse of Hinsen and shook his head grimly, staring at Arflane a little resentfully as if he blamed the captain for the barbarian attack. 'He was a good sailor, sir.'

'He was, bosun. I want you to take a party and bury the dead in the crevasse below. It should save time. Do it right away, will you?'

'Aye, aye, sir.'

Arflane looked back and saw Urquart and his band hacking at the wounded barbarians with exactly the same gusto with which they had butchered the whales the evening before. He shrugged and returned to his cabin.

Ulrica was there. He told her what had happened. She looked relieved, then she said: 'Did you speak to Janek? You were going to this morning.'

'I'll do it now.' He went out of the cabin and along the gangway. There was only one guard on duty; Arflane felt it unnecessary to have more. He signed for the man to undo the padlock chaining the door to the bar. The broken door swung inwards and Arflane saw Ulsenn leaning back in his bunk, pale but otherwise apparently fit.

'You're not eating much food they tell me,' he said. He did not enter the cabin but leaned over the bar to address the man.

'I haven't much need for food in here,' Ulsenn said coldly. He stared unfalteringly at Arflane. 'How is my wife?'

'Well,' said Arflane.

Ulsenn smiled bitterly. There was none of the weakness in his expression that Arflane had seen earlier. The man's confinement appeared to have improved his character.

'Is there anything you want?' Arflane asked.

'Indeed, captain; but I don't think you would be ready to let me have it.'

Arflane understood the implication. He nodded curtly and drew the door closed again, fixing the padlock himself.

By the time the ice schooner had been set on course the men were exhausted. A particularly dreamlike atmosphere had settled over the ship and when dawn came Arflane ordered full sail set.

The ship began to move towards the glacier range that could now be made out in detail.

The curves and angles of the ice mountains shone in the sunlight, reflecting and transforming the colours of the sky, producing a subtle variety of shades from pale yellow and blue to rich marble greens, blacks and purples. The pass soon became visible, a narrow opening between gigantic cliffs. According to Rorsefne's chart, the place would take days to negotiate.

Arflane looked carefully at the sky, his expression concerned. There seemed to be bad weather on its way, though it would pass without touching them. He hesitated, wondering whether to enter the gorge or wait; then he shrugged. New York was almost in sight; he wanted to waste no more time. Once through the pass their journey would be as good as over; the city was less than a hundred miles from the glacier range.

As they moved between the lower hills guarding the approach, Arflane ordered most of the canvas taken in and appointed six men to stay on watch in the bow, relaying sightings of any obstruction back to the wheelhouse and the four helmsmen on duty.

The mood of dreamlike unreality seemed to increase as the *Ice Spirit* drifted closer and closer to the looming cliffs of ice. The shouts of the bow lookouts now began to echo through the range until it seemed the whole world was full of ghostly, mocking voices.

Konrad Arflane stood with his legs spread on the bridge, his gloved hands gripping the rail firmly. On his right stood Ulrica Ulsenn, her face calm and remote, dressed in her best furs; beside her was Manfred Rorsefne, the only one who seemed unaffected by the experience; on Arflane's left was Urquart, harpoon cradled in his arm, his sharp eyes eagerly searching the mountains.

The ship entered the wide gorge, sailing between towering cliffs that were less than a quarter of a mile away on either side. The floor of the gorge was smooth; the ship's speed increased as her runners touched the worn ice. Disturbed by the sounds, a piece of ice detached itself from the side of one of the cliffs to starboard. It bounced and tumbled down to crash at the bottom in a great cloud of disintegrating fragments.

Arflane leaned forward to address Rorchenof, who stood on the quarter-deck looking on in some concern.

'Tell the lookouts to keep their voices down as best they can, bosun, or we might find ourselves buried before we know it.'

Rorchenof nodded grimly and went forward to warn the men in the bow. He seemed disturbed.

Arflane himself would be glad when they reached the other side of the pass. He felt dwarfed by the mountains. He decided that the pass was wide enough to permit him to increase the ship's speed without too much danger.

'All plain sail, Mr Rorchenof!' he called suddenly.

Rorchenof accepted the order with some surprise, but did not query it.

Sails set, the *Ice Spirit* leaped forward between the twin walls of the canyon, passing strange ice formations carved by the wind. The formations shone with dark colours; everywhere the ice was like menacing black glass.

Towards evening, the ship was shaken by a series of jolts; her motions became erratic.

'It's the runners, sir!' Rorchenof called to Arflane. 'They must have been damaged more than we thought.'

'Nothing to worry about, bosun,' Arflane said calmly, staring ahead. It was getting colder, and the wind was rising; the sooner they were through the pass the better.

'We could easily skid, sir, and crash into one of the cliffs. We could bring the whole thing down on top of us.'

'I'll be the judge of our danger, bosun.'

The trio beside him on the bridge looked at him curiously but said nothing.

Rorchenof scratched his head, spread his arms, and moved forward again.

The ship was wobbling badly as the sky darkened and the great cliffs seemed to close in on them, but still Arflane made no attempt to slow her and still she moved under full sail.

Just before nightfall Rorchenof came along the deck with a score of sailors at his back.

'Captain Arflane!'

Konrad Arflane looked down nearly serenely. The ship was shuddering constantly now in a series of short, rapid bumps, and the helmsmen were having difficulty in getting sufficiently fast response from the forward runners.

'What is it, bosun?'

'Can we throw out anchor lines, sir, and repair the runners? At this rate we'll all be killed.'

'There's no fear of that, bosun.'

'We feel there is, sir!' It was a new voice; one of the sailors speaking. From around him came a chorus of agreement.

'Return to your posts,' Arflane said evenly. 'You have still to understand the nature of this voyage.'

'We understand when our lives are threatened, sir,' cried another sailor.

'You'll be safe,' Arflane assured him.

As the moon rose the wind howled louder, stretching the sails taut and pushing the ship to even greater speed. They jolted and shuddered along the smooth ice of the canyon floor, racing past white, gleaming cliffs whose peaks were lost from sight in the darkness.

Rorchenof looked about him wildly as a precipice loomed close and the ship veered away from it, runners thumping erratically. 'This is insanity!' he shouted. 'Give us the boats! You can take the ship where you like – we'll get off!'

Urquart brandished his harpoon. 'I'll give this to you unless you return to your posts. The Ice Mother protects us – have faith!'

'Ice Mother!' Rorchenof spat. 'All four of you are mad. We want to turn back!'

'We cannot turn back!' Urquart shouted, and he began to laugh wildly. 'There's no room in this pass to turn, bosun!'

The red-headed bosun shook his fist at the harpooner. 'Then drop the heavy anchors. Stop the ship and give us the boats and we'll make our own way home. You can go on.'

'We need you to sail the craft,' Arflane told him reasonably.

'You *have* gone mad – all of you!' Rorchenof shouted in increasing desperation. 'What's happened to this ship?'

Manfred Rorsefne leaned forward on the rail. 'Your nerve has cracked, bosun, that's all. We're not mad – you are merely hysterical.'

'But the runners – they need attention.'

'I say not,' Arflane called, and grinned at Urquart, slipping his arm around Ulrica's shoulders, steadying her as the ship shook beneath them.

Now the wind was howling along the canyon, stretching the sails till it seemed they would rip from their moorings. The *Ice Spirit* careened from side to side of the gorge, narrowly missing the vast ragged walls of the cliffs.

Rorchenof turned silently, leading his men below.

Rorsefne frowned. 'We haven't heard the last of them, Captain Arflane.'

'Maybe.' Arflane clung to the rail as the helmsmen barely managed to turn the ship away from the cliffs to port. He looked towards the wheelhouse and shouted encouragement to the struggling men at the wheel. They stared back at him in fear.

Moments later Rorchenof emerged on deck again. He and his men were brandishing cutlasses and harpoons.

'You fools,' Arflane shouted at them. 'This is no time for mutiny. The ship has to be sailed.'

Rorchenof called up to the men in the shrouds: 'Take in the sail, lads!'

Then he screamed and staggered back with Urquart's massive

harpoon in his chest; he fell to the deck and for a moment the others paused, staring in horror at their dying leader.

'Enough of this,' Arflane began. 'Go back to your posts!'

The ship swerved again and a rattling sound came from below as the steering chains failed momentarily to grip the runner platform. The ice cliffs surged forward and retreated as the helmsmen forced the *Ice Spirit* away.

The sailors roared and rushed towards the bridge. Arflane grabbed Ulrica and hurried her into the wheelhouse, closed the door and turned to see that Urquart and Rorsefne had abandoned the bridge, vaulting the rail and running below.

Feeling betrayed, Arflane prepared to meet the mutineers. He was unarmed.

The ship seemed now completely at the mercy of the shrieking wind. Streamers of snow whipped through the rigging, and the schooner swayed on her faulty runners. Arflane stood alone on the bridge as the leading sailors began to climb cautiously towards him up the companionway. He waited until the first man was almost upon him then kicked him in the face, wrestling the cutlass from his grasp and smashing the hilt into his skull.

A sheet of snow sliced across the bridge, stinging the men's eyes. Arflane bellowed at them, hacking and thrusting. Then, as men fell back with bloody faces and mangled limbs, Urquart and Rorsefne re-emerged behind them.

Urquart had recovered his harpoon and Rorsefne was armed with a bow and cutlass. He began, coolly, to shoot arrows into the backs of the mutineers. They turned, confused.

The ship rocked. Rorsefne was flung sideways; Urquart barely managed to grasp at a ratline for support. Most of the sailors were flung in all directions and Arflane slipped down the companionway, clinging to the rail and dropping his cutlass.

Once again the ship was racked by a rapid series of jerks. Arflane struggled up, his jacket torn open by the wind, his beard streaming. With one hand he held the rail; with the other he gesticulated at the sailors.

'Rorchenof deceived you,' he shouted. 'Now you can see why

we must get through this pass as fast as we can. If we don't, the ship's finished!'

A sailor's face craned forward, his eyes as wild as Arflane's own. 'Why? Why, skipper?'

'The snow! Once caught in the main blizzard, we are blind and helpless! Loose ice will fall from the cliffs to block the pass. Snow will gather in drifts and make movement impossible. If we're not crushed we'll be snowbound and stranded!'

Above his head a sail broke loose from its eyebolts and began to flap thunderously against the mast. The howl of the wind increased; the ship was flung sideways towards the cliff, seemed to scrape the wall before it slid into the centre of the gorge again.

'But if we sail on we'll smash into a cliff and be killed!' another sailor cried. 'What have we to gain?'

Arflane grinned and spread his arms, coat swirling out behind him, eyes gleaming. 'A fast death instead of a slow one if our luck's really bad. If our luck holds – and you know me to be lucky – then we'll be through by dawn and New York only a few days' sail away!'

'You *were* lucky, skipper,' the sailor called. 'But they say you're not the Ice Mother's chosen any more – that you've gone against Her will. The woman…'

Arflane laughed harshly. 'You'll have to trust my luck – it's all you have. Lower your weapons, lads.'

'Let the wind carry us through. It's our only chance.' The voice was Urquart's.

The men began to lower their cutlasses, still not entirely convinced.

'You'd be better employed if you got into the shrouds and looked to your sails.' Manfred Rorsefne shouted above the moan of the wind.

'But the runners…' a sailor began.

'We'll concern ourselves with those,' Arflane said. 'Back to work, lads. There'll be no vengeance taken on you when we're through the pass, I promise. We must work together – or die together!'

The sailors began to disperse, their faces still full of fear and doubt.

Ulrica struggled through the wheelhouse door and made her way along the dangerously swaying deck to clutch Arflane's arm. The wind whipped her clothes and the snow stung her face. 'Are you sure the men are wrong?' she asked. 'Wouldn't it be best...?'

He grinned and shrugged. 'It doesn't matter, Ulrica. Go below and rest if you can. I'll join you later.' Again the ship listed and he slid along the deck, fighting his way back to her and helping her towards the bridge.

When she was safely below he began to make his way forward, leaning into the wind, the snow stinging his face and half blinding him. He reached the bow and tried to peer ahead, catching only glimpses of the cliffs on both sides as the ship rocked and swerved on its faulty runners. He got to the bowsprit and stretched his body along it, supporting himself by one hand curled in a staysail line; with the other he stroked the great skulls of the whales, pressing his fingers against the contours of cranium, eye-sockets and grinning jaws as if they could somehow transmit to him the strength they had once possessed.

As the snow eased slightly ahead he saw the black outlines of the ice cliffs in front of him. They seemed to be closing in, as if shifting on their bases, crowding to trap the ship. It was merely a trick of the eyes, but it disturbed him.

Then he realised what was actually happening. The gorge really did narrow here. Perhaps the cliffs had shifted, for the opening between them was becoming little more than a crack.

The *Ice Spirit* would not be able to get through.

He swung himself desperately along the bowsprit, conscious only of the careening, speeding ship, gasped and staggered across the deck till he reached the great gland of the steering pin and seized the heavy mallet that was secured beside it, began swinging at the emergency bolt. Urquart swayed towards him; he turned his head, bellowing across the deck.

'Drop the anchors! For the Ice Mother's sake, man – drop the anchors!'

Urquart raced back along the deck, finding men and ordering

them to the stanchions to knock out the pegs that kept the twin blades of the heavy anchors clear of the ice.

Arflane looked up, his heart sinking. They were nearly into the bottleneck; there was hardly a chance now of saving the ship.

The bolt was shifting. Driving his arms back and forth, he swung the mallet again and again.

Suddenly the thing flew free. There was a high-pitched squealing as the runners turned inwards, ploughshare fashion; the ship began to roll and shudder violently.

Arflane raced back along the deck. He had done all he could; now his concern was for Ulrica's safety.

He reached the cabin as the ship leaped as if in some monstrous orgasm. Ulrica was there, and her husband beside her.

'I released him,' she said.

Arflane grunted. 'Come – get on deck. There's little chance of any of us surviving this.'

There was a final violent crash; the ship's shuddering movement subsided, dying away as the heavy anchors gripped the ice and brought her to a halt.

Clambering out on deck, Arflane saw in astonishment that they were barely ten yards from the point where the ship would have been dashed against the walls of the cliffs or crushed between them.

But the *Ice Spirit*'s motion had not ceased.

Now the great schooner began to topple as her port runners gave out completely under the strain, snapping with sharp cracks. With a terrifying groan the vessel collapsed onto her side, turning as the wind caught the sails, flinging her crew in a heap against the port rail.

Arflane grabbed Ulrica and curled his hand around a trailing rope.

His one concern now was to abandon the ship and save them both. He slid down the line and leaped clear onto the hard ice, dragging the woman with him away from the ship and against the wind.

Through the blizzard he could see little of either the cliffs or the bulk of the schooner.

He heard her crash into the side of the gorge and then made out another sound from above as pieces of ice, shaken free, began to slide downwards.

Eventually he managed to find the comparative shelter of an overhang by the far wall of the gorge. He paused, panting and looking back at the broken ship. There was no way of telling if any of the others had managed to jump free; he saw an occasional figure framed near the rail as the curtain of snow parted and swirled back. Once he heard a voice above the wind. It sounded like Ulsenn's.

'He wanted this wreck! He wanted it!'

It was like the meaningless cry of a bird. Then the wind roared louder, drowning it, as a great avalanche of ice began to fall on the ship.

The two huddled together under the overhang, watching the *Ice Spirit* as she was crushed by the huge collapsing slabs, jerking like a dying creature, her hull breaking, her masts cracking and splintering, disintegrating faster than Arflane could ever have believed; breaking up in a cloud of ice splinters and swirling snow against the towering, jagged walls of the ice mountains.

Arflane wept as he watched; it was as if the destruction of the ship signified the end of all hope. He pulled Ulrica to him, wrapping his arms around her, more to comfort himself than for any thought for her.

Chapter Twenty-Two

The Trek

IN THE MORNING the snow had stopped falling but the skies were heavy and grey above the dark peaks of the glaciers. The storm had subsided almost as soon as the *Ice Spirit* had been smashed, as if destroying the ship had been its sole purpose.

Moving across the irregular masses of snow and ice towards the place where the gorge narrowed and where the main bulk of the wreck had come to rest, Arflane and Ulrica were joined by Rorsefne and Ulsenn. Neither man was badly hurt, but their furs were torn and they were exhausted. A few sailors stood by the pile of broken fibreglass and metal as if they hoped that the ship might magically restore itself. Urquart was actually in the wreck, moving about like a carrion bird.

It was a cold, bleak day; they shivered, their breath hanging white and heavy on the air. They looked about them and saw mangled bodies everywhere; most of the sailors had been killed and the seven who remained looked sourly at Arflane, blaming his recklessness for the disaster.

Ulsenn's attitude to Arflane and Ulrica was remote and neutral. He nodded to them as they walked together to the wreck. Rorsefne was smiling and humming a tune to himself as if enjoying a private joke.

Arflane turned to him, pointing at the narrow gap between the cliffs. 'It was not on the chart, was it?' He spoke loudly, defensively, as much for the benefit of the listening sailors as anyone.

'There was no mention of it,' Rorsefne agreed, smiling like an actor amused by his lines. 'The cliffs must have moved closer together. I've heard of such things happening. What do we do now, captain? There isn't a boat left. How do we get home?'

Arflane glanced at him grimly. 'Home?'

'You mean to carry on, then?' Ulsenn said tonelessly.

'That's the most sensible thing to do,' Arflane told him. 'We're only some fifty miles or so from New York and we're several thousand from home...'

Urquart held up some large slivers of ivory that had evidently come from broken hatch covers. 'Skis,' he said. 'We could reach New York in a week or less.'

Rorsefne laughed. 'Indefatigable! I'm with you, captain.'

The others said nothing; there was nothing left to say.

Within two days the party had traversed the pass and begun to move across the wide ice plain beyond the glacier range. The weather was still poor, with snow falling sporadically, and the cold was in their bones. They had salvaged harpoons and slivers of ivory to act as poles and skis; on their backs they carried packs of provisions.

They were utterly weary and rarely spoke, even when they camped. They were following a course plotted from a small compass which Manfred Rorsefne had found among the things spilled from his shattered travelling chest.

To Arflane space had become nothing but an eternal white plain and time no longer seemed to exist at all. His face, hands and feet were frostbitten, his beard was encrusted with particles of ice, his eyes were red and pouched. Mechanically he drove himself on his skis, followed by the others who moved, as he did, like automata. Thought meant simply remembering to eat and protect oneself from the cold as best one could; speech was a matter of monosyllabic communications if one decided to stop or change direction.

From habit he and Ulrica stayed together, but neither any longer felt much emotion.

In this condition it would have been possible for the party to have moved on, never finding New York, until one by one they died; even death would have seemed merely a gradual change from one state to another, for the cold was so bitter that pain could not be felt. Two of the sailors did die; the rest of the party left them where they fell. The only one who did not seem affected by exhaustion was Urquart. When the sailors died he made the sign of the Ice Mother before passing on.

None of them realised that the compass was erratic and that they were moving across the great white plain in a wide curve away from the supposed location of New York.

The barbarians were similar in general appearance to the ones who had attacked them after the whale-killing. They were dressed all in white fur and rode white, bearlike creatures. They held swords and javelins ready as they reined in to block the little party's progress.

Arflane only saw them then. He swayed on his skis, peering through red-rimmed eyes at the grinning, aquiline faces of the riders. Wearily he raised his harpoon in an attitude of defence; but the weight was almost too much for him.

It was Urquart who yelled suddenly and flung one harpoon then another, swinging his own weapon from his shoulder as two barbarians toppled from their saddles.

Their leader shouted, waving to his men; they rode swiftly down on the party, javelins raised. Arflane thrust out his own harpoon to defend Ulrica but was knocked backwards by a savage slash across the face, losing his footing in the snow. A blow on his head followed and he lost consciousness.

Chapter Twenty-Three
The Rites of the Ice Mother

THERE WAS PAIN in Arflane's head and his face throbbed from the blow he had received. His wrists were tied behind him and he lay uncomfortably on the ice. He opened his eyes and saw the barbarian camp.

Hide tents were stretched on rigid bone frames; the riding bears were corralled to one side of the camp and a few women moved about among the tents. The place was evidently not their permanent home; Arflane knew that most barbarians were nomads. The men stood in a large group around their leader, the personage Arflane had seen earlier. He was talking with them and glancing at the prisoners who had been bound together at the wrists and lay sprawled on the ice. Arflane turned his head and saw with relief that Ulrica was safe; she smiled at him weakly. Manfred Rorsefne was there and Janek Ulsenn, his eyes tightly closed. There were three sailors, their expressions wretched as they stared at the barbarians.

There was no sign of Urquart; Arflane wondered vaguely if they had killed him. Some moments later he saw him emerge from a tent with a small, obese man, striding towards the main gathering. It seemed then that Urquart had somehow gained their confidence. Arflane was relieved; with luck the harpooner might find a way to release them.

The leader, a handsome, brown-skinned young man with a beak of a nose and bright, haughty eyes, gesticulated towards Urquart as he and the short man pushed through the throng. Urquart began to speak. Arflane gathered that the harpooner was pleading for his friends' lives and wondered how the man had managed to win favour with the nomads. Certainly Urquart was considerably taller than any of them and his own primitive appearance would probably impress them as it impressed all who encountered him. Also, of course, he had been the only one to attack the barbarians; perhaps they admired him for his courage. Whatever the reason, there was no doubt that they were listening gravely to the harpooner as he spoke, waving his massive lance in the direction of the captives.

Eventually the three of them – the leader, the fat man and Urquart – moved away from the other warriors and approached Arflane and the rest.

The young leader was dressed all in fine white fur, his hood framing his face; he was clean-shaven and walked lithely, his back held straight and his hand on the hilt of his bone sword. The fat man wore reddish furs that Arflane could not identify; he pulled at his long, greasy moustachios and scowled thoughtfully. Urquart was expressionless.

The leader paused before Arflane and put his hands on his hips. 'Ha! You head north like us, eh? You are from back there!' He spoke in a strange, lilting accent, and jerked his thumb towards the south.

'Yes,' Arflane agreed, finding it difficult to speak through his swollen lips. 'We had a ship – it was wrecked.' He eyed the youth warily, wondering what Urquart had told him.

'The big sleigh with the skins on poles. We saw it – many days back. Yes.' The youth smiled and gave Arflane a quick, intelligent look. 'There are more – on top of a great hill – months back, eh?'

'You know the plateau of Eight Cities?' Arflane was surprised. He glanced at Urquart, but the harpooner's expression was frozen. He stood leaning on his harpoon, staring into the middle distance.

'We are from much further south than you, my friend,' grinned the barbarian leader. 'The country is getting too soft back there. The ice is vanishing and there is something yielding and unnatural beneath it. We came north, where things are still normal. I'm Donal of Kamfor and this is my tribe.'

'Arflane of Brershill,' he replied formally, still confused and wondering what Urquart had said at the barbarian conference.

'The ice is really melting further south?' Manfred Rorsefne spoke for the first time. 'It's vanishing altogether?'

'That's so,' Donal of Kamfor nodded. 'No-one can live there.' He gestured with his hand. 'Things – push up – from this soft stuff. Bad.' He shook his head and screwed up his face.

Arflane felt ill at the idea. Donal laughed and pointed at him. 'Ha! You hate it too! Where were you going?'

Arflane again tried to get some sign from Urquart, but the man refused even to meet his eye. There was nothing to gain by being secretive about their destination and it might capture the barbarian's imagination. 'We were going to New York,' he said.

Donal looked astonished. 'You seek the Ice Mother's court? Surely no-one is allowed there...'

Urquart gestured at Arflane. 'He is the one. He is the Mother's chosen. I told you that one of us is fated to meet Her and plead our case. She is helping him to reach Her. When he does, the melting will stop.'

Now Arflane guessed how Urquart had convinced the barbarians. They were evidently even more superstitious than the whaling men of the Eight Cities. However, Donal was plainly not a man to be duped. He nudged the fat man's shoulder with his elbow.

'We do what this Urquart says to test the truth, eh?' he said.

The fat man chewed at his lower lip, looking bleakly at Arflane. 'I am the priest,' he murmured to Donal. 'I decide this thing.'

Donal shrugged and took a step back.

The priest turned his attentions from Arflane to Ulrica and then to Manfred Rorsefne. He glanced briefly at the sailors and Janek Ulsenn, and began to tug at his moustache. He moved closer to Urquart and laid a finger on his arm. 'Those are the two, then?' he said, pointing to Ulrica and Rorsefne.

Urquart nodded.

'Good stock,' said the priest. 'You were right.'

'The line of the highest chiefs in the Eight Cities,' Urquart said. 'No better blood – and they are my kind.' He spoke almost proudly. 'It will please the Ice Mother and bring us all luck. Arflane will lead us to New York and we shall be welcome.'

'What are you saying, Urquart?' Arflane asked uneasily. 'What sort of bargain have you struck for us?'

Urquart began to smile. 'One that will solve all our problems. Now my ambition can be fulfilled, the Ice Mother mollified, your burden can be removed, we win the help and friendship of these people. At last it is possible to do what I have planned all these years.' His savage eyes burned with a disturbing brilliance. 'I have been faithful to the Mother. I have served Her and I have prayed to Her. She sent you – and you helped me. Now She gives me my right. And I, in turn, give Her Hers.'

Arflane shivered. The voice was cold, soft, terrifying.

'What do you mean?' he asked. 'How have I helped you?'

'You saved the lives of all the Rorsefne clan – my father, his daughter and his nephew.'

'That was why you befriended me, I thought...'

'I saw your destiny, then. I realised that you were the servant of the Ice Mother, though at first you did not know it yourself.' Urquart pushed back his hood, revealing his bizarre hair and his dangling bone earrings. 'You saved their lives, Konrad Arflane, so that I might take them in my own way at my leisure. The time has come for vengeance on my father's brood. I only regret that he cannot be here, also.'

Arflane remembered the funeral outside Friesgalt and Urquart's strange behaviour when he had flung the ice block down so savagely into old Pyotr Rorsefne's grave.

'Why do you hate him?' he asked.

'He tried to kill me.' Urquart's tone was distant; he looked away from Arflane. 'My mother was the wife of an innkeeper. Rorsefne's mistress. When she brought me to him, asking him to protect me as is the custom, he had his servants carry me onto the ice to expose me. I heard the story years later from her own lips. I was found by a whaling brig and became their mascot. The tale was told in the top-deck taverns and my mother realised what had happened. She sought me out and found me eventually when I was sixteen years old. From then on I planned my revenge on the whole Rorsefne brood. That was more than a score of years ago.

I am a child of the ice – favourite of the Ice Mother. The fact that I live today is proof of that.' Urquart's eyes burned brighter.

'That's what you told these people to make them listen to you!' Arflane whispered. He tested the thongs holding his wrists together, but they were tied tightly.

Urquart moved forward, ignoring Arflane. He drew his long knife from his sheath and stooped to cut the lines tying Ulrica and Manfred to the rest. Ulrica lay there, her face pale, her eyes incredulous and terrified. Even Manfred Rorsefne's face had become grim. Neither made a move to rise.

Urquart reached out and pulled the trembling woman to her feet, sheathed his knife and grabbed Rorsefne by the front of his tattered coat. Manfred stood upright with some dignity. There was a movement behind Arflane. He turned his head and saw that Ulsenn's hands had come free. In cutting the thongs, Urquart had accidentally released the man. Donal pointed silently at Ulsenn, but Urquart shrugged disdainfully. 'He'll do nothing.'

Arflane stared up unbelievingly at the gaunt harpooner. 'Urquart, you've lost your reason. You can't kill them!'

'I can,' Urquart said quietly.

'He must,' the fat priest added. 'It is the bargain he made with us. We have had bad luck with the hunting and need a sacrifice for the Ice Mother. The sacrifice must be the best blood.' He smiled a trifle sardonically and jerked his thumb at Donal. 'We need this one – he is all we have. If Urquart performs the ritual then the rest of you go free; or we come with you, whichever we decide.'

'He's insane!' Arflane tried desperately to struggle to his feet. 'His hatred's turned his brain.'

'I do not see that,' the priest said calmly. 'And even if it were true it would not matter to us. These two will die and you will not. You should be grateful.'

Arflane struggled helplessly on the ice, half rising and then falling back.

Donal turned with a shrug and the priest followed him, pushing Ulrica and Manfred Rorsefne forward. Urquart came last.

Ulrica glanced back at Arflane. The terror had left her eyes and was replaced with a look of helpless fatalism.

'Ulrica!' Arflane shouted.

Urquart called without looking at Arflane. 'I am about to cut your chains. I am paying the debt I owe you – I am freeing you!'

Arflane watched dumbly as the barbarians prepared for the ritual, erecting bone frames and tying the captives to them so that they were spreadeagled with their feet just above the ice. Urquart stepped forward, cutting expertly at Manfred's clothing as he would skin a seal until the young man was naked. In a way this was a merciful action, since the cold would soon numb his body. Arflane shuddered as he saw Urquart step up to Ulrica and begin to cut the furs from her until she, too, was bare.

Arflane was exhausting himself in his struggles to get to his feet. Even if he could rise there was nothing he could do, for the thongs held his wrists. As a precaution there were now two guards standing nearby.

He watched in horror as Urquart poised the knife close to Manfred Rorsefne's genitals; he heard Rorsefne shriek in pain and thresh in his bonds as Urquart cut his manhood from him. Blood coursed down the young man's thighs and Rorsefne fell forward, head hanging limply. Urquart brandished his trophy, hands reddened with blood, before tossing it away. Arflane remembered the old savage customs of his own people; there had not been a ritual of this kind performed for centuries.

'Urquart! No!' Arflane screamed as the harpooner turned to Ulrica. 'No!'

Urquart did not appear to hear him. All his attention was on Ulrica as, with her eyes mad with fear, she tried unsuccessfully to shrink from the knife that threatened her breasts.

Then Arflane saw a figure leap up beside him, grab a javelin from one of the guards, and impale the man. The figure moved swiftly, turning to slice at Arflane's bonds with the sharp tip of the javelin while the other guard turned bewilderedly. Arflane was up then, his fingers grasping the guard's throat and snapping his neck almost instantly.

Ulsenn stood panting beside Arflane, holding the bloody javelin uncertainly. Arflane picked up the other spear and dashed across the ice towards Urquart. As yet no-one had seen what had happened.

Then the priest shouted from where he sat and pointed at Arflane. Several barbarians leaped up, but Donal restrained them. Urquart turned, his eyes mildly surprised to see Arflane.

Arflane ran at him with the javelin, but Urquart leaped aside and Arflane only narrowly missed sticking the weapon into Ulrica's body. Urquart stood breathing heavily, the knife raised; then he moved his head slowly towards the spot where his own huge harpoon lay, ready to finish the pair after the ritual.

Arflane flung the javelin erratically. It took Urquart in the arm. Still Urquart did not move, but his lips seemed to frame a question.

Arflane ran to where the many-barbed harpoon lay and picked it up.

Urquart watched him, shaking his head bewilderedly. 'Arflane...?'

Arflane took the lance in both hands and plunged it into the harpooner's broad chest. Urquart gasped and seized the shaft, trying to pull the weapon from his body. 'Arflane,' he gasped. 'Arflane. You fool! You kill everything...' The gaunt man staggered back, his pain-filled eyes still staring unbelievingly; and it seemed to Arflane then that in killing Urquart he killed all he had ever held to be valuable.

The harpooner groaned, his great body swaying, his ivory ornaments clattering as he was racked by his agony. Then he fell sideways, attempted to rise, and collapsed in death.

Arflane turned to face the barbarians, but they did not move. The priest was frowning uncertainly.

Ulsenn ran forward. 'Two!' he called. 'Two of noble blood. Urquart was the man's cousin and the woman's brother!'

The barbarians murmured and looked questioningly at their

priest and their chief. Donal stood up, rubbing his clean-shaven chin. 'Aye,' he said. 'Two it is. It is fair. Besides, we had better sport this way.' He laughed lightly. 'Release the woman. Attend to the man if he still lives. Tomorrow we go to the Ice Mother's court!'

Ulrica wept like a child as they cut her down. Arflane took her gently in his arms, wrapping her in her ripped furs. He felt strangely calm as he passed the stiff corpse of Urquart and carried the woman towards the tent that the priest led him to. Ulsenn followed him, bearing the unconscious body of Manfred Rorsefne.

When Ulrica lay sleeping and Manfred Rorsefne's wound had been crudely dressed, Arflane and Janek Ulsenn sat together in the close confines of the tent. Night had fallen but they made no attempt to rest. Both were pondering the bond that had grown between them in the few hours that had passed; both knew in their hearts that it could not last.

Chapter Twenty-Four
New York

IT TOOK THEM two weeks to find New York and in that time Manfred Rorsefne, his nervous system unable to withstand the shock it had received, died peacefully and was buried in the ice. Konrad Arflane, Ulrica Ulsenn and Janek Ulsenn rode in a group, with Donal and his fat priest close by; they had learned to ride the huge bears without much difficulty. They moved slowly, for the barbarians had brought their tents and women with them. The weather had become surprisingly fine.

When they sighted the slender towers of New York they stopped in astonishment. Arflane felt that Pyotr Rorsefne had been peculiarly uneloquent in describing them. They were magnificent. They shone.

The party came to a straggling stop and the bears scratched nervously at the ice, perhaps sensing their riders' mixed feelings as they looked at the city of metal and glass and stone soaring into the clouds. The towers blazed; mile upon mile of shining ice reflected their shifting colours and Arflane remembered the story, wondering how tall they must be if they stretched as far below the ice as they did above it. Yet his instincts were alarmed and he did not know why. Perhaps, after all, he did not want to know the truth. Perhaps he did not want to meet the Ice Mother, for he had sinned against Her in many ways in the course of the voyage.

'Well,' Donal said quickly. 'Let's continue.'

Slowly they rode towards the many-windowed city jutting from the ice of the plain. As they moved nearer Arflane realised what it was that so disturbed him. An unnatural warmth radiated from the place; a warmth that could have melted the ice. Surely this was no city of the Ice Mother? They all sensed it and looked at one another grimly. Again they came to a halt. Here was the city that symbolised all their dreams and hopes; and suddenly it had taken on a subtle menace.

'I like this not at all,' Donal growled. 'That heat – it is much worse than the heat that came to the south.'

Arflane nodded. 'But how can it be so hot? Why hasn't the ice melted?'

'Let us go back,' said Ulsenn. 'I knew it was foolish to come here.'

Instinctively Arflane agreed with him; but he had set out to reach New York. He had told himself that he would accept whatever knowledge the city offered. He had to go on; he had killed men and destroyed a ship to get here and now that he was less than a mile away he could not possibly turn back. He shook his head and goaded his mount forward. From behind him came a muttering.

He raised his hand and pointed at the slender towers. 'Come – let's go to greet the Ice Mother!'

The riding bear galloped forward; behind him the barbarians began to increase their speed until all were galloping in a wild, half-hysterical charge on the vast city, their ranks breaking and spreading out, their cries echoing among the towers as they sought to embolden themselves. Ulrica's hood was whipped back by the wind; her unbound hair streamed behind her as she clung to her saddle. Arflane grinned at her, his beard torn by the wind. Ulsenn's face was set and he leaned forward in the saddle as if going to his death.

The towers were grouped thickly, with barely enough space between the outer ones for them to enter the city. As they reached the great forest of metal and glass they realised that there was something more unnatural about the city than the warmth that came from it.

Arflane's mount's feet skidded on the surface and he called out in amazement. 'This isn't ice!'

The stuff had been cunningly made to simulate ice in almost every detail; but now that they stood on it they could tell that it was not ice; and it was possible to look down through it and make out the dim shapes of the towers going down and down into the darkness.

Donal cried: 'You have misled us, Arflane!'

The sudden revelation had shocked Arflane as much as the others. Dumbly, he shook his head.

Ulsenn charged forward on his mount to shake his fist in Arflane's face. 'You have led us into a trap! I knew it!'

'I followed Pyotr Rorsefne's chart, that was all!'

'This place is evil,' the priest said firmly. 'We can all sense that. It matters not how we were deceived – we should leave while we can.'

Arflane shared the priest's feeling. He hated the atmosphere of the city. He had expected to find the Ice Mother and had found instead something that seemed to stand for everything the Ice Mother opposed.

'Very well,' he said. 'We turn back.' But even as he spoke he realised that the ground beneath them was moving downwards; the whole great plain was sinking slowly below the level of the surrounding ice. Those closer to the edge managed to leap their clumsy animals upwards and escape but most of them were left in panic as the city dropped lower into what was apparently a huge shaft driven into the ice. The shadows of the shaft's enormous sides fell across the group as they milled about in fear.

Arflane saw how Donal and Ulsenn were staring at him and realised that he was to be their scapegoat.

'Ulrica,' he called, turning his mount to plunge into the mass of towers with the woman close behind him. The light grew fainter as they galloped through the winding maze; behind they heard the barbarians, led by Ulsenn and Donal, searching for them. Arflane knew instinctively that in their panic they would butcher him and probably Ulrica too; they had to stay clear of them. He had two dangers to face now and both seemed insuperable. He could not hope to defeat the barbarians and he could not stop the city sinking.

There was an entrance in one of the towers; from it streamed a soft light. Desperately he rode his beast through it and Ulrica came with him.

He found himself in a gallery with ramps curving downwards from it towards the floor of the tower far below. He saw several figures lower on the ramps; figures dressed from head to foot in red, close-fitting garments, wearing masks that completely covered their faces. They looked up as they heard the sound of the bears' paws in the gallery, and one of them laughed and pointed.

Grimly Arflane sent the creature half sliding down one of the ramps. He glanced back and saw that Ulrica had hesitated but was following him. The speed of the descent was dangerous; twice the bear nearly slid off the edge of the ramp and three times he nearly lost his seat on the animal's back, but when he reached the floor of the tower the masked men were gone.

As Ulrica joined him, looking in awe at the strange devices that covered the walls, he realised that the city was no longer in motion. He stared at the things on the wall. They were instruments of some kind; a few resembled chronometers or compasses while others were alive with flickering letters that meant nothing at all to him. His main interest at that moment was in finding a door. There seemed to be none. Was this, after all, the court of the Ice Mother and the red-clad creatures ghosts? From somewhere came faint laughter again, then from above an echoing yell. He saw Ulsenn riding rapidly down the ramp towards him; he was waving a flenching cutlass while Arflane had only a javelin.

Arflane turned to look into Ulrica's face. She stared back at him, then dropped her eyes as if in consent.

Arflane rode his bear towards Ulsenn as the man lunged at him with the cutlass. He blocked the blow with the javelin but the blade sheered off the head of the spear, leaving him virtually defenceless. Ulsenn swung clumsily at his throat, missed and was taken off balance. Arflane plunged the jagged shaft into his throat.

Ulrica rode up, watching silently as Ulsenn clutched at the wound then fell slowly from the back of the bear.

'That is the end of it now,' she said.

'He saved your life,' Arflane said.

She nodded. 'But now it is over.' She began to cry. Arflane looked at her miserably, wondering why he had killed Ulsenn then and not earlier, before the man had had the chance to show that he could be courageous. Perhaps that was why; he had, towards the end, become a true rival.

'A fine piece of bloodshed, stranger. Welcome to New York.'

They turned. A section of the wall had vanished; in its place stood a thin figure. Its overlong skull was encased in a red mask. Two eyes glittered humorously through slits in the fabric. Arflane jerked up his javelin in an instinctive movement. 'This is not New York – this is some evil place.'

The figure laughed softly. 'This is New York, indeed, though not the original city of your legends. That was destroyed almost two thousand years ago. But this city stands close to the site of the original. In many respects it is far superior. You have witnessed one of its advantages.'

Arflane realised he was sweating. He loosened the thongs of his coat. 'Who are you?'

'If you are genuinely curious, then I will tell you,' replied the masked man. 'Follow me.'

Chapter Twenty-Five

The Truth

ARFLANE HAD WANTED the truth; it was why he had originally agreed to Rorsefne's scheme; but now, as he stared around the luminous chamber, Ulrica's arm on his, he began to feel that the truth was more than he could accept. The red-masked figure left the room. The walls gleamed blindingly bright and a seated man appeared at the far end of the chamber. He wore the same red garments as the other, but he was almost a dwarf and one shoulder was higher than the other.

'I am Peter Ballantine,' he said pleasantly. His pronunciation was careful, as if he spoke the words of a language he had recently learned. 'Please sit down.'

Arflane and Ulrica seated themselves gingerly on the quilted benches and were startled as the man's chair slid forward until he sat only a foot or two away from them. 'I will explain everything,' he said. 'I will be brief. Ask questions when I have finished.'

The world had grown decadent and a malaise had settled on the West so that people lost the will and eventually the means of survival. A peculiar society of stoics had grown up in the polar bases of the South Antarctican International Zone where Russian, American, British Commonwealth, Scandinavian and other research teams lived, and Camp Century, the city the Americans had established under the Greenland ice cap. Nature, unbalanced by a series of wars in Africa and Asia, had swiftly begun to draw a healing skin of ice over her ruined surface. What had precipitated the ice age was primarily the bombs and the sudden change in the various radiations in the atmosphere. The men of the two polar camps had communicated for a while by radio but the radiation was too great to risk personal contact. For one reason and another, forced by their separate circumstances, the groups of survivors had chosen different ways of adapting to the change. The men of the Antarctic learned to adapt to the ice, making use of all their resources to build ships that could travel the surface without need of fuel, dwellings where one could live without need of special heating plants. As the ice covered the planet, they moved away from the Antarctic, heading towards the equator until, at length, they reached the plateau of the Matto Grosso and decided that here was an ideal location for permanent camp. In adapting to the conditions they had neglected their learning and within a few hundred years the creed of the Ice Mother had replaced the logic of the second law of thermodynamics which had shown logically what the people now believed instinctively – that only ice eternal lay in the future. Perhaps the adaptation of the Antarcticans had been a healthier reaction to the situation than that of the Arcticans who had tended to bury themselves deeper and deeper into their under-ice caverns, searching for scientific means of survival that would preserve the way of life they knew.

Among the last messages to be sent by the Arcticans to the Antarcticans was the information that the northerners had reached the stage where they could transport their city complex further south and that they intended to site it in New York. They offered help to the Antarcticans, but they refused it, stripping their radios to make better use of them. They had grown to feel easy with their life.

So the Arcticans refined their science and their living conditions until the city of New York was the result. The rapid growth of the ice was now just as rapidly reversing.

'It will take at least another two hundred years before any great area of land is cleared,' Peter Ballantine explained. 'Wildlife is returning, though, from eastern and western areas that were never entirely ice-bound.'

Arflane and Ulrica had received the information almost expressionlessly. Arflane felt that he was drowning; his body and mind were numb.

'We welcome visitors, particularly from the Eight Cities,' Ballantine continued.

Arflane looked up at him then. 'You are lying. The ice is not melting. You speak heresies…'

'We offer only knowledge. What is wrong with that?'

Arflane said slowly: 'I believe in the ice eternal, the doctrine that all must grow cold, that the Ice Mother's mercy is all that allows us to live.'

'But you can see how wrong that idea is,' Ballantine said gently. 'Your society created those ideas to enable them to live the way they did. They needed them, but they no longer need them now.'

'I understand,' Arflane said. The depression that filled him was hard to overcome; it seemed that his whole life since he had first saved Rorsefne had led to this point. Gradually he had forsaken his old principles, allowing himself soft emotions, taking Ulrica in adultery, involving himself with others; and it was as if by forgetting the dictates of the Ice Mother he had somehow created this New York. Logically, he knew the idea was absurd but he could not shake himself clear of it. If he had lived according to his code, the Ice Mother would be comforting him at this moment; if he had listened to Urquart, last of the Ice Mother's true followers, and gone with him, they would have found the New York they expected to find. But he had killed Urquart in saving Ulrica's life. 'You kill everything,' Urquart had said as he died. Now Arflane understood what the harpooner had meant. Urquart had tried to change his course for him, but the course had led inevitably to Peter Ballantine and his logic and his vision of an Earth in which the Ice Mother was dying, or already dead. If he could find Her…

Ulrica Ulsenn touched his hand. 'He is right,' she said, 'that is why the people of the Eight Cities are changing – because they sense what is happening to the world. They are adapting in the way that animals do, though most of the animals – the land whales and the like – will not adapt in time.'

'The land whales' adaptation was artificially stimulated,' Ballantine said with some pride. 'It was an experiment that was incidentally beneficial to your people.'

Arflane sighed again, feeling completely dejected. He rubbed his sweating forehead and tugged at his clothes, resenting the heat of the place. He turned and looked at Ulrica Ulsenn, shaking his head slowly, touching her hand gently. 'You welcome this,' he said. 'You represent what they represent. You're the future, too.'

She frowned. 'I don't understand you, Konrad. You're being too mysterious.'

'I'm sorry.' He glanced away from her and looked at Ballantine as he sat in the moving chair, waiting patiently. 'I am the past,' he said to the man. 'You can see that, I think.'

'Yes,' said Ballantine sympathetically. 'I respect you, but...'

'But you must destroy me.'

'Of course not.'

'I have to see it so.' Arflane sighed. 'I am a simple man, you see. An old-fashioned man.'

Ballantine told him: 'We will find accommodation for you both while you rest.' He chuckled. 'Your barbarian friends are still chasing around on the surface of the city like frightened lice. We must see how we can help them. In their case our hypnomats will doubtless be of more use than conversation.'

Chapter Twenty-Six

North

THE NEXT DAY Peter Ballantine walked in the artificial gardens of the city with Ulrica Ulsenn. Arflane had looked at the gardens and declined to enter. He sat now in a gallery staring at the machines Ballantine had told him were the life-giving heart of the city.

'Just as your ancestors adapted to the ice,' Ballantine was saying to the woman, 'so you must re-adapt to its disappearance. You came north instinctively because you identify the north with your homeland. All this is natural. But now you must go south again, for your own good and the good of your children. You must give your people the knowledge we have given you; though it will take time they will gradually come to accept it. If they do not change they will destroy themselves in a reversion to savagery.'

Ulrica nodded. She looked with growing enjoyment at the multitude of brightly coloured flowers around her, sniffed their scents in wonder, her nostrils the keener for never having experienced such perfume before. It made her feel light-headed. She smiled slowly at Ballantine, eyes shining.

'I realise Arflane is disturbed just now,' Ballantine continued. 'There is a lot of guilt in his attitude; but there is no need for him to feel this. There was a purpose to all those inhibitions, but now it does not exist. That is why you must go south again, to tell them what you have learned.'

Ulrica spread her hands and indicated the flowers. 'This is what will replace the ice?' she said.

'This and much more. Yours and Arflane's children could see it if they wished to journey even further south. They could live in a land where all these things grow naturally.' He smiled, touched by her childlike enjoyment of his garden. 'You must convince him.'

'He will understand,' she said confidently. 'What of the barbarians? Donal and the rest?'

'We have had to use less subtle and possibly less lasting methods on them. But they will help spread the ideas.'

'I wish Arflane had not refused to come here,' Ulrica said. 'I'm sure he would like it.'

'Perhaps,' said Ballantine. 'Shall we return to him?'

When Arflane saw them come back he rose. 'When you are ready,' he said distantly, 'I would like to be taken back to the surface.'

'I have no intention of keeping you here against your will,' Ballantine said. 'I will leave you together now.'

He left the gallery. Arflane began to walk back to the apartment that had been set aside for them. He moved slowly, Ulrica beside him.

'When we go back to Friesgalt, Konrad,' Ulrica said, taking his arm, 'we can marry. That will make you Chief Ship Lord. In that position you will be able to guide the people towards the future, as Ballantine wants us to. You will become a hero, Konrad, a legend.'

'I do not trust legends,' he said. Gently he took her hand from his arm.

'Konrad?'

He shook his head. 'You go back to Friesgalt,' he told her. 'You go back.'

'What will you do? You must come back with me.'

'No.'

He moved as if to kiss her, then he checked himself.

'Our love...' Her voice shook. 'Oh, Konrad!'

'Our love was immoral. We paid our price. It is over. I –'

He frowned as if he heard his own voice for the first time. He continued, almost amused. 'I give myself to the Ice Mother. She has all my loyalty now.'

She kissed his shoulder. She turned back towards the garden.

The city rose to ground level and they disembarked. A storm was beginning to rise over the ice plains. The wind whistled through the tall towers of the city. Peter Ballantine helped Ulrica into the cabin of the helicopter that would take her most of the way back to Friesgalt.

There was a general confused bustling as the barbarians mounted up and began to turn their steeds towards the south. With a wave Donal led his men away across the plain.

Arflane watched them as they rode. There were skis on his feet, two lances in his gloved hands, a visor pushed up from his face; on his back was a heavy pack.

Ulrica looked out from the cabin. 'Konrad…'

He smiled at her. 'Goodbye, Ulrica.'

'Where are you going?' she asked.

He gestured into the distance. 'North,' he said. 'To seek the Ice Mother.'

As the rotors of the machine began to turn he pushed himself around on his skis and dug the lances into the ice, sending his body skimming forward. He leaned into the wind as he gathered momentum; it had begun to snow.

The helicopter bumped as it rose into the air and tilted towards the south. Ulrica stared through the glass and saw him moving swiftly northwards. His figure grew smaller and smaller. Sometimes it was obscured by drifting snow; sometimes she glimpsed him, the lances rising and falling as he gathered speed.

Soon, he was out of sight.

The Black Corridor

To the memory of Bob Calvert, a rare talent

Chapter One

Space is infinite.
It is dark.
Space is neutral.
It is cold.

Stars occupy minute areas of space. They are clustered a few billion here. A few billion there. As if seeking consolation in numbers.

Space does not care.

Space does not threaten.
Space does not comfort.

It does not sleep; it does not wake; it does not dream; it does not hope; it does not fear; it does not love; it does not hate; it does not encourage any of these qualities.

Space cannot be measured. It cannot be angered. It cannot be placated. It cannot be summed up.

Space is there.

Space is not large and it is not small. It does not live and it does not die. It does not offer truth and neither does it lie.

Space is a remorseless, senseless, impersonal fact.

Space is the absence of time and of matter.

THROUGH THIS SILENCE moves a tiny pellet of metal. It moves so slowly as to seem not to move at all. It is a lonely little object. In its own terms it is a long way from its planet of origin.

In the solid blackness it gives off faint light. In that great life-denying void it contains life.

A few wisps of gas hang on it; a certain amount of its own waste matter surrounds it: cans and packages and bits of paper, globules of fluid, things rejected by its system as beyond reconstitution. They cling to its side for want of anything better to cling to.

And inside the spacecraft is Ryan.

Ryan is dressed neatly in regulation coveralls which are light grey in colour and tend to match the vast expanse of controls, predominantly grey and green, which surround him. Ryan himself is pale and his hair is mainly grey. He might have been designed to tone in with the ship.

Ryan is a tall man with heavy grey-black eyebrows that meet near the bridge of his nose. He has grey eyes and full, firm lips that at the moment are pressed tightly together. He seems physically very fit. Ryan knows that he has to keep himself in shape.

Ryan paces the spaceship. He paces down the central passageway to the main control cabin and there he checks the co-ordinates, the consumption indicators, the regeneration indicators and he checks all his figures, at length, with those of the ship's computer.

He is quietly satisfied.

Everything is perfectly in order; exactly as it should be.

Ryan goes to the desk near thc ship's big central screen. Although activated, the screen shows no picture. It casts a greenish light onto the desk. Ryan sits down and reaches out towards the small console on the desk. He depresses a stud and, speaking in a clear, level voice, he makes his standard log entry.

'Day number one thousand, four hundred and sixty-three. Spaceship *Hope Dempsey* en route for Munich 15040. Speed holds steady at point nine of *c*. All systems functioning according to original expectations. No other variations. We are all comfortable.

'Signing off.

'Ryan, Acting Commander.'

The entry will be filed in the ship's records and will also be automatically broadcast back to Earth.

Now Ryan slides open a drawer and takes from it a large red book. It is his personal logbook. He unclips a stylus from a pocket in his coveralls, scratches his head and writes, slowly and carefully. He puts down the date: 24 December, AD 2005. He takes another stylus from his pocket and underlines this date in red. He looks up at the blank screen and seems to make a decision.

He writes:

The silence of these infinite spaces frightens me.

He underlines the phrase in red.

He writes:

I am lonely. I am controlling a desperate longing. Yet I know that it is not my function to feel lonely. I almost wish for an emergency so that I could wake at least one of them up.

Mr Ryan pulls himself together. He takes a deep breath and begins a more formal entry, the third of his eight-hourly reports.

When he has finished, he gets up, puts the red logbook away, replaces his stylus neatly in his pocket, goes over to the main console and makes a few fine adjustments to the instruments.

He leaves the main control cabin, enters a short companionway, opens a door.

He is in his living quarters. It is a small compartment and very tidy. On one wall is a console with a screen that shows him the interior of the main control cabin. Set in the opposite wall is a double bunk.

He undresses, disposes of his coveralls, lies down and takes a sedative. He sleeps. His breathing is heavy and regular at first.

He goes into the ballroom. It is dusk. There are long windows looking out onto a darkening lawn. The floor gleams; the lights overhead are dim.

On the ballroom floor formally dressed couples slowly rotate in perfect time to the music. The music is low and rather sombre. All the couples wear round, very black spectacles. Their faces are pale, their features almost invisible in the dim light. The round black glasses give them a mask-like appearance.

Around the floor other couples are sitting out. They stare forward through their dark glasses. As the couples move the music becomes quieter and quieter, slower and slower, and now the couples revolve more slowly too.

The music fades.

Now a low psalmlike moaning begins. It is in the room but it does not come from the dancers.

The mood in the room changes.

At last the dancers stand perfectly still, listening to the song. The seated men and women stand up. The chanting grows louder. The people in the room become angry. They are angry with a particular individual. Above the chanting, louder and faster, comes the beating of a rapid drum.

The dancers are angry, angry, angry…

Ryan awakes and remembers the past.

Chapter Two

Ryan and Mrs Ryan shyly entered their new apartment and laid down the large, nearly brand-new suitcase. It came to rest on the floor of the lobby. They released the handle. The suitcase rocked and then was still.

Ryan's attention left the case and focused on the shining tub in which grew a diminutive orange tree.

'Mother's kept it well watered,' murmured Mrs Ryan.

'Yes,' said Ryan.

'She's very good about things like that.'

'Yes.'

Awkwardly Ryan took her in his arms. Mrs Ryan embraced him. There was a certain reserve in her movements as if she were frightened of him or of the consequences her action might provoke.

A feeling of tenderness overwhelmed Ryan. He smiled down at her upturned face, reached out his hand to stroke her jawline. She smiled uncertainly.

'Well,' he said. 'Let's inspect the family mansion.'

Hand in hand they wandered through the apartment, over the pale gold carpets, past the simulated oak furniture of the living room to stare out through the long window at the apartment blocks opposite.

'Not too close,' said Ryan with satisfaction. 'Wouldn't it be terrible to live like the Benedicts – so near the next block that you can see right into their rooms. And they can see right into yours.'

'Awful,' agreed Mrs Ryan. 'No privacy. No privacy at all.'

They wandered past the wall-to-wall television into the kitchen. They opened cupboards and surveyed the contents. They pressed buttons to slide out the washing machine and the refrigerator. They turned on the infragrill, played with the telephone, touched the walls. They went into the two empty bedrooms, looking out of the windows, turning on the lights, their feet noisy on the tiles of the floors.

Last of all they went into the main bedroom, where the coloured lights of the walls shifted idly in the bright sunshine from the windows. They opened the wardrobes in which their clothes had been neatly laid out.

Mrs Ryan patted her hair in front of the huge convex mirror opposite the bed. Shyly they stood, looking out of the window.

Ryan pressed the button on the sill and the blinds slid down.

'Aren't the walls beautiful?' Mrs Ryan turned to look at the multicoloured lights playing over the flat surfaces.

'Not as beautiful as you.'

She looked around at him. 'Oh, you…'

Ryan reached out and touched her shoulder, touched her left breast, touched her waist.

Mrs Ryan glanced at the windows as if to reassure herself that the blinds were drawn and no-one could see in.

'Oh, I'm so happy,' she whispered.

'So am I.' Ryan moved closer, drew her to him, holding her buttocks cupped in his heavy hands. He kissed her lightly on the nose, then strongly on the mouth. His hand left her buttock and moved down her thigh, pushing up the skirt, feeling her flesh.

A flush came to Mrs Ryan's face as he eased her towards the new bed. She opened her lips and stroked the back of his neck. She sighed.

His thumb traced the line of her pelvis. She trembled and moved against him.

Then the Chinese jazz record started in the next apartment. The Ryans froze. Mrs Ryan was bent backwards with Mr Ryan's face buried in her neck. The clangour of the record, every note and every phrase, was as audible as if the music poured from their own glowing walls.

They broke apart. Mrs Ryan straightened her skirt.

'Damn them!' Mr Ryan raised his fists impotently. 'Good God! Don't tell me that's the kind of neighbours we've got.'

'Hadn't you better…?'

'What?'

'Couldn't you...?' She was confused.

'You mean...?'

'... go and speak to them?'

'Well, I...' He frowned. 'Maybe this time I'll just hammer on the wall.'

Slowly he took off his shoe. 'I'll show them.' He went to the wall and banged on it vigorously, stood back, shoe in hand, and waited.

The music stopped.

He grinned. 'That did it.'

Mrs Ryan took a deep breath and said, 'I'd better unpack.'

'I'll help you,' said Ryan.

He left the bedroom and approached the suitcase. He took the handle in both hands and staggered back to where she was waiting.

Together they unpacked the residue of their honeymoon – the suntan lotions, the damp bathing suits, the tissue-wrapped gifts for their parents. They talked and they laughed as they took things out of the suitcase and put them away, but secretly they were sad as article after article came out. All the souvenirs of that sunny three weeks on an island where no-one else lived, where there was freedom from observation, the noise and demands of other people.

The suitcase was empty.

Mrs Ryan reached into the waterproof pouch at the back and produced the tapes they had processed when they reached the mainland heliport. He fetched the player from the dressing table and they went into the living room to play the tapes on the television.

In silence they looked at the pictures, drinking in the landscapes they showed. There were the mountains, there the great blue expanse of the sea, there the heaths.

There were almost no shots of Mr or Mrs Ryan. There were only the views of the silent crags, the sea and the moors of the island where they had been so happy.

A bird cried.

Somewhat shakily the picture swept upward towards the cloud-slashed sky. A kittyhawk dived into the distance. There was the sound of the breakers in the background.

Suddenly the picture cut out.

Mrs Ryan looked at Mr Ryan with tears in her eyes.

'We must go back there soon,' she said.

'Very soon,' he smiled.

And the Chinese jazz, as loud as ever, shrieked through the room.

The Ryans sat rigidly in front of the television screen.

Ryan clenched his teeth. 'Jesus God, I'll –' he stood up – 'I'll kill the bastards!' He gestured irresolutely. 'There are laws. I'll call the police.'

Mrs Ryan held his hand. 'There's no need to speak to them, darling. Just put a note through their door. Warn them. They must have heard of the Noise Prevention Act. You could write to the caretaker as well.'

Ryan rubbed his lips once.

'Tell them they could be heavily fined,' said his wife. 'If they're reasonable, they'll...'

'All right.' Ryan pursed his lips. 'This time that's what I'll do. Next time – and I mean it – I'll knock on the door and confront them.'

He went into the living room to write the notes. Mrs Ryan made tea.

The Chinese jazz went on and on. Ryan wrote the notes with short, jerky movements of his pen.

... And I warn you that if this noise continues I will be forced to contact the police and inform them of your conduct. I have also told the caretaker of my intention. At very least you will be evicted – but you must also be aware of the heavy penalties you could receive under Section VII of the Noise Prevention Act of 1978.

He read back over the letter. It was a bit pompous. He hesitated. Perhaps if he...? No. It would do. He finished the letters, put them into envelopes and sealed them as Mrs Ryan directed the tea trolley into the living room. 'That will do, thank you,' she told it.

Suddenly the music stopped in mid-bar. Ryan looked at his wife and laughed. 'Maybe that's the answer. Maybe it's robots making that row.'

Mrs Ryan smiled. She picked up the teapot.

'Look, I'll do that,' said Ryan, 'if you'll just put these into the internal mail slot outside the front door.'

'All right.' Mrs Ryan replaced the pot. 'But what shall I do if I meet them?' She nodded towards the neighbouring flat.

'Ignore them completely, of course. They surely won't try to involve you in conversation. You might as well ignore anybody else you meet outside. If we start making contact with all the people in this block we'll never have any bloody privacy.'

'That's what mother said,' said Mrs Ryan.

'Right.'

She took the two letters and went out of the living room and into the lobby. Ryan heard the front door click open.

He straightened his head as he heard another voice. It was a woman's voice, high-pitched and cheerful. He heard Mrs Ryan mumble something, heard her footsteps as she entered hastily and shut the front door firmly.

'What on earth was that?' he asked as she returned to the living room. 'It's like living in a zoo. Maybe it was a mistake...'

'It was the woman who lives on the other side of us. She was coming back with her shopping. She welcomed me to the block. I said thank you very much and slid back in here.'

'Oh, Christ, I hope they're not going to pester us,' said Ryan.

'I don't think so. She seemed quite embarrassed to be chatting with a stranger.'

In cosy, uninterrupted silence the Ryans drank their tea and ate their sandwiches and cake.

When they had finished Mrs Ryan ordered the trolley back to the kitchen and she and Ryan sat together on the couch watching the tapes on the television. They were beginning to feel at ease in their little home.

Mrs Ryan smiled at the screen and pointed. There was a scene of cliffs, a cave. 'Remember that old fisherman we found in there that day? I was never so startled in my life. You said –'

A steady knocking began.

Ryan swung around, seeking the source of the noise.

'Over here,' said a voice.

Ryan got up. Outside the window was the head and torso of a man in overalls. His grinning red face was capped by a mop of clashing ginger hair. His teeth were ragged and yellow.

Mrs Ryan put her hand to her mouth as Ryan dashed to the window.

'What the bloody hell do you think you're doing, pushing your fucking face in our window without warning?' Ryan trembled with rage. 'What's the matter with you? Haven't you ever heard of privacy? Can't we get a moment's peace and quiet? It's a bloody conspiracy?'

The man's grin faded as Ryan ranted on. His muffled voice came through the pane. 'Look here,' he said. 'There's no need to be like that. I never knew you was back, did I? I was asked by the old lady to keep the windows clean while you was away. Which I have done without, if I may say so, any payment whatsoever. So before you complain about my bloody habits, I suggest you settle up.'

'How much?' Ryan put his hand in his pocket. 'Come on – how much?'

'Thirty pounds seven.'

Ryan opened the window and put some five-pound coins on the outside sill. 'There you are. Keep the change. And while you're at it don't bother to come back. We don't need you. I'm going to clean the windows myself.'

The man grinned cynically. 'Oh, yeah?' He tucked the money into his overall pocket. 'I hope you've got a head for heights, then. They're all telling me they're going to clean their own windows from now on. Have you seen them? Half of them don't do the outsides. They can't stand the height, see? You should see 'em. Filthy. You can hardly see out for the dirt. It must be like the black hole of Calcutta in most of them flats. Still, it's none of my business, I'm sure. If people want to live in the dark that's their affair, not mine.'

'Too right,' said Ryan. 'You nosy bloody –'

The window cleaner's eyes hardened. 'Look, mate –'

'Clear off,' said Ryan fiercely. 'Go on!'

The man shrugged, gave his yellow grin again and touched his carroty hair sardonically in a salute. 'Cheerio, then, smiler.' He began to lower himself down the wall towards the distant ground.

Ryan turned to look at his wife. Mrs Ryan was not on the couch any more. He heard sobs and followed the sound.

Mrs Ryan was stretched across the bed, face down, weeping hysterically.

He touched her shoulder. 'Cheer up, love. He's gone now.'

She shrugged off his hand.

'Cheer up. I'll –'

'I've always been a *private* person,' she cried. 'It's all right for you – you weren't brought up like me. People in our neighbourhood never intruded. They didn't come poking their faces through windows. Why did you bring me here? *Why*?'

'Darling, I find it all just as distasteful as you do,' Ryan told her. 'Honestly. We'll just have to sort it out step by step. Show people that we like to keep to ourselves. Be calm.'

Mrs Ryan continued to cry.

'Please don't cry, darling.' Mr Ryan ran his hands through his hair. 'I'll straighten things out. You won't see anyone you don't know.'

She turned on the bed. 'I'm sorry... One thing after another. My nerves...'

'I know.'

He sat down on the edge of the bed and began to stroke her hair. 'Come on. We'll watch a musical on TV. Then we'll...'

And as Mrs Ryan's sobs abated there came the familiar sound of the Chinese jazz. It was muted now, but it was still loud enough to lacerate the Ryans' sensitive ears.

Mrs Ryan moaned and covered her head as the tinkling, the jangling, the thudding of the music beat against her.

Ryan, helpless, stood and stared down at his weeping wife.

Then he turned and began to bang and bang and bang and bang on thc wall until all the colours disappeared.

But the music kept on playing.

Chapter Three

MR RYAN HAS done his exercises, bathed, dressed and breakfasted.

He has left his cabin and has paced down the main passageway to the central control cabin. He has checked the co-ordinates, the consumption indicators, the regeneration indicators and run computations through the machine.

He seats himself at the tidy steel desk below the big screen that has no picture. Around him the dials and the indicators move unobtrusively.

Mr Ryan takes out the heavy red-covered logbook from its steel drawer. He unclips his pen.

Using the old-fashioned log appeals to his imagination, his sense of pioneerdom. It is the one touch of the historic, the link with the great captains and explorers of the past. The logbook is Ryan's poem.

He enters the date: 25 December, AD 2005. He underlines it. He begins to write the first of his eight-hourly reports:

Day number one thousand, four hundred and sixty-four. Spaceship Hope Dempsey *en route for Munich 15040. Speed steady at point nine of c. All systems functioning according to original expectations. No other variations. All occupants are comfortable and in good health.*

Under this statement Ryan signs his name and rules a neat line. He then stands up and reads the entry into the machine.

Ryan's report is on its way to Earth.

He likes to vary this routine. Therefore when he makes his next report he will do it orally first and write it second.

Ryan stands up, checks the controls, glances around and is satisfied that all is in order. Since embarkation on the *Hope Dempsey* three years ago he has lost weight and, in spite of his treatments under the lamps, colour. Ryan exercises and eats well and relatively speaking he is in the best possible condition for a man living at two-thirds Earth gravity. On Earth it would be doubtful if he could run a hundred yards, walk along the corridor of a train, move a table from one side of a room to another. His muscles are maintained, but they have forgotten much. And Ryan's mind, basically still the same, has also forgotten much in the narrow confines of the perfectly running ship.

But Ryan has his will. His will makes him keep to the perfect routine which will take the ship and its occupants to the star. That will has held Ryan, the ship and its instruments and passengers together for three years, and will hold them together, functioning correctly, for the next two.

Ryan trusts his will.

Thus, in the private and unofficial section of the red logbook, the section which is never read over to Earth, Ryan writes:

Today is Alex's ninth birthday – another birthday he will miss. This is very saddening. However it is the kind of sacrifice we must make for ourselves and for others in our attempt to make a better life. I find myself increasingly lonely for the company of my dear wife and children and my other old friends and good companions. Broadcasts from Earth no longer reach us and soon I shall be reduced, for stimulation, to those old shipmates of mine, my videotapes, my audiotapes and my books. But all this must be if we are to achieve our end – to gain anything worthwhile demands endurance and discipline. In three minutes it will be time to perform the duty I find most painful emotionally – and yet most essential. Every day I am seized by the same mixture of reluctance, because I know the distress it will cause me. And yet there is an eagerness to fulfil my task. I shall go now and do what I have to.

Ryan closes the red logbook and places it back in the steel drawer so that the near edges of the book rest evenly against the bottom of the drawer. He replaces his pen in his pocket and stands up. He glances once more at the controls and with a firm step leaves the room.

He walks up the metallic central corridor of the ship. At the end there is a door. The door is secured by heavy spin screws. Ryan presses a button at the side of the door and the screws automatically retract. The door swings open and Ryan stands for a moment on the threshold.

The room is a small one, instantly bright as the heavy door opens. There are no screens to act as portholes and the walls gleam with a platinum sheen.

The room is empty except for the thirteen long containers.

One of the containers is empty. Plastic sheets are drawn two thirds of the way up over the twelve full containers. Through the semi-transparent material covering the remainder of the tops can be seen a thick, dark green fluid. Through the fluid can be seen the faces and shoulders of the passengers.

The passengers are in hibernation and will remain so until the ship lands (unless an emergency arises which will be important enough for Ryan to awaken them). In their gallons of green fluid they sleep.

At their heads is a panel revealing the active working of their bodies. On the plastic cover is a small identification panel, giving their names, their dates of birth and the date of their engulfment into suspended animation. On the indicator panel is a line marked DREAMS. On each panel the line is steady.

Ryan looks tenderly down into the faces of his family and friends.

> JOSEPHINE RYAN. 9/9/1960. 7/3/2004. His wife. Blonde and plump-faced, her naked shoulders still pink and smooth.

> RUPERT RYAN. 13/7/1990. 6/3/2004. The dark face of his son, so like his, the bony shoulders just beginning to broaden into manhood.

> ALEXANDER RYAN. 25/12/1996. 6/3/2004. The fairer face of his younger son. Eyes, amazingly, still open. So blue. Thin shoulders of an active small boy.

Ryan, looking on the faces of his closest relatives, feels close to tears at their loss. But he controls himself and paces past the other containers.

SIDNEY RYAN. 2/2/1937. 25/12/2003. His uncle. An old man. False teeth, very white, revealed through open mouth. Eyes closed. Thin, wrinkled shoulders.

JOHN RYAN. 15/8/1963. 26/12/2003. Ryan's brother. Ryan thinks that now he is thinner, less muscular, he must look more like John than he has ever done, even when they were children. John has the same short face, thick brows. His exposed shoulders are narrow, knotted.

ISABEL RYAN. 22/6/1962. 13/2/2004. His brother John's first wife, her crowned teeth exposed in a snarl in her narrow jaw. Pale face, pale hair, pale, thin shoulders. Ryan feels a spasm of relief that Isabel is lying in her container instead of around him, erect and needlelike, talking to him in her high voice. Ryan does not notice the passing thought, does not need to correct himself.

JANET RYAN. 10/11/1982. 7/5/2004. So lovely. His brother John's second wife. Soft cheeks, soft shoulders, long wavy black hair suspended in the green fluid, a gentle smile through pink, generous lips, as if she were dreaming pleasant dreams.

FRED MASTERSON. 4/5/1950. 25/12/2003. Narrow face. Thin, narrow shoulders. Furrowed brow.

TRACY MASTERSON. 29/10/1973. 9/10/2003. Masterson's wife. A pretty woman, looking as stupid in her container as she did out of it.

JAMES HENRY. 4/3/1957. 29/10/2003. Shock of red hair floating, sea-green eyes open in the green fluid. Looking like some drowned merman.

Ryan moves past him and stops at the eleventh container.

IDA HENRY. 3/3/1980. 1/2/2004. Poor girl. Matted hair, pale brown. Sunken young cheeks, drooping mouth.

There are two arrested lives in that container, Ryan thinks. Ida, Henry's wife, and her coming child. What would be the result of that long gestation of mother and child, both in foetal fluid?

FELICITY HENRY. 3/3/1980. 1/2/2004. Henry's other wife and Ida's twin sister. Her hair is smoother and shinier, her cheeks less sunken than her sister's. Not pregnant.

Ryan reaches the last container and looks into it. The white bottom of the container shines up at him. Surrounded by his sleeping companions he has the urge to get into the container and try it out.

Suspecting his impulse, he squares his shoulders and walks firmly from the room. The door hisses shut behind him. He touches the stud that replaces the screws. He walks back down the silent corridor and re-enters the control cabin. He makes rapid notes on a small pad of paper he takes from his breast pocket. He moves to the computer and runs his calculations through.

If necessary the computer could be switched to fully automatic, but this is not considered good for the psychology of crew members.

Ryan nods with satisfaction when the replies come. He returns to the desk and puts the charts back in the drawer.

As he does this another spurt of paper comes from the computer. Ryan examines it.

It reads:

REPORT ON PERSONNEL IN CONTAINERS NOT SUPPLIED.

Ryan purses his lips and punches in the reports:

JOSEPHINE RYAN. CONDITION STEADY.

RUPERT RYAN. CONDITION STEADY.

ALEXANDER RYAN. CONDITION STEADY.

SIDNEY RYAN. CONDITION STEADY.

JOHN RYAN. CONDITION STEADY.

ISABEL RYAN. CONDITION STEADY.

JANET RYAN. CONDITION STEADY.

FRED MASTERSON. CONDITION STEADY.

TRACY MASTERSON. CONDITION STEADY.

JAMES HENRY. CONDITION STEADY.

IDA HENRY. CONDITION STEADY.

FELICITY HENRY. CONDITION STEADY.

****

*******YOUR OWN CONDITION****

suggests the computer.

Ryan pauses and then reports:

I AM LONELY.

The computer tells him instantly:

*******FILL YOUR TIME ACCORDING TO THE SUGGESTED PROGRAMME. IF THE CONDITION CONTINUES INJECT 1CC PRODITOL PER DIEM. DO NOT TAKE MORE. DISCONTINUE THE DOSAGE AS SOON AS POSSIBLE AND AT ALL COSTS AFTER 14 DAYS***

Ryan straightens his shoulders, signs off and walks away from the computer.

He walks down the corridor to his own accommodation. He inflates a red easy chair, sits down and presses a stud on the wall. The TV screen in front of him begins to roll off a list of its offerings. Films, plays, music, dancing and discussion and educational programmes. In his weakness Ryan does not choose the agricultural information he is committed to studying. He selects an old Polish film.

Soon the screen is full of people walking, talking, eating, getting on streetcars, watching scenery, kissing and arguing.

Ryan feels tears on his cheeks but he has an hour of relaxation due to him and he will take it, in whatever form it comes.

As Ryan watches, bearing his expected melancholy with stoicism, his mind wanders. He hears, echoing in his head, the report on his undead companions in their cavernous containers:

Josephine Ryan. Condition steady. Rupert Ryan. Condition steady. Alexander Ryan... Sidney Ryan... John Ryan... Isabel Ryan... Janet Ryan... Fred Masterson... Tracy Masterson... James Henry... Ida Henry... Felicity Henry...

The parade of the faces he once knew passes in front of him. He imagines them as they were, before they were immersed in their half-life in the sea-green fluid.

Chapter Four

JAMES HENRY'S PALE hands, stubby and freckled, shook as he bent forward in his chair and stared into Fred Masterson's face. '*Do* something, Fred, *do* something – that's what I'm saying.'

Masterson gazed back, thin eyebrows raised cynically, long forehead creased by parallels of wrinkles. 'Such as?' he asked after a pause.

Henry's hands clenched as he said: 'Society is polluted physically and morally. Polluted by radioactivity we're continually told is within an acceptable level – though we see signs every day that this just isn't so. I cannot allow Ida or Felicity to bear children with the world as it is today. And worse, in a way, than the actual environment is the infinite corruption of man himself. Each day we grow more rotten, like sacks of pus, until the few of us who try to cling to the old standards, try to stay decent, are more and more threatened by the others. Threatened by their corruption, threatened by their violence. We're living in a mad world, Masterson, and you're advising patience...'

Beside him on the Ryans' couch were his two wives, tired, identically pale, identically thin, as if the split cell which produced them had only contained the materials for one healthy woman and had been forced to make two. As Henry spoke they both gazed at him from their pale blue eyes and followed every word as if he was speaking their thoughts.

Masterson did not reply to James Henry's tirade. He merely stared about him as if he were thoroughly tired of the discussion.

The furniture of the Ryans' living room had been pushed back against the walls to seat the group which met there every month. The blinds were drawn and the lights were on.

Seated with his back to the window was Ryan's Uncle Sidney, a thin, obstinate old man with a tonsure of brown hair around his bald head. The rest of the group was seated around the other walls. The seat in front of the window, like the front row at public meetings, was always the last to be filled.

Fred Masterson and his wife, Tracy, who wore a well-cut black floor-length dress, the conservative fashion of the moment, and fully made-up black lips, sat opposite the Henry family on their sofa.

Next to Masterson sat John Ryan's first wife, Isabel. She was a dowdy, pinch-faced woman. On John's left sat his other wife, the beautiful Janet. Against the fourth wall were Ryan and his wife Josephine.

The women wore blacks and browns, the men were quietly dressed in dark-coloured tunics and trousers. The room, bare in the centre, entirely without ornament, had a dull look.

Ryan sat and worked out in his head some estimates for a new line of product. As a silence fell between James Henry and Fred Masterson, he turned his mind away from his business problems and said:

'This is, after all, only a discussion group. We haven't the power or the means to alter things.'

Henry opened his green eyes wider and said urgently: 'Can't you see, Ryan, that the days of discussion are practically over? We're living in chaos and all we're doing is talking about it. At the meeting next month –'

'We haven't agreed to a meeting next month yet,' said Masterson.

'Well, if we don't we'll be fools.' Henry crossed his legs in an agitated manner. 'At the meeting next month we must urge that pressure –'

Tracy Masterson's face was taut with stress. 'I've got to go home now, Fred.'

Masterson looked at her helplessly. 'Try to hang on…'

'No…' Tracy hunched her shoulders. 'No. It's people all around me. I know they're all friends… I know they don't mean to…'

'A couple more minutes.'

'No. It's like being shut up in a box.'

She folded her hands in her lap and sat with her eyes downcast. She could say no more.

Josephine Ryan rose and took her by the arm. 'I'll give you some pills and you can sleep in our bed. Come on, dear…' She drew the younger woman up by the arm and led her into the kitchen.

Henry looked at Masterson. 'Well? You know why your wife is like this. It all dates from the time when she was caught up in that UFO demonstration in Powell Square. And that's an experience any one of us could have at any time – as things are now.'

As he spoke there came the sound of chanting from nearby streets. A window broke in the distance and there were shouts. A noisy song began.

From the bedroom Tracy Masterson started to scream.

Fred Masterson got up, paused for a moment and then ran towards the sound.

The rest of the group sat frozen, listening as the hubbub came closer. In the bedroom Tracy Masterson screamed and shouted.

'NO.NO.NO.NO.NO.NO.NO.NO.NO.'

Josephine Ryan came back, leaning against the doorway. 'The pills will take effect soon. Don't worry about her. Who are the people in the street?'

No-one replied.

Tracy screamed again.

'Who are the people in the street?' Josephine moved further into the room. 'Who?'

The noisy voices subsided, giving way to the same low chanting, in a minor key, which had begun the procession.

Now Ryan and his friends could hear some of the words.

Shut up the land,
Shut up the sky.
We must be alone.
Strangers, strangers all must die.
We must be alone.
Alone, alone, alone.
Shut out the fearful, darkening skies.

Let us be alone.
No strangers coming through the skies.
We must be alone.
No threats, no fears,
No strangers here,
No thieves who come by night.
Alone, alone, alone.

'It's them, then. The Patriots.' Mrs Ryan looked at the others. Again no-one replied.

The chanting was close under the windows now.

The lights went out. The room was left in complete darkness.

Tracy Masterson's screams had diminished to a whimper as the drug took hold.

'Bloody awful verses, whatever else...' Uncle Sidney cleared his throat.

The group sat surrounded by a chanting which seemed, in the utter darkness, to be coming from all over the room.

Suddenly it stopped.

There was the sound of running and sharp cries. Then a pitiful high screaming like the sound of an animal being killed.

Uncle Sidney stirred in his chair by the window and stood up. 'Let's have a look out, then,' he said calmly. His finger went to the button on the window sill.

As James Henry shouted *'No!'* Ryan was halfway across the room, arms stretched toward his uncle.

It was too late.

The blind shot up.

The window covering the whole of one wall was open to the night.

Ryan stood petrified in the middle of the floor as the flickering light cast by a thousand torches in the street played over him. Henry, half out of his seat, stood up and was completely still.

Josephine Ryan stood in the middle of the floor with the bottle of pills in her hand.

The dark-clad women sat in their seats without moving.

The cries and the terrible high scream went on.

Uncle Sidney looked down into the street. On the other side, in the high block opposite, all the windows were blinded.

'Oh, my God,' said Uncle Sidney. 'Oh, my God.'

There was silence until Josephine Ryan said: 'What is it?'

Uncle Sidney said nothing. He looked downwards.

Mrs Ryan took a deep breath. She walked firmly over to the window. Ryan watched her.

She steeled herself, looked swiftly down into the street, stepped back. 'It's too horrible. That really is too horrible.'

Uncle Sidney's face was hard. He continued to watch.

The crowd had caught a young man of twenty, one of the people who lived in the block opposite. They had tied him to an old wooden door, propped the door against a great steel power supply post, drenched the door and the young man with petrol and set light to him.

The young man lay at an angle on the blazing door. He writhed and he screamed as the flames consumed him. The crowd pressed closely around, those in front being perpetually pushed too close to the flames by the people at the back who wanted to see. Their torches and the light cast over them by their human bonfire revealed chiefly men, most of them in their thirties and forties. The women among them were younger. All were dressed in dark, long clothing. In the front the people were crouched, tensely watching the young man burn.

A young woman with cropped blonde hair yelled: 'Burn, stranger, burn.' The men about her took up the cry. 'Burn, burn, burn, burn!'

The young man writhed in the flames, gave a final, frantic twist of his body and was still.

When he had stopped screaming, the crowd became quiet. Apparently they were exhausted. They sat or stood about, breathing heavily, wiping their faces and hands and mouths.

Uncle Sidney pressed the blind button in silence. The blind slid down, blotting out the torches, the fire, the silent crowd below. He sat heavily in his chair.

The crackling of the fire could be heard in the Ryans' living room.

Mrs Ryan took her hand from her eyes, walked out to the kitchen and went to the sink. The men and women in the room heard her running water into a tumbler, heard her drink and put the tumbler into the dishwasher, heard the door of the washer close.

Uncle Sidney sat in his chair, looking at the floor.

'What did you want the blind open for?' James Henry demanded. 'Eh?'

Uncle Sidney shrugged and continued to stare at the floor.

'Eh?'

'What difference does it make?' said Uncle Sidney. 'What bloody difference…?'

'You had no right to expose us to that – particularly the women,' said James Henry.

Uncle Sidney looked up and there were a few tears in his eyes. His voice was strained. 'It happened, didn't it?'

'What's that got to do with it? We don't want to get involved. It's not even your home. It was Josephine's window which was uncovered when – this thing – took place. She'll be the one accused!'

Uncle Sidney didn't reply. 'It happened, that's all I know. It happened – and it happened here.'

'Very horrifying to see, no doubt,' said Henry. 'But that doesn't make any difference to the fact that the Patriots have got some of the right ideas, even if they do put them into practice in a very distasteful way.' He sniffed. 'Besides, some people enjoy watching that sort of thing. Revel in it. As bad as them.'

Uncle Sidney's eyes expressed vague astonishment. 'Do what?'

'What did you want to watch it for, then?'

'I didn't *want* to watch it.'

'So you say…'

Masterson appeared in the doorway and said, 'Tracy's gone to sleep at last. What's been happening? Patriots, was it?'

Ryan nodded. 'They just burnt a man. Outside. In the street.'

Masterson wrinkled his nose. 'Bloody lunatics. If they really want to get rid of them there's plenty of legal machinery to help them.'

'Quite,' said Henry. 'No need to take the law into their own hands. What bothers me is this odd anti-space notion of theirs.'

'Quite,' said Masterson. 'They've been reassured time and time again that there are no alien bodies in the skies. They've been given a dozen different kinds of proof and yet they continue to believe in an alien attack.'

'There could be some truth in it, couldn't there?' Janet said timidly. 'No smoke without fire, eh?'

The three men looked at her.

'I suppose so,' Masterson agreed. He made a dismissive gesture. 'But it's extremely unlikely.'

Mrs Ryan directed the trolley through the door. The group sat drinking coffee and eating cake.

'Drink up while it's hot.' Mrs Ryan's voice had an edge to it.

Isabel Ryan flinched and said, 'No thank you, Josephine. It doesn't agree with me.'

Josephine's mouth turned down.

'Isabel hasn't been very well,' her husband John said defensively.

Ryan tried to smooth things over. He smiled at Isabel.

'You're quite right to be careful,' he said.

The whole group knew, from Isabel's demeanour, although no-one would have stated it, that Isabel was experiencing a phase where she supposed people were trying to poison her. She would eat and drink nothing she had not prepared herself.

Most of them knew what it was like. They had gone through the same thing at one time or another. It was best to ignore it.

Anyway, it wasn't unheard of for people who believed that sort of thing to be perfectly right. They all knew men and women who had imagined that they were being poisoned who later had died inexplicably.

'One of us ought to attend the next big meeting of the Patriots,' said Ryan. 'It would be interesting to know what they're up to.'

'It's dangerous.' John Ryan's face was stern.

'I'd like to know, though.' Ryan shrugged. 'It's best to investigate a thing, isn't it? We ought to find out what they're really saying.'

'We'll go in a band, then,' said James Henry. 'Safety in numbers, eh?'

His wives looked at him fearfully.

'Right,' said Masterson. 'Time to tune into the report of the Nimmoite rally at Parliament. The government will fall tonight.'

They watched the Nimmoite rally on the television. They watched it while more cries and shouts sounded from the street below. They watched as a group passed playing drums and pipes. They did not look around. They watched the Nimmoite rally until the President appeared in the House of Commons and offered his resignation.

Chapter Five

THAT NIGHT THERE were riots and fires all over the city.

The Ryans and their friends watched the riots and fires, sitting behind their closed blinds, staring at the large, bright wall which was their television.

The city was being ripped and battered and bloodied.

They drank their coffee and they ate their cake and they watched the men fall under the police clubs, watched the girls and boys savaged by the police dogs, heard the hooting and yelling of the looters, saw the fire service battling to control the fires.

The Ryans and their friends had seen a great many riots and fires in their lives, but never so many at a single time. They watched almost critically for a while.

But as the programmes wore on, Mrs Ryan became quieter and quieter, more mechanical in her presentation of coffee, of sugar, of things to eat.

It was when she saw her favourite department store go up in flames that she finally put her head in her arms and sobbed…

Mrs Ryan had been married for fourteen years.

For fourteen years she had carried the weight of her vigorous husband's moods and ambitions. She had reared children, battled with her fear of other people, of the outside, had made almost all family decisions.

She had done her best.

Now she wept.

Ryan was startled.

He went over and patted her, tried to comfort her, but she could not be stopped. She went on crying.

Ryan looked up from his wife and stared at Uncle Sidney. In front of them, unheeded, glass was smashing into the streets, crowds were running and shouting, the top of the Monument, built to commemorate the Great Fire of 1666, was crowned with flames.

'Put her to bed,' said Uncle Sidney. 'You can't do or say anything effective. It's the situation that's getting her down. Put her to bed.'

The group watched as sensible Josephine Ryan was supported out of the room by her husband. Josephine Ryan was about to be sedated and put to bed next to the unconscious Tracy Masterson.

Ida and Felicity Henry, seeing their senior woman carried off, became alarmed. Ida shuddered and Felicity said, 'Where will it end?'

'You're becoming inhuman,' said Uncle Sidney. 'Switched off.'

'In the grave unless we do something fast,' James Henry said brutally. Apparently he hadn't heard Uncle Sidney.

'In the grave,' he said again. 'What are you two going to do, eh?' And he laughed nastily into the pale, identical faces of his two hapless wives.

Fred Masterson looked at Uncle Sidney and Uncle Sidney looked at Fred Masterson. They shrugged almost at the same time.

And there was Henry laughing as usual. As usual, leaning forward in his chair. As usual, springy, full of ideas, head crowned by that energetic mass of red hair which gave the impression of a man getting extra fuel from somewhere.

As James Henry pushed his features aggressively towards the faces of his tired twin girl-brides it seemed impossible not to think that he was somehow plugged into their vital forces, in some manner draining off energy before it could reach the women to power their thin, narrow feet, their stooped backs, their limp hair, their lacklustre eyes.

Uncle Sidney, possessed by this thought, laughed heartily into the room.

'What the hell are you laughing at, Sidney?' demanded James Henry.

Uncle Sidney shook his head and stopped.

James Henry glared at him. 'What was so funny, then?'

'Never mind,' said Uncle Sidney. 'It's enough to be able to laugh at all, the way things are.'

'Then keep laughing, Sidney,' said James Henry. 'Keep at it, chum. You'll be fucking crying soon enough.'

Sidney grinned. 'So much for the good old values. Didn't you know there were ladies present?'

'What d'you mean?'

'Well, when I was a young man, we didn't use that sort of language in front of ladies.'

'What sort of language, you old fool?'

'You said "fucking", James,' said Uncle Sidney, straight-faced.

'Of course I didn't. I don't believe in… A man has to have a very limited vocabulary if he needs to resort to swearing like that. What are you trying to prove, Sidney?'

Again the look of vague astonishment crept into Uncle Sidney's eyes. 'Forget it,' he said at length.

'Are you trying to start something?'

'I don't want to start anything more, no,' said Uncle Sidney.

The television screen jumped from one scene to another. Fires and riots. Riots and fires.

James Henry turned to his wives. 'Did I say anything objectionable?'

In unison they shook their heads.

He glared again at Uncle Sidney. 'There you are!'

'Okay. All right.' Uncle Sidney looked away.

'I proved I didn't say anything,' said James Henry insistently.

'Fair enough.'

'They're my witnesses!' He pointed back at his wives. 'They told you.'

'Sure.'

'What do you mean, "sure"?'

'I meant I believe you. I'm sorry. I must have misheard you.'

James Henry relaxed and smiled. 'You might apologise, then. To all of us, I should have thought.'

'I apologise to all of you,' Uncle Sidney said. 'All of you.'

Ryan watched from the doorway and he was frowning. He

looked at Uncle Sidney. He looked at James Henry. He looked at Ida and Felicity. He looked at Fred Masterson. Then he looked at the television screen.

It was not so different. It was frightening. Nothing seemed real. Or perhaps it was that nothing seemed any more real than anything else.

He went towards the television with the intention of switching it off. Then he paused. He was overwhelmed with the feeling that if he turned the switch not just the television picture would fade, but also the scene in the room. He shuddered.

Mr Ryan shuddered, full of fear and hopelessness. Full of depression. Full of doubt.

It had been a bad day.

The day was really something of an historic day, he thought. Today marked a turning point in his country's history – perhaps the world's history.

Perhaps it was the beginning of a new Dark Age.

He came to a decision and reached forward to switch off…

Chapter Six

SEATED IN HIS little cabin, the television flickering gently in front of him, the foreign voices speaking their lines, Ryan falls, against his will, into a doze.

Surely he knew, when he sat down, when he selected a film in an alien language, that this would be the result. Perhaps he did but would not acknowledge the thought.

Ryan, a man tormented by nightmares during his official hours of sleep, who rises every morning with the indefinable despair of a man who has dreamed of horrors he cannot even remember – Ryan is desperate for rest.

Through the caverns of his brain pound the sounds of heart and blood, the drums of life. He hears them dimly at first.

Ryan is standing in the ballroom.
The dance floor has a dull shine.
The lights in the candelabra are low.
They give off a bluish light.
Black streamers decorate the walls.
There are masks suspended at eye level on them.
The masks show human faces.

K
E
E
P
GOING
P
E
E
K

The spaceship is on course for Munich.
Travelling at just below the speed of light.
The spaceship is on course for Munich.
I KNOW THAT I DES...
... DES SCIENCES – HISTOIRE DES SCIENCES – HISTOIRE DES SCIENCES...
IT IS TRUE, HOWEVER
I AM WILLING TO TELL
WHOEVER WISHES TO KNOW
(there is no need to tell – there is no-one to tell – it does not matter...)

K
E
E
P
GOING
P
E
E
K

WHICH WAY?

In the ballroom the masks show human faces. Faces distorted by anger, lust and greed.

Suddenly one of the masks shows his wife Josephine, her face ferociously distorted. There is his youngest child, Alexander. His mouth is open, his eyes are blank. Alexander – a drooling idiot.

The couples are circling to the chanting music. It grows slower and slower and they revolve more and more slowly. They are dressed in dark clothes. They have the firm and well-defined faces of the practical, self-interested, well-fed middle classes. They are people of substance.

Their eyes are masked by the round sunglasses. The long closed windows at the end of the room look out into blackness. The music gets slower, the men and women revolve more slowly, so slowly they barely move at all.

The music almost stops.

There is the slow beating of a drum.

The music is heard more loudly. It is like a psalm sung by a chorus of monks. It is a funeral dirge, the song sung when a man is about to be buried.

The drums beat louder, the music quickens.

A high screaming note comes in and holds steady through the dirge.

The drum beats faster, the music quickens.

The high screams grow louder.

The dancers bunch in the middle of the room, staring towards the window through their round, black, covered eyes. They begin to talk quietly among themselves. They are discussing something and looking at the window.

ON THE NIGHT OF THE FAIR THERE WAS AN ACCIDENT
Q: WHAT WAS THE EXACT NATURE OF THE CATASTROPHE?
ON THE NIGHT OF THE MARINOS AN ACCIDENT
Q: WHAT WAS THE EXACT NATURE OF THE CATASTROPHE?
ON A NIGHT IN MAY AN ACCIDENT
Q: WHAT WAS THE EXACT NATURE OF THE CATASTROPHE?
ON AND ON MAY ACCIDENT
Q: WHAT WAS THE EXACT NATURE OF THE CATASTROPHE?
ONE MAY ACCIDENT
Q: WHAT WAS THE EXACT NATURE OF THE CATASTROPHE?
ONE MAY ACCEPT
Q: WHAT WAS THE EXACT NATURE OF THE CATASTROPHE?
ONE MACE IT

Q: WHAT WAS THE EXACT NATURE OF THE CATASTROPHE?
ONE ACED
Q: WHAT WAS THE EXACT NATURE OF THE CATASTROPHE?
ONE A
Q: WHAT WAS THE EXACT NATURE OF THE CATASTROPHE?
ONE
Q: WHAT WAS THE EXACT NATURE OF THE CATASTROPHE?
WON
Q: WHAT WAS THE EXACT NATURE OF THE CATASTROPHE?
WIN
Q: WHAT WAS THE EXACT NATURE OF THE CATASTROPHE?
IN
Q: WHAT WAS THE EXACT NATURE OF THE CATASTROPHE?
N
Q: WHAT WAS THE EXACT NATURE OF THE CATASTROPHE?
NO ANSWER AVAILABLE
NO ANSWER AVAILABLE
NO ANSWER AVAILABLE
END OF SESSION. PLEASE CLEAR ALL PREVIOUS JUNK AND RESET IF REQUIRED.

They are still looking at the window.

Ryan finds himself and his wife and their two children standing in front of the window. His arm is around Josephine on one side and his other arm spans the shoulders of the two boys on the other.

The crowd is talking about them. Ryan feels fear for his wife and children. The crowd talks more angrily, looks at Ryan and his family.

The scream behind the music is louder, the singing more urgent, the drum beats faster, faster, faster.

THE SPACESHIP IS ON COURSE FOR MUNICH. ON COURSE TRAVELLING AT JUST BELOW THE SPEED OF LIGHT.

THE SPACESHIP IS ON COURSE FOR MUNICH.

CONDITION STEADY
CONDITION STEADY
CONDITION STEADY

The light flashes on and off as if trying to warn him of something rather than to reassure him. He frowns at the big sign. Is there something wrong with the hibernating personnel? Something he has not noticed? Something the instruments have not registered?

And Ryan awakes sweating in his red, inflatable chair and stares blindly at the minute, flat figures on the television screen.

His body is limp and his mouth is dry.

He licks his lips and sighs aloud.

Then he sets his mouth in a firm line, switches off the set and leaves the room.

His feet echo along the passageway. He reaches a cubicle containing a long white bed. He straps himself on and is massaged.

When he is finished his body aches and his mind is still not clear. It is now time for Ryan to eat. He returns to his room and gets food. He eats and he tastes nothing.

When he has finished he raises the cover over the porthole screen in his room and looks out through the simulated window into the vastness of space.

For a second he feels that he sees a dark figure out there in the void. He clears his vision rapidly and stares out at the stars.

He cannot see the planet that he and his companions are bound for. He has been in space for three years. He will be in space for another two years. And he cannot see his destination yet. He has only the word of the space physicists that it exists and that it can support the thirteen lives he carries with him.

A planet of Barnard's Star, Munich 15040.

He is alone in space, in charge of his ship and the lives of the other twelve. He is more than halfway to his destination.

The sudden remembrance of what he has done sweeps over him. Along with his fear, with the torment caused by the solitude, Ryan feels pride. He causes the cover to sweep down over the 'porthole'. He leaves his room and walks into the control room to continue his duties.

But he cannot get rid of the lingering feeling of depression, the sense of something not done.

This sense of a task unfulfilled makes him work with even greater intensity, even greater efficiency.

He frowns.

There is still something left undone.

He rechecks everything. He runs tests through the computer. He inspects every instrument and double-checks it to make sure it is reading accurately.

Everything is perfect.

He has forgotten nothing.

The feeling almost disappears.

Chapter Seven

When he has read his report into the machine Ryan goes to the desk beneath the screen and opens the drawer where his red logbook is lying ready for his remarks.

First he sits down at his desk and hums a song as he completes some calculations. He works quickly and mechanically to complete his task. He lays it aside, satisfied.

He has fifteen minutes free now. He produces the red logbook from the drawer again, rules a line under his formal report and writes:

Alone in the craft I experience the heights and depths of emotion untempered by the needs of less mechanical work than I do now, uninterrupted by the presence of others.

He reads this over, frowns, shrugs, continues:

This means deep pain and being a prey to my own feelings. It also means great joy. An hour ago I stared out of my porthole at the enormous vista and recollected what I – what we as a group – have done to save ourselves. My mind goes back to how we were, and forward to what we will be.

Ryan's stylus hovers over the page. He makes writing motions over the book, but he cannot phrase his thoughts.

At length he gives up, rules another line under his entry, shuts the book and replaces it in the drawer.

He changes his mind, gets the book out again and begins to write rapidly:

The world was sick and even our group was tinged with unhealthiness. We were not lilywhite. We sold out some of our ideals. But perhaps the difference was that we knew we were selling out. We admitted what we were doing and so remained rational when almost everyone else had gone insane.

It is true, too, that we became somewhat hardened to the horrors around us, shut them out – even condoned some of them – even fell in with the herd from time to time. But we had our objectives – our sense of purpose. It kept us going. However, I don't deny that we dirtied our hands sometimes. I don't deny that I got carried away sometimes and did things that I now am inclined to regret. But perhaps it was worth it. After all, we survived!

Perhaps that is all the justification needed.

We kept our heads and we are now on our way to colonise a new planet. Start a new society on cleaner, more decent, more rational lines.

Cynics might think that an impossible ideal. It will all get just as bad in time, they'd say. Well, maybe it won't. Maybe this time we really can build a sane society!

None of us is perfect. Especially this crew! We all have our rows and we all have qualities that the others find annoying. But the point is that we are a family. Being a family, we can have our arguments, our strong disagreements – even our hatreds, to a degree – and still survive.

That is our strength.

Ryan yawns and checks the time. He still has a few minutes of free time to spare. He looks at the paper and begins to write again:

When I look back to our days on Earth, particularly towards the end, I realise just how tense we were. The ship routine has relaxed me, allowed me to realise just what I had become. I don't like what I became. Perhaps one has to become a wolf, however, to fight wolves. It will never happen again. There were times, I cannot deny, when I lost hold of my ideals – even my senses. Some of the events are hazy – some are almost completely forgotten (though doubtless one of my relatives or friends will be able to remind me). I can hardly believe that it took such a short time for society to collapse.

That was what caused the trauma, of course – the suddenness of it all. Obviously, there were signs of the coming crises, and perhaps I should have taken more heed of those signs – but then all chaos suddenly broke loose throughout the world! What we tut-tutted at in the manner of older people slightly disconcerted by the changing times I now realise were much more serious indications of social unrest. Sudden increases in population, decreases in food production – they were the old problems that the Jeremiahs had been going on about for years – but they were suddenly with us.

Perhaps we had been deliberately refusing to face the problem, just as people had refused to consider the possibility of war with Germany in the late thirties. We Homo sapiens *have a great capacity for burying our heads in the sand while pretending to face out the issue.*

Ryan smiles grimly. It's true, he thinks. People under stress usually start dealing with half a dozen surrogate issues, leaving the real issues completely untouched because they're too difficult to cope with. Like the man who lost the sixpence in the house but decided to look for it outside because the light was better and he would thus save his candles.

He adds in his log:

And there's always some bloody messiah to answer their needs – someone whom they will follow blindly because they are too fearful to rely on their own good sense. It's like Don Quixote leading the Gadarene Swine!

Ryan chuckles aloud.

Leaders, führers, duces, prophets, visionaries, gurus... For a hundred years the world was ruled by bad poets. A good politician is only something *of a visionary – essentially he must be a man who sees the needs of people in practical and immediate terms and tries to do something about them. Visionaries are fine for inspiring people – but they are the worst choice as leaders – they attempt to impose their rather simple visions on an extremely complicated world! Why have politics and art become so mixed up together in the last hundred years? Why have bad artists been given nations as canvases on which to paint their tatty, sketchy, rubbish? Perhaps because politics, like religion before it, was dead as an effective force and something new had to be found. And art stood in until whatever it was turned up. Will something turn up? It's hard to say. We'll probably never know on Munich* 15040 *if the world survives or not.*

Thank God we had the initiative to get this ship on her way to the stars!

No more time for writing. Ryan puts the logbook away quickly and begins his regular check of the ship's nuclear drive, running a check on virtually every separate component.

He taught himself the procedure for running the ship. He was not trained as an astronaut. No-one planned that he should be the man standing in the control cabin at that particular moment.

Until comparatively recently Ryan was, in fact, a businessman. A pretty successful businessman.

As he does the routine checking, he thinks about himself before he even conceived the idea of travelling into space.

He sees himself, a strongly built man of forty, standing with his back to the vast plate-glass window of his large, thickly carpeted office. His heavy, healthy face was pugnacious, his back was broad, his thick, stubby-fingered hands were clasped behind his back.

Where Ryan is now a monk – a man dedicated to his ship and his unconscious companions, a man charged, like a cleric in the Dark Ages, with preserving the knowledge and lives contained in this moving monastery – then he was a man almost perpetually in a state of combat.

Ten thousand years before he would have been a savage standing in front of his pack, hair bristling, teeth bared, bone club in hand.

Instead, Ryan had been a toymaker.

Not a kindly old peasant whittling puppets in a pretty little cottage. Ryan had owned a firm averaging a million pounds a year in profits, producing toy videophones, plastic hammers, miniature miracles of rocketry, talking life-size dolls, knee-high cars with automatic gear changes, genuine all-electric cooking machines, real baaing sheep, things which jumped, sped, made noises and broke when their calculated life-span was over and were thrown secretly and with curses by parents into the rapid waste disposal units of cities all over the western world.

Ryan pressed the button which connected him with the office of his manager, Owen Powell.

Powell appeared on the screen. He was on his hands and knees on the office floor watching two dolls, three feet high, walk about the carpet. As he heard the buzz of the interoffice communicator he was saying to one of the dolls: 'Hello, Gwendolen.' As he said 'Hello, Ryan', the doll replied, in a beautifully modulated voice, 'Hello, Owen.'

'That's the personalised doll you were talking about, is it?' Ryan said.

'That's it.' Powell straightened up. 'I knew they could do it if they tried. Lovely, isn't she? The child voice-prints her in the shop on its birthday, say. After that she can give any one of twenty-five responses to the child's questions – but only to the one child. Imagine that – a doll which can speak, apparently intelligently, *but only to you*. The kids go mad about it.'

'If the price is right,' Ryan said.

Powell was an enthusiast, a man who would really, if he had not had a twenty thousand pound a year job with Ryan, have been perfectly happy carving toys in an old peasant's hut. He looked disconcerted by Ryan's discouraging remark.

'Well, maybe we can get the price down to twenty pounds retail. What would you say to that?'

'Not bad.' Ryan deliberately gave Powell no encouragement. Powell was a man who would work hard for a smile and stop working when you gave it, reasoned Ryan. Therefore it was better to smile seldom in his direction.

'Never mind all that now.' Ryan rubbed his eyebrows. 'There's plenty of time to get it right before Christmas when we'll try a few out, see how they go and produce a big line by spring for the following Christmas.'

Powell nodded. 'Agreed.'

'Now,' said Ryan, 'I want you to do two things for me. One – get in touch with the factory and tell Ames to use the Mark IV pin on the Queen of Dolls. Two – ring Davies and tell him we're stopping all deliveries until he pays.'

'He'll never keep going during August if we do that,' objected Powell. 'If we stop delivering, he'll have to close down, man. We'll only get a fraction of what he owes us!'

'I don't care.' Ryan gestured dismissively. 'I'm not letting Davies get away with another ten thousand pounds' worth of goods so that he'll pay us in the end, if we're lucky. I will not do business on that basis. That's final.'

'All right.' Powell shrugged. 'That's reasonable enough.'

'I think so.' Ryan broke the connection.

He reached into his desk and took out a bottle of green pills.

He poured water into a glass from an old-fashioned carafe on his immaculate desk. He swallowed the pills and put the glass down. Unconsciously he resumed his stance, head jutting slightly forward, hands behind back. He had a decision to make.

Powell was a good manager.

A bit sloppy sometimes. Forgetful. But on the whole efficient. He was not quarrelsome, like the ambitious Conroy, or withdrawn, like his last manager, Evers.

What he had mistaken at first for decent behaviour, respect for another man's privacy, had gone beyond reason in Evers.

When a manager refused to speak to the firm's managing director on the interoffice communicator – broke the connection consistently, in fact – business became impossible.

Ryan could certainly respect his feelings, sympathise with them as it happened – so would any other self-respecting person. But facts were facts. You could not run a business without talking to other people. Strangers they might be, uncongenial they might be, but if you couldn't stand a brief conversation on the communicator, then you were no use to a firm.

Ryan reflected that he himself was finding it increasingly distasteful to get in touch with many of his key workers but, since it was that or go under, he forced himself to do so.

Powell was certainly a good manager.

Inventive and clever, too.

On the other hand, Ryan thought, he had come to hate him.

He was childish. There was no other word for it. That open countenance, that smile, a smile which said that he would take to anybody who took to him. There was something doglike about it. Just pat him on the head and he would wag his tail to and fro, jump up and lick your face. Sickening, really, Ryan thought to himself. It made you feel sick to think about it. He had no reticences, no reserves. A man shouldn't be so friendly.

And, of course, Ryan thought, when you looked at the facts, it all came down to Powell's being Welsh. That was the Welshman for you – open-faced and friendly when they spoke to you and clannishly against you behind your back.

The Welsh gangs were some of the worst in the city. Ryan reflected that he had not bought his machine gun, and taught his wife and elder son how to use it, just for fun. That was the Welsh – all handshakes and smiles when you met them, and all the time their sons were stoning your relatives three streets away.

Ryan tapped his teeth together. Old Saunders of Happyvoice had shaken him a bit when he had got on the communicator just to warn him about Powell.

'It might help,' he had said, 'if that manager of yours, Powell, changed his name. You can't deny it sounds Welsh and there's been an awful lot of trouble with those Welsh Nationalists recently. Between ourselves, it only needs one word from a competitor of yours – say Moonbeam Toys – via their PRO, and you'll be branded in the Press as an employer of Welsh labour. And that's never likely to help sales – because people remember. Just at that critical moment when they're choosing between one of your products and one of another firm's – they remember. And then they don't buy a Ryan Toy. See what I mean? One word from you to old Powell and he'll change his name to Smith and you're in the clear.'

Ryan had smiled and made bluff assurances. When he had cut off the communicator two thoughts came to him.

One, he knew Powell would be first confused and then obstinate about changing his name.

Two, and worse, Saunders did not think for one instant that Powell was a Welshman. He just thought he had an unfortunate name.

Ryan realised that he was right out on a limb. Where his competitors refused to take on employees with suspect names, however impeccable their backgrounds, Ryan had an actual living, breathing Welshman working for him. Someone who could quite easily be a Nationalist, working for the Welsh cause (a somewhat obscure cause as Ryan saw it). It was bloody ridiculous. How could he have got so out of touch? Why hadn't he thought of it?

Ryan frowned. No – it was stupid. Powell was too absorbed in his work to worry about politics. He was the last person to get involved in anything like that.

Still, a name was a name. The Nationalists had been causing quite a bit of trouble lately and things had really got bad with the assassination of the King. The Welsh Nationalists had claimed it was their work. But other groups of extremists had also made the same claim.

From a practical point of view, Ryan thought, Powell was an embarrassment. No question of it. Yet he couldn't fire a man on suspicion.

Ryan's face took on an over-rosy tinge and his thick hands gripped each other a little more firmly behind his back.

I'm in fucking trouble here, he thought.

He pinched his nose and then reached out to buzz for his personnel manager.

Frederick Masterson was sitting at his desk working on a graph. Masterson was, in physical terms, the exact complement to Ryan. Where Ryan was thickset and ruddy, Masterson was tall, thin and pale. As the communicator buzzed in his office he dropped the pencil from his long, thin hand and looked at the screen in alarm. Seeing Ryan, a thin smile came to his lips.

'Oh, it's you,' he said.

'Fred. I want details of any staff we employ with foreign or strange-sounding names – or foreign backgrounds of any kind. Just to be on the safe side, you realise. I'm not planning a purge!' He laughed briefly.

'Just as well.' Masterson grinned. 'Your name's Irish, isn't it, begorrah!'

Ryan said, 'Come off it, Fred. I'm no more Irish than you are. Not a single relative or ancestor for the past hundred years has even seen Ireland, let alone come from it.'

'I know, I know,' said Fred. 'Call me Oirish agin and Oi'll knock ye over the hade wid me shillelagh.'

'Skip the funny imitations, Fred,' Ryan said shortly. 'The firm's at stake. You know how bloody small-minded a lot of people are. Well, it seems to be getting worse. I just don't want to take any chances. I want you to probe. If necessary turn the whole department over to examining personnel records for the slightest hint of anything peculiar. Examine marriages, family background, schooling, previous places of employment. No action at this stage. I'm not planning to victimise anyone.'

'Not at the moment,' said Masterson, a funny note in his voice.

'Oh, come off it, Fred. I just want to be prepared. In case any competitors start going for us. Naturally I'll protect my employees to the hilt. This is one way of making sure I can protect them – against any scandal, for a start.'

Masterson sighed. 'What about those with Negro blood? I mean the West Indians got around a bit before they were all sent back.'

'Okay. I don't think anyone's got anything against blacks at the moment, have they?'

'Not at the moment.'

'Fine. But you never know…'

'No.'

'I want to protect them, Fred.'

'Of course.'

Ryan cut the communicator and sighed.

An image flashed into his mind and with a start he remembered a dream he had had the previous night. It was funny, the way you suddenly remembered dreams long after you had dreamed them.

It had been to do with a cat. His old house where he had lived with his parents. It had had a big, overgrown back garden and they had kept several cats. The dream was to do with the air rifle he had had and a white-and-ginger cat – an interloper – that had entered the garden. Someone – not himself, as he remembered the dream – had shot the cat. He had not wanted to shoot the cat himself, but had gone along with this other person. They had shot the cat once and it had been patched up by neighbours. There had been a piece of sticking plaster on its left flank. The person had fired the gun and badly wounded the cat but the animal had not appeared to notice. It had still come confidently along the wall, tail up and purring, towards the French windows. It had had a big bloody wound in its side, but it hadn't seemed to be aware of it.

The cat had entered the house and come into the kitchen, still purring, and eaten from the bowl of one of the resident cats.

Ryan had not known whether to kill it to put it out of its misery or whether to let it be. It hadn't actually seemed to be in any misery, that was the strange thing.

Ryan shook his head. A disturbing dream. Why should he remember it now?

He had never, after all, owned a white-and-ginger cat.

Ryan shrugged. Good God, this was no time for worrying about silly dreams. He would have to do some hard thinking. Some realistic thinking. He prided himself that if he was nothing else he was a pragmatist. Not an ogre. He was well-known for his good qualities as an employer. He had the best staff in the toy industry. People were only too eager to come and work for Ryan Toys. The pay was better. The conditions were better. Ryan was much respected by his fellow employers and by the trades unions. There had never been any trouble at Ryan Toys.

But he had the business to consider. And, of course, ultimately the country, for Ryan's exports were high.

Or had been, thought Ryan, before the massive wave of nationalism had swept the world and all but frozen trade, save for the basic necessities.

Still, it would pass. A bit of a shake-up for everybody. It wasn't a bad thing. Made people keep their feet on the ground. One had to know how to ride these peculiar political crises that came and went. He wasn't particularly politically minded himself. A liberal with a small 'l' was how he liked to describe himself. He had an excellent profit-sharing scheme in the factory, lots of fringe benefits, and an agreement with the unions that on his death the workers would take over control of the factory, paying a certain percentage of profits to his dependants. He was all for socialism so long as it was phased in painlessly. He steadfastly refused to have a private doctor and took his chances with the National Health Service along with everybody else. While he was not over-friendly with his workers, he was on good terms with them and they liked him. This silly racialistic stuff would come and go. The odds were that it wouldn't affect the factory at all.

Ryan took a deep breath. He was getting overanxious, that was his trouble. Probably that bloody Davies account preying on his mind. It was just as well to take a stiff line with Davies, even if it meant losing a few thousand. He would rather kiss the money goodbye if it meant kissing goodbye to the worries that went with it.

He buzzed through to Powell again.

Powell was once again on his knees, fiddling with a doll.

'Ah,' said Powell, straightening up.

'Did you take care of those couple of items, Powell?'

'Yes. I spoke to Ames and I phoned Davies. He said he'd do his best.'

'Good man,' Ryan said and switched off hastily as a delighted grin spread over Powell's face.

Chapter Eight

RYAN IS WORKING on a small problem that has come up concerning the liquid regeneration unit in the forward part of the ship. It is malfunctioning slightly and the water has a slight taste of urine in it. A spare part is needed and he is instructing the little servorobot to replace the defunct element.

That was what had saved him, of course, he thinks. His pragmatism. He had kept his head while all around people were losing theirs, getting hysterical, making stupid decisions – or worse, making no decisions at all.

He smiles. He had always made quick decisions. Even when those decisions were unpalatable or possibly unfashionable in terms of the current thinking of the time. It was his basic hardheadedness that had kept him going longer than most of them, allowed him to hang on to a lot more, helped him to the point where he was now safely out of the mess that was the disrupted, insane society of Earth.

And that is how he intends to remain. He must keep cool, not let the depression, the aching loneliness, the weaker elements of his character, take him over.

'I'll make it,' he murmurs confidently to himself. 'I'll make it. Those people are going to get their chance to start all over again.'

He yawns. The muscles at the back of his neck are aching. He wriggles his shoulders, hoping to limber the muscles up. But the ache remains. He'll have to do something about that. Must stay fit at all costs. Not just himself to think of.

He isn't proud of everything he did on Earth. Some of those decisions would not have been made under different circumstances.

But he didn't go mad.

Not the way so many of the others did.

He stayed sane. Just barely, sometimes, but he made it through to the other side. He kept his eyes clear and saw things as they really were while a lot of other people were chasing wild geese or phantom tigers. It was a struggle, naturally. And sometimes he had made mistakes. But his common sense hadn't let him down – not in the long run.

What had someone once said to him?

He nodded to himself. That was it. *You're a survivor, Ryan. A natural bloody survivor.*

It was truer now, of course, than ever before.

He was a survivor. *The* survivor. He and his friends and relatives.

He was making for the clean, fresh world untainted by mankind, leaving the rest of them to rot in the shit heap they had created.

Yet he mustn't feel proud. Pride goeth before a fall... Mustn't get egocentric. There had been a good deal of luck involved. It wasn't such a bad idea to test himself from time to time, run through that Old Time Religion stuff. The seven deadly sins.

Check his own psyche out the way he checked the ship.

CHECK FOR *Pride.*

CHECK FOR *Envy.*

CHECK FOR *Sloth.*

CHECK FOR *Gluttony.*

... and so forth. It didn't do any harm. It kept him sane. And he didn't reject the possibility that he *could* go insane. There was always a chance. He had to watch for the signs. Check them in time. A stitch in time saves nine.

That was how he had always operated.

And he hadn't done badly, after all.

REPAIR COMPLETED reports the computer. Ryan is satisfied.

'Congratulations,' he says cheerfully. 'Keep up the good work, chum.'

The point was, he thinks, that he, unlike so many of the rest, had never been to a psychiatrist in his life. He'd been his own psychiatrist. *Gluttony*, for instance, could indicate some kind of disturbance that came out in obsessive eating. Therefore if he found himself overeating, he searched for a reason, hunted out the cause of the problem. It was the same with work. If it started to get on top of you, then stop – take a holiday. It meant you could work better when you got back and didn't spend all your time bawling out your staff for mistakes that were essentially your own creation.

He presses a faucet button and samples the water. He smacks his lips. It's fine.

He is relaxing. The disturbing dreams, the sense of depression, have been replaced by a feeling of well-being. He has compensated in time. Instead of looking back at the bad times, he is looking back at the good times. That is how it should be.

Chapter Nine

MASTERSON FLASHED RYAN about a week after he had begun his check-up.

Ryan had been feeling good for days. The Davies matter was settled. Davies had paid up two thirds of the amount and they had called it quits. To show no hard feelings Ryan had even paid off the mortgage on Davies's apartment so that he would have somewhere secure to live after he had sold up his business.

'Morning, Fred. What's new?'

'I've been doing that work you asked for.'

'Any results?'

'I think all the results are in. I've drawn up a graph of our findings on the subject.'

'How does the graph look?'

'It'll come as a shock to you.' Masterson pursed his lips. 'I think I'd better come and talk to you personally. Show you the stuff I've got. Okay?'

'Well – of course – yes. Okay, Fred. When do you want to come here?'

'Right away?'

'Give me half an hour.'

'Fine.'

Ryan used the half-hour to prepare himself for Masterson's visit, tidying his desk, putting everything away that could be put away, straightening the chairs.

When Masterson arrived he was sitting at his desk smiling.

Masterson spread out the graph.

'I see what you mean,' said Ryan. 'Good heavens! Just as well we decided to do this, eh?'

'It confirms what I already believed,' said Masterson. 'Ten per cent of your employees, chiefly from the factories in the North, are actually of wholly foreign parentage – Australian and Irish in the main. Another ten per cent had parents born outside England itself, i.e. in Scotland, Wales and the Republic of Ireland. Three per cent of your staff, although born and educated in England, are Jewish. About half a per cent have Negro or Asiatic blood. That's the general picture.'

Ryan rubbed his nose. 'Bloody difficult, eh, Masterson?'

Masterson shrugged. 'It could be used against us. There are a number of ways. If the government offers tax relief to firms employing one-hundred-per-cent English labour, as they're talking of doing, then we aren't going to benefit from the tax relief. Then there are wholesalers' and retailers' embargoes if our rivals release this information. Lastly there're the customers.'

Ryan licked his lips thoughtfully. 'It's a tricky one, Fred.'

'Yes. Tricky.'

'Oh, fuck, Fred.' Ryan scratched his head. 'There's only one solution, isn't there?'

'If you want to survive,' said Fred, 'yes.'

'It means sacrificing a few in order to protect the many. We'll pay them generous severance pay, of course.'

'It's something like twenty-five per cent of your employees.'

'We'll phase them out gradually, of course.' Ryan sighed. 'I'll have to have a talk with the unions. I don't think they'll give us any trouble. They'll see the sense of it. They always have.'

'Make sure of it,' said Masterson, 'first.'

'Naturally. What's up, Fred? You seem fed up about something.'

'Well, you know as well as I do what this means. You'll have to get rid of Powell, too.'

'He won't suffer from it. I'm not a bloody monster, Fred. You've got to adjust though. It's the only way to survive. We've got to be realistic. If I stood on some abstract ideal, the whole firm would collapse within six months. You know that. The one thing all political parties are agreed on is that many of our troubles stem from an over-indulgent attitude towards foreign labour. Whichever way the wind blows in the near future, there's no escaping that one. And the way our rivals are fighting these days, we can't afford to go around wearing kid gloves and sniffing bloody daffodils.'

'I realise that,' said Masterson. 'Of course.'

'Powell won't feel a thing. He'd rather be running a doll hospital or a toyshop anyway. I'll do that. I'll buy him a bloody toyshop. What do you say? That way everybody's happy.'

'Okay,' said Masterson. 'Sounds like a good idea.' He rolled up the charts. 'I'll leave the breakdown with you to go over.' He made for the door.

'Thanks a lot, Fred,' Ryan said gratefully. 'A lot of hard work. Very useful. Thanks.'

'It's my job,' said Masterson. 'Cheerio. Keep smiling.' He left the office.

Ryan was relieved that he had gone. He couldn't help the irrational feeling of invasion he had whenever anyone came into his office. He sat back, humming, and studied Masterson's figures.

You had to stay ahead of the game.

But Masterson had put his finger on the only real problem. He disliked the idea of firing Powell in spite of the man's unbearable friendliness, his nauseating candour, his stupid assumption that you only had to give one happy grin to open the great dam of smiles swirling about in everyone.

Ryan grinned in spite of himself. That summed up poor old Powell, all right.

As a manager, as a creative man, Powell was first class. Ryan could think of no-one in the business who could more than half fill his place. He wasn't any trouble. He was content. A willing worker putting in much longer hours than were expected of him.

But was that just his good-heartedness? Ryan wondered. A light was dawning. Now he could see it. Powell was probably just grateful to have a job! He knew that no-one in any business would employ him.

Just like a bloody Welshman to hang on and on, not letting you know the facts, creeping about, getting good money out of you, not letting you know that his very presence was threatening to ruin your business. Trying to make himself indispensable in the hopes that you'd never find out about him and fire him. Pleasant and agreeable and co-operative. Maybe even a front for some sort of Welsh Nationalist sabotage. Then – the knife in the back, the bullet from the window, the enemy in the alley.

Stop it, Ryan told himself. Powell wasn't like that. He didn't need to build the man up into a villain to justify sacking him. There was only one reason for sacking him. He was an embarrassment. He could harm the firm.

Ryan relaxed.

He sat down at his desk, opened a drawer and took out his packed lunch. He opened the thermos flask and poured himself a cup of coffee. He placed his meal on the miniature heater in the lower compartment of the luncheon box.

Thank God, he thought, for the abolition of those communal lunches with other businessmen, or the firm's executives.

Thank God that communal eating had finally died the death. What could have been more disgusting than sitting munching and swallowing with a gang of total strangers, sitting there staring at their moving mouths, offering them items – wine, salt, pepper, water – to make their own consumption more palatable, talking to them face to face as they nourished themselves. The conversion of the canteens had provided much-needed office space as well.

Ryan took a fork and dug into the plate. The food was now thoroughly heated.

Once he had eaten he felt even more relaxed. He had thought it all out. He didn't waste time when it came to decisions. No point in moralising.

He wiped his lips.

The problem had assumed its proper proportions. It would cost him a bit in golden and silver handshakes, but it was worth it. He could probably get cheaper staff anyway, considering the huge volume of unemployment, and recoup his losses by the end of the year.

This way everybody gains something. Nobody loses.

He picked up the sheets of names and figures and began to study them closely.

Chapter Ten

THAT'S HOW IT *was*, thinks Ryan. A cop-out, now he looked back, but a graceful cop-out. No-one got badly hurt. It could have been worse. It was the difference between a stupid approach and an intelligent approach to the same problem.

It had been the same when he had got the group out of that riot at the Patriot meeting. When had that been? January. Yes, January, 2000. The civilised world had been expecting the end. There had been all the usual sort of apocalyptic stuff, which Ryan had dismissed as a symptom of radical social change. He had not been able to believe then that things were going to get worse. There had been penitential marches through the streets. Even scourgings, public confessions.

And January had been the month of that oddball move to close the camps for Foreigners. The camps had been decently maintained. The people lived as well as anyone outside the camps – perhaps better in certain circumstances. It had also been the month when the Patriots had tried to open the camps up to more people – to a more sinister, less identifiable group.

Ryan remembers the crowd in Trafalgar Square. A crowd of fifty thousand strong, covering the square, pushed up the steps of the National Gallery and St Martin's, pushed inside the gallery and the church, right up against the altar. The crowd had blocked the streets all around. It was horrifying. Disgusting. People like rats in a box.

Even now Ryan feels sick, remembering how he felt then.

He and the group had gone along, but they were now regretting it.

Whenever the crowd got too noisy or violent the troops fired over their heads.

It had been snowing. The searchlights played over the plinth where the leading Patriots stood and they flashed over the heads of the crowd, picked up large flakes of snow as they drifted down on the dense mass of people.

The Patriot leaders, collars of their dark coats turned up, stood in the snow looking over the crowd. And as they spoke their voices were enormously amplified. Deafeningly amplified; reaching all the way up the Mall to where Queen Anne sat in her lonely room, hearing the words on TV and from the meeting itself a quarter of a mile away; reaching all the way down Whitehall to Parliament itself.

Parliament. That discredited institution.

They are turning on each other now, thought Ryan, looking at the faces of the Patriots. There were signs of dissension there if he wasn't mistaken. There would be a split soon.

But meanwhile there were the usual speeches, coming distorted into the mind partly because of the amplification system, partly because of the wind, partly because of the usual ungraspable political clichés the speakers used.

The snow kept falling on the upturned faces of the crowd – an orderly crowd of responsible people. There were few interrupters. The presence of the troops and the paid Patriot Guards made sure of that.

Dennis Beesley, Patriot leader and Member of Parliament, stood up to speak.

Beesley, a large, thickset man in a long black overcoat and a large hat, was an extremist. His political manner was of the old school – the Churchillian school which still touched many people who wanted their politicians to be 'strong'. His tone was ponderous. His words, spoken slowly and relatively clearly, were portentous.

Unlike the others, he did not speak generally about the Patriot cause, for he had come to make a fresh statement.

As he began to speak the wind dropped and his words came through with a sudden clarity – over the crowd in the square, the crowds in the streets, down as far as Westminster, along to Buckingham Palace, as far as Piccadilly Circus in the other direction.

'Aliens among us,' he said, his head lowered and thrust towards the crowd. 'There are aliens among us. We do not know where they come from. We do not know how they landed. We do not know how many there are. But we do know one thing, my friends, people of England – they are among us!'

Ryan, standing uncomfortably in the middle of the crowd in the square grimaced sceptically at his friend Masterson who stood beside him. Ryan couldn't believe in a group of aliens contriving to land on Earth without anyone's knowledge. Not when the skies were scanned for invaders from special observation posts built all over the country. But Masterson was listening seriously and intently to Beesley.

Ryan turned his attention back to the platform.

'We cannot tell who they are, yet they are among us.' Beesley's voice droned on. 'They look like us, sound like us – in every respect they are human – but they are not human. They are non-human – they are anti-human.' He paused, lowered his voice. 'How, you say, do we know about the aliens? How have we found out about the existence of this pollution, of these creatures who move about our society, like cancer cells in a healthy body? We know by the evidence of our own eyes. We know the aliens exist because of who they are, what happens when they are about.

'Otherwise how can we explain the existence of chaos, blood-lust, law-breaking, riot, revolution in our midst? How can we explain the little children battered to death by the fanatics of Yorkshire? The waves of rioting and looting all over the West Country? The satanic practices of religious maniacs in the Fens? How can we explain the hatred and the suspicion, the murder rate – now three times what it was five years ago, a full ten times what it was in 1990? How can we explain the fact that we have so few children when a few years ago the birth rate had doubled? Disaster is upon us! Who is stirring up and fomenting all this disorder, bloodshed and ruin? Who? Who?'

Ryan, glancing into the faces of the people about him, could almost believe they were listening seriously. Were they? Or was the presence of the troops and the Patriot Guards preventing them from catcalling or just walking away from this nonsense?

He looked at the faces of the police around the platform. They were staring up at Beesley – brute-faced men listening to him with close attention. Ryan, scarcely able to believe it, realised that Beesley's story of the hidden invaders was being taken seriously by the majority of the vast crowd. As Beesley went on speaking, describing the hidden marauders, makers of chaos in their midst, the crowd began to murmur in agreement.

'Their bases are somewhere,' Beesley went on. 'We must find them, fellow patriots. We must eliminate them, like wasp nests...'

And there came from the crowd a great hissed susurrus 'Yesssss.'

'We must find the polluters and wipe them out for ever. Whether they come from space or are the agents of another Power, we do not know as yet. We must discover where they originate!'

And the crowd, like a cold wind through the ruins, answered 'Yessssss.'

He's lost them, thought Ryan sceptically, *if he doesn't give them something a bit more concrete than that. He's got to tell them how to pick out these menacing figures they have to destroy.*

'Who are they? How do we find them?' asked Beesley. 'How? How? How indeed?' His tone became divinely reasonable. 'You all know, in your heart of hearts, who they are. They are the men – and women, too; make no mistake, they are women as well – who are different. You know them. You can tell them at a glance. They look different. Their eyes are different. They express doubt where you and I know certainty. They are the men who associate with strangers and people of doubtful character, the men and women who throw suspicion on what we are fighting for. They are the sceptics, the heretics, the mockers. When you meet them they make you doubt everything, even yourself. They laugh a lot, and smile too often. They attempt, by jesting, to throw a poor light on our ideals. They are the people who hang back when plans are suggested for purifying our land. They defend the objects of our patriotic anger. They hang back from duty. Many are drunkards, licentious scoffers. You know these people, friends. You know them – these men who have been sent here to undermine a righteous society. You have always known them. Now is the time to pluck them out and deal with them as they deserve.'

And, before he had finished speaking, the crowd was in uproar. There were shouts and screams.

Ryan poked Masterson, who was staring incredulously at the platform, in the ribs. 'Let's get out,' he said. 'There's going to be trouble.'

'Only for the aliens,' said James Henry at his other elbow. 'Come on, Ryan. Let's sniff 'em out and snuff 'em out.'

Ryan looked at Henry in astonishment. Henry's green eyes were ablaze. 'For crying out loud, Henry...'

He turned to his brother John. John looked back vaguely and suddenly, under the gaze of his elder brother, seemed to pull himself together. 'He's right,' said John. 'We'd better think of getting home. This is real mass hysteria. Jesus Christ.'

Henry's mouth hardened. 'I'm staying.'

'Look –' Ryan was jolted by the crowd. Snow fell down his neck – 'Henry. You can't possibly –'

'Do what you like, Ryan. We've heard the call to deal with these aliens – let's deal with them.'

'They wouldn't be likely to come here tonight, would they?' Ryan shouted. Then he stopped, realising that he was beginning to answer in Henry's terms. That was the first step towards being convinced. 'Good God, Henry – this is too classic for words. We're rational men.'

'Agreed. Which makes our duty even clearer.'

The crowd was pushing the four men backwards and forwards. The men had to shout to be heard over the roar of the rabble.

'James – come home and talk it over. This isn't the place...' Ryan insisted, standing his ground with difficulty. From somewhere came the sound of gunfire. Then the gunfire stopped. Ryan found he was shouting into relative silence. 'You won't take that "aliens" nonsense seriously when you've got a drink inside you back at our flat!'

A man put his head over Henry's shoulder. His red face was flushed. 'What was that, friend?' he said to Ryan.

'I wasn't talking to you.'

'Oh, no? I heard what you said. That's of interest to *everyone* here. You're one of them, if you ask me.'

'I didn't.' Ryan looked contemptuously at the sweating face. 'But we're all entitled to our own opinions. If you think it's true, I won't argue with you.'

'Shut up,' Masterson cried, tugging at Ryan's sleeve. 'Shut up and come home.'

'Bloody alien!' the red-faced man shouted. 'A bloody nest of them!'

Instantly, it seemed to Ryan, the crowd was on them. He came rapidly to a decision, keeping his head even in this situation.

'Calm down, all of you,' he said in his most commanding voice. 'My point is that we might make mistakes in this situation. The aliens have to be found. But we need to work systematically to find them. Use a scientific approach. Don't you see – the aliens themselves could be stirring things up for us – making us turn on each other.'

The red-faced man frowned. 'It's a point,' he said grudgingly.

'Now I believe that if there are aliens here tonight they are not going to be in the middle of the crowd. They are going to be on the edges, trying to sneak away,' Ryan continued.

'That seems reasonable,' said James Henry. 'Let's get after them.'

Ryan led the way shouting with the rest.

'Aliens! Aliens! Stop the aliens! Get them now. Over there – in the streets!'

Pushing through the crowd was like trying to trudge through a quagmire. Every step, every breath Ryan took was painful.

Ryan led them, pace by pace, through the packed throng, up the steps into the National Gallery and, as the crowd thinned out in the galleries themselves, through a window at the back, through yards, over walls and car parks until they escaped the red-faced man and his friends and were finally in the moving mass of Oxford Street.

Only James Henry didn't seem aware of what Ryan had done. As they reached Hyde Park he pulled at Ryan's torn coat.

'Hey! What are we supposed to be doing? I thought we were going after the aliens.'

'I know something about the aliens that wasn't mentioned tonight,' Ryan said.

'What?'

'I'll tell you when we get back to my place.'

When they finally reached Ryan's flat they were exhausted.

'What about the aliens, then?' James Henry asked as the door closed behind them.

'The worst aliens are the Patriots,' said Ryan. 'They are the most obvious of the anti-humans.'

Henry was puzzled. 'Surely not...'

Ryan took a deep breath and went to the drinks cabinet, began fixing drinks for them all as they sat panting in the chairs in the living room.

'The Patriots...' murmured Henry. 'I suppose it's just possible...'

Ryan handed him his drink. 'I thought,' he said, 'that the discoveries in space would give us all a better perspective. Instead it seems that the perspective has been even more narrowed and distorted. Once people only feared other races, other nations, other groups with opposed or different interests. Now they fear everything. It's gone too far, Henry.'

'I'm still not with you,' James Henry said.

'Simply – paranoia. What is paranoia, Henry?'

'Being afraid of things – suspecting plots – all that stuff.'

'It can be defined more closely. It is an *irrational* fear, an *irrational* suspicion. Often it is in fact a refusal to face the *real* cause of one's anxiety, to invent causes because the true cause is either too disturbing, too frightening, too horrible to face or too difficult to cope with. That's what paranoia actually is, Henry.'

'So?'

'So the Patriots have offered us a surrogate. They have offered us something to concentrate on that is nothing really to do with the true causes of the ills of society. It's common enough. Hitler supplied it to the Germans in the form of the Jews and the Bolsheviks. McCarthy supplied it to the Americans in the form of the Communist Conspiracy. Even our own Enoch Powell supplied it in the form of the West Indian immigrants in the sixties and seventies. There are plenty of examples.'

James Henry frowned. 'You say they were wrong, eh? Well, I'm not so sure. We were right to get rid of the West Indians when we did. We were right to restrict jobs to Englishmen when we did. You have to draw the line somewhere, Ryan.'

Ryan sighed. 'And what about these "aliens" from space, then? Where do they fit in. What are they doing to the economy? They are an invention – a crude invention, at that – of the Patriots to describe anyone who is opposed to their insane schemes. Where do you think the term "witch-hunt" comes from, Henry?'

James Henry sipped his drink thoughtfully. 'Perhaps I did get a bit over-excited...'

Ryan patted him on the shoulder. 'We all are. It's the strain, the tension – and it is particularly the uncertainty. We don't know where we're going. We've no goals, because we can't rely on society any longer. The Patriots offer certainty. And that's what we've got to find for ourselves.'

'You'd better explain,' John Ryan said from his chair. 'Have you got any suggestions?'

Ryan spread his hands. 'That was my suggestion. That we find a goal – a rational goal. Find a way out of this mess...'

And Ryan, now sitting at his desk in the great ship, reflects that it was that evening which was the turning point, that decision which brought him to where he is now, aboard the spaceship *Hope Dempsey*, heading towards Munich 15040, Barnard's Star, at point nine of *c*...

Chapter Eleven

THERE IS NO sound here in space. No light. No life. Only the dim glow of distant stars as the tiny craft moves, so slowly, through the great neutral blackness.

And Ryan, as he goes methodically about his duties, thinks with a heavy heart of the familiarity and warmth of his early years – of the births of his children, of studying their first schoolbooks, talking to his friends in the evenings at their apartment, of his wife, now resting like some comfortable Sleeping Beauty, unaware of him in the fluids of her casket.

Just a pellet travelling through space, thinks Ryan. Nearly all the living tissue contained in the pellet is unconscious in the waters of the caskets. Once they had moved and acted. They had been happy, until the threats had become obvious, until life had become unbearable for them…

Ryan rubs his eyes and writes out his routine report. He underlines it in red, reads it into the machine, sits down again before the logbook.

He writes:

Another day has passed.

I am frightened, sometimes, that I am becoming too much of a vegetable. I am an active man by nature. I will need to be active when we land. I wonder if I have become too passive. Still, this is idle speculation…

His speculations were never idle, he reflects. The moment the problem was clearly seen, he began to think along positive lines. The problem was straightforward: society was breaking down and death and destruction were becoming increasingly widespread. He wished to survive and he wished for his friends and family to survive. There was nowhere in the world that could any longer be considered a safe refuge. Nuclear war was bound to arise soon. There had been only one answer: the stars. And there had been only one project for reaching the stars. Unmanned research craft had brought back evidence that there was a planetary system circling Barnard's Star and that two of those planets were in many respects similar to Earth.

The research project had been United Nations sponsored – the first important multilateral project between the Great Powers...

It had been a last attempt to draw the nations of the world together, to make them consider themselves one race.

Ryan shakes his head.

It had been too late, of course.

Ryan writes:

... I keep fit as best I can. An odd thought just popped into my head. It gives some idea of how closely one has to watch oneself. It occurred to me that a way of keeping fit would be to wake one of the other men so that we could have sparring matches, play football or something like that. I began to see the 'sense' of this and began to rationalise it so that it seemed advantageous to all concerned to wake, say, my brother John. Or even one of the women... There are several ways of keeping fit and alert – getting exercise. Ridiculous, undisciplined ideas! It is just as well I keep the log. It helps me keep perspective.

He grins. A great way of cheating on old John. He'd never know...

He shudders.

Naturally, he couldn't...

There was Josephine, too. It would betray the whole idea of the mission if he betrayed them...

I think I'll go and take a cold shower! he writes jokingly. He signs the book, underlines his entry in red, closes the book, puts it neatly away, gets up, makes a last check of the instruments, asks the computer a couple of routine questions, is satisfied by the answers, leaves the control cabin.

True to his word, Mr Ryan has his cold shower. It does the trick. He feels much better. Humming to himself he enters his own cabin, selects the tape of Messiaen's Turangalîla *Symphony* and sits down to listen to the strange and beautiful melodies of the Ondes Martenot.

By the sixth movement ('Jardin du sommeil d'amour') he is asleep...

The gallery is vast and made of solid platinum.

He paces it.

It is the bridge of a massive ship. But the ship does not sail across the ocean. It sails through foliage. Dark, tangled foliage. Foliage that the Douanier himself might have painted. Menacing foliage.

Perhaps it is a jungle river. A river like the Amazon or one of those mysterious, unmapped rivers of New Guinea that, as a boy, he had wished to explore.

Ship... foliage... river...

He is alone on the ship, but for the sound of the engines, strangely melodic, and the cries of the unseen birds in the jungle.

He leans over the rail of the bridge, looking for the waters of the river. But there are no waters. Beneath the ship is only vegetation, crushed and bent by the passage of the great vessel.

The ships rolls.

He falls and from somewhere comes a sound that is oddly sympathetic. Something is pitying him.

He rejects the pity.

He falls to the ground and the ship passes on.

He is alone in the jungle and he hears the sounds of lumbering monsters in the murk. He searches with his eyes for the monsters, but he cannot see them, cannot trace the origin of their noise.

A woman appears. She is dark, lush, exotic. She parts her red lips and takes him by the hand into the shadowy darkness of the tropical foliage. Birds continue to cry and to squawk. He begins to kiss her wet, hot mouth. He feels her hand on his penis. He runs his hand into her crutch and her pants are wet with her juices. He tries to make love to her, but for some reason she is wary, expecting discovery. She will not remove her clothing. They make love as best they can. Then she gets up and leads him through the dark jungle corridors into a clearing.

They are in a bar. Girls – club hostesses or prostitutes, he cannot tell – fill the place. There are a few men. Probably ponces or gigolos. He feels at ease here. He relaxes. He puts his arm around the dark woman and puts his other arm around a young blonde with a lined, decaying face. Someone he knew.

All the faces, in fact, are familiar. He tries to remember them. He concentrates on remembering them. Dimly he begins to remember them...

AFTER THE FAIR THEY WERE ALL LEAD
Q: PLEASE DEFINE SPECIFIC SITUATION
ARDOUR THE MORE THEY SANG AHEAD
Q: PLEASE DEFINE SPECIFIC SITUATION
AH DO RE ME FA SO LA TI DI
Q: PLEASE DEFINE SPECIFIC SITUATION
ARIA ARIADNE ANIARA LEONARA CARMEN AMEN
A: AMEN

AMEN
AMEN. AMEN. AMEN.
AMEN.

SUGGEST HOLD ON TIGHT
SUGGEST HOLD ON TIGHT
SUGGEST HOLD ON TIGHT

KEEP GOING
E O
E I
P N
G
G
O K
I E
N E
GOING KEEP

THE SPACESHIP HOPE DEMPSEY IS EN ROUTE
FOR MUNICH 15040
THE SPACESHIP
HOPE DEMPSEY IS EN ROUTE FOR MUNICH 15040
IS GOING
EN ROUTE FOR MUNICH 15040 THE SPACESHIP
NOWHERE
FOR MUNICH 15040 THE SPACESHIP
MUST
HOPE DEMPSEY IS EN ROUTE
BE SAFE
FOR MUNICH 15040
MUST
THE SPACESHIP
KEEP THEM
SPACESHIP
SAFE
SPACESHIP
SPACE SAFE
SHIP KEEP THEM
SAFE SAFE
SHIP THE SPACESHIP HOPE DEMPSEY IS EN
ROUTE
SAFE FOR MUNICH 15040 AND TRAVELLING
AT POINT
SHAPE NINE OF C
SHIP WE ARE ALL COMFORTABLE
SHAPE WE ARE ALL
SPACE SAFE
SHAPE SPACESHIP SAFE
SHIP SAFESHIPSAFE
SHAPE SAFESHIPSHAPE

SAFE

SAFE

SAFE

SAFE

SAFE

SHIP

SHIP

SHIP

SHIP

SHAPE

SAFE

SHIP

SHIP

SAFE

SAFE

SHIP

SHIP

SAFE

SAFE

SHIP

SHIP

SAFE

SAFE

SHIP

SHIP

SAFE

SAFE

SHIP

SWEET

SAFE

SHIP

SPACE

SAIL

SPACE

SNAIL

PACE

SAFE

PACE

SNAIL

PACE

SPACE

SHIP

SAFE

PLACE

SPACE

SAFE

SMELL

TASTE

HASTE

RACE

WASTE

SPACE

SAVE

SPACE

SAFE

PLACE

SAFE CASE SPACE PLACE

HATE HEAT SWEET SAFE

BRAIN
SHIP
TAME
WHIP
GOOD
TRIP
SPACE
SHIP
LET
RIP
SPACE
TRIP
HATE
TASTE
SPACE
FACE
HATE
HASTE
SPACE
RACE
HATE
FACE
SPACE
PLACE
HOT
DRIP
SPACE
SHIP
HATE
HEAT SPACE HEAT SAFE FEAT
SWEET HATE SAFE HAZE

NOT TRUE * * * * * * * * *
NOT TRUE * * * * * * * * *
* * * * * * * * * NOT TRUE*

NOT TRUE

'It's not fucking true!'

Ryan screams.

He wakes up.

The tape machine is humming rhythmically.

He shudders.

He has an erection.

His mouth is dry.

He has a pain above his left temple.

His legs are trembling.

His hands are gripping the plastic of his chair, pinching it in handfuls like a housewife inspecting a chicken.

The muscles at the back of his neck ache horribly.

He shakes his head.

What wasn't true?

The symphony has come to an end.

He gets up and switches off the machine, frowning and massaging his neck. He yawns.

Then he remembers the dream. The jungle. The women.

He grins with relief, recognising the source of the exclamation – the denial with which he had woken himself up.

Just simple, old-fashioned guilt feelings, obviously.

He had considered waking Janet, cheating on his brother, had dreamed accordingly, had denied his feelings and had come awake with a start.

All that proved was that he had a conscience.

He stretches.

Scratching his head he leaves the cabin and goes to take another shower.

As he washes, he smiles again. It's just as well to let those secret thoughts out into the open. No good burying them where they can fester into something much worse, catch him off his guard and possibly wreck the entire mission, maybe make him wake up the others. That would be fatal.

A wave of depression hits him. *It's bloody hard*, he thinks. *Bloody.*

He pulls himself together. His old reflexes are as good as ever. Keeping fit isn't just a matter of exercising the body. One has to exercise the brain, too. Make constant checks to be sure it's working smoothly.

He must be getting unduly sensitive, however, for his conscience was never that much of a burden to him!

He laughs. He knows what he must do.

It's the old trouble. The problem of leisure. It was unhealthy not to put your mind to something other than its own workings. He was developing the neuroses of the rich, the non-workers – or would start to, if he wasn't careful.

The dream is a warning.

Or rather his reaction to the dream is a warning. Tomorrow he will start studying the agricultural programmes, get interested in something other than himself.

Refreshed, his aches and pains vanishing, he returns to his cabin and sorts out the agricultural programmes ready for the next day.

Then he goes to bed.

Chapter Twelve

ALTHOUGH HE IS alone on board, he faithfully follows all the rituals as if there were a full crew in attendance.

As a boy I used to swim through cold water in the streams that ran between the pines, he thinks.

At the time set for the daily conferences, he sits at the head of the table and reviews the few events and projected tasks with which he is involved.

He eats at the formal mealtimes, uses formal language in all his dealings with the ship, makes formal checks and radios formal log entries back to Earth. His only break with formal routine is the red logbook he keeps in the desk.

He makes the formal tours to the Hibernation Section (nick-named 'crew storage' by the personnel when they first came aboard).

As a young man I stood on hills in the wind and stared at moody skies, he thinks, *and I wrote awful, sentimental, self-pitying verse until the other lads found it and took the piss out of me so much I gave it up. I went into business instead. Just as well.*

He touches the button and the spin screws automatically retract.

I wonder what would have happened to me. Art thrives in chaos. What's good for art isn't good for business...

He pauses by the first container and looks into the patient face of his wife.

Mrs Ryan washed down the walls of her apartment. She was using the appropriate fluid. All the time she cleaned she kept her face averted from the long window forming the far wall of the apartment.

When she had finished cleaning she took the can of fluid back to the kitchen and put it on the right shelf.

Frowning uncertainly, she stood in the middle of the kitchen.

Then she drew a deep breath and she reached towards the shelf again, touching another can. The can was labelled PLANT-FOOD.

She grasped the can.

She lifted it from the shelf.

She coughed and covered her mouth with her free hand.

She drew another breath.

She walked into the lobby and sprayed the orange tree that stood in its shining metallic tub. She went back into the living room, with its coloured walls, expensive, cushiony plastic chairs, the wall-to-wall TV.

She turned on the TV.

The wall opposite the window was instantly alive with whirling, dancing figures.

Watching them gyrate, Mrs Ryan relaxed a trifle. She looked at the can in her hand and put it down on the table. She watched the dancers. Her eyes were drawn back to the can, still lying on the table. She began to sit down. Then she stood up again.

Mrs Ryan's fresh forty-year-old's face crumpled slightly. Her lips moved. She had the expression of a resolute but frightened child, half-ready to cry if the expected accident occurred.

She picked up the can and walked to the wall-long window. With her eyes half-closed she located the button which controlled the raising and lowering of the blinds. With the room in darkness, she sprayed the plants on the window sill.

She took the can back to the kitchen and placed it on the shelf. She stood in the kitchen doorway for a while, staring into the darkness of the living room, lit only by the flicker of the TV. Then she crossed the room to the window and placed her hand on the button controlling the blind.

She turned her back to the window and found the button with her left hand.

There was a big production number on TV. She stared at it, unmoving.

Then she pressed the button and sprang away from the window

as the blinds rushed up and the room was flooded with daylight again.

She hurried into the kitchen, turning off the TV as she went past. She made some coffee and sat down to drink it.

The room was silent.

The empty window looked out onto the apartment blocks opposite. Their empty windows stared back.

Few cars ran in the street between the blocks.

Inside the apartment, in the kitchen, Mrs Ryan sat with her coffee cup raised, like a puppet whose motor had cut out in mid-action.

The telephone buzzed.

Mrs Ryan sat still.

The telephone went on buzzing.

Mrs Ryan sighed and approached the instrument, set at head height on the kitchen wall. She ducked down against the wall and reached up to remove the mouthpiece.

'It's me. Uncle Sidney,' said the voice from the screen above her head.

'Oh, it's you, Uncle Sidney,' said Mrs Ryan. She backed away from the wall, still holding the mouthpiece, and sat down near the kitchen table.

'Don't come too close,' said Uncle Sidney.

'Uncle Sidney,' said Mrs Ryan pitifully. 'I've asked you not to call during the day, when no-one's at home. After all, I don't know who you are. It might be anyone.'

'I'm sorry, I'm sure. I just wanted to ask if you'd like to come over tonight.'

'The car's being repaired,' said Mrs Ryan. 'He had to go by bus this morning. I told him not to, but he insisted. I don't know…'

Mrs Ryan broke off, a sadly bewildered look on her face.

There was silence.

Then she and Uncle Sidney spoke together:

'I've got to clean –' Mrs Ryan said.

'Can't you come –' said Uncle Sidney.

'Uncle Sidney. I've got to clean the front door today. And I know – I *know* that as soon as I open the door the woman from the next apartment will come out and pretend she's going to use the garbage disposal. Do you realise what it's like living next to a woman like that?'

Uncle Sidney's lined face dropped. 'Well, if you won't visit your uncle you won't,' he said. 'Do you know how long it's been since I saw you and him and the kids? Three months.'

'I'm sorry, Uncle Sidney.' Mrs Ryan looked at the floor, noticing a smear on one of the tiles. 'You wouldn't come to see us, I suppose…?'

'On my own?' Uncle Sidney said contemptuously.

He cut the connection. Mrs Ryan sat by the kitchen table holding the mouthpiece in her hand. She stood up slowly and replaced it.

It seemed to her that she could not get the cleaner and the spray from the cupboard. She could not cross the kitchen and go through the living room. She could not, alone, open the front door.

She could not open the front door.

She might…

Mrs Ryan's mind became dark, fearful, confused.

She was swept around the whirlpool of her brain, helpless and still, in spite of herself, struggling.

She could not open the door.

She could not.

Mrs Ryan uttered a low moan and went into the bedroom.

Even in daylight the walls shimmered with many colours. The bed was neatly covered with the white bedspread. The shining dressing table was clear. Mrs Ryan picked up the only sign of occupancy, a pair of Mr Ryan's outdoor shoes. She opened a concealed cupboard and threw them in violently. She ran to the window, pressed the button on the sill.

The blinds came down quickly.

The walls of the room glowed and flickered.

Mrs Ryan paced to and fro. Past the bed to the darkened window. Back from the window to the bed. Back and forth.

She stopped and turned on soft, soothing music.

She ran out of the room and locked the front door.

She came back into the bedroom, shut that door, lay down on the bed, listening to the music.

Even the music seemed slightly harsh today.

She closed her eyes and the faces came. She opened her eyes and reached towards the bedside cupboard, took out her sleeping pills, swallowed a pill and lay down again.

The music was almost raucous. She turned it off.

She lay in silence, waiting for sleep.

It was 11.23 a.m.

Chapter Thirteen

Mrs Ryan began to dream.

She was walking across the field away from the house she had lived in when she was eight. If she turned around she could see her mother framed in the kitchen window, her head bent over the stove. Behind her she could hear the shouts of her brothers playing hide-and-seek.

Mrs Ryan trod over the springy turf, dreamily floated over the bright grass. She could hear birds singing in the trees at the edges of the field.

Mrs Ryan was floating, floating over the fields, far from the house. How sunny it was. How the birds sang. She was walking again. She turned to look for the house but she was too far away. She could not see it. The sky was darkening. She could only dimly see the trees on either side of the field. She seemed to hear a noise; a babble of talk. At once, ahead of her, she saw a dark crowd approaching, talking among themselves. As they came closer she could still not distinguish one person from another. She had the impression that there were men, women and children. But the mass was still a dark blur of heads, bodies, limbs, formless and faceless. The crowd advanced, the cackle of voices growing louder.

She stood transfixed in the field.

She could not move.

And the voices grew clearer.

'Look. There she is. She's there. She's really there.'

She felt the mood of the crowd change.

She felt a terrible fear.

'She's there. That's her. That's her. She's there. She's there.'

She stood rooted to the spot, her legs too heavy to carry her.

'She's there. She's there. That's her. That's her.'

The dark crowd began to run towards her. It yelled and cried out.

She could hear high, vengeful screams from the women. The crowd was almost on her.

And Mrs Ryan awoke with a start in her bedroom in the light of the shimmering walls. She looked at the clock.

It was 11.31 a.m.

Trembling, she lay there on the white bedspread, fighting her way out of the dream. She gazed blankly at the walls, blinking her eyes to rid herself of the image of the black, blank faces of that terrible crowd. She rose and walked heavily from the room.

She went into the kitchen and took a pill to clear her head. Sighing, she removed the can of cleaner from the shelf, walked through the living room, out into the lobby and up to the front door. She put her hand on the latch.

Mrs Ryan hesitated, stiffened her back and opened the front door. She crept outside, into the long corridor.

The corridor was bright and white. It stretched away from her on either side. Set in the walls were the doors, all painted in fresh, dark colours.

Slowly Mrs Ryan began to spray cleaner on the surface of the door. Once the door was covered with the white film she began to rub it off, faster and faster.

Nearly done, she thought to herself, *nearly done. Thank God, thank God. Soon finished. Thank God.*

Very slowly the blue door of the apartment opposite began to open. A woman looked through the crack of the door. She and Mrs Ryan stared at each other in shock. The woman's hand went to her mouth. Mrs Ryan recovered herself first.

Leaving the door half covered in white cleaning fluid she ran back inside her apartment and slammed the door. Almost at the same moment the other woman shut her own door.

Mrs Ryan stood in the middle of her kitchen, gasping for breath. 'That bitch,' she said aloud. 'That bitch. What docs she want to persecute me for? Why does she always do that to me? Spying on me all the time. Bitch, bitch, bitch.'

She went to the shelf, took down a bottle of capsules and swallowed two. She went into the living room and fell down on the plastic couch. She switched on the TV.

There was a picture of a family eating a turkey dinner. The turkey and its trimmings were laid out brightly on a gay table. The family – parents and three teenage children – were joking. Mrs Ryan watched the programme with a faint smile curling around her mouth.

She was soon asleep.

It was 11.48 a.m.

The boys woke her up.

She told them what had happened and they told Ryan.

Ryan was sympathetic.

'You need a holiday, old girl,' he said. 'We'll see what we can do.'

'I'd rather not,' she said. 'I prefer to stay at home. It's just – the *interference* from the neighbours. I'm proud of my home.'

'Of course you are. We'll see what we can do.'

It was 7.46 p.m.

'Time passes so slowly,' she said.

'It depends how you look at it,' he replied.

She suffered a lot, thinks Ryan. *Maybe I could have been more helpful.*

He shrugs the thought off. A pointless exercise. There was nothing to be gained from self-recrimination. If one didn't like what one had done, the best thing was to decide not to do it again and leave it at that. That was the pragmatic attitude. The scientific attitude.

He looks down at the sleeping face of his wife and he smiles tenderly, touching the top of the container.

Even her condition improved once they had decided on their goal. She was basically a sensible woman. Her condition was no different from that of millions of others in the cities all over the world.

If they had taken one of the abandoned houses in the country, perhaps she would have been happier. But probably not. The isolation of the places beyond the cities was pretty unbearable.

She had liked the country as a girl, of course. That was partly what the dream was about, he guessed. That dream of hers. It had recurred relatively frequently. Not unlike that recurring dream of his.

He starts to pace between the containers, checking them automatically.

What is time, after all? Do we meet in our dreams?

Pointless, mystical speculation.

Everything seems to be in order. The containers are functioning correctly. Ryan yawns and stretches, fighting off the sinking feeling in his stomach, ignoring the impulse to wake at least some of the occupants of the containers. They must not be awakened until the ship nears the planet that is its destination.

This is his penance, his test, his reward.

He has one last look at his sleeping boys, then he leaves the compartment and makes his way back to the main control cabin, sends his report back to Earth. All is well aboard the spaceship *Hope Dempsey.*

He writes a short entry in his red logbook:

On the other side of those thin walls is infinite space. There is no life for billions of miles. No man has ever been more alone.

In his cabin he takes three pills, disposes of his clothes, lies down.

As he begins to fall asleep a numb, desperate feeling tells him that tonight could be another of those nights of fitful, nightmare-ridden sleep. His routine demands that he sleep regularly. His health will break if he does not. Ryan lies on his narrow couch willing himself not to rise. The pills take effect and Ryan sleeps.

He dreams that he is in his office. It is dark. He has drawn the blinds to shut out the city noise and the view of the shining office towers opposite. He sits at his desk doing nothing. His hands are curled on the desk before him. The fingernails are torn. He is afraid.

He sees his wife in their apartment. She is sitting in the darkened living room doing nothing.

He sees the bedroom in which his two sons lie sleeping under heavy sedation. The youngest, five-year-old Alexander, groans in his sleep, thrusts an arm, thin as a Foreigner's, out of the covers. The arm dangles lifelessly down from his bed. He moans again. His brother Rupert, who is twelve, lies on his back, eyes half open in his coma, staring blindly at the ceiling.

Back in the living room Ryan sees the hunched figure of his wife. Again he sees himself sitting at his office desk staring into the half dark.

The family is waiting.

It is waiting in fear.

It does not know what to expect.

There is a scratching noise behind him. Ryan, half-paralysed with terror, turns slowly around to see what it is. He faces the window now. The blind is shaking, as if it were being blown by the wind. There is something behind the blind, something from outside, trying to enter the office. Ryan breathes in, holds his breath hard in some animal instinct to make himself so immobile that he will not be noticed. The blind shakes and shakes. A bony hand comes through the fabric, leaving no gap or tear, merely sliding through as if the material were smoke, or air. Ryan gazes at the hand. It belongs to an old woman, thin-fingered, with pronounced tendons. The nails are painted red. There are three large rings: two diamond ones on the middle finger, a large amethyst on the slender, slightly curved, little finger. The hand appears to part the blind and a face peers in.

It is the face of an old woman. The wrinkled eyelids are carefully painted blue. The mouth is blackened, the lined cheeks powdered. The old woman looks Ryan straight in the eyes and smiles, revealing yellow teeth, the edges slightly serrated with age. Ryan stares at the old woman. She continues to give him a confidential, intimate smile.

Her hand appears again, through another part of the blind.

It holds a pair of round, dark glasses.

The hand moves towards her face. It places the glasses over her eyes. Then the hand disappears through the blind again, leaving no gap or rent in it.

The old, blackened mouth continues to smile below the obliterated eyes.

Then the old woman's face, in the centre of the blind, begins to droop. The smile disappears, the lips begin to curve in a snarl.

Ryan is terrified.

He cannot scream.

He wants to say the following words:

I – DID – NOT

– but he cannot.

He cannot say the…

I —

He gets up from his bed. He is sweating. Naked, he leaves the cabin and walks down the bright corridor, enters the main control cabin and stares at the dancing, shifting indicators, at the ever busy computer.

He listens to the faint hum of the engine which is propelling the little pellet of steel through the void.

The computer has left him a message. He walks over to the machine and reads it.

It says:

*******THERE IS A LOSS OF COMMUNICATION**************************987654321000000000000,,,,,,,,,,,,,,,/*********************A LOSS**,,,,,,,,,,,,,,,,,,,,,,,,PLEASE ENSURE THAT IN FUTURE***INFORMATION IS GIVEN IN THE CORRECT FORM,,,,,,,,REPEAT THE**CORRECT FORM,,,,,,,,,,,,,,WHAT IS THE EXACT NATURE OF THE******SITUATION REPEAT WHAT IS THE EXACT NATURE OF THE******SITUATION REPEAT WHAT IS THE EXACT NATURE OF THE********SITUATION,,*********

Uncomprehendingly Ryan stares at the message.

What has gone wrong?

He has carried out his duties impeccably.

His days have been dedicated to order, the routine of the ship.

What has he done wrong?

Or – worse – what mistake can be occurring inside the computer?

He rips off the printout and reads it, seeking a clue. It has all the fluency and random lack of sense of a message from a Ouija board.

And as he reads the computer spills out more:

******I CANNOT READ YOUR LAST MESSAGE UNLESS****** *******INFORMATION IS GIVEN IN THE CORRECT FORM’’’’’’’’ I CANNOT**ASSIST’’’’’’’’’’’’PLEASE REPEAT YOUR LAST MESSAGE IN THE****CORRECT FORM**********************************

Wearily Ryan organises the machine to rerun his last message. It reads:

******TRIUMPHANT IN THE BLOODY SKY AND THE HUMAN FORM*IS NO MORE**************************************

I must control this sort of thing, thinks Ryan.

He wanders to the desk and takes out his red logbook. He writes:

I must keep better control of things.

He struggles back to the computer and realises he has left his red logbook on the desk. He weaves back to the desk and carefully, but with great difficulty, puts the book in its drawer. Slowly, he closes the door. He returns to the computer. He erases the messages as best he can by condemning them to the computer's deepest memory cells. He walks wearily from the control room.

I must control this sort of thing.

I must forget these nightmares.

I must maintain order.

It could wreck the computer and then I would be finished.

Everything depends on me.

Triumphant in the bloody sky and the human form...

Ryan weeps.

He paces the corridor, back to his prison, takes three more pills and sleeps.

He dreams of the factory. A huge hall, somewhat darker in Ryan's dream than it was in reality. It is filled with large silent machines. Only the throbbing of the tiled floor indicates the activity of the machines.

At the end of each machine is a large drum into which spill the parts used in the making of Ryan Toys.

There are the smooth heads, legs, arms and torsos of dolls; the woolly heads, legs and torsos of lambs, tigers and rabbits; the metal legs, heads and torsos of mechanical puppets. There are the tiny powerpacs for the bellies of Ryan Toys; there are the metal parts for Ryan Toys dredgers, oilpumps, spacecraft; there are the great, shining grinning heads of Rytoy Realboys and Rytoy Realgirls; the great probosces of Rytoy Realphants.

The vast machines turn out their parts steadily and inexorably. As each drum fills it glides away and is replaced by another which is, in turn, steadily filled.

Ryan is a witness to this scene. He knows that he will be involved if they find out.

He sees a white-coated mechanic walk along the files of machines and disappear through a door at the end of the hall.

Did the mechanic notice him?

The drums roll away and are replaced by empty ones.

Suddenly Ryan sees the parts rise, as if in weightlessness. They join together, assembling in mid-air. As each toy is completed, or as completed as it can be with the parts available, it sinks to the floor of the hall and begins to operate.

A row of golden-haired Realboys, life-size but armless, revolve slowly, singing 'Frère Jacques' in their high voices.

A cluster of woolly lambs gambol mechanically, raising and dipping their heads.

On the floor the large trunks of the Realphants plunge and rise.

The spacecraft hover a foot above the floor, emitting humming noises.

Ryrobots strut and clank about, running into the machines and toppling over. Two great heaps of musical building blocks chime out the letters printed on their sides —

I AM *A*

I AM *M*

I AM *U*

The piles fall and tumble as Ryan kicks them.

The Realgirls link hands and dance around him, tossing their blonde curls. The Ryan Battlewagons run about the floor, shooting their miniature missiles.

Ryan looks fondly at the action, music and chatter of his toys. The whole of the tiled floor is being gradually covered with toys in motion. All these things are Ryan's – made and sold by Ryan.

He looks at the building blocks and smiles. Some have fallen and spelled out: AMUSEMENT.

In the middle of this cheerful scene, Ryan ceases to dream and falls fast asleep.

In accordance with the regulations ensuring that no member of the government or the civil service could be identified save by his rank (thus ensuring the absence of blackmail, bribery, favour-seeking and/or giving and so forth) the Man from the Ministry wore a black cloth over his face. It had neat holes for his eyes and his mouth.

Ryan, sitting behind his office desk, contemplated the Man from the Ministry somewhat nervously.

'Will you have a cup of tea?' he asked.

'I think not.'

Ryan could almost see the expression of suspicious distaste on the man's face. He had made a tactical blunder.

'Ah...' said Ryan.

'Mr Ryan...' began the official.

'Yes,' said Ryan, as if in confirmation. 'Yes, indeed.'

'Mr Ryan – you seem unaware that this country is in a state of war...'

'Ah. No.'

'Since Birmingham launched its completely unprovoked attack on London, Mr Ryan, and bombed the reservoirs of Shepperton and Staines, the official government of South England has had to requisition a great deal of private industry if it has been discovered that it has not been contributing to our war effort as efficiently as it might...'

'That's a threat, is it?' Ryan said thickly.

'A friendly tip, Mr Ryan.'

'We've turned over as fast as we can,' Ryan explained. 'We *were* a bloody toy factory, you know. Overnight we had to change to manufacturing weapons parts and communications equipment. Naturally we haven't had a completely smooth ride. On the other hand, we've done our best...'

'Your production is not up to scratch, Mr Ryan. I wonder if your heart is in the war effort? Some people do not seem to realise that the old society has been swept away, that the Patriots are bent on ordering an entirely new kind of nation now that the remnants of the alien groups have been pushed back beyond the Thames. Though attacked from all sides, though sustaining three hydrogen bomb drops from France, the Patriots have managed to hold this land of ours together. They can only do it with the full co-operation of people like yourself, Mr Ryan.'

'We aren't getting the raw materials,' Ryan said. 'Half the things we need don't arrive. It's a bloody shambles!'

'That sounds like a criticism of the government, Mr Ryan.'

'You know I'm a registered Patriot supporter.'

'Not all registered supporters have remained loyal, Mr Ryan.'

'Well, I *am* loyal!' Ryan half believed himself as he shouted at the Man from the Ministry. He and the group had decided early on that the Patriots would soon hold the power and had taken the precaution of joining the party. 'It's just that we can't work more than ten bloody miracles a day!'

'You've got a week, I'm afraid, Mr Ryan.' The official got up, closing his briefcase. 'And then it will be a Temporary Requisition Order until our borders are secure again.'

'You'll take over?'

'You will continue to manage the factory, if you prove efficient. You will enjoy the status of any other civil servant.'

Ryan nodded. 'What about compensation?'

'Mr Ryan,' said the official grimly, wearily, 'there is a discredited cabinet that fled to Birmingham to escape retribution. Among other things that was discovered about that particular cabinet was that it was corrupt. Industrialists were lining their pockets with the connivance of government officials. That sort of thing is all over now. All over. Naturally, you will receive a receipt guaranteeing the return of your business when the situation has been normalised. We hope, however, that it won't have to happen. Keep trying, Mr Ryan. Keep trying. Good luck to you.'

Ryan watched the official leave. He would have to warn the group that things were moving a little faster than anticipated.

He wondered how things were in the rest of the world. Very few reports came through these days. The United States were now Disunited and at war. United Europe had fragmented into thousands of tiny principalities, rather as England had. As for Russia and the Far East the only information he had had for months was that a horde thousands of times greater than the Golden Horde was sweeping in all directions. Possibly none of the information was true. He hoped that the town of Surgut on the Siberian Plain was still untouched. Everything depended on that.

Ryan got up and left the office.

It was time to go home.

Chapter Fourteen

When he awakes he feels relieved, alert and refreshed. He eats his breakfast as soon as he has exercised and walks to the control room where he runs through all the routine checks and adjustments until lunch time.

After lunch he goes to the little gym behind the main control cabin and vaults and climbs and swings until it is time to inspect Hibernation.

He unlocks the door of Hibernation and makes a routine and unemotional check. A minor alteration is required in the rate of fluid flow on Number Seven container. He makes the alteration.

Again the routine checks, the reiteration during the normal conference period.

He then does two hours' study of the agricultural programmes. He learns a great deal. It is a much more interesting subject than he would have guessed.

Then it is time to report to the computer and read the log through to Earth, if anyone is left on Earth to hear it.

He makes the last of his reports for this period:

'Day number one thousand four hundred and sixty-six. Spaceship *Hope Dempsey* en route for Munich 15040. Speed steady at point nine of *c*. All systems functioning according to original expectations. No other variations. All occupants are comfortable and in good health.'

Ryan goes to the desk and takes out his red logbook. He frowns. Scrawled across a page are the words:

I MUST KEEP BETTER CONTROL OF THINGS.

It hardly looks like his writing. Yet it must be.

And when did he write it? He has not had time to make any

entries in the log until now. It could have been at any time today. Or last night. He frowns. When…?

He cannot remember.

He takes a deep breath and he rules two heavy red lines under the entry, writes the date below it and begins:

All continues well. I maintain my routine and am hopeful for the future. Today I feel less bedevilled by loneliness and have more confidence in my ability to carry out my mission. Our ship carries us steadily onwards. I am confident that all is well. I am confident

He stops writing and scratches his head, staring at the phrase, above the entry.

I MUST KEEP BETTER CONTROL OF THINGS.

I am confident that my period of nightmares and near-hysteria is over. I have regained control of myself and therefore

He considers tearing out this page and beginning it afresh. But that would not be in accord with the regulations he is following. He sucks his lower lip…

am doubtless much more cheerful. The above phrase is something of a puzzle to me, for at this point I cannot remember writing it. Perhaps I was under even greater stress than I imagined and wrote it last night after finishing the ordinary entry. Well, it was good advice – the advice of this stranger who could only have been myself!

It gives me a slightly eerie feeling, however, I must admit. I expect I will remember when I wrote it. I hope so. In the meantime there is no point in my racking my brains. The information will come when my unconscious is ready to let me have it!

Otherwise – all okay. The gloom and doom period is over – at least for the time being. I am in a thoroughly constructive and balanced state of mind.

He signs off with a flourish and, humming, puts the book in the desk, closes the drawer, gets up, takes a last look around the control room and goes out into the passage.

Before returning to his cabin, he goes to the library and gets a couple of educational tapes.

In his cabin, he studies the programmes for a while and then goes to sleep.

He dreams again.

He is on the new planet. A pleasant landscape. A valley. He is working the soil with some sort of digging instrument. He is alone and at peace. There is no sign of the spaceship or of the other occupants. This does not worry him. He is alone and at peace.

Next morning he continues with his routine work. He eats, he makes his formal log entries, he manages to get an extra hour of study. He is beginning to understand the principles of agriculture.

He returns to the control room to make the last of his reports – the standard one – which, according to his routine, he first enters in his logbook and then reads out to the computer. He then sits down and picks up his stylus to begin his private entry. He enters the date.

Another pleasant and uneventful day spent largely in the pursuit of knowledge! I am beginning to feel like some old scholar. I can understand the attraction, suddenly, in the pursuit of information for its own sake. In a way, of course, it is an escape – I can see that even the most sophisticated sort of academic activity is at least in part a rejection of the realities of ordinary living. My studies, naturally, are perfectly practical, in that I will need a great deal of knowledge about every possible kind of agriculture when we

The computer is flashing a signal. It wants his attention.

Frowning, Ryan gets up and goes over to the main console.

He reads the computer's message.

*******CONDITION OF OCCUPANTS OF CONTAINERS NOT *****REPORTED***

Ryan gasps. It is true. For the first time he has not checked the hibernation compartment. He realises now that he was so caught up in his studies he must have forgotten. He replies to the computer:

******REPORT FOLLOWS SHORTLY**********************************

Reproving himself for this stupid lapse, relieved that the

computer is programmed to check every function he performs and to remind him of any oversights, he marches along the corridor to the hibernation room.

He touches the stud to open the door.

But the door remains closed.

He presses the stud harder.

Still the door does not open.

Ryan feels a moment's panic. Could there be someone else aboard the ship? A stowaway of some kind who...?

He rejects the notion as stupid. And then he returns to the main control cabin and gives the computer a question.

******HIBERNATION COMPARTMENT DOOR WILL NOT OPEN *****PLEASE ADVISE***

There is a pause before the computer replies:

******EMERGENCY LOCK EFFECTIVE,,,,,,,,,,,,,,,,,,,,YOU MUST******* *****DEACTIVATE AT MAIN CONSOLE*************************

Ryan licks his lips and goes to the main console. He scans the door plan and sees that the computer is correct. He touches a stud on the console and cuts off the emergency lock. Was the mistake his or the computer's? Perhaps the emergency lock was activated at the same time as he made the mysterious log entry.

He returns to the hibernation room and opens the door.

He enters the compartment.

Chapter Fifteen

THE CONTAINERS GLEAM a pure, soft white.

He walks to the first and inspects it. It contains his wife.

JOSEPHINE RYAN. 9/9/1960. 7/3/2004.

His blonde, pink-faced wife, blue eyes peacefully closed, lies in her green fluid. She looks so natural that Ryan half expects her to open her eyes and smile at him. Josephine, heart of the ship, so glad to be setting out on her great adventure, so glad to be free from the torture of living in the city with its unbearable atmosphere of hostility.

Ryan smiles as he remembers the eager step with which she came aboard on the day of the take-off, how she had lost, almost overnight, the sadness and the fear which had afflicted her – indeed, which had been afflicting them all. He sighs. How pleasant to be together again.

RUPERT RYAN. 13/7/1990. 6/3/2004.

ALEXANDER RYAN. 25/12/1996. 6/3/2004.

Ryan walks fairly quickly past the containers where his two sons' immature faces gaze in startlement at the bright ceiling.

SIDNEY RYAN. 2/2/1937. 25/12/2003.

Ryan stares for a while at the wrinkled old face, lips slightly drawn back over the false teeth, the thin musclely old shoulders showing above the plastic sheet drawn over the main length of the containers.

JOHN RYAN. 15/8/1963. 26/12/2003.

ISABEL RYAN. 22/6/1962. 13/2/2004.

Isabel. Still weary-looking, even though at peace…

JANET RYAN. 10/11/1982. 7/5/2004.

Ah, Janet, thinks Ryan with a surge of affection.

He loved Josephine. But, by God, he loved Janet passionately.

He frowns. The problem had not been over, when they went into hibernation. It would take a great deal of self-discipline on his part to make sure that it did not start all over again.

FRED MASTERSON. 4/5/1950. 25/12/2003.

TRACY MASTERSON. 29/10/1973. 9/10/2003.

JAMES HENRY. 4/3/1957. 29/10/2003.

IDA HENRY. 3/3/1980. 1/2/2004.

FELICITY HENRY. 3/3/1980. 1/2/2004.

Everything is as it should be. Everybody is sleeping peacefully. Only Ryan is awake.

He blinks.

Only Ryan is awake because it is better for one man to suffer acute loneliness and isolation than for several to live in tension.

One strong man.

Ryan raises his eyebrows.

And leaves Hibernation.

Ryan reports to the computer:

JOSEPHINE RYAN. CONDITION STEADY.

RUPERT RYAN. CONDITION STEADY.

ALEXANDER RYAN. CONDITION STEADY.

SIDNEY RYAN. CONDITION STEADY.

JOHN RYAN. CONDITION STEADY.

ISABEL RYAN. CONDITION STEADY.

JANET RYAN.

CONDITION STEADY.

FRED MASTERSON. CONDITION STEADY.

TRACY MASTERSON. CONDITION

STEADY.

JAMES

HENRY

CONDITION STEADY.

IDA HENRY. CONDITION STEADY

FELICITY HENRY. CONDITION

STEADY.

The computer says:

******EARLIER YOU REPORTED YOURSELF LONELY*****

,,,,,,,,,,,,DOES THIS CONDITION STILL / OBTAIN*******************

Ryan replies:

******CONDITION EASIER SINCE THEN***************************

He moves to his desk and picks up his diary.

He writes:

land.

A short while ago the computer reported an oversight of mine. I'd forgotten to report on the condition of the personnel. The first time I've done anything like that! And the last, I hope. Then I discovered that the emergency locks in Hibernation had been sealed and I had to come back and unseal them. I must have done that, too, when I made the above entry. I feel relaxed and at ease now. The previous mistakes and, I suppose, mild blackouts must have been the result of the strain which I now seem to have overcome.

Ryan winds up the entry, closes the log, puts it away, leaves the control room.

He goes to his cabin and sets aside the educational tapes. *Too much concentration,* he thinks. *Mustn't overdo it. It's incredible how one has to watch the balance. A very delicate equilibrium involved here. Very delicate.*

He starts to watch an old Patriot propaganda play about the discovery of a cell of the Free Yorkshire underground and its eventual elimination.

He turns it off.

He hears something. He turns his head from the viewer.

It is a year since he heard a footstep not his own.

But now he can hear footsteps.

He sits there, feeling sweat prickle under his hair, listening to what seems to be the sound of echoing steps in the passage outside.

There is some stranger aboard!

He listens as the steps approach the door of the compartment. Then they pass.

He forces himself out of his chair and gets to the door. He touches the stud to open the door. It opens slowly.

Outside the passageway stretches on both sides, the length of the ship's crew quarters. The only sound is the faint hum of the ship's system.

Ryan gets a glass of water and drinks it.

He switches the viewer back on, half smiling. Typical auditory hallucination of a lonely man, he thinks. The programme ends.

Ryan decides to get some exercise.

He leaves his cabin and makes for the gym.

As he walks along the corridor he feels footsteps moving behind him. He ignores the feeling with a shrug.

Then comes a moment's panic. He gives way to the impulse to turn sharply.

There is, of course, no-one there.

Ryan reaches the gym. He has the impression that he is being watched as he runs through his exercises.

He lies down on a couch for fifteen minutes before beginning the second half of the exercise routine.

He remembers family holidays on the Isle of Skye. That was in the very early years, of course, before Skye was taken over as an experimental area for research into algae food substitutes. He remembers the pleasant evenings he and Josephine used to have with Tracy and Fred Masterson. He remembers the evening walks through the roof gardens with his wife. He remembers Christmases, he remembers sunsets. He remembers the smell of the rain on the fields of the place where he was born. He remembers the smell of his toy factories – the hot metal, the paint, the freshly cut timber. He remembers his mother. She had been one of the victims of the short-lived Hospitals Euthanasia Act. The act had been repealed by the Nimmoites during their short period of power. The only sensible thing they did, thinks Ryan.

He sleeps.

Once again he is on the planet, in the valley. But this time he is panic-stricken that the ship and the others have left him. He begins to run. He runs into the jungle. He sees a dark woman. He is in his own toy factory among the dancing toys.

He takes pleasure at the sight of these things he has made. They all function together so joyfully. He sees the musical building blocks. They still spell out a word.

AMU...

With dawning fear he hears, above the bangs and clangs of the mechanical toys, the drone of the dirgelike music which in other dreams accompanies the dancers in the darkened ballroom.

The music rises, almost drowning out the sounds made by the moving toys. Ryan feels himself standing rooted with fear in the middle of his gyrating models. The music grows louder. The toys spin to and fro, round and round. They begin to climb on top of each other, lamb on dredger, girl doll on piles of bricks, making a huge pyramid close to him. The pyramid grows and grows until it is at the level of his eyes. The music grows louder and louder.

In his terror Ryan anticipates a point in the music when the pyramid of still-moving toys collapses on him.

He struggles to free himself from the toils of little mechanical bodies.

As he struggles he awakes. He lies there and hears himself groan:

'I thought they were over. I've got to do something about it.'

He gets off the couch and abandons the idea of exercise.

He stares around at the exercising machines. 'I can remain master of myself,' Ryan says.

'I can.'

He goes back to the control room, adjusts various dials, checks that his time devices are working accurately and makes the following statement to the computer:

********I AM TROUBLED BY NIGHTMARES**********************

The computer replies:

******I KNOW THIS’’’’’’’’’’’’INJECT 1CC PRODITOL PER** ***DIEM’’’’’’’’’’’’DO NOT TAKE MORE’’’’’’’’’’’’DISCONTINUE THE DOSE** AS SOON AS POSSIBLE AND AT ALL COSTS AFTER 14 DAYS****

Ryan rubs his lips.

Then he bites the nail of his right forefinger.

Ryan paces the ship.

Passageways, engine room, supplies room, exercise room, control room, own cabin, spare cabins, observation room, library...

He does not look at the door of the hibernation room. He does not walk along the passage towards the door.

He continues his angry prowling for half an hour or more, trying to collect his thoughts.

The footsteps follow him most of the time. Footsteps he knows do not exist.

Echoing up and down the passageways he begins to hear fragments of the voices of his companions, the men and women now suspended in green fluid in the containers that must remain sealed until planetfall.

'Daddy! Daddy!' cries his youngest child Alexander.

Ryan hears the thud of his feet in the passage. He overhears an argument between Ida and Felicity Henry: 'Don't keep telling me how you feel. I don't want to know,' Felicity snaps at her pregnant twin sister. 'You don't realise what it's like,' says the other on a familiar note of complaint. 'No, no. I don't,' he hears Felicity say hysterically. He hears the noise of a slap and Ida's weeping. A door bangs. 'Let me see to it, Ryan,' he hears James Henry say impatiently. The voice seems to echo all over the ship. He hears Fred and Tracy Masterson's feet coming rapidly along the passageway. His wife Josephine is behind them. 'Daddy! Daddy!' The child's feet come scudding up to him. Ryan turns his head this way and that. Where are the sounds coming from?

Janet Ryan sings, far away.

'Homeward bound, where the fields are like honey…'

Ryan cannot hear the words properly. He cranes his neck to listen, but the words are still indistinct. Uncle Sidney is singing too. 'There was a man who had a mouse, hi-diddle-um-tum-ti-do; he baked it in an apple pie; there was a man who had a mouse…'

Isabel Ryan's voice comes from somewhere around him. 'I can't bear any more!'

Then the rumble of John Ryan, his brother, talking to her, saying something Ryan cannot catch.

Janet singing.

Both boys are running, running, running…

And Ryan, in the centre of all this noise, sinks to the floor of the passage, cocks his head, listening to the voices.

As he crouches there it seems to him that the voices must be coming from the room at the end of the passage. Automatically he gets to his feet and with a stiff gait starts to walk up the passageway towards the door.

The voices grow louder.

'I hate to see a man playing at being indispensable. It benefits neither him nor the people about him,' says James Henry.

'The Lord thy God is a jealous God and thou shalt have no other God than Him,' advises Uncle Sidney.

'Never mind, dear, never mind,' Isabel Ryan is telling someone.

Alexander is crying muffled sobs into the pillow.

Janet Ryan is singing in her high, clear voice: 'Homeward bound, we're homeward bound, where the singing birds welcome such lovers as we…'

Ida and Felicity Henry are still arguing: 'Take it.' 'I don't want to take it.' 'You must take it. It's what you need.' 'I know what I need.' 'Be sensible. Drink it now.'

As Ryan reaches the door, the voices rise. As he touches the stud, they are louder still.

Conversations, statements, songs, sobs, laughter, arguments, all coming towards him in an indistinguishable medley.

Then the door is open.

The noises cease abruptly and Ryan is left in the silence, staring at the thirteen containers, twelve full and labelled with the names and dates of the occupants.

The owners of the voices lie there quietly in their pale fluid. Ryan stands there in the doorway, suddenly realising again that he is alone, that the noise has ceased, that he has opened the door at an unscheduled time…

His companions continue to sleep. Peaceful and unaware of the torment he is undergoing, they are all at CONDITION STEADY.

Which is more than I am, thinks Ryan. Tears come to his eyes.

From the door he cannot see the people in the containers.

He counts the containers. There are still thirteen. He looks at the thirteenth, his own. He draws in his breath. His lips curl back in a frightened, feral snarl. He steps out into the passageway and slams the heel of his hand against the door, shutting it.

He begins to run very slowly down the passage until he comes to the end.

Then he leans against a bulkhead, breathing heavily.

He gasps and gasps again. Then he straightens his back and sets off slowly for the control room.

I shall have to think about that injection. I might not be able to carry on without it. I'd hoped to hold out longer than this. Doesn't do to get too reliant on that sort of thing. It is supposed to be addictive, after all.

Maybe one dose will do the trick. One might be all I need.

At any rate, I daren't go on without it.

Ryan decides to have his first injection the next morning.

The Proditol is an enzyme-inhibiting substance that works directly on new cell matter entering the brain. It has the effect of preventing the release of harmful substances into the cells, substances causing lack of connection with the outside world and, thus, delusions. Ryan, partly for pride's sake, partly for reasons he does not fully understand, is very unwilling to take the drug.

But Ryan is dedicated to the ship, its occupants, its goal.

There is little he would not do in order to be able to continue with the steady schedule of the ship and fulfil his responsibility towards its occupants.

Ryan has made his decision.

Plenty of sleeping pills tonight and the Proditol tomorrow.

He goes to his sleeping compartment but then wanders back to the main control room.

He asks for details of the action of the drug.

*******1CC PRODITOL’,’,’,1CC PRODITOL ALSO MA-19:::USSR*1CC PRODITOL IS A FAST ACTING DRUG OF THE ENZYME*****INHIBITOR VARIETY’’’’’’’’’’’’IT BEGINS TO TAKE EFFECT*****WITHIN TEN MINUTES OF INJECTION’’’’’’’’’’’’ITS FULL EFFECT*IS FELT WITHIN THE HOUR FOLLOWING’’’’’’’’’’’’AFTER THIS****THE MIND OF THE PATIENT SHOULD BE RELIEVED OF ALL****IMPRESSIONS OF A DELUSORY NATURE’’’’’’’’’’’’IN THE**********SEVEREST CASES THE DRUG WILL CONTROL ADVERSE**********SYMPTOMS FOR 24 HOURS AFTER WHICH: IF DELUSIONS*******RETURN:A FURTHER INJECTION SHOULD BE ADMINISTERED*****IN MANY CASES THIS WILL NOT BE NECESSARY’’’’’’’’’’’IN NO**CIRCUMSTANCES: HOWEVER: SHOULD THE DRUG BE ADMINISTERED*DAILY FOR MORE THAN 14 DAYS*****

Ryan acknowledges the message and walks to the control room's main ‘porthole’. He activates the screen and looks out at space. The holographic illusion is complete.

Space and the distant suns, the tiny points of light so far away.

Ryan's brows contract.

He notices trails in the blackness. They appear to be wisps of vapour and yet they are plainly not escaping from the ship. It is something like smoke from an open fire, trailing in the dark.

He passes his hand across his eyes and peers forward again. The trails are still there.

He is alarmed. He casts his mind over the data he has accumulated, hoping to think of something that will account for the vapour.

Could it be left by the ships of another space-travelling race?

It must be a possibility.

Meanwhile the wisps continue to rise. There are more and more of them now. They swirl together, break apart and reform.

Ryan, to his horror, begins to hear a faint noise, a kind of buzzing and ringing in his ears. As the noise begins the gases begin to unite, to shape themselves. Once again Ryan passes a hand over his eyes.

The noises in his ears continue. As he looks out of the porthole once more a terrible suspicion comes over him.

And instantly, staring at him gravely, with a small, malicious smile on her lips, is the old woman. Her eyes are shielded by the round dark glasses. She is black-lipped, her old skin covered in powder. She puts the clawlike hand to the window and is gone.

Ryan gasps and is about to turn from the window in panic when he sees the shapes ahead of him. Out there in space are the whirling figures of his nightmare, the figures of the insane dancers in the darkened ballroom.

They are far away.

Ryan hears their music in his ears. As they dance, slowly and proudly, to the distant chant he watches, paralysed, as they come closer to the ship.

He sees their stiff bodies, their plump, respectable faces, the expensive dark brocades of the women's dresses, the good dark suits of the men. He observes the well-nurtured upright bodies, the straight backs, the air of dignity and comportment with which they circle, so correctly, in time to the music.

The dark circles which are their eyes stare blindly at each other. Their faces are rigid below the dark glasses. They circle through the void towards Ryan and the music becomes louder, more solemn, more threatening.

'Daddy! Daddy!'

Alexander is crying.

Ryan is unable to move. Cold light falls on the dancers. They come closer to the ship, closer to Ryan, standing terrified at his window.

'Daddy!'

Ryan hears the insistent voice and frowns. Is Alex really up?

Ryan smiles. The boy was never one to stay in bed if he could help it.

But Alexander Ryan is not in bed. He is in hibernation.

The dancers dance on.

They are not real. Ryan realises that he should give his attention to his son, not to the illusory dancers out there in space. They can't get in. They can't confront him. They can't take off, in one terrible gesture, the glasses which encircle their eyes, revealing...

'Get back to bed, Alex!'

They are very close now. The music slows. They are just a few paces from the ship. They turn to face Ryan with their blinded eyes. Slowly they take a step.

One step...

Two steps...

Three steps towards Ryan.

They are clustered, some thirty of them, a foot from Ryan, standing just outside the window. And then Ryan realises with greater terror that it has been an illusion. The dancers are not outside. What he was seeing was a reflection in the window. The dancers are actually *behind* him. They have been in the ship all the time. He dares not turn. He stares instead into the mirror.

They stare back.

Then Ryan sees the others. Behind the crowd of dancers are his friends and relatives. All stare at him from blank eyes. All stare at him as if they do not know him. As if, indeed, he does not exist for them.

Josephine – her plump face expressionless, her blonde hair tumbling to her plump shoulders, cruel in her indifference.

His two sons, Alexander and Rupert, startled expressions in their round eyes. Uncle Sidney, his stringy arm gripping the two boys around their thin shoulders, his lips drawn back in a snarl, his eyes on an object somewhere above Ryan's head.

There are the Henry twins, one healthy, one tired by pregnancy, but hand in hand and staring through Ryan with identical hazel eyes. There is Tracy Masterson, looking vacuously past Ryan's left shoulder. There is Fred Masterson, Ryan's oldest friend, a sympathetic expression on his face. There is brother John, puzzled, tired, uncomprehending. There is Isabel, looking bitterly at John. There is James Henry, red hair gleaming in the mirror-light, glaring meaninglessly through Ryan.

And as he looks, Ryan sees the dancers in front take their last step towards him. He wheels to face them.

He stares into the cool, orderly control room. The screens, the dials, the indicators, the instruments, the computer console. Grey and green, muted colours, quiet…

He looks back at the porthole. There is only blackness.

In one way this seems worse to Ryan. He begins to beat at the porthole, howling and cursing.

'Where are you? Where are you? You shits, you cunts, you bastards, you bleeders, you fuckers, you horrors…'

They are there again. Not the dancers. Only his friends and relatives. But they still cannot see him.

He waves to them, mouths friendly words at them. They do not understand. They come a little closer.

And suddenly Ryan feels their malice, is shocked and horrified. He looks at them and his expression is puzzled. He tries to signal to them – that they know him, that he is their friend.

They crowd closer.

'*Let us in!*' they cry. 'Let us in. Let us in. Let us in. Let us in. Let us in. Let us live. Let us in.'

The clamour around the ship increases. Hands claw at the window. Hands tear their way through the fabric of the porthole.

'You fools! You'll destroy the ship. Be sensible. Wait!' Ryan begs them. 'You'll bring the deaths of all of us! Don't – don't – don't!'

But they are ripping the whole of the wall away, exposing it to frigid space.

'You'll wreck the expedition! Stop it!'

They cannot hear him.

His throat is tight.

He faints.

Chapter Sixteen

RYAN IS LYING on the floor of the control room. His sleeve is rolled up and an ampoule of 1cc Proditol lies near him. The ampoule is empty.

He blinks. At some point he must have realised what he had to do to stop the hallucinations. He is impressed by his own strength of will.

'How are you now?'

He knows the voice. He feels fear, then relief. It is his brother John's voice. He looks up. His jacket has been folded under his head.

John, stalwart and stolid, looks down at him.

'You *were* in a bad way, old son!'

'John. How did you wake up?'

'Something to do with the computer, I think. There's probably an emergency waking system if anything happens to the man on duty.'

'I'm glad of that. I was a real idiot to carry on on my own. I realised everything else about my condition except the extent of the strain. I was insisting to myself that I didn't need anyone else to help me.'

'Well, you're okay now. I'll help you. You can go into hibernation if you like…'

'No, that won't be necessary,' Ryan says hastily. 'I'll be able to manage now I've got someone to share my troubles with.' He laughs feebly. 'It's just plain old-fashioned loneliness.' He shudders. He still thinks he can see things in the corners of his eyes. 'I hope.'

'Of course,' says John. He is convinced; he isn't just trying to humour Ryan. John was always a hard man to convince, therefore Ryan is satisfied.

'Thank God for the emergency system, eh?' says John a trifle awkwardly.

'Amen to that,' says Ryan.

He wishes the emergency system had awakened that other member of John's family, his young wife Janet. If someone had to be awake... He dismisses the thought and gets up. Being with John is almost like being alone, he thinks, for John is not the most voluble of men. Still...

Ryan gets up. John is efficiently checking the instruments.

'You'd better get off to your bed, old chap,' says John. 'I'll look after things here.'

Gratefully Ryan goes to his cabin.

He lies in the dark, grateful for the drug which has driven away his visions, slightly nervous of the fact that John has joined him.

John probably knows about the affair he had with Janet, John's younger wife. Perhaps he doesn't care.

Then again, perhaps he does. John isn't a particularly vengeful man, but it would be just as well to be on guard.

Ryan remembers the other affair he'd had. The affair with Sarah Carson – old Carson's daughter...

Carson's toy business had been Ryan's closest competitor. Carson was chairman of Moonbeam Toys and had known Ryan for years. They had both started off with Saunders Toys in the old days and had been running pretty much neck and neck ever since. Their rivalry had been a friendly one and they often met for lunch or dinner before the habit of communal eating became unfashionable. When that happened they would still converse over the video.

Carson became a fanatical Patriot one day and, as far as Ryan was concerned, no longer worth speaking to. But by this time it was evident that the Patriots were by far the most powerful political group in the country and Ryan decided it would do him no harm to be Carson's friend. He even attended some meetings with Carson and other Patriots, registering himself as a member.

It was at one of these meetings that he met Sarah, a tall, beautiful girl of twenty-two, who did not seem convinced by her father's views.

Josephine was going through a particularly bad time, as were the two boys. All three of them spent two thirds of the day under sedation and Ryan himself, though he sympathised with their problems, needed some form of relaxation.

The form of relaxation he chose was Sarah Carson. Or, rather, she chose him. The moment she saw him, she made a heavy play for him.

They took to meeting at an all but finished hotel. For a few pounds they could hire a whole suite. The bottom had dropped out of the hotel business by that time. Very few people trusted hotels or liked to leave home.

Sarah pulled Ryan out of his depression and gave him something to look forward to at night. She was passionate and she had stamina. Ryan took to sleeping during the day.

Ryan used the Patriot meetings as an excuse and continued, with Sarah and her father, to turn up at several.

Then Carson had an argument with the rest of his group. Carson had lately formed the opinion that the Earth, far from being a planet circling through space, was in fact a hollowed-out 'bubble' in an infinity of rock. Instead of walking about on the outside of a sphere, we were walking about on the inside of one.

Carson went off to form his own group and soon had a healthy following who shared the Hollow Earth belief with him. Sarah continued to go with her father to his meetings (she knew he had a weak heart and also acted, sometimes, as his chauffeur).

Then Carson formed the impression that Ryan was an enemy. Sarah told Ryan this.

'It's the old story – if you're not with me, you're against me. He's getting a bit funny lately,' she said. 'I'm worried about his heart.' She stroked Ryan's chest as they lay together in the hotel bed. 'He's told me to stop seeing you, darling.'

'Are you going to?'

'I think so.'

'Just to humour him? He's eligible for a nut-house now, you know. Even the bloody Patriot fanatics think he's barmy.'

'He's my old dad,' she said. 'I love him.'

'You're hung up on him, if you ask me.'

'Darling, I wouldn't have gone for you if I didn't have a hefty father complex, would I?'

Ryan felt anger. Stupid old fool, Carson! And now his daughter trying to put him down.

'That was clever,' he said bitterly. 'I didn't know you had such sharp knives in your arsenal.'

'Come off it, darling. You brought it up. Anyway, I was only joking. You're not at all bad for your age.'

'Thanks.'

He got up, scowling.

He put a glass under the tap in the washbasin and filled it with water. He sipped the water gingerly and then threw it down the sink. 'Christ, I'm sure they're putting something in the water, these days.'

'Haven't you heard?' She stretched out in the bed. Her body was near-perfect. She seemed to be taunting him with it. 'There's everything in the water – LSD, cyanide, stuff to rot your brain – you name it!'

He grunted. 'Sure. I think it's probably just dead rats...' He got his shirt and began to put it on. 'It's time we were going. It's nine o'clock. The curfew starts at ten.'

'You don't want one last fuck? For old times' sake?'

'You mean it, then? About not seeing each other again?'

'I mean it, darling. Make no mistake. The condition he's in, it would kill him...'

'He'd be better off dead.'

'That's as may be.' She swung her long legs off the bed and began to dress. 'Will you give me a lift home?'

'For old times' sake...'

The mixture of rage and depression was getting on top of him. He tried to shrug it off, but it got worse. With all his business worries – production falling, custom declining, debts unpaid – he didn't need this. He knew there was no chance of her changing her mind. She was a direct girl. Her pass at him had been direct. Now the brush-off was direct. He hadn't realised how much she had been bolstering his ego. It was ridiculous to rely on something like that. But he had been. His feelings now told him so.

They left the hotel. The sun was red in the sky. His car was in the street outside. The curfew seemed pretty pointless, for there was hardly anyone in Oxford Street at all.

Ryan stood by the car looking at the ruins of the burned-out department stores, the gutted office blocks, mementoes of the Winter Riots.

Sarah Carson looked out of the window. 'Admiring the view?' she said. 'You're a bit of a romantic on the quiet, aren't you?'

'I suppose I am,' he said as he climbed into the car and started the engine. 'Though I've always considered myself a realist.'

'Just a selfish romantic.'

'You're making it harder than you need to,' he said as he took the car down the street.

'Sorry. I'm not much of a sentimentalist. You can't afford to be, these days.'

'You want me to take you all the way back to Croydon?'

'You don't expect me to *walk* through the Antifem zone, do you?'

'Zone? Have they got control of a whole area now?'

'All but. They're trying to set up their own little state in Balham – allowing no women in at all. Any woman they catch, they kill. Lovely.'

Ryan sniffed. 'They might have the right bloody attitude.'

'Don't get morbid, sweetie. Can we go around Balham?'

'It's the quickest route since the Brighton Road got blown to bits in Brixton.'

'Try going around the other side, then.'

'I'll see.'

They drove for a while in silence.

London was bleak, blackened and broken.

'Ever thought of getting out?' Sarah said as he drove down

Vauxhall Bridge Road, trying to avoid the potholes. He had begun to feel slightly sick. Partly her, he thought, and partly the damned agoraphobia.

'Where is there to go?' he said. 'The rest of the world seems to be worse off than England.'

'Sure.'

'And you need money to live abroad,' he said. 'Since nobody recognises anyone else's currency any more, what would I live on?'

'You think people are going to buy a lot of toys this Christmas?' She was looking at the completely flattened houses on the right.

His depression and his anger grew. He shrugged. He knew she was right.

'You and my old dad are in the wrong business,' she said cheerfully. 'At least he had the sense to go into politics. That's a bit more secure – for a while, at any rate.'

'Maybe.' He drove over the bridge. It shook as he crossed.

'A strong wind'll finish that,' she said.

'Shut up, Sarah.' He gripped the wheel hard.

'Oh, God. Try to finish this thing off gracefully, darling. I thought you were such a good businessman. Such a cunning bastard. Such a cool bird, working out all the odds. That's what you told me.'

'No need to throw it in my face. I've got plans, my love, that you haven't an inkling of.'

'Not the spaceship idea!' She laughed.

'How —?'

'You didn't tell me, darling. I went through your briefcase a couple of weeks ago. Are you really serious? You're going to take thirteen people to Siberia and steal that UN spaceship that's been standing idle for the last year?'

'It's ready to go.'

'They're still bickering over who owns what bit of it and whose nationals have got a right to go in it. It'll never take off.'

Ryan smiled secretly.

'You're nuttier than my old man, sweetie!'

Ryan scowled.

'Wait till I tell my friends,' she said. 'I'll be dining out on it for weeks.'

'You'd better not tell anyone, my love.' He spoke through his teeth. 'I mean it.'

'Come *on*, darling. We all have our illusions, but this is ridiculous. How would you fly one of those things?'

'It's fully automatic,' he said. 'It's the most sophisticated piece of machinery ever invented.'

'And you think they're going to let you pinch it?'

'We're already in touch with the people at the station,' he said. 'They seem to agree we can do it.'

'How are you in touch with them?'

'It's not hard, Sarah. Old-fashioned radio. For some time a few scientifically minded pragmatists like myself have been working towards a way of getting out of this mess, since it seems impossible to save the human race from sinking back to the Dark Ages...'

'You could have saved it once,' Sarah said, turning to look directly at him. 'If you hadn't been so bloody careful. So bloody selfish!'

'It wasn't as simple as that.'

'Your generation and the generation before that could have done something. The seeds of all this ridiculous paranoia and xenophobia were there then. God – such a waste! This century could have been a century of Utopia. You and your mothers and fathers turned it into Hell.'

'It might look like that...'

'Darling, it *was* like that.'

He shrugged.

'And now you're getting out,' she said. 'Leaving the mess behind. Your talk of "pragmatism" is so much bloody balls! You're as much an escaper as my poor daft old dad! Maybe more of one – and less pleasant, for that – because you might fucking succeed!'

They were driving through Stockwell. The sun was setting but no street lighting came on.

'You feel guilty because you're letting me down, don't you?' he said. 'That's what all this display is about, isn't it?'

'No. You're a good fuck. But I never cared much for your character, darling.'

'You'll have to go a long way to find a better one in these dark days.' He tried to say it as a joke, but it was evident he believed it.

'Selfish and opinionated,' she said. 'Pragmatism. Ugh!'

'I'll drop you off here then, shall I?'

He stopped the car. It sank on its cushion of air.

She peered out into the darkness. 'Where's "here"?'

'Balham,' he said.

'Don't play games, darling. Let's get this over with. You were taking me all the way to Croydon, remember.'

'I'm a bit tired of your small-talk – darling.'

'All right.' She leaned back. 'I'll button my lip, I promise. I'll say nothing until we get to Croydon and then I'll give you a sweet "thank you".'

But he had made his decision. It wasn't malice. It was self-preservation. It was for Josephine and the boys, and for the group. He wasn't enjoying what he was doing.

'Get out of the car, Sarah.'

'You take me bloody home the way you said you would!'

'Out.'

She looked into his eyes. 'My God, Ryan...'

'Go on.' He pushed her shoulder, leaned over her and opened the door. 'Go on.'

'Jesus Christ. All right.' She picked up her handbag from the seat and got out of the car. 'It's something of a classic situation. But a bit too classic really. The sex war's hotted up in this part of the world.'

'That's your problem,' he said.

'I'm not likely to get out of this alive, Ryan.'

'That's your problem.'

She took a deep breath. 'I won't tell anyone about your stupid spaceship idea, if that's what's worrying you. Who'd believe me, anyway?'

'I've got a family and friends to worry about, Sarah. They believe me.'

'You dirty shit.' She walked off into the darkness.

They must have been waiting for her all the time because she screamed – a high-pitched, ugly scream – she cried out for him to help her. Her second scream was cut short.

Ryan closed the door of the car and locked it. He started the engine and switched on the headlights.

He saw her face in the lights. It stuck out above the black mass of Antifems in their monklike robes.

It was only her face.

Her body lay on the ground, still clasping her handbag.

Her head was on the end of a pole.

Chapter Seventeen

Ryan lies in his bunk with his logbook and his stylus. He has been there for two days now. John comes in occasionally, but doesn't bother him, realising that he does not want to be disturbed. He lets Ryan get his own food when he wants to and looks after the running of the ship. To make sure that Ryan rests, he has even turned off the console in Ryan's cabin.

Ryan spends most of his time with the logbook. He removed it from the desk originally to make sure that John didn't come across it.

He reads over the first entry he made when he brought it back to the cabin.

What I did to Sarah can be justified, of course, in that she could have ruined this project. I had to be sure nothing wrecked it. The fact that we are all safe and aboard is evidence that I took the right precautions – trusting no-one outside the group – making sure that everything was done with the utmost secrecy. We kept contact only with the Russian group – about the last outpost of rational humanity that we knew about.

Would I have done it in that way if she had not turned me down in such an unpleasant manner? I don't know. Considering the state of things at the time, I behaved no worse, no less humanely, than anyone else. You had to fight fire with fire. And if it – and certain other things – is on my conscience, at least it isn't on anyone else's conscience. The boys are clean. So is Josephine. So are most of the others…

He sighs as he reads the entry over. He shifts his body in the bunk.

'All right, old chap?'

John has come, as silently as ever, into the cabin. He looks a trifle tired himself.

'I'm fine.' Ryan closes the book quickly. 'Fine. Are you all right?'

'I'm coping very well. I'll let you know if anything crops up.'

'Thanks.'

John leaves. Ryan returns his attention to the log, turning the pages until he comes to a fresh one.

He continues writing:

There is no doubt about it. I have blood on my hands. That's probably the reason I've been having bad dreams. Any normal, halfway decent man would. I took it on myself to do it, at least. I didn't involve anyone else.

When we hijacked the Albion transport, I had hoped there would be no trouble. Neither would there have been, I think, if the crew had been all English. Incredible! I always knew the Irish were excitable, but that stupid fellow who tried to get the gun from me in mid-air deserved all he got. He must have been Irish. There's no other explanation. I was never a racist, but one has to admit that there are certain virtues the English have which other races don't share. I suppose that is racialism of a sort. But not the unhealthy sort. I was horrified when I heard that the Foreigners in the camps were being starved to death. I would have done something about it if I could. But by that time it had gone too far. Maybe Sarah was right. Maybe I could have stopped it if I hadn't been so selfish. I always considered myself to be an enlightened man – a liberal man. I was known for it.

He stops again, staring at the wall.

The rot had set in before my day. H-bombs, nuclear radiation, chemical poisoning, insufficient birth control, mismanaged economics, misguided political theories. And then – panic.

And no room for error. Throw a spanner in the works of a society as sophisticated and highly tuned as ours was and – that's it. Chaos.

They tried to bring simple answers to complicated problems. They looked for messiahs when they should have been looking at the problems. Humanity's old trouble. But this time humanity did for itself. Absolutely.

It is odd, he thinks, *that I will never know how it all turned out. Just as well, of course, from the point of view of our kids. We left just in time. They were bombing each other to smithereens...*

Another few days, he writes, *and we wouldn't have made it. I timed it pretty well, all things considered.*

Ryan had led the party out to London Airport, where the big Albion transport was preparing to take off on its bombing mission over Dublin. They were all in military kit for Ryan was posing as a general with his staff.

They had driven straight out onto the runway and were up the steps and into the plane before anyone knew what had happened.

At gunpoint Ryan had told the pilot to take off.

Within a quarter of an hour they were heading for Russia...

It had been over the landing strip on the bleak Siberian Plain that the Irishman – he must have been an Irishman – had panicked. How an Irishman had managed to remain under cover without revealing his evident racial characteristics, Ryan would never know.

For two hours Ryan had sat in the co-pilot's seat with his Purdy automatic trained on the pilot while Henry and Masterson looked after the rest of the crew and John Ryan and Uncle Sidney stayed with the families.

Ryan was tired. He felt drained of energy. His body ached and the butt of the gun was slippery with the sweat from his hands. He felt filthy and his flesh was cold. As the Albion came down through the clouds he saw the huge spaceship standing on the launching field. It was surrounded by webs of gantries, like a caged bird of prey, like Prometheus bound.

His attention was on the ship when the Irish pilot leaped from his seat.

'You damned traitor! You disgusting renegade –' The pilot lunged for the gun, screaming at the top of his voice, his face writhing with his hatred and his insanity.

Ryan fell back, pressing the trigger. The Purdy muttered and a stream of tiny explosive bullets hit the pilot all over his chest and face and his bloody body collapsed on top of Ryan.

Pilotless, the big transport began to shake.

Ryan pushed the body off him and reached up to throw the

lever that would put the plane automatically on Emergency Landing Procedure. The plane's rockets fired and the transport juddered as its trajectory was arrested. It began to go down vertically on its rockets.

Ryan wiped the sweat from his lips and then retched. He had smeared the pilot's blood all over his mouth. He cleaned his face with his sleeve, watching as the plane neared the ground, screaming towards the overgrown airstrip to the north of the launching field.

John Ryan put his head into the cabin. 'My God! What happened?'

'The pilot just went mad,' Ryan said hoarsely. 'You'd better check everyone's got their safety belts on, John. We're going to make a heavy landing.'

The Albion was close to the ground now, its rockets burning the concrete strip. Ryan buckled his own safety belt.

Five feet above the ground the rockets cut out and the plane bellyflopped onto the concrete.

Shaken, Ryan got out of his seat and stumbled into the crew section. Alexander was crying and Tracy Masterson was screaming and Ida Henry was moaning, but the rest were very quiet.

'John,' Ryan said. 'Get the doors open and get everybody out of the plane as soon as possible, will you?' He still held the Purdy.

John Ryan nodded and Ryan went aft to where Masterson and Henry were covering the rest of the crew.

'What was all that about?' James Henry said suspiciously. 'You trying to kill us all, Ryan?'

'The pilot lost his head. We had to make an emergency rocket-powered landing – vertical.' Ryan looked over the rest of the crew – four boys and a woman of about thirty. They all looked scared. 'Did you know your captain was Irish?' Ryan asked them. 'And you were going to bomb Dublin? You can bet your life he was going to try to make a landing.'

The crew stared at him incredulously.

'Well, it was true,' Ryan said. 'But don't worry. I've dealt with him.'

The woman said, 'You murdered him. Is that what you did?'

'Self-defence,' said Ryan. 'Self-defence isn't murder. All right, Fred – Henry – you go and help everybody get off this bloody plane.'

The woman said, 'He was no more Irish than I am. Anyway, what does it matter?'

'No wonder your people are losing,' Ryan answered contemptuously.

When everyone was off the ship Ryan shot the crew. It was the only safe thing to do. While they were alive there was a chance that they would seize control of the Albion and do something foolish.

Tishchenko was a harried-looking man of about fifty. He gravely shook hands with Ryan and then guided him by the elbow across the barren concrete towards the control buildings. The wind was cold and moaned. Beyond the launching site, the plain stretched in all directions, featureless and green-grey. Ryan's people trudged behind them.

Tishchenko was the man whom Ryan had contacted originally. The contact had been made through Allard, who had been one of the people vainly trying to keep the UN together in the last days. Allard, an old schoolfriend of Ryan's, had been sent to a Patriot camp not long after he had put Ryan in touch with Tishchenko.

'It is a great pleasure,' said Tishchenko as they entered the building that had been converted to living quarters. It was cold and gloomy. 'And something of an achievement that, in the midst of all this insane xenophobia, a little international group of sane men and women can work together on a project as important as this one.' He smiled. 'And it's good to be able to look at a woman again, I can tell you.'

Ryan was tired. He nodded, rubbing his eyes. One of the reasons the Russian group had been so eager to deal with his group was because of the number of women he could bring with him.

'You are weary?' Tishchenko said. 'Come.'

He led them up two flights of stairs and showed them their accommodation. Camp-beds had been lined around the walls of three rooms. 'It is about the best we can provide,' Tishchenko apologised. 'Amenities are few. Everything had to go to the ship.' He went to the window and drew back the blankets that covered it. 'There she is.'

They gathered around the window and looked at the spacecraft. She towered into the sky.

'She has been ready to fly for two years.' Tishchenko shook his head. 'It has taken two years to provision her. The civil war here, and then the Chinese invasion, is what protected us. We were all but forgotten about...'

'Who else is here now?' Ryan asked. 'Just Russians?'

Tishchenko smiled. 'Just two Russians – myself and Lipche. A couple of Americans, a Chinese, two Italians, three Germans, a Frenchman. That's it.'

Ryan drew a deep breath. He felt odd. The shock of the killings, he supposed.

'I'll be back in a few minutes to take you down to dinner,' Tishchenko told him.

Ryan looked up. 'What?'

'Dinner. We all eat together on the floor below.'

'Oh, I see...'

'I couldn't,' said Josephine Ryan. 'I really couldn't...'

'We're not used to it, you see,' said James Henry. 'Our customs – well...'

Tishchenko looked puzzled and very slightly perturbed. 'Well, if you'd like to arrange to bring the food up here, I suppose we can do that... Then perhaps we can meet after meals. You have been in the thick of things, of course. We have been isolated. We haven't really experienced...'

'Yes,' said Ryan, 'it has been very nasty. I'm sorry. Some of our social sicknesses have rather rubbed off on us. Give us a day or two to settle. We'll be all right then, I'm sure.'

'Good,' said Tishchenko.

Ryan watched him leave. He sensed a certain antipathy in the Russian's manner. He hoped there would not be trouble with him. Russians could not always be trusted. For one moment he wondered if they had been led into a complicated trap. Could this team of scientists just be after the women? Would they dispense with the men now that they had served their purpose?

Ryan pulled himself together. An irrational idea. He would have to watch himself more carefully. He had had no sleep for two nights. *Get some rest now*, he told himself, *and you'll be your old self in the morning.*

The thirteen English people and the eleven scientists toured the ship.

'It is all completely automatic,' said Schonberg, one of the Germans. He smiled and patted Alexander on the head. 'A child could run it.'

The English party, rested and more relaxed, was in better spirits. Even James Henry, who had been the most suspicious of all, seemed better.

'And your probes proved conclusively that there are two planets in the system capable of supporting human life?' he said to Boulez, the Frenchman.

The French scientist smiled. 'One of them could be Earth. About the same amount of land and sea, very similar ecology. There was bound to be a planet like it somewhere – we were just lucky to discover one this early.'

Buccella, one of the Italians, was taking a strong interest in pointing out certain features of the ship to Janet Ryan.

Typical Italian, thought Ryan.

He glanced at his brother John, who was listening carefully as Shan, the Chinese, tried to explain about the regeneration units. Shan's English was not very good.

Back in their own quarters, Ryan asked his brother: 'Did you notice that Italian, Buccella, and Janet together?'

'What do you mean, "together"?' John said with a grin.

Ryan shrugged. 'It's your problem.'

The preparations continued swiftly. News came in of massive nuclear bombardments taking place all over the globe. They took to working night and day, resting when they could no longer keep their eyes open. And at length the ship was ready.

Buccella, Shan and Boulez were going on the ship with the others. The rest were staying behind. Their job was to get the ship off the ground. They were taking over the duties of some fifty technicians.

Lift-off day arrived.

Chapter Eighteen

RYAN SCRATCHES HIS nose with the tip of his stylus. He writes: *One could not afford to be sentimental in those days. Perhaps when we land on the new planet we can relax and indulge all those pleasant human vices. It would be nice to feel at peace again, the way one did as a child.*

He shifts in his bunk and looks up.

'Good God, Janet. You're up!'

Janet Ryan smiles down at him. 'We're all up. John thought it wisest.'

'I suppose he knows what he's doing. It's not part of the original plan.'

'John wants to see how it works out. Can I get you anything?'

He grins. 'No thanks, love. I've got my Proditol to keep me cool. It seems to be working fine. I've been doing some pretty sober thinking since I decided to stay in bed for a bit.'

'John says you'd got pretty obsessive – following ship routine to the point of your own breakdown...'

'I can see I was half crazy now. I'm very well – very relaxed.'

'You'll soon be in control of things again.' She smiles.

'I certainly will!'

Janet leaves the cabin.

Ryan writes:

Janet has just been in to see me. Apparently brother John feels it's best for everybody to be up and about. I expect Josephine and the boys will be along soon. Janet looks as beautiful as ever. You couldn't really blame that Italian chap for going overboard for her... A sick joke that, I suppose. When I caught him with her in John's own cabin, I felt sick. The man was a complete stinker, playing around like that. He had to be dealt with. His friends had their eyes on the girls, too, that was plain. They were only waiting for a chance to get their hands on them while our backs were turned. I was a fool to trust a pack of Foreigners. I know that now. It became evident that his friends were in on the plot with him, the way they took his part. They threatened the security of the whole mission with their utterly irrational intentions on the girls – and the boys, too, I shouldn't wonder. I suppose it was that they hadn't seen any women for so long. It went to their heads. They couldn't control themselves. In a way one can sympathise, of course. It showed just what a threat to the safety of the ship they were when they tried to steal my gun. I had to shoot Buccella then and his friends, when they wouldn't stop coming at me. We pushed the corpses through the air-lock. Everybody agreed I had done the right thing.

He sighs. It has been hard, keeping control of everything for so long. Making unpleasant decisions…

Strange that Josephine and the boys haven't come in, yet. John is probably staging the wake-up procedure.

He closes the log and puts it and the stylus under his pillow. He leans back, looking forward to seeing his wife and children.

He dozes.

He sleeps.

He dreams.

Q: WHO ARE YOU KIDDING?
A: HAD A NOISE TROUBLE

He stands in the control room. He is sure he has forgotten something, some crucial operation. He checks the computer, but it is babbling nonsense. Puns and facetious remarks flow from it. He casts around for the source of the trouble, looks for a way to switch off the computer. But it will not switch off. The life of the ship depends on the computer. But it is the ship or Ryan, as Ryan sees it. He starts to batter at the computer with a chair.

*****YOURE KILLING ME**********HAHAHAHAHAHA***********

says the computer.

Ryan turns. Through the porthole he sees the dancers again, their faces pressed against the glass.

'You're in league with them,' he tells the computer. 'You're on their side.'

*******I AM ON EVERYONES SIDE**************I AM A***** SCIENTIFIC INSTRUMENT******I AM UTTERLY PRAGMATIC**

says the computer.

'You're laughing at me now,' Ryan says almost pathetically. 'You're taking the piss out of me, aren't you?'

*******MY DUTY IS TO LOOK AFTER YOU ALL AND KEEP YOU SAFE AND SOUND""""REPEAT SAFE AND SOUND*****************

'You cynical bugger.'

He sees a sweet old lady shaking her head, a wry smile on her face. 'Language,' she says. 'Language.'

It is his mother. Her maiden name was Hope Dempsey. He christened the ship after her.

'You tell the computer to stop getting at me, Ma!' he begs.

'Naughty thing,' says his mother. 'You leave my little boy alone.'

But the computer continues to mock him.

'You were never a sweet old lady anyway,' says Ryan. She turns into the hag who haunts him and he screams.

Josephine stands over him. She is holding an empty ampoule of Proditol. 'You'll feel better in a moment, darling,' she says. 'How are you now?'

'Better already,' he says, smiling in relief. 'You don't know how pleased I am to see you, Jo. Where are the boys?'

'They're not quite awake yet. You know it takes a bit of time.' She sits on the edge of his bunk. 'They'll be here soon. You should have woken us up earlier, you know. It's too much of a strain for one man – even you.'

'I realise that now,' he says.

She gives the old slightly nervous, slightly tender smile. 'Take it easy,' she says. 'Let the Proditol do its stuff.'

She catches sight of the red logbook sticking from under his pillow. 'What's that, darling?'

'My logbook,' he says. 'A sort of private diary, really.'

'If it's private...'

'I'd rather keep it that way until I've had a look through it. When I feel better.'

'Of course.'

'It's the only thing that kept me halfway sane,' he explains.

'Of course.'

With one hand supporting his head, Ryan lies in his bunk and writes:

Alexander and Rupert both look fit and well and everybody seems singularly cheerful. It seems as if we have all benefited from rest and with breaking ties with Earth. We feel free again. I can hear them bustling about in the ship. Laughter. A general mood of easy co-operation. What a change from the early days on the ship, when even Uncle Sidney seemed jealous of my command! Even sullen, suspicious old James Henry has an almost saintly manner! My morbid thoughts melt like snow in springtime. My obsession for Janet has disappeared – part of the same morbid mood, I suppose. James Henry's new attitude surprises me most. If it wasn't for the fact that everybody is in better spirits I'd suspect that he was once again harbouring plans to get rid of me and run the ship himself. It is amazing what a change of environment can do! John was wise to awaken everybody. Plainly, I had become too worried that the tensions would start up again. We're going to make a fine colony on New Earth. And thank God for Proditol. Those scientists certainly covered every angle. I've decided to put all morbid thoughts of the past out of my mind. I was a different person – perhaps a sick person – when I did what I did. To indulge in self-recrimination now is stupid and benefits nobody.

My breakdown was caused by the chaos that crept over society. It reflected the breakdown of that society. I could almost date its beginning for me – when our own air force (or, at least, what had been our own air force) dropped napalm and fragmentation bombs on London. My psyche, I suppose, reflected the environment.

But enough of that! I've made up my mind. No more morbid self-examination. No need for it now, anyway.

The days will pass more quickly now that everybody is up and about and so cheerful. We'll be landing on that planet before we realise it!

He signs the page, closes the book and tucks it under his pillow. He feels a little weak. Doubtless the effects of the drug. He sleeps and dreams that the ship has landed on the Isle of Skye and everyone is swimming in the sea. He watches them all swim out. James Henry, Janet Ryan, Josephine Ryan, Rupert Ryan, Sidney Ryan, Fred Masterson, Alexander Ryan, Ida and Felicity Henry, Tracy Masterson, Isabel Ryan, John Ryan. They are laughing and shouting. They all swim out into the sea.

A week passes.

Ryan spends less time writing in his logbook and more time sleeping. He feels confident that John and the others are running the ship well.

One night he is awakened by pangs of hunger and he realises that nobody has thought to bring him any food. He frowns. An image of the Foreigners comes into his mind. He saw a camp only once, but it was enough. They were not being gassed or burned or shot – they were being systematically starved to death. The cheapest way. His stomach rumbles.

He gets up and leaves his cabin. He enters the storeroom and takes a meal pack from a bin. Chewing at the pack, he pads back to his cabin.

He has a slight headache – probably the effects of the Proditol. They have given him a dose every day for the past ten days or so. It will be time to finish the doses soon.

He sleeps.

Chapter Nineteen

RYAN MAKES AN entry in his log.

I have now been resting for two weeks and the difference is amazing. I have lost weight – I was too heavy anyway – and my brain has cleared. I have had insights into my own behaviour (amazing what a clever rationaliser I am!) and my body is relaxed. I will soon be ready to resume control of the ship.

Josephine enters. She is holding an ampoule of Proditol in her hand.

'Time for your shot, dear,' she smiles.

'Hey! What are you trying to do to me?' He grins at her. 'Fourteen days is the maximum period for that stuff. I don't need it any more.'

Her smile fades. 'One more shot can't do you any harm, dear, can it?'

He swings himself out of the bunk. 'What's up?' he jokes. 'Is there something you don't want me to know about?'

'Of course not!'

Ryan unfolds a suit from the pack in the cupboard. He lays it on the bed. 'I'm going to take a shower,' he says. 'Then I'll go into the control room and see how everyone's getting along without me.'

'You're not well enough yet, dear,' says Josephine, her pink face anxious. 'Please stay in bed a bit longer, even if you won't let me give you the Proditol.'

'I'm fine.' Ryan frowns. He feels a return of his old feelings of suspicion. Maybe he should have something more to keep him calm – yet if he has any more Proditol, he exceeds the dose and risks his life. 'I'd like to stay in my bunk all the time.' He smiles. 'Honest, I would. But the suggested dosage period is over, Jo. I've got to get up sometime.'

He leaves the cabin and takes his shower. He comes back in.

Josephine has gone. She has laid out a fresh disposable suit on the bed. He puts it on.

He walks along the passage towards the main control room and he remembers that he has left his diary under his pillow. There is a chance that someone will give in to the temptation to read it. It would be better if no-one saw his comments. After all, some of them were pretty insane. Some of it was a bit like a prisoner of the Inquisition, confessing to anything that is suggested to him!

He smiles and returns to his cabin. He picks up the logbook and puts it in his locker, sealing the locker.

He still feels weak. He sits on the edge of the bunk for a moment.

For some time now he has been aware of a sound. Now it impinges on his consciousness. A high-pitched whine. He recognises the noise. An emergency in the control room.

He gets up and runs out of his cabin, down the passage, into the main control room.

The computer is flashing a sign:

URGENT ATTENTION REQUIRED

URGENT ATTENTION REQUIRED.

James Henry is at the controls. He turns as Ryan enters. 'Hello, Ryan. How are you now?'

'I'm fine. What's the emergency?'

'Nothing much. I'm coping with it.'

'What is it, though?'

'A new circuit needed in the heat control unit in the hydroponics section. Cut out the emergency signal, would you?'

Ryan automatically does as Henry asks him.

Henry makes a few adjustments to the controls then turns to Ryan with a smile. 'Glad to see you're okay again. I've been managing pretty well in your absence.'

'That's great...' Ryan feels a touch of anger at Henry's slightly patronising tone.

Ryan looks around the control room. Everything else seems to be as he left it at the time of his breakdown. 'Where's everybody else?' he asks.

'Studying – resting – checking out various functions – standard ship routine.'

'You seem to be working together very well,' Ryan says.

'Better than before. We've got something in common now, after all.'

Ryan feels a touch of panic. He doesn't know why. Is there something in Henry's tone? A sort of triumph? 'What do you mean?'

Henry shrugs. 'Our great mission.'

'Of course,' says Ryan. He sucks his lower lip. 'Of course.'

But what did James Henry really mean? Is it that they have got rid of him? Do they believe that he was the cause of their tension? Is that what Henry is insinuating?

Ryan feels his throat go dry. He feels his anger rising.

He controls himself. He isn't thinking clearly. He still needs to rest. Josephine was right.

'Well, keep up the good work, James,' he says, turning to leave. 'If there's anything I can do...'

'You could check the hibernation room some time,' Henry says.

'What?' Ryan frowns.

'I said you could check the hydration loom – in hydroponics.'

'Sure. Now?'

'Any time you feel like it.'

'Okay. I'm still a bit shaky. I'll get back to my bunk, I think.'

'I think you'd better.'

'I'm perfectly all right now.'

'Sure. But you could still do with some rest.'

Ryan again controls his temper. 'Yes. Well – I'll see you later.'

'I'm here whenever you need me, captain.'

Again the feeling that James Henry is mocking him, just as he used to, before it became intolerable...

He feels faint. No. Henry is right. He's still not properly recovered. He staggers back to his cabin.

He falls into his bunk.

He sleeps and he dreams.

He is in the control room again. James Henry stands there. James Henry is trying to supersede him. James Henry has always wanted to take over command of the group and of the spaceship. But James Henry is not stable enough to command. If he takes over from Ryan the whole safety of the ship becomes at risk. Ryan knows that there is only one thing to do to stop Henry's plotting against him.

He raises the Purdy automatic – the same gun that he used on the aircraft. He levels it at James Henry. He takes a deep breath and begins to squeeze the trigger.

The computer flashes:

URGENT ATTENTION REQUIRED

URGENT ATTENTION REQUIRED.

Henry turns. Ryan hides the gun behind his back. Henry signals to him to have a look at the computer. Ryan approaches it suspiciously.

******YOU ARE IN NO CONDITION TO COMMAND THIS****** CRAFT’’’’’’’’’’’’REPEAT YOU ARE IN NO CONDITION TO** *****COMMAND THIS CRAFT’’’’’’’’’’’’REPEAT YOU ARE IN NO** *****CONDITION TO COMMAND THIS CRAFT’’’’’’’’’’TAKE ONE DOSE*1CC PRODITOL INSTANTLY AND REPEAT DOSE DAILY FOR***FOURTEEN DAYS’’’’’’’’’’’’YOU ARE IN NO CONDITION TO******COMMAND THIS CRAFT’’’’’’’’’’’’YOU ARE ENDANGERING THE****ENTIRE EXPEDITION IF YOU DO NOT FOLLOW THESE*******INSTRUCTIONS AT ONCE’’’’’’’’’’’’REPEAT AT ONCE***

Ryan looks contemptuously at Henry. 'You'll use anything to try to discredit me, won't you?'

Henry says calmly: 'You are a sick man, Ryan. The computer's right. Why don't you…?'

Ryan raises the Purdy automatic and fires one bullet into Henry's skull. The man's head jerks back. He opens his mouth to say something. Ryan fires again. James Henry falls.

Ryan scowls at the computer. 'The next one's for you if you go on playing games with me, chum.'

He turns the cut-out switch.

*******YOU ARE IN NO CONDITION TO COMMAND THIS******

URGENT ATTENTION REQUIRED

URGENT AT

Tension, tension everywhere

Nor any time to think

CRAFT’’’’’’’’’’’’REPEAT YOU ARE IN NO CONDITION TO*************

There is d…

Q: WHAT IS THE EXACT NATURE OF THE CATASTROPHE?

Ryan wakes up, sweating. His suit is torn. The bunk is in a mess. He climbs off the bunk and stands on the floor, shaking. The Proditol just hasn’t been enough. But he can’t risk taking any more. He strips the bunk and disposes of the covers. He takes off his clothes and disposes of them.

A feeling of desperation engulfs him. Is he really incurable? Will he never shake the nightmares? He was sure he was better. And yet…

Suppose they haven’t been giving him Proditol. Suppose they are deliberately poisoning him. No. Not his friends. Not his family. They couldn’t be so cruel.

And yet hasn’t he been cruel? Hasn’t he done as much for expediency’s sake?

He sobs, drawing in huge breaths.

Ryan falls on his bunk and weeps.

He weeps for a long while before he hears his brother John’s voice.

‘What’s the matter, old chap?’

He looks up. John’s face is sympathetic. But can he trust him?

‘I’m still getting the nightmares, John. They’re just as bad. Worse, if anything.’

John spreads his hands helplessly. ‘You must try to rest. Take some sleeping pills. Try to sleep, for God’s sake. There’s nothing to worry about. The responsibility was too much for you. No one man should have to bear such a burden. You’re afraid that you might weaken – but it is right to weaken sometimes. You expect too much of yourself, old son.'

'Yes.' Ryan rubs at his face. 'I've done my best, John. For all of you.'

'Of course.'

'What?'

'Of course you have.'

'People are never grateful.'

'We're grateful, old chap.'

'I'm a murderer, John. I murdered for your sake.'

'You took too much on. It was self-defence.'

'That's what I think, but…'

'Try to rest.'

More tears fell from Ryan's eyes.

'I'll try, John.'

The music has started again. The drums are beating. Ryan watches the dancers circle about the control room. They are smiling fixed, insincere smiles. James Henry dances with one of them. He has two holes in his forehead.

Ryan wakes up.

The dream is so vivid that Ryan can hardly believe he did not shoot James Henry. Obviously he didn't. John would have mentioned it. He gets out of his bunk and pulls on a new suit of coveralls. He leaves the cabin and goes to the control room.

It is empty, silent save for the muted noises of the instruments. There is no sign of any sort of struggle.

Ryan smiles at his own stupidity and leaves the control room.

Only when he is back in his bunk does he realise that there should have been someone on watch.

He frowns.

Things are relaxed. But should they be lax?

He feels he should go and check, but he is sleepy…

He awakes to find the smiling face of his wife Josephine bending over him.

'How are you?'

'Still rough,' he says. 'You were right. I should have stayed in my bunk longer.'

'You'll be fit and well soon.'

He nods, but he is not confident. She seems to understand this.

'Don't worry,' she says softly. 'Don't worry.'

'I suspect everyone, Jo – even you. That's not healthy, is it?'

'Don't worry.'

She goes towards the door. 'Fred Masterson's thinking of dropping in later. Do you want to see him?'

'Old Fred? Sure.'

Fred Masterson sits on the edge of Ryan's bunk.

'You're still feeling a bit under the weather, I hear,' Fred says. 'Still got the old persecution stuff, eh?'

Ryan nods. 'I once heard someone say that if you had persecution feelings it usually meant you were being persecuted,' he says. 'Though not always from the source you suspect.'

'That's a bit complicated for me.' Fred laughs. 'You know old Fred – simple-minded.'

Ryan smiles slowly. He is pleased to see Fred.

'I cracked up once,' Fred continues. 'Do you remember? That awful business with Tracy?'

Ryan shakes his head. 'No...'

'Come on – you remember. When I thought Tracy was having it off with James Henry. You must remember. When we'd only been on the ship for a month.'

Ryan frowns. 'No. I can't remember. Did you mention it?'

'Mention it! I should think I did! You helped me out of that one. It was you who suggested that Tracy would be better off if she was in hibernation.'

'Oh, yes. Yes, I do remember. She was overwrought...'

'We all were. We decided that in order to ease the tension she should enter her container a bit earlier than scheduled.'

'That's right. Of course...'

'Off course,' says Masterson.

Ryan looks at him. 'You're not... you're not having a joke with me are you, Fred?'

'Why should I do that?'

'I'm still getting a touch of the trouble I had earlier. Auditory hallucinations. It's nasty.'

'I bet it is.'

Ryan turns in the bunk. 'I'm a bit tired now, Fred.'

'I'll be off, then. See you. Keep smiling.'

'See you,' says Ryan.

When Masterson has gone, he frowns. He really doesn't remember much about Tracy and Masterson's problems with her.

It begins to dawn on him that he might not be as disturbed as he thinks. If he is in a bad way, might not some of the others be in equally poor shape? Maybe Fred Masterson has a few delusions of his own to contend with?

It is a likely explanation. He had better be careful. And he had better humour Fred next time he sees him.

He begins to worry.

If they are all in bad shape, then that could threaten the smooth running of the ship. It is up to him to get well soon, keep a careful eye on the others.

People under stress do odd things, after all. They get peculiar paranoid notions. Like James Henry's...

Next time he sees John, he'll suggest, reasonably, that James Henry have another spell of hibernation. For his own sake and the sake of the rest of them. It could be suggested quite subtly to James.

Chapter Twenty

RYAN'S DREAMS CONTINUE.

Once again he is in the control room. Most of his dreams take place in the control room now. He stares through the porthole at the void, at the dancers with their round black glasses, at his friends and family who stand behind the dancers. Sometimes he sees the old woman.

When occasionally he wakes – and it is not very often now – he realises that he must be under heavy sedation.

He hears the music – the high-pitched music – and it makes his flesh crawl. Dimly he wonders what is happening to him, what his one-time friends, his treacherous family are doing to him. There is now no question in his mind that he is the victim of some complicated deception, that he has been victim to this deception perhaps even before the spaceship took off, certainly after it left Earth.

He does not know why they should be working against him, however; particularly since he is the chief engineer of their salvation.

He is too weak, too drugged to do more than speculate about their plans.

Was that why they were all originally put into hibernation?

He seems to remember something about that now. Was that why he was so insistent that they should not be wakened until the end of the journey? Could be.

But he had to crack up temporarily. The ship's emergency system awakened John, who awakened the others, and now they are in control, they have him in their power.

It is even possible that they are not his family and friends at all, but could have brainwashed him into thinking they are. He remembers that old Patriot rally.

'They look like us, sound like us – in every respect they are human – but they are not human...'

God! It couldn't be true!

But what other explanation is there for the strange behaviour of the rest of the personnel on board the *Hope Dempsey*?

Ryan moves restlessly on the bunk. He has cracked up – no doubt about that. And the reason, too, is obvious – strain, overwork, too much responsibility. But there is no such explanation, when he thinks about it, for the behaviour of the others.

The others are mad.

Or they are...

... not human.

'No,' he murmurs. 'Not Josephine and the boys. I'd realise it, surely. Not Janet, warm little Janet. Not Uncle Sidney and John and Fred Masterson and the women. And James Henry half believed the Patriots. He couldn't be one. Unless he was so cunning he...'

He rolls on the bunk.

'No,' he groans. 'No.'

John comes into the cabin. 'What's the matter, old son? What's bothering you now?'

Ryan looks up at him, wanting to trust his brother, wanting to confide in him, but he can't.

'Betray me...' he mutters. 'You've betrayed me, John.'

'Come off it.' John tries to laugh. 'What would I want to betray you for? How could I betray you? We're on your side. Remember the old days? Us against the world? The only ones who could see the terrible state the world was in. The only ones who had a plan to deal with it. Remember your apartment? The last bastion of rationalism in an insane world...'

But John's tone seems to be mocking. Ryan can't be sure. His brother was always straightforward. Not like him to take that tone – unless this man is not his brother John.

'We were an élite, remember?' John smiles. 'Sane, scientific approaches to our problems…'

'All right!'

'What did I say?'

'Nothing.'

'I was only trying to help.'

'I bet you were. You're not my bloody brother. My brother wouldn't… couldn't…'

'Of course I'm your brother. East Heath Road. Remember East Heath Road where we were born? There was actually a heath there in those days. Hampstead Heath. There used to be a fair there on Bank Holidays. You must remember that…'

'But do you?' Ryan looks directly at the man. 'Or are you just very good at learning that sort of information? Eh?'

'Come on, old son…'

'Leave me alone, you bastard. Leave me alone or I'll –'

'You'll what?'

'Get out.'

'You'll what?'

'Get out.'

AFTER THE FAIR WE KIDDED HER…

Q: PLEASE DEFINE SPECIFIC SITUATION

AFTER THE PAIR WE KIDS WERE…

Q: PLEASE DEFINE SPECIFIC SITUATION

AFTER A PEAR WE DID THE…

Q: PLEASE DEFINE SPECIFIC SITUATION

AFTER A LAIR WE RID THE…

Q: PLEASE DEFINE SPECIFIC SITUATION

AFTER THE AFFAIR WE KILLED HER.

******THANK YOU***

‘NO!’

NO   O   NO   NO   NO
NO   N   NO   NO   NO
NO   O   NO   NO   NO
NO   N   NO   NO   NO
NO   O   NO   NO   NO
NON   NO   NO   NO
NO   O   NO   NO   NO
NO   N   NO   NO   NO
NO   O   NO   NO   NO
NO   N   NO   NO   NO
NO   O   NO   NONONONO   NONONONO

‘NO!’

Ryan rises from his bunk. He is weak, he is trembling. He vomits. He vomits over the floor of his cabin.

I need help.

He staggers from the cabin into the main control room.

It is empty.

No-one on watch.

The computer is flashing its signal:

URGENT ATTENTION REQUIRED
URGENT ATTENTION REQUIRED
URGENT ATTENTION REQUIRED.

He is suspicious of the computer.

Warily he approaches it.

The computer says:

*******CONDITION OF OCCUPANTS OF CONTAINERS NOT****
REPORTED’’’’’’’’’’’’REPEAT CONDITION OF OCCUPANTS OF
*****CONTAINERS NOT REPORTED’’’’’’’’’’’’REPORT YOUR OWN****
*****CONDITION’’’’’’’’’’’’REPEAT REPORT YOUR OWN CONDITION
******LOG NOT FILED*SIXTEEN DAYS’’’’’’’’’’’’CONDITION OF
OCCUPANTS OF***

Ryan is astonished.

It is plain to him that whoever else is running the ship, they are not running it as efficiently as he had been doing.

He replies to the computer:

*******OCCUPANTS NO LONGER IN CONTAINERS’’’’’’’’’’’’MY *****OWN CONDITION IS POOR’’’’’’’’’’’’I HAVE BEEN OUT OF ********OPERATION FOR SIXTEEN DAYS’’’’’’’’’’’’WILL FILE REPORTS AS*SOON AS POSSIBLE’’’’’’’’’’’’PLEASE ACKNOWLEDGE*********

He waits for a second. The computer replies.

*******THANK YOU’’’’’’’’’’’’LOOKING FORWARD TO HEARING** ***YOUR LOG ENTRIES’’’’’’’’’’’’HOWEVER YOU ARE WRONG ABOUT****OCCUPANTS OF CONTAINERS’’’’’’’’’’’’THEY ARE STILL IN*******CONTAINERS’’’’’’’’’’’’SORRY TO HEAR YOUR OWN CONDITION*****POOR’’’’’’’’’’’’SUGGEST YOU SWITCH ME TO FULLY AUTOMATIC***UNTIL YOUR CONDITION IMPROVES’’’’’’’’’’’’DID YOU TAKE******RECOMMENDED DOSE PRODITOL’’’’’’’’’’’’REPEAT DID YOU TAKE***RECOMMENDED DOSE PRODITOL****************

Ryan is staring incredulously at the second part of the message. Automatically he replies:

*******YES I TOOK RECOMMENDED DOSE PRODITOL*************

and before the computer replies he leaves the main control room and runs through the dark corridors of the ship until he comes to the hibernation room. He touches the stud and nothing happens. The emergency locks must again be operating. Someone has switched them on.

John?

Or someone pretending to be John?

He runs back to the main control room and switches off the emergency locks, runs back down the corridors to the hibernation room. He opens the door and dashes in.

There they are. As they were when he last saw them. Sleeping in the peace of the hibernation fluid.

Has he imagined…?

No. Someone locked the hibernation room before. Someone locked it again. There is at least one other person aboard. Probably the person posing as John.

He knew there was something odd about him.

An alien aboard.

It is the only explanation.

He realises that he does not remember seeing any of the people together. Doubtless the creature can change shape.

He shudders.

He couldn't have imagined the creature because the Proditol cleared his delusions, at least for a while.

He stares around the hibernation room and he sees the Purdy pistol hanging on the wall. It is odd that it should be here. But providential. He goes to the wall and removes the pistol. It is low on ammunition, but there is some.

He leaves the hibernation room and returns to main control. Hastily he reports on the occupants of the containers.

Then he goes to look for the alien.

Just as he has on his routine inspections, he paces the ship, gun in hand. He checks every cabin, every cabinet, every room.

He finds no-one.

He sits down at the desk below the blank TV screen in the main control room and he frowns.

He realises that he has no idea of the characteristics the alien may possess. He could live outside the ship in some ship of his own – attached like a barnacle, perhaps covering the airlock of the *Hope Dempsey*.

The big TV screen above his head is used for scanning the hull. Now he puts it into operation. It scans every inch of the hull. Nothing.

Ryan realises he has eaten virtually nothing for two weeks. That explains his weakness. The creature, he remembers now, never brought him food. He only brought him drugs – and tried, in the shape of his wife Josephine, to administer more. Perhaps it was not Proditol at all...

Ryan clutches the back of his neck, massaging it. He holds the gun firmly in his other hand.

There is a polite cough from behind him.

He wheels.

Fred Masterson stands there – or a creature that has assumed the shape of Fred Masterson.

Ryan covers it with his gun, but he does not shoot at once.

'Ryan,' says Fred Masterson. 'You're the only one I can trust. It's Tracy.'

Ryan hears himself saying, 'What about Tracy?'

'I've killed her. I didn't mean to. We were having an argument and – I must have stabbed her. She's dead. She was having an affair with James Henry.'

'What do you intend to do, Fred?'

'I've already done it. But I need your help as commander. I can't hide it from you. I put her in her container. You could say you suggested it. You could tell everybody she needed rest so you suggested she hibernate a little earlier than scheduled.'

Ryan screams at him. 'You're lying! You're lying! What do you know about that?'

'Please help me,' says Masterson. 'Please.'

Ryan fires the pistol, careful not to waste ammunition.

'Masterson' falls.

Ryan smiles. His headache blinds him for a moment. He rubs his eyes.

He goes to see if 'Masterson' is dead.

'Masterson' has vanished. The alien cannot be killed.

Again Ryan feels sick. He feels defeated. He feels impotent.

His headache is worse.

He looks up.

The dancers are there. The group is there. The old woman is there.

Ryan screams and runs out of the control room, down the passage, into his cabin. He seals the cabin door.

He collapses on his bunk.

Chapter Twenty-One

SITTING IN THE sealed cabin, Ryan tries to think things out.

There is no alien aboard. I am merely hallucinating. That is the most obvious explanation.

But it does not explain everything.

It does not explain why the door to the hibernation room was locked.

It does not explain why the Proditol did not work.

He blinks. *Of course. I had no Proditol. I merely deceived myself into believing I had had it. That was why I invented John's sudden awakening.*

And I suppose I could have switched on the emergency locks without realising it.

The strain was too much for me. Some mechanism in my own brain tried to stop me working so hard. It invented the 'help' so that I could relax for a couple of weeks, not worry about running the ship.

Ryan grins with relief. The explanation fits.

And thus I felt guilty about the personnel in the containers. Because I had 'abandoned' them. My talk of their betrayal of me was really my belief that I had betrayed them…

Ryan looks down at the gun still clutched in his hand.

He shudders and throws it to the floor.

Uncle Sidney stands near the door.

'You're doing fine, aren't you?' he says.

'Go away, Uncle Sidney. You are an illusion. You are all illusions. Your place is in your container. I'll wake you up when we reach the new planet.' Ryan leans back in his bunk. 'Go on. Off you go.'

'You're a fool,' Uncle Sidney says. 'You've been deceiving yourself all along. Well before you got into this predicament. You were as paranoid as anyone else on Earth. You were just better at rationalising your paranoia, that's all. You don't deserve to have escaped. None of us deserves it. You're clever. But you're all alone now.'

'It's better than having you lot around all the time.' Ryan grins. 'Go on. Get out.'

'It's true,' says Josephine Ryan. 'Uncle Sidney's right. We were humouring you towards the end, you know. It didn't seem to make much difference to me and the boys whether we went up in an H-bomb attack or up in a spaceship. In a way I think I'd have preferred the H-bomb. I wouldn't have had to listen to your self-righteous pronouncements day in and day out until you…'

'Until I what?'

'Until…'

'Go on. Say it!' Ryan laughs in her face. 'Go on, Jo – say it!'

'Until I went into hibernation.'

'Bloody shrinking violet!' Ryan sneers at her. 'If I'd had a stronger woman…'

'You needed one,' she says. 'I'll admit that.'

'Shut up.'

'You got rid of the strong one, didn't you?' says Fred Masterson. 'Did her in, eh?'

'Shut up!'

'Just like you did James Henry in,' says Janet Ryan, 'after you helped Fred cover up Tracy's death. Shot him in the control room with that gun, didn't you?'

'Shut up!'

'You got worse and worse,' says John Ryan. 'We tried to help you. We put you under sedation. We humoured you. But you had to do it, didn't you?'

'Do what? Tell me?'

'Put me in hibernation,' says John Ryan.

Ryan laughs. 'You, too?'

Ida and Felicity Henry laugh harshly. Ida's hands are folded over her swollen abdomen. 'You lost all your friends, didn't you, Ryan?' says Felicity. 'You sold yourself the alien story, didn't you, in the end? After being so scornful about it, you swallowed it when you could least afford to.'

'Shut up. You'll go, too.'

'You've put us all in hibernation,' says James Henry. 'But we can still talk to you. We'll be able to talk to you again, when we wake up.'

Ryan laughs.

'What are you laughing about, Dad?' says Alexander Ryan.

'Let us in on it, Dad. Go on!' says Rupert Ryan.

Ryan stops laughing. He clears his throat.

'Out you go, boys,' he says. 'You don't want to be involved in this.'

'But we are involved,' says Alex. 'It's not our fault our dad's a silly old fart.'

'She turned you against me,' says Ryan.

'Anyone can see you're a silly old fart, Dad,' Rupert says reasonably.

'I did my best for you,' Ryan says. 'I gave you everything.'

'Everything?' says Josephine. She sniffs.

'Things will be different on the new planet. I'll have time for you and the boys.' His tone is placatory. 'I had so much work to do. So many plans to make. I had to be so careful.'

'And you were.' Isabel Ryan winks at him. 'Weren't you?'

'You'd better shut up, Isabel. I warned you before to keep your mouth shut about that…'

He glances at Janet. Janet bursts out laughing. 'I slept with you because I was shit-scared of you,' she says.

'Shut up!'

'I was afraid you'd do it to me, too.'

'Do what?' He dares her. 'What?'

She looks at the floor. 'Put me in hibernation,' she murmurs.

Ryan sneers at them all. 'Not one with guts, is there? You all wanted to get rid of me. You all thought you could plan behind my back. But you forgot –' he taps his head – 'I've got brains – I'm rational – I worked it out scientifically – pragmatically… I used a system, didn't I? And I beat you *all*!'

'You didn't get me,' says Tracy Masterson.

Ryan screams.

Chapter Twenty-Two

RYAN IS BETTER now.

The hallucinations have passed. Some dreams still disturb him, but not seriously.

He paces the spaceship. He paces down the central passageway to the main control cabin and there he checks the co-ordinates, the consumption indicators, the regeneration indicators and he checks all his figures, at length, with those of the ship's computer.

Everything is perfectly in order; exactly as it should be.

Near the ship's big central screen is a desk. Although activated the screen shows no picture, but it casts a greenish light onto the desk. Ryan sits down and depresses a stud on the small console on his desk. In a clear, level voice he makes his standard log entry.

'Day number one thousand, four hundred and ninety. Spaceship *Hope Dempsey* en route for Munich 15040. Speed holds steady at point nine of *c*. All systems functioning according to original expectations. No other variations. We are all comfortable.

'Signing off.

'Ryan, Commander.'

Ryan now slides open a drawer and takes from it a large red book. It is a new book, with only one page filled in. He enters the date and underlines it in red.

He writes:

Another day without much to report. I am a little depressed, but I felt worse yesterday and I think my spirits are improving. I am rather lonely and sometimes wish I could wake someone else up so that we could talk a little together. But that would be unwise. I persevere. I keep myself mentally active and physically fit. It's my duty.

All the horror and humiliation and wretchedness of Earth is far behind us. We shall be starting a new race, soon. And the world we'll build will be a cleaner world. A sane world. A world built according to knowledge and sanity – not fear and guilt.

Ryan finishes his entry and neatly puts his book away.

The computer is flashing at him.

He goes over to it and reads.

REPORT ON PERSONNEL IN CONTAINERS NOT SUPPLIED.

A stupid oversight. Ryan punches in the reports:

JOSEPHINE RYAN. CONDITION STEADY

RUPERT RYAN. CONDITION STEADY

ALEXANDER RYAN. CONDITION STEADY

SIDNEY RYAN. CONDITION STEADY

JOHN RYAN. CONDITION STEADY

ISABEL RYAN. CONDITION STEADY

JANET RYAN. CONDITION STEADY

FRED MASTERSON. CONDITION STEADY

He hesitates for a moment, then he continues:

TRACY MASTERSON. CONDITION STEADY.

JAMES HENRY. CONDITION STEADY

IDA HENRY. CONDITION STEADY

FELICITY HENRY. CONDITION STEADY******

****

****YOUR OWN CONDITION

suggests the computer.

Ryan shrugs.

CONDITION STEADY

he reports.

Ryan sleeps.

He is in the ballroom. It is dusk and long windows look out onto a darkening lawn.

Formally dressed couples slowly rotate in perfect time to the music, which is low and sombre. All the couples have round, very black glasses hiding their eyes. Their pale faces are almost invisible in the dim light…

Ryan awakes. He smiles, wondering what the dream can mean.

He gets up and stretches. For some reason he remembers old

Owen Powell, the man he had to dismiss, the man who killed himself. That gave him a bad turn at the time. Still...

He dismisses the thought. No point in dwelling on the past when the future's so much more important.

He switches on the agriculture programme. Might just as well do a bit of homework until he can get back to sleep.

He falls asleep in front of the screen.

The spacecraft moves through the silence of the cosmos. It moves so slowly as to seem not to move at all.

It is a lonely little object.

Space is infinite.
It is dark.
Space is neutral.
It is cold.

MICHAEL MOORCOCK (1939–) is one of the most important figures in British SF and Fantasy literature. The author of many literary novels and stories in practically every genre, he has won and been shortlisted for numerous awards including the Hugo, Nebula, World Fantasy, Whitbread and Guardian Fiction Prize. He is also a musician who performed in the seventies with his own band, the Deep Fix; and, as a member of the space-rock band, Hawkwind, won a platinum disc. His tenure as editor of NEW WORLDS magazine in the sixties and seventies is seen as the high watermark of SF editorship in the UK, and was crucial in the development of the SF New Wave. Michael Moorcock's literary creations include Hawkmoon, Corum, Von Bek, Jerry Cornelius and, of course, his most famous character, Elric. He has been compared to, among others, Balzac, Dumas, Dickens, James Joyce, Ian Fleming, J.R.R. Tolkien and Robert E. Howard. Although born in London, he now splits his time between homes in Texas and Paris.

For a more detailed biography, please see Michael Moorcock's entry in *The Encyclopedia of Science Fiction* at: http://www.sf-encyclopedia.com/

For further information about Michael Moorcock and his work, please visit www.multiverse.org, or send S.A.E. to The Nomads Of The Time Streams, Mo Dhachaidh, Loch Awe, Dalmally, Argyll, PA33 1AQ, Scotland, or P.O. Box 385716, Waikoloa, HI 96738, USA.